EDWARD MARSTON was born and brought up in South Wales. A full-time writer for over forty years, he has worked in radio, film, television and theatre and is a former chairman of the Crime Writers' Association. Prolific and highly successful, he is equally at home writing children's books or literary criticism, plays or biographies.

edwardmarston.com

By Edward Marston

THE RAILWAY DETECTIVE SERIES

The Railway Detective • The Excursion Train • The Railway Viaduct
The Iron Horse • Murder on the Brighton Express
The Silver Locomotive Mystery • Railway to the Grave • Blood on the Line
The Stationmaster's Farewell • Peril on the Royal Train
A Ticket to Oblivion • Timetable of Death
Signal for Vengeance • The Circus Train Conspiracy

Inspector Colbeck's Casebook

THE RESTORATION SERIES

The King's Evil • The Amorous Nightingale • The Repentant Rake
The Frost Fair • The Parliament House • The Painted Lady

THE BRACEWELL MYSTERIES

The Queen's Head • The Merry Devils • The Trip to Jerusalem
The Nine Giants • The Mad Courtesan • The Silent Woman
The Roaring Boy • The Laughing Hangman
The Fair Maid of Bohemia • The Wanton Angel
The Devil's Apprentice • The Bawdy Basket
The Vagabond Clown • The Counterfeit Crank
The Malevolent Comedy • The Princess of Denmark

THE HOME FRONT DETECTIVE SERIES

A Bespoke Murder • Instrument of Slaughter • Five Dead Canaries
Deeds of Darkness • Dance of Death • The Enemy Within • Under Attack

THE BOW STREET RIVALS SERIES

Shadow of the Hangman • Steps to the Gallows
Date with the Executioner

THE CAPTAIN RAWSON SERIES

Soldier of Fortune • Drums of War • Fire and Sword
Under Siege • A Very Murdering Battle

SIGNAL FOR VENGEANCE

EDWARD MARSTON

Allison & Busby Limited
12 Fitzroy Mews
London W1T 6DW
allisonandbusby.com

First published in Great Britain by Allison & Busby in 2016.
This paperback edition published by Allison & Busby in 2017.

A CIP catalogue record for this book is available from
the British Library.

10 9 8 7 6 5 4 3 2 1

ISBN 978-0-7490-2011-8

Typeset in 10.5/15 pt Adobe Garamond Pro by
Allison & Busby Ltd.

The paper used for this Allison & Busby publication
has been produced from trees that have been legally sourced
from well-managed and credibly certified forests.

Printed and bound by
CPI Group (UK) Ltd, Croydon, CR0 4YY

CHAPTER ONE

Dorset, 1860

It was just before midnight when she left. There was no need to be quiet while she dressed or to tiptoe down the narrow staircase. No matter how much noise she made, her husband would not wake up. It was always the same on a Saturday night. He would roll back home, stagger into the lodge and make an effusive declaration of love before lurching forward to grope her. As she more or less carried him up to the bedroom, she had to endure the stink of beer on his breath and the cumbersome weight of his body. She was forced to listen to the crude words that dribbled out of his mouth like so much slime then submit to the painful squeezing of her breasts and some slobbering kisses. By the time they finally reached the top of the stairs, he'd lapse into a drunken stupor. Hauling him on to the bed, she'd remove his coat, boots and trousers before pulling the blanket over him. The deafening sound of his snores was, as always, accompanied by outbursts of flatulence. With a sigh of resignation, she'd climb unwillingly in beside him and grit her teeth.

Marriage to a crossing-keeper had brought much sadness and disappointment for Rebecca Tullidge. Though she lived in a neat, compact, two-storey, brick-built lodge in the Dorset countryside, it had soon lost its appeal. Other women might envy her well-tended garden and covet the steady wage that her husband earned but she took pleasure from neither. She hated the isolation, the dull repetition of each day and, above all, the fact that she was shackled to a brutish man she'd mistakenly imagined she could love, honour and obey. It was a continuous ordeal.

She had to escape.

It was pitch-dark when she let herself out of the lodge but she soon picked her way to the railway line. Once she felt the sleepers under her feet, her confidence grew and she strode off with mingled relief and excitement. No trains would come for hours. Rebecca was certain of that because the timetable was graven on her heart. It was just as well. When her husband had been drunk or incapable or simply unable to wake up, she'd had to take over his duties, closing the gates before an approaching train and watching it flash past in a heady mixture of wind, smoke, steam, stench and tumult. But she was not on duty now. If only for a short time, she was gloriously free. She was on a very special journey, moving between one life and another. Drudgery and despair were left behind her; love and hope lay ahead.

Though she knew the risk she was taking, she scorned danger. Nobody else would be abroad on such a cold, unforgiving, starless night. With her hat pulled down, her coat buttoned up and her shawl around her shoulders, she felt invisible. All she had to do was to walk a few hundred yards and he would be there. That thought warmed her body and set her blood racing. She had finally found some relief from the misery of her existence. In place of a blundering oaf of a husband, she had someone who was kind, gentle and understanding. Instead of shrinking from the touch of a man with legitimate access to her body, she would give herself wholeheartedly to someone who had no rightful claim on her. His love for Rebecca obliterated the impediments of holy matrimony. Nothing could hold them back.

Desperate to see him and emboldened by passion, she broke into a trot, running from sleeper to sleeper with sure-footed joy. It would only be a matter of minutes before she flung herself into his arms once again. She quickened her pace even more. Her haste, however, was her downfall. Before she even saw the body stretched across the rails, she tripped over it and fell headlong to the ground. Her jarring pain was intensified by her utter desolation. Rebecca knew at once that it was him. All of their plans had suddenly been ripped to shreds. All of their promises and intimacy and tenderness lay sprawled lifelessly across a deserted stretch of track.

There was no escape, after all.

CHAPTER TWO

'I've just spoken to Inspector Vallence,' said Colbeck, angrily. 'Is it true that you've given him an assignment in Dorset?'

'Yes, it is,' replied Tallis.

'But he has no experience of dealing with a railway crime.'

'That's why Sergeant Leeming will be at his side. After all the cases he's worked on with you, the sergeant is something of an expert.'

'This investigation should be *mine*, sir.'

'Calm down, man.'

'Inspector Vallence is too young and untried.'

'I need you here in London.'

'But this is a case for which I'm ideally suited.' Conscious that he was almost shouting, Colbeck took a deep breath before speaking more softly. 'I beg you to reconsider your decision.'

'Too late – it's already made.'

'Then you must change your mind.'

Tallis bridled. 'Don't you dare tell me what to do!'

'This is *important* to me,' said Colbeck, earnestly, 'and I can assure you that it's equally important to the London and South Western Railway. When they sent a telegraph to Scotland Yard, I'll wager that I was mentioned by name.'

Edward Tallis shifted uneasily in his seat. They were in his office, a place that Robert Colbeck only ever entered after a polite knock. That formality had been swept aside this time. He'd flung open the door and stormed into the room to lean across the desk and fire his question at the superintendent. Tallis went on the attack.

'You're forgetting yourself, Inspector,' he said, sharply. 'You should respect my rank and only come in here by invitation or summons. Granted, there is something in what you say. By dint of your success, you've rightly earned the appellation of the Railway Detective but the railway system of this country should not be your only sphere of activity. Broaden your horizons. Tackle crime elsewhere.'

Colbeck held out his hand. 'Let me see the telegraph, please.'

'It was addressed to me.'

'I have a right to see it, sir.'

'The only right you have is to obey my instructions. The matter is settled. You will stay here while Vallence and Leeming go to Dorset.'

Hand still extended, Colbeck held his ground and met the superintendent's glare without flinching. It was a battle of wills. As a rule, Tallis would have asserted his authority and sent him on his way but he couldn't do that in this instance. He could see the hurt and indignation in Colbeck's eyes and read the dire warning that was there. This was no ordinary argument between the two men. They'd had dozens of those in the past and Tallis had, more often than not, won them. Here was one trial of strength, however, that he was destined to lose. Colbeck was not merely insisting on taking over the investigation, he was, in effect, threatening to resign if he were not allowed to do so.

That – the superintendent knew – would be a catastrophe for Scotland Yard. Colbeck was the finest detective there. If the inspector were forced to leave, Tallis would face a roasting at the hands of the commissioner and ridicule in the press. Editors would crucify him for sending a novice inspector on an assignment that self-evidently called for the unique skills of Robert Colbeck. Tallis glanced at the outstretched hand in front of him and eventually capitulated. Reaching into his desk, he took out the telegraph and thrust it at his visitor.

'You *were* asked for by name,' he admitted, grumpily.

'So I see,' said Colbeck, reading the terse message. 'A railway policeman has been murdered.' He looked up. 'Do you really wish to send Inspector Vallence to Wimborne in place of me? He's never even heard of Castleman's Corkscrew.'

Tallis blinked. 'Nor more have I. What the deuce is it?'

'The line is now under the aegis of the LSWR but – when the Southampton to Dorchester Railway was first built in 1847 – it was known as Castleman's Corkscrew because it followed a circuitous route through the New Forest and on into Dorset. Mr Castleman was the driving force behind the formation of the SDR. His name will for ever be associated with the tortuous route taken.'

'You are embarrassingly well informed,' conceded Tallis.

'Inspector Vallence had the grace to say the same thing.'

'Don't denigrate him. He's a good man.'

'He's also a good detective and may well become an outstanding one. I have high hopes of him,' said Colbeck, 'but I'll not yield a yard of my territory to him.'

Putting the telegraph down on the desk, he adopted a pose of mute defiance.

Visibly under pressure, Tallis reached for the comfort of a cigar, taking one from its box and going through his usual ritual. As the smoke billowed, Colbeck took a few cautionary steps backwards.

Tallis's mood changed. In place of his gruff and peremptory tone, he was uncharacteristically reasonable and apologetic. Compassion was not a word that Colbeck would ever use of his superior yet he heard a distinct trace of it in the other man's voice.

'I thought that you'd prefer to stay in London,' he explained.

'I go wherever I'm needed, sir.'

'My feeling is that you're needed here at the moment.'

'We've had an urgent request from the LSWR and I must respond to it at once. The murder of a railway employee is a matter of . . .'

His voice tailed off and he gaped at the superintendent. At last understanding what Tallis had been trying to do, he was both amazed and touched. Colbeck did indeed have a good reason to remain in the capital. His pregnant wife, Madeleine, was due to give birth before long. Colbeck was astonished that the superintendent even knew about his domestic situation. Ordinarily, Tallis would never talk about family matters. He believed that in order to do their job properly and without distraction, detectives should be – like him – unmarried. He frowned on those who took a wife and made no special allowances for them. When his wife, Estelle, was about to give birth to their two children, Victor Leeming had been shown scant sympathy. On the day that the first child came into the world, the sergeant had been helping Colbeck to solve a murder in Northampton.

Yet here was this crusty, old bachelor actually showing consideration for once. Tallis might not be the confirmed misogynist that everyone took him for, after all. At the time, the superintendent had been upset to hear that the Railway Detective was about to get married and he made no secret of his disapproval. And yet – to Colbeck's astonishment – he had turned up at the wedding, indicating a token sign of acceptance. Though he never referred to Madeleine or once asked after her, he'd clearly got his information from somewhere.

'You understand me at last, I see,' observed Tallis.

'Yes, sir, and I'm . . . grateful to you.'

'Under any other circumstances, nothing would tempt me to send another detective on an assignment like this. It's yours by right. Nobody here can challenge you. At present, however . . .'

'I still wish to go to Dorset,' said Colbeck, firmly.

'Are you sure?'

'Wimborne is less than four hours away by train. I checked.'

'That's not the point. It's a question of priorities.'

Tallis was right and it was a sobering reminder. When Colbeck first heard that he'd been supplanted, as he saw it, by another detective, he'd been deeply wounded. Only now did he realise what the superintendent had been doing. Tallis was deliberately keeping him in London so that he would be on hand when Madeleine gave birth to their first child. Colbeck chided himself for misunderstanding the other man's motives. Ideally, Madeleine would love to have her husband by her side at such a critical time yet she'd never asked him to request a leave of absence. She knew that Colbeck was wedded to his work as well as to her. The decision had been left to him and he was now forced to confront it.

His duty to his wife should come first. He accepted that. But the appeal of solving another railway murder was very strong. Colbeck consoled himself with the words of the doctor attending Madeleine. Unable to give a precise date, he'd said that the baby might not be due for another week or so, perhaps even a fortnight. That gave Colbeck some leeway. He was confident that the killer could be caught within that time. Dorset was a predominantly rural county with a sparse population. It would be easier to hunt a killer there than in a major city with abundant hiding places. That, at least, was what he was now telling himself. As a prospective father, he wanted to be with his wife when she delivered the baby; as a detective, however, his immediate response to a murder was to leap into action. After agonising over it for some while, he finally announced his decision.

'Sergeant Leeming and I will be on the next train to Wimborne,' he said.

'You're under no obligation to take on this investigation.'

'I believe that I am, sir.'

'What about . . . Mrs Colbeck?' asked the other, tentatively.

'My wife is in good hands, Superintendent. Thank you for asking.'

Madeleine Colbeck was not lacking for company during her pregnancy. Her father, Caleb Andrews, had called at the house regularly, each time urging her to name the boy – he was certain of its gender – after him. A retired engine driver, Andrews had been given a new lease of life by the news of the impending arrival of a new member of the family. Filled with pride, he was also conscious of the dangers that even a healthy young woman like his daughter would face during childbirth. Much as she loved her father, what Madeleine prized most was the company of another woman. Estelle Leeming had therefore been a welcome visitor. Having two children of her own, she was able to offer advice and comfort. Since her husband worked alongside Colbeck, she understood the frustration of being deprived of him when his work took him far from London. During confinement, that frustration had been edged with fear and she talked honestly about it to Madeleine.

But there was another female visitor to the house and she offered a rather different kind of support. Lydia Quayle was an attractive, intelligent, young spinster with a great affection for Madeleine. They'd met when Colbeck was trying to solve the murder of Lydia's father in a suburb of Derby. Vivian Quayle had, in fact, been estranged from his daughter at the time and she'd moved to London to lead an independent life, sharing a house with an older female companion. Taking part in the investigative process at her husband's request, Madeleine had met and befriended Lydia, helping her through a difficult time and earning her gratitude as a result. They'd been quickly drawn together. When she heard about the forthcoming birth, Lydia was delighted for Madeleine and intensely curious on her own behalf.

'You're going to have anaesthesia?' she asked.

'It's what the doctor advised, Lydia.'

'Is it safe?'

'It was safe enough for Her Majesty, the Queen,' said Madeleine with a smile. 'There's a rumour that she has been given chloroform during the birth of more than one of her children.'

'Even so – the thought worries me.'

'Why?'

'I don't know, Madeleine. I suppose that I don't trust anaesthesia. You're putting yourself at the mercy of a powerful drug. You . . . lose control.'

Madeleine was about to suggest that her friend might think differently when she faced childbirth herself but, since that was an unlikely prospect, she said nothing. Nor did she touch on the problem of labour pains. It was too indelicate a subject. Estelle Leeming had been frank about her own experience. Since she and her husband lacked the financial advantages enjoyed by Colbeck, anaesthesia had never even been an option. In order to relieve her pangs, therefore, she'd had to put up with repeated bloodletting. Afraid of upsetting her, it was a piece of information that Madeleine decided not to pass on to Lydia.

'How do you feel?' asked the visitor.

'To tell the truth, I'm a trifle uncomfortable.'

'That's normal at this stage, isn't it?'

'I suppose that it is, Lydia.'

'Have you talked about names?'

'We've left that to my father. He wants our son to be called Caleb.'

'What if it's a daughter?'

'He's going to be very disappointed.'

'Yet he had a daughter of his own,' argued Lydia. 'He must be very proud of you, Madeleine. You've not only married a famous detective, you've developed into a talented artist.'

Madeleine smiled wanly. 'I haven't been able to stand in front of an easel for some time. I miss it badly.' She heaved a sigh. 'Though not as much as I'm going to miss my husband.'

'Why – where is he going?'

'He's been put in charge of a murder investigation.'

Lydia was taken aback.

'But it's a *Sunday*.'

'That makes no difference. Robert often has to work seven days a week. A letter from Scotland Yard arrived not long before you did. He's on his way to Dorset.'

The tables had been turned for once. By virtue of his superior rank, education and skill as a detective, Colbeck had always held the whip hand over his sergeant. Victor Leeming deferred to him readily. Now, however, he was in the dominant position. Fatherhood was the one area in which Colbeck could not maintain his status as the natural leader. It fell to him to be deferential.

'Did it make a big difference to you, Victor?' he wondered.

'Oh, yes, sir.'

'In what way?'

'Well, you must remember the time when I was in uniform.'

'I do,' said Colbeck, grinning. 'You were fearless to the point of sheer recklessness. You lusted after action. No matter how strong or dangerous a criminal might be, you tackled him with ferocity.'

'That was before I had children, Inspector.'

'Have you learnt that discretion is the better part of valour?'

'I learnt that Estelle and the two boys depend on me for everything. As a result, I think twice before doing anything rash.'

'I daresay that being a father will moderate *my* behaviour as well.'

'Oh, it will – and in ways that you don't foresee.'

'I hope that it won't impair me in any way.'

'Nothing could do that, sir.'

They were sharing an empty carriage of a train that was speeding away from Waterloo Station, the LSWR's London terminus. Colbeck was ready to take any advice that the sergeant was able to offer him. In appearance, they presented a strange contrast. The handsome inspector was renowned at Scotland Yard for his elegance while his ugly companion was often mocked for his scruffiness. Even in a tailcoat and a top hat, Leeming contrived to look dishevelled and vaguely sinister. Whatever fatherhood had done for him, it had not taught him how to dress properly.

'What do we expect to find in Dorset, sir?' asked Leeming.

'I think we'll find something we've never encountered before,' said Colbeck. 'Most railways are built to connect cities with thriving industries in them and a need to move raw materials quickly and cheaply. The Castleman Corkscrew, on the other hand, is an essentially rural line that links a number of small market towns and, in some cases, mere villages.' He unfolded the map that lay beside him. It was one of a large collection he kept in his office so that he could familiarise himself with a new destination on his way there. 'Let me show you. This is the route we'll take.'

Leeming followed the progress of Colbeck's finger as it traced the route from Southampton to Wimborne and on to Dorchester. Time and again, it seemed to loop back on itself. The sergeant was mystified.

'I thought the shortest distance between two places was a straight line.'

'You won't find many of those on our journey.'

'Why not choose a more direct route?'

'There are all sorts of reasons, Victor. Rights of access over Crown land had to be taken into account, major obstructions posing especial difficulties for the contractors had to be avoided for financial reasons, and there's the eternal problem of vested interests.'

'What do you mean?'

'People expect a return on their money,' said Colbeck. 'If they invest a large amount of it in a new railway, they do so in order to ensure that the town where they live or conduct their business is incorporated into the network.'

'But some of these places along the line look as if they're no more than a hole in the hedge, sir,' noted Leeming, peering at the map. 'The station at Beaulieu, for instance, looks as if it's miles from the village itself. Did they run out of track?'

Colbeck shook his head. 'There's another explanation. It involves the Commissioners for the Royal Woods and Forests. They'll have had an influence.'

'I still think that Mr Castleman has a lot to answer for. His railway is a mess.'

'Strictly speaking, he wasn't responsible for the mess. The sinuous route was actually designed by an engineer. I recall reading somewhere that Mr Castleman favoured a route that would have been eight miles shorter in length. However,' Colbeck emphasised, 'we're not here to criticise anyone. We must simply adapt to the conditions that we find and make the most of them.'

'What sort of place is Wimborne?'

'I imagine that it will seem very parochial after London.'

'That's a pity,' said Leeming. 'I only feel at home in a big city.'

'There are no large centres of population in Dorset, Victor. You must be prepared to inhale country smells for a change and get mud on your boots.'

'Who asked for us?'

'Mr Ambrose Feltham. He's a director of the LSWR and lives in Wimborne. It was he who sent the telegraph to the superintendent.'

'I just wish we had more detail. All we know so far is that a railway policeman was murdered.'

'That's enough for me,' said Colbeck.

CHAPTER THREE

Seen from a distance, the two men on the platform at Wimborne Station bore a marked similarity to each other. Roughly equal in height and girth, both were in uniform and exuded a sense of authority. Closer examination showed that there were considerable differences between them. Older, more weather-beaten and with a greying beard, Bertram Maycock was a local constable, a man with a philosophical cast of mind who brought a degree of tolerance to the work of law enforcement in the town. It endeared him to most, but not all, of the inhabitants. Richard Satchwell, by contrast, was a tense individual in his late twenties with flashing eyes and a hooked nose, overzealous in discharging his duties as one of the two railway policemen assigned to the station. His jurisdiction only stretched as far as railway property and a little beyond but he tended to behave as if he had the same power and scope as Maycock.

'It was bound to happen sooner or later, Bert,' he said, solemnly.

'I don't agree.'

'John Bedloe upset too many people.'

'I've upset a few in my time,' said Maycock, smiling, 'and ye've gotten the wrong side of even more, from what I've heerd, but nobody feels that Wimborne would be better off wi'out ye and I. Ye need a lot more'n bein' upset to kill a man.'

'I think that someone was settling an old score.'

'Then 'e were a strong man – either that or 'e weren't alone. John was as tough as teak. There's not many as'd tek 'im on on 'is own.'

'He was probably caught off guard.'

'Let this fella from Lun'un decide that, Dick. That's why 'e's a-comin'.'

'I've never heard of this Inspector Colbeck.'

'Mr Felt'am says 'e's famous. We're lucky to get 'im.'

'Speak for yourself,' said Satchwell, resentfully. 'You and I could solve this crime between us, Bert. We don't need a famous detective from Scotland Yard. By rights, I should make the arrest. Me and John Bedloe were colleagues. It's my duty to catch his killer.'

'Ye'll 'ave to fight it out wi' the inspector and ye won't 'ave long to wait to do that. The train is comin'. 'E'll be wi' us in no time at all.'

Satchwell cupped a hand to his ear. 'I don't hear anything.'

'Then ye should wash out your lug'oles. It's puffin' fit to burst.'

'Ah,' said the other, listening more intently, 'I think I can hear it now.'

It was not long before they saw it as well. Advertised beforehand by plumes of smoke, it suddenly came into view with a sense of purpose, chugging determinedly along until it began to lose speed and spew out clouds of smoke less aggressively. When it finally pulled into the station, it came to a surprisingly smooth halt. Anxious to meet the detectives, Maycock moved forward but his companion hung back until they actually

22

stepped out on to the platform. While the constable gave them a cordial welcome, Satchwell took stock of the newcomers. He was not impressed. In his eyes, Leeming had the build of a farm labourer dressed incongruously in fine clothes and Colbeck was a dandy whose appearance made Satchwell sneer. In response to Maycock's gesture, the railway policeman came forward to be introduced to the newcomers and discovered that both men – especially Colbeck – had a very firm handshake.

'Mr Feltham is expecting you,' he said, officiously. 'He's booked rooms for you at the King's Head. I'm to take you there right now, then conduct you to Mr Feltham's house.'

Maycock chuckled. ''Tis no 'ouse, Dick. 'Tis a manshun.'

'Mr Feltham is eager to see you as soon as possible, Inspector.'

'If he were that eager,' said Colbeck, drily, 'he'd have been here to greet us in person. I sent a telegraph to warn him of the time of our arrival.' He turned to Maycock. 'Where is the body, Constable?'

'Oh, it's at Dr Keddle's, sir.'

'Were you the first to discover it?'

'No, Inspector.'

'What about you, Satchwell?'

'I only learnt there'd been a murder when I was roused from my bed,' said the other, defensively.

'Who actually found it?'

'Sim Copsey. He's a shepherd.'

'Then that's the person I wish to speak to first,' decided Colbeck.

Satchwell was taken aback. 'What about Mr Feltham?'

'He can wait his turn. Help the sergeant with our luggage and take him to the King's Head. I'll join him there in due course.'

'Mr Feltham will be most upset if you go somewhere else first.'

'That's his prerogative.'

23

'He more or less insists.'

'We take no orders from him,' said Colbeck, smoothly. 'Copsey is the person I need to see. He can tell me something useful about this crime.' He handed Satchwell his valise. 'All that Mr Feltham can do is to repeat hearsay.'

'Come on,' said Leeming, moving away. 'Take me to the King's Head.'

After a surly glance at the inspector, Satchwell fell in beside Leeming.

'Ye must excuse Dick,' said Maycock. ''Im an' Bedloe was coaliggs.'

'That's no excuse for bad manners.'

'Dick Satchwell's a good man at 'eart, sir.'

'What about Mr Copsey?'

Maycock cackled. 'Oh, Sim is a wicked ole devil.'

'Which farm does he work on?'

''Tis out near God's Blessin' Green.'

Colbeck was amused. 'Is there really such a place?'

'Oh, yes.'

'Is it far away?'

'Sim won't be there, Inspector.'

'Then where is he?'

Maycock's eyes sparkled. 'I'll show ye.'

Wimborne Station was in a rural setting near the bank of the River Stour. Trains going on from there to Poole and beyond crossed the river by means of a timber viaduct. Since the town was some distance away, Satchwell had acquired a trap to take the visitors there. As it set off at a leisurely pace, he and Leeming sat side by side. It was a mode of transport that suited the sergeant. He hated travelling by train and complained bitterly whenever he was forced to set off on yet another long, noisy, uncomfortable journey.

The only thing that reconciled him to regular use of the railway network was the privilege of working beside Colbeck. Of the many things he'd learnt from the inspector, one was the importance of gathering intelligence at every opportunity. Satchwell was patently sulking beside him. Having worked alongside the murder victim, he was bound to have valuable knowledge about him. Leeming set about chiselling it out of the railway policeman.

'What sort of man was Bedloe?' he asked.

'He did his job well.'

'I'm asking about his character.'

Satchwell shrugged. 'John was all right when you got to know him.'

'Was he friendly, supportive, easy to work with?'

'We got along.'

'Was he married?'

'Oh, no,' said the other, crisply. 'He was not the marrying type.'

'How long had he worked here?'

'Two years. He was transferred from Dorchester.'

'And how long have *you* been here?'

'Three and a half years.'

'So you had seniority.'

'That wasn't quite the way it happened,' said Satchwell with a hint of sourness. 'Because he was older and had worked in the county town, John felt that he should be in charge.'

'Are you saying that he liked to throw his weight around?'

'That's one way of putting it.'

'We have a superintendent like that,' confided Leeming. 'Did you see much of Bedloe when you were off duty?'

'Not really – I'm a family man.'

'Whereas he was single and fancy-free.' Satchwell said nothing. 'Was he the type of man who made enemies?'

'Well, he didn't make friends easily, I can tell you that. John never learnt how to be off duty. When he wasn't wearing a uniform, he behaved as if he still was. Some people didn't like that.'

'Some people?' echoed Leeming. 'Can you give me any names?'

'No, Sergeant, I can't.'

'Why not?'

'There was just this general feeling against him. When he came into a pub, most of those who were there looked the other way.'

'How do you know? I thought you never spent time with him off duty.'

'You hear things.'

'Had he always worked on the railways?'

'Oh, no, he'd spent some years as a gamekeeper on a big estate the other side of Sherborne. John would have loved that, strutting about with a shotgun under his arm. He was always boasting about his knack of catching poachers.'

'That's good training for a railway policeman.'

'He kept telling me the same thing.'

'You said earlier that you were hauled out of bed this morning.'

'It was just before dawn. Bert Maycock sent someone to bang on my door. I got dressed and rushed straight to the scene.'

'How was Bedloe killed?'

'John had been stabbed in the back and . . .' There was a lengthy pause.

'And?' prompted Leeming.

Satchwell stared straight ahead. 'And his mouth had been prised open. A corkscrew had been driven through his tongue and into his jaw.'

The sergeant winced. 'A *corkscrew*?'

'Yes, Sergeant – a large one.'

Though Satchwell did his best to conceal it, Leeming could swear that he'd heard something in the man's voice bordering on quiet satisfaction.

Simon Copsey had seen death in many forms. When the railway had first been built some thirteen years earlier, he'd lost sheep who'd strayed on to the line in front of an approaching train. He killed vermin on a regular basis and snared rabbits to vary his diet. Dead animals were a common sight. What he'd never done before, however, was view the corpse of a murdered man, especially one who'd been treated in such a bizarre way. He'd puzzled over the corkscrew for a long time before summoning help. Copsey had acquired an instant fame and he sought to exploit it. Instead of going back to his flock, he'd made his way to The Jolly Shepherd, a small, shabby, unappealing pub on the road out of Wimborne. Its thatched roof was badly neglected and two of its windows were cracked but that didn't deter Copsey. He banged on the door until the landlord finally opened it, letting him in on the strength of the tale he had to tell.

Over a free pint, the visitor had explained how he'd stumbled on the body of John Bedloe, omitting to mention that, in fact, it was his dog, Sam, who'd actually found it. Sam didn't contradict him. He was happy curling up at his master's feet. When the pub opened for business, people drifted in, each one mesmerised by the story of a foul murder told with macabre gusto. Copsey was in his element, the image of a jolly shepherd. He not only had a captive audience, each new visitor bought him a fresh pint and treated him with exaggerated respect. By the time that Colbeck arrived at the pub with Maycock, the wizened, old shepherd was snoring contentedly away with his dog beside him. Maycock exchanged a few words with the landlord, introduced the detective, then shook Copsey awake.

'What's goin' on?' demanded the shepherd, slurring his words.

'Time to wake up, Sim,' said Maycock, pleasantly.

'Who says so?' Opening an eye, he saw the police uniform. 'It wasn't me,' he protested. 'I've not been near them chickens and neither has Sam.'

The dog barked in agreement. After helping him to sit upright again, Maycock explained why they were there. For his part, Colbeck was wondering how reliable a witness the drunken shepherd would be. He noticed that the man's mud-covered smock had traces of blood on the sleeve and asked himself how anyone could wear a misshapen hat that had been pounded so hard over the years by wind, rain and snow that it was threatening to fall apart at the seams. He gave Copsey time to compose himself. The promise of more beer helped to concentrate the old man's mind and he thrust out a skeletal hand.

'You can have it *afterwards*,' said Colbeck, firmly, 'when you've told me what I came to hear. Now then, when and how did you find the murder victim?'

'It were in West Moors,' said Copsey, shaking himself fully awake. 'I saved 'im, sir, that I did. I saved John Bedloe.'

'But he was already dead, wasn't he?'

'Oh, yes, but 'e were stretched across the track. The poor man's neck was on the line itself. If a train'd come, it'd tek off 'is 'ead.' He made a vivid gesture. 'Then, o' course, there was the corkscrew.'

'Ye never told me John'd been on the line itself,' complained Maycock. 'When I got there, 'e were lyin' beside the track.'

'I were too shocked to tell ye all, Bert.'

'Then tell us everything now,' said Colbeck, patiently, 'and remember as much detail as you possibly can.'

Pleased to have another audience, Copsey cleared his throat and launched into his story. In the course of its repetition, it had picked up all kinds of embellishments but it was not difficult for Colbeck to separate fact from fanciful decoration. The shepherd added some significant new details to the version that Maycock had already given the detective. When it was all over, Colbeck bought a pint of beer for Copsey but kept it tantalisingly out of reach on the bar counter. Reaching inside his coat, he took out a notebook and pencil.

'Before I pass you your drink,' said Colbeck, opening the pad to a blank page, 'I want you to do something for me.'

'What is it, sir?'

'Do you know what this is?'

Colbeck drew two parallel lines then joined them together with a series of smaller lines set apart at regular intervals. He showed the drawing to the shepherd.

''Tis a railway track,' said the old man.

'Take the pencil and draw in the body exactly as you found it.'

'I'm no hartist, sir.'

'Was he at an angle like this?' asked Colbeck, sketching in a matchstick figure.

'No, no, ye've got it all wrong.'

'Then what about this?'

Colbeck created a few more corpses on the paper before he finally put one in exactly the right position. The man's head – a tiny circle – was over one line while his legs were over the one parallel with it.

Copsey nodded excitedly and Sam added a few celebratory barks for good measure. Putting his pad away, Colbeck reached for the tankard and gave it to the old man. The detective felt that he now had something on which to work. Not long after John Bedloe had been dragged off the track, the milk train had thundered through. Had the body been in its original position, it would have been sliced into three parts. The shepherd had not only prevented a gory mess from disfiguring the track, he'd spared the driver and the fireman of the milk train from having nightmares about what they'd inadvertently done. Killing stray animals was one thing, always regrettable but an occupational hazard. Mangling a human body was on a different scale altogether.

When he left the pub with Colbeck, the policeman was curious.

'Why did ye ask about the position 'e was in?'

'I thought it might give me a useful clue.'

'And did it?'

'Oh, yes,' said Colbeck. 'The shepherd did the right thing in pulling the body clear. My guess is that Bedloe was killed elsewhere, then taken to a particular point on the track. Instead of being tossed across the line, he was placed there very carefully.'

Maycock hunched his shoulders. 'I don't foller ye, sir.'

'He wasn't just a murder victim. He was a sacrifice.'

Notwithstanding his dislike of being away from home, Leeming was favourably impressed by Wimborne. It was a pretty town, dominated by a minster with two towers, each built in different architectural styles. He was struck by the oddness of its appearance because it was constructed of limestone interspersed with a dark, rust-coloured stone that gave it a strangely mottled look. The King's Head Hotel was in the main square. It featured a series of square columns protruding from the facade and had both a reassuring symmetry and a uniform colour. The interior was equally pleasing. Taking charge of Colbeck's valise, Leeming was booked in and shown up to a room so commodious that it was bigger than the entire floor space of his house in London. As he looked around what were for him luxurious facilities, he thought wistfully of his family and wished that he could afford to bring them to stay in such a place. His window looked out on the square and he spent several minutes just gazing out at the busy scene below.

After removing his hat and coat, he flopped into an armchair and enjoyed a rare moment of relaxation. Once the investigation gathered pace, there would be little time to rest because he knew how keen Colbeck was to solve the murder in the shortest time possible. That would entail long hours and hard work. Meanwhile, he could bask in a moment of idleness. It did not last long. There was a rapping on the door and he opened it to find himself staring at the face of Richard Satchwell. The railway policeman was smirking like a mischievous boy who'd just got a fellow pupil into serious trouble by betraying him to the headmaster.

'You're wanted downstairs at once,' he warned.

'Has the inspector returned?'

'No, Sergeant. It's Mr Feltham who wants to see you and he wasn't at all happy when I told him that you were delayed. He's waiting. You'd better come quickly.'

After retrieving his coat, Leeming put it on and followed him down to the lounge. Ambrose Feltham was standing there with one hand on the back of a chair and the other on his hip. A short, slim, well-dressed man in his fifties, he increased his height by wearing an exceptionally tall top hat. Piggy eyes glinted above a bushy moustache. A flick of the wrist dismissed Satchwell.

'So,' said Feltham, looking him up and down with evident misgivings, 'you are Sergeant Leeming.'

'Yes, Mr Feltham.'

'I expected you to come straight to me.'

'Inspector Colbeck had other priorities.'

'I find that very annoying.'

'There was no intention of upsetting you, sir. It's just that the inspector wished to speak to the man who actually found the body.'

Feltham snorted. 'That will be a complete waste of time.'

'Why?'

'He'll get no sense out of Sim Copsey. That old reprobate is probably as drunk as a lord by now. He's not very articulate at the best of times.'

'Do you know him, sir?'

'I should do, Sergeant,' said the other, grandiloquently. 'I'm a magistrate here and I've lost count of the number of times that Copsey has been up before me. I've sentenced him for everything from causing an affray to stealing chickens. He might *claim* that he was the first to find Bedloe,' he added, tapping the side of his nose, 'but there might be another explanation altogether.'

'You mean that he's a suspect?'

'What was he doing in such a place at that time of night? Ask yourself that. Copsey lives miles away. He had no reason to be anywhere near West Moors.'

'What about Mr Bedloe himself. Does he live close by?'

'No, he has a cottage here in Wimborne.'

'So what was *he* doing out in the dead of night?'

'I'm counting on you and the inspector to find out.' He wagged a finger. 'By and large, this is a law-abiding town. We have our share of petty crime, as I know only too well, but we don't usually have anything as serious as this. Murder leaves a nasty stain. I summoned you here to clean up the mess.'

'We came in the interests of justice, Mr Feltham.'

'Well, yes, that goes without saying.'

'In view of your comments,' said Leeming, tartly, 'I rather felt that it needed to be said.' The piggy eyes flashed. 'Satchwell tells me that the murder victim had very few relations. The only one he knew of is a cousin in Dorchester.'

'If he's next of kin, you'll have to get in touch with him.'

'We don't need him to identify the body. Apparently, that's already been done by a number of people. Mr Bedloe seems to have been well known.'

'Well known, perhaps, but not well liked,' said Feltham. 'He was a handsome devil, by all accounts, and something of a ladies' man. I wouldn't be at all surprised if the killer was a jealous husband whose wife caught Bedloe's eye.'

'Is Mr Copsey married?'

'Heavens, no! He's repulsive. What woman would look twice at him?'

'Then that destroys your theory about him being a suspect, sir,' Leeming pointed out. 'If we're after a vengeful husband, we can rule Copsey out. In any case, murder is a big step up from causing an affray and stealing chickens.'

'I hope that you're not being sarcastic, Sergeant.'

Leeming was stony-faced. 'It would never cross my mind, sir.'

'How long have you worked with Inspector Colbeck?'

'It must be ten years at least.'

'Is he always this wayward?'

'He would call it being methodical.'

'I left orders that he should come to see me straight away. I need to impress upon him the importance of ridding Wimborne of this awful stigma as soon as is humanly possible.'

'You don't need to tell him that, sir. He has his own reasons for a speedy resolution. Meanwhile, may I thank you for booking us into this hotel. The accommodation is excellent.'

'I didn't bring you to Dorset for a holiday, Sergeant,' snapped Feltham. 'You're here for a specific purpose.'

'We're well aware of that, sir.'

Feltham looked up as Satchwell reappeared in the lounge.

'Well,' he demanded. 'Have you tracked down the inspector?'

'Yes, sir,' replied the other, 'I've just seen him going into Dr Keddle's house.'

'Damn the fellow!' exclaimed Feltham, slapping the back of the chair with the flat of his hand. 'First, it's that flea-ridden shepherd and now it's the doctor. Why is the man dodging me all the time? I brought him here to solve a murder, not to play hide-and-seek.'

Leeming could not suppress a wild laugh.

After examining the corpse and noting the single entry wound in the man's back, Colbeck drew the shroud over the naked body and moved across to a small table. Standing in a bowl was a blood-covered corkscrew. He picked it up to inspect it then turned to the doctor with a raised eyebrow.

'Don't ask me, Inspector,' said Keddle, raising both palms. 'I haven't got a clue why the killer felt it necessary to add that gruesome touch.'

'A corkscrew murder on Castleman's Corkscrew,' mused Colbeck. 'Is that what we have here?'

'We have evidence of a heinous crime. That's all I can say.'

Oliver Keddle was a tubby man of middle years with a bald head fringed with hair in a style reminiscent of a tonsure. There was nothing monastic about his manner, however. He was an ebullient man who shunned solemnity. Instead of praying over the victim, his response was almost light-hearted.

'Well, this has certainly livened up my day,' he said. 'I usually spend my time diagnosing minor ailments or advising people against overindulgence. The human body is capable of contracting an infinite number of diseases but I only seem to get a limited share, most of them depressingly dull. Bedloe is the most interesting patient I've had in years.'

'He's not exactly a patient, Dr Keddle,' said Colbeck, replacing the corkscrew.

'In one sense, I suppose that he's not. He's way beyond the reach of the humble medical skills that I possess.' He indicated the door. 'Why don't we step into the drawing room and leave Bedloe in peace?'

'That's a good idea, sir.'

'Unhappily, he's in no position to solve the riddle of the corkscrew.'

Keddle led the way to the drawing room then turned to Colbeck.

'You must have seen a lot of murder victims in your time.'

'I have,' said the other, 'but none quite as intriguing as this one.'

'Wimborne will be in a state of shock over this business. It's an unwelcome novelty for us,' explained Keddle. 'We've had murders in Dorset before but they tend to be further west. I never know whether to be relieved or disappointed. In the last decade, we've had two. The more notorious of them was the one involving Martha Brown who bludgeoned her husband with an axe. He was twenty years younger but he was clearly no match for her. The crime took place near Beaminster. Martha was hanged in Dorchester four years ago in front of a huge crowd.'

'I'm opposed to the idea of public executions,' said Colbeck, seriously.

'So am I, Inspector – it excites the wrong emotions.' They heard the doorbell ring. Keddle ran a hand over his pate. 'I'm still puzzling over that corkscrew.'

'I think that it was symbolic, sir.'

'That may well be but . . . symbolic of *what*?'

'It went through his tongue,' recalled Colbeck. 'Was someone trying to tell us that he was prone to lying? Or is there some other meaning?'

They heard approaching footsteps. The door opened and a manservant showed in a panting Ambrose Feltham. Having had to walk a hundred yards from the hotel, he'd had time to work up his anger. Hat still on his head, he pointed at Colbeck.

'There you are, at last!' he cried. 'I was beginning to think that you were a phantom. Why have you been avoiding me?'

'This is Mr Feltham,' said Keddle, introducing them. 'And there's no need to shout, Ambrose. The inspector has excellent hearing.'

'That may be so,' retorted Feltham, 'but he falls woefully short when it comes to consideration. That's a grave fault in my book.'

'I'm sorry that you feel that way, sir,' said Colbeck with a disarming smile. 'I was not being deliberately impolite. I'm most grateful that you called on us to take on this fascinating case. It's just that I felt it important to speak to the person who found the body first. After him, I was anxious to view the cadaver.'

'So I take third place to a drunken shepherd and a dead body, do I? Or was there something else you wished to do before deigning to report to me?'

'Oddly enough, sir, there was. As a matter of urgency, I'd like to see the scene of the crime.'

'When will you take notice of *me*?' wailed Feltham.

'The inspector is only following procedure,' said Keddle, trying to mollify him. 'He's been in this situation many times before.'

'I have,' confirmed Colbeck, 'but I've not been avoiding you, sir. If you're that eager to see me, I suggest that you accompany me to West Moors. You can examine the scene of the crime alongside me. Will that content you?'

'That's a very sensible idea, Ambrose.'

'Keep out of this, Oliver,' muttered Feltham.

'I'm professionally involved.'

'Then save any comments for the inquest.' Drawing himself up to his full height, he looked at Colbeck. 'I expect to be part of this investigation at every stage. Do you understand?'

'I understand you perfectly, sir,' said Colbeck.

'I want to be there when you arrest the man who committed this murder.'

'How do you know that it was a man?'

Feltham spread his arms. 'Who else could it have been?'

'It could just as easily have been a woman,' argued Colbeck. 'It only needed one thrust of a knife to kill him and most women would be capable of using a corkscrew in the way that it was employed.'

'That's arrant nonsense, Inspector. This is a crime of patent brutality.'

'So?'

'I'll wager anything that it's the work of a man.'

'Why do you say that?'

'Women simply don't do such things.'

'As a rule, they don't,' agreed Colbeck. 'But just before you arrived, Dr Keddle was telling me about a recent domestic murder in Dorset in which a wife hacked her husband to death with an axe. Her name was Martha Brown, I believe.' He looked Feltham in the eye. 'I'd call *that* a crime of patent brutality – wouldn't you?'

CHAPTER FOUR

Not for the first time, Caleb Andrews reflected that it had been so different in his day. When his wife had been awaiting the birth of their only child, the care she received was based solely on what he could afford and he'd earned a low wage at the time. Madeleine's situation was infinitely better. Married to a detective inspector who had independent means as well, she lived in a fine house and had the best medical attention. Though he was pleased for his daughter, he wished that his wife had been able to enjoy similar treatment and comfort. Andrews had been convinced that he was about to become the father of a son. When Madeleine had come into the world, however, he was thrilled and soon found that there were special joys in raising a daughter. The roles were eventually reversed. At the untimely death of his wife, Andrews had been so heartbroken that he'd been unable to cope and it was Madeleine who then became like a parent to him. He never forgot the way that she'd carried him through a difficult time and wondered if any son could have done that so well and so uncomplainingly.

'How are you feeling, Maddy?' he asked.

'Much the same.'

'What does the doctor say?'

'He's happy with the way that everything is going.'

In fact, he'd said a great deal more but it was not the kind of information that she wished to pass on to her father. While she confided everything in Colbeck, she felt too embarrassed to discuss certain details with her father and, for his part, Andrews was too embarrassed to ask for them. When he called in to see her that morning, she was reclining in bed in a dressing gown. He felt uneasy.

'You must tell me if I'm in the way, Maddy.'

She laughed. 'Don't be silly.'

'You know what I mean.'

'I'm always pleased to see you, Father.'

'But the time will soon come when . . .' He let his words hang in the air and she nodded. Andrews glanced around. 'Where's Robert?'

'He's at work.'

He sat up. 'Your husband should be here, looking after you.'

'Where were you when I was born?'

'I was working.' She gave a knowing smile. 'Don't blame me, Maddy. I had no choice. I just couldn't take time off. Robert is more senior than I was at the time. He could take leave whenever he wants.'

'The trouble is that he never actually wants it.'

'You and the baby should come first.'

'Robert appreciates that. He's promised to be back in London well in time.'

Andrews stiffened. 'Back from where?'

40

'He's had to go to Dorset to lead an investigation.'

'That's dreadful, Maddy!' he exclaimed. 'He doesn't have time to go gallivanting around the countryside. His place is here beside you.'

'He's not exactly gallivanting, Father. He's gone to solve the murder of a railway policeman. Surely, you'd approve of that? Robert was outraged when they tried to send someone instead of him. He told me so in his letter.'

'How long does he think it will take him?'

'He and Victor Leeming will do everything to make it a short visit.'

'What happens if the case drags on?'

'I have faith in Robert.'

'Some of his cases have taken weeks, Maddy.'

'This is not one of them.'

She spoke with a breezy confidence that she didn't really possess. Every morning she awoke, she felt that the day might at last have arrived. It was only when the doctor called to examine her that she was reassured that the birth was not, after all, imminent. However, the uncertainty remained. Madeleine would have loved to have her husband close but she knew that he had a missionary zeal for his work and admired him for it. She just hoped that his latest investigation could be terminated quickly.

'Dorset,' said Andrews with a contemptuous sniff. 'That must mean the LSWR. I've never heard a good word about them. Why can't they look after their policemen?'

'Don't be so critical,' she told him. 'Just because you were an engine driver for a different company all those years, it doesn't mean that you have to attack every one of its rivals.'

'Facts are facts.'

'It's so unfair.'

'I worked for the very best railway company, Maddy. I take pride in that.'

'That's understandable. As for Robert, he makes no distinction between different companies. If one of them sends for him, he feels that he has to go.'

'And is that more important than being here for the birth of his child?'

'Robert will be here,' she said, firmly. 'He promised.'

But the doubts were already starting to swirl inside her mind.

Set in heathland, West Moors was only a couple of miles away from Wimborne. It was a scattered community of less than a hundred souls, dispersed among cottages that were, in some cases, little better than hovels. The carriage got them to the site quickly. Feltham had put his vehicle at Colbeck's disposal and accompanied him. The inspector was not happy to have someone keeping such a close eye on him but he tolerated the situation. Dr Keddle went with them because he knew where the body had been found. Alighting from the carriage, they were in an isolated spot beside the railway line. The doctor indicated the exact place where the corpse had been when he came to examine it. Colbeck studied the scene with great care. Keddle looked on with interest but Feltham was impatient.

'There's nothing to see here,' he said.

'Yes, there is,' argued Colbeck. 'We're looking into the mind of a killer. He or she chose this specific point on the line. Why?' He looked down the track in one direction and saw a shed. 'What's that?'

'It's used for storage, I should imagine.'

Colbeck looked in the opposite direction. Less than three hundred yards away was the crossing-keeper's lodge. It was one of many he'd noticed on the train journey there and it looked identical to many of the others.

'I'll need to speak to the crossing-keeper,' he decided.

'Why?'

'He was the person closest to the scene when the crime was committed. After that, I'll have a word with some of the people living in the vicinity.'

'That could take ages,' protested Feltham.

'Knocking on doors is an essential part of my trade, sir.'

'Well, I'm not traipsing around after you.'

'I thought you wished to be involved at every stage.'

'All I insist is that I'm there when something important is going to happen. I've no time for the tedium of talking to the local bumpkins.'

'Something important already *has* happened,' Colbeck pointed out.

'Has it?' Feltham looked around. 'I didn't notice it.'

'Neither did I,' added Keddle.

'Are you playing tricks with us, Inspector?'

'No, sir,' replied the other. 'I simply meant that, in coming here, we've made a significant discovery.'

Feltham laughed harshly. 'All that we've discovered,' he said, 'is that it's cold and miserable out here. It's such a bare and forbidding place.'

Colbeck snapped his fingers. '*That's* the discovery,' he explained. 'Nobody in their right minds would come out to such a spot on a chilly night unless they had a very good reason, and that reason, I suggest, is the obvious one.'

'It's not obvious to me,' admitted Keddle.

'Two people came for an assignation, Doctor.'

'What – on a deserted railway line?'

'It's not entirely deserted,' said Colbeck. 'The crossing-keeper's lodge is within easy walking distance and that shed is even closer. If we take a closer look at it, we may well find that it was the place for the rendezvous.' He extended an arm. 'Shall we go, gentlemen?'

He set off at a steady pace. Eager to keep up with him, Keddle waddled as fast as he could. Puffing noisily behind them, Feltham kept tripping over tufts of grass or scuffing his shoes. At one point, he stepped on some animal excrement and swore under his breath. By the time they reached the shed, he was spitting with fury. Detective work was rapidly losing its appeal for him. Colbeck tried the door of the shed but found it locked. It took him less than a minute to find the key. It had been hidden at the rear of the shed.

'How on earth did you know that it was there?' asked Keddle. 'I'd never have dreamt of looking behind it.'

'My guess was that the shed would be full of tools for maintenance of the track. A lot of people would need to use them, if only infrequently, and they wouldn't all have wanted to carry a key around with them. So,' he opened his palm to display the key, 'they keep it hidden here. It was in the most ingenious place, I must admit.'

'Well done, Inspector!'

'Open the door,' said Feltham, irritably.

Colbeck handed him the key. '*You* can have the honour, sir.'

Taking it from him, Feltham inserted it in the lock and turned it. When he pulled the door open, he goggled at what he saw. Picks, shovels and other tools hung from nails in the walls so that the floor space could be taken up by an old mattress and a couple of blankets. There was an oil lamp on the little table.

'*This* is where they were going to meet,' suggested Colbeck, 'only a vengeful man found out about the arrangement and got here ahead of Bedloe. At least, that's one explanation. There is, of course, another one.'

'I don't see it,' said Feltham, testily.

'Then you'll never make a detective,' teased Keddle.

'Do *you* know what the devil he's talking about, Oliver?'

'I think I do. The inspector is saying that it might not have been a man. The killer could have been the very woman that Bedloe intended to . . . entertain in here.'

'Either that,' said Colbeck, 'or it could have been a discarded lover who knew she'd been supplanted. You know what they say about a woman scorned. And such a person would know about this place from her previous encounters here. She could have lurked in readiness last night. So you see, Mr Feltham, we mustn't assume that we're looking for a male killer.' He took the key from him and locked the door. 'I'll just put this back in its hiding place, then we can introduce ourselves to the crossing-keeper.'

'I've no time to exchange tittle-tattle with him,' said Feltham.

'Then you might as well return to Wimborne with the doctor.'

'Oh, I'm staying with you,' Keddle put in. 'I'll need no introduction to Tullidge and his wife because they're patients of mine. As it happens, I've got a good reason to drop in on them.' He put a hand on Feltham's shoulder. 'Leave us to it, Ambrose. We'll find someone with a trap to take us back to town.'

Colbeck replaced the key then all three of them set off. Feltham cleaned the mess off his shoe by rubbing it in a clump of grass. He grumbled all the way back to the carriage then took his leave. They waved him off.

'For all his bluster,' said Keddle, 'Ambrose Feltham is a decent man. His bark is far worse than his bite. This murder has really upset him. It's almost as if he takes it personally. That's why he sent for you.'

'I'm grateful to him. It's an interesting case.'

'And do you really think it was a crime of passion?'

'Oh, it's too soon to make a firm judgement yet,' said Colbeck, warily. 'But you didn't have to stay with me. You could have returned with Mr Feltham.'

'I'm interested to see you in action. Besides, I really would like a word with Michael and Becky Tullidge. They suffered the kind of tragedy from which it's very difficult to recover.'

'Oh?'

'As a result, the husband took to drink. I didn't want to say that in front of Ambrose or he'd demand that Tullidge was sacked. He's never drunk on duty, I'm sure of that, but there's only one place you'll find him on a Saturday night and that's quaffing beer at the local tavern.' He gave a sympathetic smile. 'If the murder had occurred right under his nose, he wouldn't have seen or heard a thing. Tullidge would have been dead to the world.'

'You mentioned a tragedy.'

'It was very sad. They'd been so keen to have a baby.'

'What happened?'

'It was stillborn,' said Keddle, sadly, 'and that was not the end of it. Let me just say that complications set in that made it impossible for her ever to conceive again. That kind of blow can be crippling.' He pursed his lips and shook his head. 'Becky Tullidge was a healthy young woman who'd have made a good mother. Nature can be so cruel at times.'

Colbeck thought about Madeleine and his heart missed a beat.

Victor Leeming had not been idle. After being deserted by Feltham, he asked Richard Satchwell to take him to the pub where John Bedloe had been a regular customer. The sergeant was soon sipping his first pint at the Mermaid Tavern but Satchwell politely refused the offer of a drink.

'We're not likely to see any mermaids around here,' said Leeming.

'The sea is not that far away, Sergeant. From time to time, I take my family to Weymouth.'

'How many children have you got?'

'Two – both of them boys.'

'I've got two boys as well,' said Leeming, proudly. 'They can be real devils if you don't keep an eye on them but, then, I was the same at their age.'

The pub was buzzing with speculation about the murder. Theories were being advanced on all sides and the sergeant thought that some of them were worth noting. What he didn't hear was anyone speaking well of Bedloe. The consensus of opinion was that the town was better off without the railway policeman.

Satchwell felt obliged to speak up for him. 'John Bedloe was not the villain you all seem to think,' he declared, raising his voice. 'He was a hard worker and he knew how to protect railway property.'

''Tis the reason we 'ated the bugger so much,' said a swarthy, middle-aged man, producing a rumble of agreement from his friends. 'We 'ad rich pickin's till Bedloe come along and spoilt our fun.'

'Long before *he* turned up, I caught you pilfering.'

'Aye, but ye 'ad the sense to look t'other way, Dick.'

'I did nothing of the kind, Jed Baber. I kicked your bony arse.'

'I didn't mind that,' said the other, airily. 'Bedloe was diff'rent. When 'e got 'is bleedin' 'ands on me, I ended up in gaol.'

'It's the best place for you.'

But the man didn't hear him. He was already involved in another lively discussion about the murder victim. Leeming kept one ear cocked to pick up the banter around him. He was learning more about John Bedloe all the time.

'Shouldn't you be at work?' he asked Satchwell.

'Looking after you *is* work, Sergeant.'

'Won't the stationmaster be missing you?'

'I'm taking my orders from Mr Feltham.'

'He looks as if he enjoys giving them,' said Leeming. 'Our superintendent is like that. He has to keep reminding you that he's in charge.' He took a long sip of his beer. 'This is strong stuff,' he went on. 'I like it.'

'I'm not allowed to drink on duty.'

'Neither am I.'

They shared a laugh. Leeming was slowly warming to him. When he'd first met the detectives, Satchwell had been rather spiky. Like so many of the railway policemen they'd met in the course of their work, he resented their interference in a crime he felt he was best placed to solve. The fact that Satchwell was a family man with two sons, however, had softened the sergeant's antipathy towards him.

'What did you do before you came to work here?' asked Leeming.

'I was doing the same job at Poole. There were four of us there as well as two clerks and six porters. As the newcomer, I got to do the work nobody else wanted.'

'Is that why you moved here?'

'It was one of the reasons. The main one was that my wife's family live in Wimborne. She'd always wanted to come home.'

'Do you *like* being a railway policeman?'

'I don't like the long hours,' said Satchwell, 'and the pay could certainly be better but the work suits me. No two days are the same. I look after an allocated section of line. I'm there to prevent pilferage and vandalism, report defects in the track, clear obstructions, remove trespassers, supervise the points and give hand signals to drivers to indicate that the line is clear. If there's a crash, of course, I'm duty-bound to lend a hand.'

'You've had to shoulder a lot of responsibilities.'

'I don't mind that. I like a job where something happens all the time.'

'Murder, for instance?'

'That's different. When I started here, the last thing I ever expected was that a colleague of mine would be killed. As policemen, we can never be popular but that doesn't mean we become targets for murder. What about you, Sergeant?' he asked. 'Do you like being a detective?'

'No,' replied Leeming. 'Most of the time, I don't.'

'Why not?'

'Like you, I work long hours and deserve a lot more than the money I earn. I have to travel all over the country and beyond it. We even had to follow a suspect to New York on one occasion. Going everywhere by train is bad enough, but if you want to scare yourself to death, try sailing across the Atlantic in a storm.'

Satchwell was envious. 'It sounds far more exciting than what I do.'

'It's also a lot more dangerous. I've had to fight my way out of trouble dozens of times. I've had broken bones, stab wounds, dislocated fingers and I've lost count of the times I've been knocked out. I don't call any of that exciting. No,' he went on, 'all in all, I suppose that I hate the job.'

'Then why do you keep doing it?'

'There's an easy answer to that – Inspector Colbeck.'

'Does he really deserve his reputation?'

'Oh, yes,' said Leeming with a fond smile. 'There's nobody

quite like him. Whenever we take on a new case, I'm completely bewildered but he always manages to see things that nobody else would. Watching him is an education.' He helped himself to another mouthful of beer. 'That's why I'm still a detective.'

As they were approaching the lodge, the door opened and Michael Tullidge came trudging out. He was wearing a crumpled uniform and hat. He didn't seem to notice that he had visitors and simply went about his work, closing the gates on either side of the line to block access when the next train steamed through. Colbeck noticed the man's sagging shoulders and the lugubrious expression on his face. When he was hailed by the doctor, Tullidge blinked in surprise and turned towards them.

'Oh,' he apologised, 'I didn't see you there, Dr Keddle.'

'We'd like a word with you,' said the other.

After introducing the inspector, the doctor let him take over.

'You can guess why I'm here,' said Colbeck.

'Yes, sir.'

'Someone was murdered within sight of your lodge.'

'Yes, sir.'

'Did you see or hear anything untoward during the night?'

'No, sir.'

'Are you quite sure?'

'Yes, sir.'

'Have you seen any unusual activity here in the last few days?'

'No, sir.'

'You must know who John Bedloe was.'

'Yes, sir.'

'Did he ever come near your lodge?'

'No, sir.'

'So you've never seen him on this stretch of the line.'

'No, sir – never.'

There was a bovine simplicity about Tullidge. Though he was a muscular man with wide shoulders, he appeared to have no life in him. Grief had etched deep lines into his face, adding years to his actual age. Knowing about his tragedy, Colbeck felt a surge of compassion for him.

'Do many people come here?' asked Colbeck.

'Only if they wants to cross the line, sir.'

'What about your neighbours' children?' said Keddle.

'Oh, they're always playing about. They can be a nuisance sometimes.'

'In what way, exactly?'

'All sorts of ways, Doctor,' replied Tullidge. 'Some of them likes to put coins on the line so that the train runs over them. Others try to bounce a ball off a passing carriage. That's just fun. The real nuisances are them as likes to climb over the gate and charge across the line at the last possible moment. Sooner or later, one of them will trip up on the line and be sliced to death by the train.'

'I'd like to meet some of these children,' said Colbeck.

'They're easy to find, sir.'

'And I'd like to speak to your wife, if I may.'

Tullidge became defensive. 'There's nothing Becky can tell you, sir.'

'I'd like to meet her, nevertheless.'

'So would I,' said Keddle. 'It's well over nine months since she last came to my surgery. How is she?'

'Becky's fine,' said Tullidge, watchfully.

'Is she at home?'

'Yes, Doctor.'

'Presumably,' said Colbeck, 'you'll have to stay out here until the train has passed.' The crossing-keeper nodded. 'Then we'll pay her a call.'

Before the husband could object, Colbeck and the doctor strolled towards the lodge. As they did so, they heard the distant sound of an approaching train, on its way from Wimborne to Ringwood. There was no need to knock on the door of the house. Rebecca Tullidge had been peering anxiously at them through the window. The moment they reached it, the door opened.

Keddle introduced his companion and asked if they could step inside to speak to her. Frightened and flustered, she let them in and followed them into a neat, well-kept living room with a collection of small china ornaments on the mantelpiece. When she tried to speak, the train shot past and her voice was lost in the cacophony. Colbeck could see how tense she was. Her pretty features were distorted by a deep frown and darting eyes. Her trim figure reminded him of Madeleine. The women were roughly the same age but Rebecca looked much older.

As soon as the train had passed, she was ready with her apology.

'I'm sorry, Inspector,' she said, 'but there's nothing I can tell you.'

'With respect,' he told her, 'you don't know that. Without realising it, you may have seen something in the last few days that could furnish me with valuable clues. Let's start with last night.'

'I saw nothing. As soon as Michael came home, we went straight to bed.'

'Where had he been?'

'He'd been to . . . see some friends.'

A glance from the doctor told Colbeck that the friends had been fellow revellers in the local tavern. Evidently, Rebecca had been left at home alone. Colbeck suspected that she was accustomed to loneliness. There was an air of neglect about her and an abiding sense of resignation. He asked her several questions but she fended off each one. Realising that he was getting nothing of use from her, he let himself out so that Keddle could have a private word with his patient. Having reopened the gates, Tullidge was talking to a carrier who'd stopped to ask directions. When he'd sent the man on his way, the crossing-keeper turned to Colbeck.

'What did my wife tell you?'

'Nothing at all, really.'

'I could have warned you that would happen.'

'I just hoped that she might have . . . picked up gossip about Bedloe.'

'Becky doesn't go far from here, sir,' he explained. 'She's not one to listen to tittle-tattle. We prefers our own company.'

'I gathered that.'

'We likes living at the lodge.'

'I'm not surprised. It's a nice house. Your wife keeps it spick and span.'

'Becky's got standards.'

Colbeck pointed down the line. 'Do you have a key to that shed?'

'No, sir. Why should I?'

'Who uses it?'

'Them as comes to make repairs and that.'

'Have you seen anyone using it recently?'

'No, sir.'

'But you must know who they are.'

'It's not always the same men.'

Colbeck was confused. Ordinarily, he could tell if someone was lying to him but not in this case. Michael Tullidge was impassive and spoke in a dull undertone. His eyes gave nothing away. Colbeck could not work out if he was being deceived or if the crossing-keeper had lapsed into a state of torpor that allowed him to do little more than work at a repetitive job in a bleak outpost on the line. After failing to draw him out, Colbeck gave up. He was pleased to see Keddle emerging from the lodge.

'I'm going to call on some of the neighbours,' he said, 'but you're not obliged to stay with me, Doctor. I'm sure you'll find transport back to Wimborne somehow.'

'I'm staying,' insisted Keddle. 'Things are starting to get interesting.'

'Very well – I'll be glad of your company.'

'Do you want to speak to anyone in particular?'

'Yes,' said Colbeck. 'I'd like to talk to some of those naughty children we heard about. They can often see things that their parents miss.'

When they walked away, Colbeck could feel Tullidge's eyes watching them intently. He turned to Keddle.

'How did you get on with your patient?'

'Poor woman is no better, really. There's a profound sadness in her that she can't seem to shake off. Living with that husband hardly helps the situation.'

'He's so dour and uncommunicative.'

'Tullidge was never what you might call a sparkling conversationalist. When you look at him, walking through life as if in a bad dream, it's hard to believe that he persuaded two attractive young women to marry him.'

Colbeck was astonished. 'Two?' he echoed.

'The first wife died of consumption. He was devastated. Becky had been a close friend of the wife. After her death, she used to run errands for him. The next thing I knew, they were walking out together. If you ask me,' he went on, 'she married him because she felt sorry for him.'

'She must regret that now.'

'Oh, I think she's too loyal to admit that. Becky went into the marriage with the kind of hopes that all young women have but

54

they never came to fruition, alas.' He looked shrewdly at Colbeck. 'You must have had to impart a lot of bad news in your job, Inspector.'

'It's the thing I hate most.'

'Understandably.'

'Passing on the news that a loved one has been brutally murdered is a harrowing experience. Few people can cope with sudden loss.'

'That's what it was like for me with Becky and her husband. Not that it involved murder, of course,' said Keddle, 'but there was a profound loss. In effect, I was pronouncing a death sentence on their hopes of having a family. She wept for hours and he turned into the shambling wreck that you saw today.'

Colbeck pondered. 'I'm not certain that he *is* a shambling wreck,' he said at length. 'He's hiding something. I'd very much like to know what it is.'

After leaving the Mermaid Tavern on his own, Victor Leeming elected to make a short tour of the town so that he could familiarise himself with its geography. It was an interesting walk. Notwithstanding the changes that the railway had brought to Wimborne, it was still essentially a rural town. Horse-drawn vehicles predominated and, while the sergeant was surprised when a dozen sheep were herded along a narrow passageway, the inhabitants accepted it as if it were a daily event. After the hectic pace of the capital, he found Wimborne quaint and restful. Even the pungent country smells did not affront him. Though he could not understand why, five minutes inside the minster gave him something close to inspiration.

Feltham had been right. Murder had defaced the town. It was up to the detectives to restore it to normality by solving a shocking crime. Leeming was ready for the task. He decided to return to the King's Head in case Colbeck had arrived there but it was not the inspector who greeted him. It was Bertram Maycock who stepped towards him as soon as he entered the building. At the policeman's elbow was a gaunt, wild-eyed man in the uniform of a railway employee.

'I've brought someone to meet ye,' said Maycock.

But his companion could not wait for an introduction. Pushing Maycock aside, he lunged forward to grab Leeming impulsively by the arm.

'My name is Harry Wills,' he gasped. 'I'm John Bedloe's cousin.'

CHAPTER FIVE

The burgeoning friendship with Madeleine Colbeck had been of great importance to Lydia Quayle, coming, as it did, after a series of dramatic changes in the latter's life. The murder of her father had allowed her to achieve a measure of reconciliation with the rest of her family, though she had no wish to move back into the Quayle mansion. Her mother's death had caused her far more anguish than that of her father and she had been overwhelmed by the subsequent discovery that she was, in fact, the principal beneficiary of the old woman's will. One of the most difficult changes to which she had to adapt related to Beatrice Myler, the female companion with whom she'd lived in quiet contentment in her friend's London house. Shared interests had brought them together and each believed that they'd found a permanent mode of existence. Murder had effectively pushed them apart, however, because it brought Lydia's family back into her life. Unable to cope with a threat to their friendship, the possessive Beatrice drove away the very person she wished to keep beside her.

The passage of time had acted as a balm to their respective wounds. Though the friendship had been renewed, Lydia had insisted on renting rooms elsewhere but, whenever she visited Beatrice, she was prey to a wave of regret. She'd been so happy when living at the house and missed its many comforts.

'How are you, Lydia?' asked her friend, kissing her lightly on both cheeks. 'It's so wonderful to see you again.'

'It's good to be here,' said the other, smiling.

'I was expecting you a little earlier.'

'I felt the need of a long, bracing walk. That delayed me.'

They were in the hallway of the house. Lydia allowed the maid to remove her coat, then she handed the woman her hat before following Beatrice into the drawing room. They stood and appraised each other with a blend of affection and timidity, both keenly aware that their wounds had by no means healed completely. Beatrice was a short, plump, handsome woman of middle years and, although she'd never married or had children, she evinced a natural motherliness. It was one of the things that had attracted Lydia to her in the first instance.

Beatrice sat down. 'Tell me what you've been doing since we last met.'

'Heavens!' said Lydia, taking a seat opposite her. 'I can't possibly remember everything and, in any case, most of it is so mundane that you'd be bored to tears.'

'You could never bore me.'

'I suppose the main thing is that I've read a couple of books.'

Her friend tittered. 'Both by Dickens, I'll wager.'

'You're wrong, Beatrice. One was by him, I admit, because I relish just about everything he's written but I actually enjoyed the other one rather more. It was *Adam Bede* by George Eliot.'

'I don't know it.'

'It was published last year and features a case of infanticide.' Pulling a face, Beatrice flinched. 'There's no need to be squeamish. It's a beautifully written novel with some memorable characters. In no way is it rooted in sheer sensation.'

'Well, I've been reading a new book about Italy,' said Beatrice, smiling. 'It has the most remarkable illustrations.'

A frisson of pleasure passed between them. They'd first met in Rome when each was on a sightseeing tour and a bond had formed immediately. It had been sorely tested by events in the Quayle family but, as they searched each other's eyes, they realised that it had been far from broken. How completely it could be restored, however, was an open question. Beatrice seemed ready to make compromises but Lydia still had reservations.

'So you haven't been gadding about with friends, then?' said Beatrice, probing gently.

'Yes, I have, actually.'

'Oh?'

'Their names are Charles Dickens and George Eliot.'

'There's nothing to touch the pleasure of reading a good novel,' said the older woman, complacently.

Another memory was conjured up. One of the joys of living at the house had been having access to Beatrice's well-stocked collection. During the time that Lydia had lived there, it had been supplemented by books they both borrowed from a library in central London. Endless happy hours had been spent discussing what they'd read.

Back in the house, Lydia felt the seductive warmth of its welcome. It was starting to envelop her. What kept her from surrendering to its pull, however, was the fact that she intended to keep an important new development in her life entirely to herself. While she was prepared to talk freely to Beatrice Myler on any other subject, she was not going to mention her regular visits to see Madeleine Colbeck or her growing fascination with the forthcoming birth of her child.

It took them a few minutes to calm Harry Wills down so that he became intelligible. He was so excited that the words came spurting out like steam from the spout of a kettle. Wills was a tall, wiry, sharp-featured man in his late twenties with a sense of guilt animating him.

'I'm sorry I didn't come earlier,' he said, gesticulating madly, 'but I only found out about it when my shift ended in Dorchester. I've been on a goods train all day. I'm ashamed to think that I've been working while my cousin was lying dead here in Wimborne.'

'You weren't to know,' said Leeming, kindly.

'I'll never forgive myself, sir.'

'You've nothing to blame yourself for, Mr Wills.'

'John, murdered – I still can't believe it!'

'You have my sympathies.'

He grabbed Leeming again. 'Can I see him?'

'I'm not sure that it's a good idea,' said the other, detaching himself.

'But he's my own flesh and blood.'

''Tis not the point,' Maycock interjected. 'Ye've every right to view the body, sir, but you're not in the right frame of mind to do it. D'ye agree, Sergeant?'

Leeming signalled that he did.

'John would expect it of me,' said Wills.

'The first thing ye needs to do, sir, is to catch your breath.'

'That's good advice,' said Leeming, winking at the policeman to indicate thanks. 'You're very important to us, Mr Wills. As his cousin, you can tell us things about Mr Bedloe that nobody else knows and that might, in time, lead us to the person who killed him.'

Wills nodded energetically. 'Yes, yes, I want to help. That's why I came.'

'Then why don't you and I step into the bar and have a drink? We don't need to detain Constable Maycock. I'm sure that he has plenty to do.' Maycock accepted his dismissal without complaint and slipped away. 'Come with me, Mr Wills.'

But the man was suddenly frozen with fear. It was as if he'd just realised where he was and what he was wearing. In the normal course of events, he would never have dreamt of crossing the threshold of somewhere like the King's Head Hotel. Socially and financially, it was hopelessly beyond his reach. And he would certainly never have ventured into the bar in the grubby uniform he was wearing. It was stained with oil and flecked with coal dust. The filth covered his hands and face as well. A day on the footplate and in various marshalling yards had left him dirty and bedraggled. The landlord might well refuse to serve him in that state. On reflection, Leeming decided, it was better to take him up to his room where they could enjoy some privacy. Yet even that was a challenge for the newcomer. He held out blackened palms in a gesture of apology.

'I'll find somewhere for you to wash,' Leeming assured him.

Wills was overawed. 'I don't belong here, sir.'

'Right this minute, there's nobody I'd rather see in this hotel. Let's go upstairs and get you cleaned up. I have lot of questions to ask of you, Mr Wills.'

'When can I see my cousin?' bleated the other.

'Later,' promised Leeming. 'You'll see him later.'

* * *

Colbeck was disappointed. The brief tour of West Moors was fruitless. Nobody who lived there could offer anything that resembled useful information about the deceased. Talkative children somehow became mute and none of them dared to confess that they enjoyed climbing on to the shed where the tools were kept or swinging on the crossing gates when Tullidge and his wife had their backs turned. It was almost as if a conspiracy of silence had descended upon the place. Since some of the inhabitants were his patients, Keddle was able to prevail upon one of them to drive them back to Wimborne on his cart. It was a jolting journey but it got them to their destination. While the doctor returned to his house, Colbeck made his first visit to the hotel. When he asked after Leeming, he was told that the sergeant had last been seen going up to his room with a visitor. Colbeck went swiftly upstairs after them. He tapped on the door and it was opened by Leeming. Relieved to see him, the sergeant ushered him into the room and closed the door.

'You've come just in time, sir,' he said, indicating the visitor. 'This is John Bedloe's cousin – Harry Wills.'

'I'm pleased to meet you, Mr Wills,' said Colbeck, offering his hand. 'Please accept my condolences.'

Having jumped to his feet, Wills shook his hand nervously then backed away. Though he'd removed his hat and washed himself thoroughly, he was still self-conscious about his appearance. Colbeck tried to put him at his ease.

'I'm used to spending time with railwaymen,' he said. 'My father-in-law was an engine driver for the LNWR for many years. He had a sense of pride when he got dressed for work. He felt that it was an honour to be employed on the railways. He called himself a pioneer of progress.' He smiled amiably. 'Do please sit back down, Mr Wills.'

'Thank you, sir,' said Wills, perching on the edge of an upright chair.

'What have I missed so far, Sergeant?'

'Very little, sir,' replied Leeming. 'I was just hearing about the Bedloe family. They seem to have had rather more than their share of bad luck. Would you mind repeating what you told me, Mr Wills?'

Wills nodded and ran a tongue over his dry lips. He was clearly dazzled by Colbeck's appearance and by his reputation. Bertram Maycock had told him how lucky they were to get the services of the Railway Detective. Wills spoke haltingly and apologetically, as if embarrassed to be taking up the time of so esteemed a person as Colbeck. He explained how Bedloe had lost his immediate family and how he, Wills, was his only living relative. While admitting that they were not exactly close friends, he stressed that he'd stepped in to help Bedloe when the latter left his job as a gamekeeper. As a result of his cousin's intervention, Bedloe was taken on as a railway policeman in Dorchester.

'So you must have seen a lot of him,' said Leeming.

'Not really, sir,' explained Wills. 'We lived different sorts of lives. He came to us for a meal once or twice and, of course, I'd see him at work but we never spent much time together. John had . . . other interests.'

'So we've gathered.'

'Did he enjoy his job as a gamekeeper?' asked Colbeck.

'Oh, yes, sir,' said Wills.

'Then why did he leave it?'

'I don't know.'

'Didn't he tell you?'

'John simply said that it was time for a change.'

'How long did he work in Dorchester?'

63

'It must have been eighteen months or so, sir.'

'Why did he move from there to Wimborne?'

'Well,' said Wills, 'he told me he'd always wanted to live here but I think the truth of it was that he fell out with someone in Dorchester. Who it was, I don't know. John was always getting into arguments with people, especially when he'd had a drink or two.'

'Are you saying that someone drove him away from Dorchester?'

'I'm not sure, Inspector.'

'But it's a possibility.'

'Yes, sir.'

'Then I daresay it's a possibility that he left his earlier employment as a result of falling out with someone?' Wills nodded. 'We'll need to know on which estate he worked as a gamekeeper,' Colbeck went on. 'The sergeant will call there first thing tomorrow.'

'I can tell him how to get there,' volunteered Wills, 'because my wife and I called on John once at his little cottage. When I've done that . . .' He looked from one man to the other, 'can I please see my cousin?'

'I'll take you there myself, Mr Wills.'

'Thank you, Inspector.'

'Afterwards, I have an important job for you to do . . .'

Michael Tullidge was more alert than usual. His day was controlled by the train timetables and he discharged his responsibilities without fail. Rebecca was pleasantly surprised. Expecting to take his place from time to time, she found that she was not needed. During a break between trains, her husband came into their kitchen. She was standing at the sink, peeling potatoes.

'What did you tell him?' he grunted.

'Who?'

'That there inspector.'

'I didn't tell him anything, Michael.'

'What did he ask you?'

'He wanted to know if I knew anything about . . . what happened last night. How could I?' she said, turning to face him. 'I was in bed with you.'

'That's right.'

She quailed slightly under the intensity of his glare. Being interviewed by Colbeck – albeit for a short time – had been something of a trial but her husband's interrogation was far worse. Looming over her, he posed a physical threat.

'What did the doctor say?' he demanded.

'He asked me how I was.'

'And what did you tell him?'

'I told him the truth. Nothing has changed.'

'He always did like to poke his nose in,' said Tullidge, scornfully.

'Dr Keddle is a kind man.'

'He couldn't save our baby.'

'That wasn't his fault, Michael.'

'I wonder.'

Rebecca had accepted the doctor's diagnosis without question at the time but her husband had lingering doubts about his abilities. Tullidge found it easier to blame Keddle for their misfortune than to recognise that they were victims of a malign fate. Since he was still staring at her with a glint in his eye, she turned back to the sink and reached for another potato.

'Don't speak to anyone about this,' he warned.

'What do you mean?'

'That inspector will have talked to some of the neighbours. If they ask what he said to us, don't tell them.'

'Why not?'

'Because I said so,' he hissed in her ear. 'Do you understand?'

The knife slipped in her hand and cut into a finger.

When the shroud was pulled back, Harry Wills gazed at the corpse of his cousin with tears in his eyes. Feeling that they were in the way, Colbeck and Dr Keddle withdrew into the next room. They did, however, leave the door slightly ajar. Several minutes passed but there was no sign of Wills. At length, Colbeck peeped into the room and saw that the man was kneeling in prayer beside the body. It was some while before he got to his feet and joined the two men.

'Thank you,' he said to them.

'There's something we'd like you to do, Mr Wills,' said Colbeck. 'As his next of kin, you should take charge of his effects. That's the things found on him. They include the key to his cottage. I assume that you know where that is?'

'Yes, Inspector.'

'Would you be kind enough to take me there?'

Wills was perplexed. 'Why?'

'It's the important job I referred to earlier.'

'What makes you want to go to the cottage?'

'I might find some clues. At the very least, it will give me a more rounded picture of your cousin. The more I know about him, the better.'

'Ah, yes . . .' He needed a moment to think it through. 'I suppose so.'

'Mr Bedloe didn't have much in his pockets,' explained Keddle. 'He was wearing a suit and that, by rights, should be yours.'

'It's John's,' said Wills, stoutly. 'I'll take it back to his cottage.'

'As you wish.'

'I don't want to keep anything belonging to him.'

'That's your choice, sir,' said Colbeck, 'but I would like to see where he lived. Is it far from here?' Wills shook his head. 'Then let's gather up his effects and we can be on our way.'

Wills didn't move. He seemed to have lapsed into a reverie. Fresh tears began to course down his cheeks. The other men watched in silence. Neither of them made any attempt to catch his attention. They waited until he jerked himself awake. After wiping the tears away with the cuff of his sleeve, he apologised profusely.

'Would you like more time to recover?' asked Colbeck, considerately.

'No, no, Inspector.'

'Then we can think about going to Mr Bedloe's cottage.'

'Yes,' said Wills, steeling himself. 'Let's do that right now.' He bit his lip. 'I want to get it over with as soon as possible.'

While he was waiting for Colbeck to return to the hotel, Leeming went into the bar. He was nursing a tankard of beer when Ambrose Feltham descended on him. The newcomer was in a much more emollient mood.

'Excellent,' he said. 'I'm glad that I found you, Sergeant.'

'The inspector is not here at the moment, sir. He's with Mr Bedloe's cousin.'

'Then you can pass on the message to him.'

'What message?'

'It's more of an apology, really,' explained Feltham, sitting opposite him at the table. 'I was less than welcoming when you first arrived in the town. I must have struck you as being far too high-handed.'

Leeming was tactful. 'We always make allowances for people's reaction to a murder, sir,' he said. 'It's a distressing experience. You may have no direct link to the victim but he worked for the railway company of which you're a director. You were bound to take a personal interest.'

'Actually, there's more to it than that.'

'Go on.'

'I'm not offering this as an excuse, mind you, but it may help you to understand the way that I acted. As I've mentioned before, Wimborne means everything to me, Sergeant.'

'I realise that, sir.'

'The fact is . . .' Leaning forward, he lowered his voice. 'The fact is that, in all likelihood, I'm to be the next mayor.'

'Congratulations, Mr Feltham!'

'It's not exactly a foregone conclusion,' conceded the other. 'I face a stern challenge so it's imperative that I'm seen to be doing good things for the town.' He beamed. 'I need to put my wares on display in the shop window, so to speak. That's why I summoned Inspector Colbeck. If he solves this crime – and I've every faith in his ability – then I will get some of the kudos.'

Leeming frowned. 'That's not a word I know.'

'It means that people will admire me for taking such prompt action.'

'That's beside the point, sir.'

'I don't understand.'

'Well, we didn't come here to help you win an election.'

'No, no, I appreciate that.'

'We came to solve a vile murder,' asserted Leeming. 'If you're expecting us to take time off to deliver leaflets for you, then you'll be disappointed. The fact that you want to be mayor means nothing to us. Inspector Colbeck will say the same.'

Feltham's face hardened. 'There's no need to be so obstructive.'

'I'm just being honest, sir.'

'And so was I. Foolishly, it now appears, I confided in you so that you'd understand the necessity of proceeding apace with your enquiries.'

'That's not true, sir.'

Feltham coloured. 'Do you dare to question my integrity?'

'It was your intentions that I question,' said Leeming, levelly. 'John Bedloe has a cousin. He must also have *some* friends who'll mourn his death. While they're suffering his loss, all you can think about is becoming the Mayor of Wimborne.'

'I've earned that right.'

'Then you don't need us to help you. If you're the best man for the job, you're sure to be elected. Our only interest is in the murder victim.'

'Why do you have to be so wilfully obtuse?'

'I'm just trying to do my job.'

'Solve the crime and we *both* profit.'

'I'm glad you didn't put that in your telegraph, sir,' said Leeming, angrily. 'If the inspector realised that we were being hauled here for your benefit, he'd never have considered taking on the case. You might care to know that Mrs Colbeck will soon be bringing their first child into the world. If you're a father yourself, you'll understand what a trying time it is for the inspector. It's only because he's such a dedicated person that he agreed to come here.'

Feltham's jaw dropped. 'I didn't realise that.'

'You know the facts now, sir, and the inspector will soon know about this conversation. He won't be pleased. If he *had* a vote to cast in the election,' he warned, 'then it certainly wouldn't be for Mayor Feltham!'

The walk to the cottage took them past the minster. Wills paused involuntarily to look up at it with an amalgam of sorrow and awe.

69

'Are you all right?' asked Colbeck, coming to a halt.

'Yes, I am, sir.'

'Why did you stop?'

'Let's walk on.' He set off again and Colbeck fell in beside him. 'I'm sorry but I always do that when I see the minster and it's the same with Sherborne Abbey. It comes of the way I was brought up.'

'Really?'

'The vicar ran the school in our little village,' said Wills, nostalgically, 'and he made us respect the Church. There was even a time when I thought I could follow in his footsteps. It was very silly of me. I mean, I don't have the brains for anything like that. All that studying's not for me. I belong on the railways. I can look no higher. In any case,' he went on with a first smile, 'I soon met Letty – that's my wife, sir – and I stopped thinking about religion. I had other things on my mind. But it sort of . . . well, it catches me out now and again. That's what it did just now.'

'There's nothing wrong in that.'

'Letty teases me about it sometimes.'

'That's the privilege of a wife. Do you have children?'

'Just the one, sir – a girl.'

'How old is he?'

'Helen is six. All she talks about is being an engine driver one day. I've told her that it's not a job any woman could ever do. But she won't believe me. She wants to drive a train.'

'That's a dream for lots of boys her age,' said Colbeck, letting his mind drift for a moment to the possibility that he might soon have a son. 'I can see its appeal.'

They walked on in silence. It was Wills who eventually broke it.

'The doctor mentioned an inquest,' he said.

'It's mandatory in the case of a violent death.'

'Will I have to be there?'

'I would have thought you'd be eager to do so.'

'Oh, I would, I would. It's just that . . . getting the time off is always a problem.'

'This is an emergency. Your boss surely appreciates that.'

'You don't know him, Inspector.'

'Then I'll be happy to meet him,' said Colbeck. 'At a time like this, you need support from your employer. Apart from the inquest, there'll be the funeral.'

'That's what worries me the most.'

'Are you troubled by the expense?'

'Oh, no,' replied Wills, 'I'm a careful man. I've always got something put aside. No, my fear is that . . .' he grimaced '. . . that nobody will turn up.'

They walked on until they came to a lane that went slightly downhill. The slippery cobblestones made them watch where they put their feet. Bedloe's house was the last in a row of little cottages, each one overhung by a thatched roof. Wills used the key to open the door and, after inhaling deeply, he stepped inside. Colbeck was at his heels. They were standing in a living room that was too small to accommodate the various pieces of furniture. There was hardly space to move. The first things that Colbeck noticed were the two weapons hanging above the fireplace. One was a shotgun with gleaming barrels. Below it was a rifle. In the scullery at the rear of the house, they found a brace of wood pigeons dangling from a hook. Bedloe's guns were clearly not only for display.

Wills had been carrying his cousin's clothing and effects. He took them up to the front bedroom and laid them sadly out on the bed. Colbeck, meanwhile, had been conducting a quick search of the living room and scullery. He opened drawers, lifted the lid of the settle beside the fireplace and poked into every nook and cranny. He was examining the contents of a large box when Wills returned.

'It seems wrong to be doing that, Inspector,' he said.

'I don't think so. I'm learning something new about your cousin with every second. He wasn't the tidiest of men, was he?'

'John always looked smart in his uniform.'

'That was his public face. In private, he was slovenly.'

'He had nobody to look after him, Inspector.'

'That was the choice he made, obviously. He relished his freedom.'

'It wouldn't suit me.'

'As you saw,' said Colbeck, 'there's food in the scullery. It shouldn't be allowed to rot. Why don't you take it away with you?'

Wills was affronted. 'That would be stealing.'

'In a sense, you're his heir.'

'I couldn't touch anything.'

'It's a shame to let it go to waste. Give it to the neighbours.'

Wills at least agreed to consider the idea. He went into the kitchen to see how much food there was. Colbeck took the opportunity to climb up the circular steps. It took him less than a minute to search the tiny back bedroom. When he turned to the front one, he had an equally frustrating time. There was nothing there that he wouldn't have expected to find in the home of a single man like Bedloe. Crouching down, he looked under the bed but all he could see was a chamber pot and a battered case. On examination, the latter turned out to be empty. He was just about to leave when he remembered the murder victim's reputation as a ladies' man. The bed had been an important part of his life and Colbeck suspected that more than one woman had shared it with him from time to time. Since it was so central to Bedloe's life, it was the most likely place where he'd hide anything of value.

Taking hold of the mattress, Colbeck lifted it carefully until he could look under it. The search at last paid a handsome dividend. Tucked away under the bed was a sheaf of letters tied up with a piece of ribbon. Grabbing them quickly, he tucked them inside his coat and lowered the mattress. He heard feet clattering up the staircase and turned to see Wills stepping into the doorway.

'I saw it in that bowl,' said Wills, dully.

'What are you talking about?'

'When I was in the doctor's house, I saw that corkscrew lying in the bowl. It was covered in blood.'

'Yes,' admitted Colbeck. 'The killer screwed it into his mouth.'

Wills gulped. 'Why would anyone *do* such a thing to my cousin?'

CHAPTER SIX

Caleb Andrews was in a quandary. Desperate to know how his daughter was faring, he wanted to make a second visit to the house that day. He even got as far as walking to within yards of the property but was held back from ringing the bell by the thought that he might be in the way and that Madeleine might prefer female company. Though it was his right as her father to have privileged access to her, he had to weigh up the consequences of calling on her again. On balance, he decided, the last thing that Madeleine would want under her roof at such a time was an overanxious parent. He therefore resigned himself to returning home and speculating on the choice of present that he'd buy his grandson when the latter finally chose to appear. Back in his little house in Camden Town, he was lost in thoughts of his role as a doting grandfather when there was a knock on the door. Believing that it might be a message to say that Madeleine was at last in labour, he pulled himself quickly out of his armchair and scurried to the door. When he opened it, however, he saw that he simply had a visitor. Estelle Leeming was standing on the doorstep.

'I thought someone had brought news,' he said, hand to his pounding heart.

'I called in to ask if there *was* any news, Mr Andrews.'

'No, Maddy is still waiting.'

'Have you seen her today?'

'Yes, I have. She's in good spirits.'

'The waiting is always the worst bit,' recalled Estelle.

He invited her into the house and they sat down opposite each other. Andrews was very fond of Estelle and of her two boys. In fact, he could relate to the Leeming family much more easily than he could to his own son-in-law. After all this time, he still felt out of place whenever he visited the Colbeck house in John Islip Street. It was far bigger and more luxurious than anything he could ever have aspired to and the presence of servants had at first intimidated him.

'I think it's wrong,' he began.

'What is, Mr Andrews?'

'Them going off to Dorset like that.'

'Victor sent me a note. He said he had no choice.'

'Robert did. He could have turned down the case.'

She smiled. 'Can you imagine him ever doing that?'

'He's going to be a *father*, Estelle.'

'The inspector is unlikely to forget that. He thinks of little else. Victor said that he keeps asking him what it's like to have a child.'

'A son,' corrected Andrews. 'Maddy will have a son.'

'You can't count on that happening.'

'I feel it in my bones.'

'We didn't mind if we had sons or daughters,' she said. 'I was just grateful to bring two healthy children into the world.'

'I've got plans for a grandson. Maddy won't let me down.'

'It's not up to her, Mr Andrews.'

As they chattered happily away, Estelle kept one eye on the painting of a locomotive that adorned the wall. It was one of Madeleine's earliest ventures into art and it had had so much promise that Colbeck had encouraged her to develop her talent. Constant application had eventually taken her to the point where she was able to sell her paintings. Estelle had always admired Madeleine's work and envied the fact that she had the time needed to produce it. When the baby was born, she reflected, days at the easel would be few and far between. Andrews seemed to read her mind.

'Oh, Maddy will manage to find the time somehow,' he said, airily. 'She'll hold the baby in one arm and the paintbrush in the other hand.'

'It's not that easy, Mr Andrews.'

'I know. Babies have a nasty habit of squirming out of your grasp. Maddy was like that. I felt as if I was holding a bar of soap sometimes.'

'She'll need a lot of rest after the birth. I certainly did.'

'Who looked after the baby – Victor?'

'No, he did his best but he was always too busy on his beat. Luckily, my mother moved in with us for a while. She's looking after the boys now.'

Andrews nodded soulfully. Having the support of a mother was not an option available to Madeleine. The forthcoming birth had reminded him how much he missed his wife and how much his daughter would miss her at such a crucial time in her life. Since Colbeck's parents had both died as well, Andrews would be in a unique position. As the only grandparent, he would have to take on especial responsibility.

'You don't need to come here for news, Estelle,' he said. 'You could always call on Maddy herself. I know how much she'd welcome a visit.'

'To be honest,' she said, 'I've been keeping my distance. The last time I went to the house, it was . . . well, I felt a bit uncomfortable.'

'Why?'

'That friend of hers was there – Miss Quayle.'

'Yes, I've met her. She's a nice woman.'

'She's very nice,' agreed Estelle, 'but we just didn't . . . get on, somehow. To put it another way, she comes from a different world. I have no idea what to say to her. It's my own fault,' she stressed. 'I don't blame Miss Quayle in any way. In fact, I'm glad that she visits as often as she can. At a time like this, Madeleine needs all the friends that she can get.'

The search of John Bedloe's cottage had been a revelation. In finding the letters, Colbeck not only had a much clearer idea of the character of the man, he'd made what he believed was a valuable discovery. It was one that he kept from Harry Wills, reasoning that the cousin was too grief-stricken to be of much use in the investigative process. If taken completely into the inspector's confidence, Wills might well prove to be a hindrance and speed was of the essence. Colbeck therefore walked back with him to the town square and said nothing about the correspondence he'd found under the mattress. As they parted, he assured the man that he'd keep in touch with him and report any progress he and Leeming made. Wills was pathetically grateful.

The first thing that Colbeck did when he got back to the King's Head was to go up to his room and let himself in. Without even bothering to assess the quality of his accommodation, he took out the letters and undid the ribbon. There were almost a dozen in all and they were patently written by three different women. Colbeck felt slightly guilty to be looking at private correspondence filled with endearments but, in the interests of solving the case, it was vital that he did so. Two things were clear. None of the three women was educated. One could barely scrawl her messages and the others, though writing in a neater hand, made grammatical and spelling mistakes. The shortcomings did not in any way distract from the intensity of the feelings that were expressed. All three sets were love letters written by women who'd surrendered to Bedloe's charms. Evidently, he'd kept them as trophies.

The second thing Colbeck noticed was that one woman had written twice as many letters as either of the others. Unlike their missives, hers were unsigned. They were brief but suffused with longing. Each one specified a date and time when they could next meet. Colbeck had the familiar feeling of excitement that he got when he believed he'd made a breakthrough in an investigation.

Twenty minutes later, he and Leeming were settling down for a meal in the dining room. When he heard about the cache of letters, the sergeant was at once pleased yet scandalised, delighted with the find yet critical of the clear evidence of adultery that it exposed.

'What about their marriage vows?' he asked.

'They chose to ignore them.'

'That's dreadful, sir!'

'It's reprehensible,' conceded Colbeck, 'but we don't know the full details. Not all marriages are as happy as the ones that we enjoy, Victor. That's in no way a justification for adultery, I grant you, but we must accept that some wives lead lives of utter desperation.'

'What they did was wrong.'

'I prefer to see them less as scarlet women and more as victims of a practiced philanderer. Bedloe obviously exerted a hold over them and enjoyed doing so. That's why he kept the letters as souvenirs.'

Leeming forked a piece of potato. 'I'm not sure I want to read them.'

'You don't have to, Victor. My job is to identify the three women. That might be problematical. One of the names was illegible and the other was little better. The third woman was careful not to sign her letters and she's the important one.'

'Why is that, sir?'

'I fancy that she had an assignation with Bedloe last night.'

'Then she must have had a terrible shock when she turned up to meet him.'

'Yes,' said Colbeck. 'The chances are that it wasn't that old shepherd who first found the body. It was Bedloe's latest conquest. She'll be distraught.'

They broke off the conversation for a couple of minutes and addressed themselves to the meal. While Colbeck was musing on the contents of the letters, Leeming's thoughts went in another direction.

'What about the danger, sir?' he asked.

'All three of them were married so there was a definite risk. It's a measure of how infatuated they must have been that they took it.'

'That's not what I meant.'

'Oh?'

'I was thinking about . . . consequences.'

'Ah, I'm with you now. You're talking about the possibility of impregnation. They must have been aware of that and taken steps to avoid it.'

'John Bedloe was a monster.'

'He wasn't the most appealing individual, perhaps, but I don't think he was quite that bad. His cousin did say that there was a good side to him. I believe that Wills was really upset at his murder. I got the feeling that he wished he'd spent more time with Bedloe when the latter was still alive.'

'So did I. Harry Wills was racked with guilt.'

'We must leave him to deal with it on his own,' said Colbeck. 'Anyway, enough of what I found at Bedloe's cottage – tell me what you've been doing.'

'I had a row with the next Mayor of Wimborne.'

'Oh – and who might that be?'

'It's our arch-enemy, Mr Feltham. Except that he's now trying to be friendly towards us. He cornered me in the bar.'

As he listened to details of the encounter between the two men, Colbeck was both angered and curious. The idea that their presence in Wimborne was related to an election made him seethe.

'Does he realise the situation I'm in?' he asked.

'Yes, sir. I explained that you were close to becoming a father.'

'What did he say to that?'

'I think he was embarrassed.'

'Men like Feltham are never properly embarrassed, Victor. They display the appropriate emotions on the surface but they're only skin-deep.' He sipped from his wine glass. 'But you say that he has a rival for the position of mayor.'

'That's right, Inspector. The result of the election could be close.'

'Then we must find out who is standing against him. Both must be town councillors. It will be up to their colleagues to choose between them.'

'Mr Feltham would never get my vote.'

'But he might win over a few people,' Colbeck pointed out. 'The local newspaper will have details of the murder on its front page tomorrow and I'll guarantee that Feltham will have contrived to get his photograph displayed there. He wants to be portrayed as the hero of the hour for summoning us. We're being *used*, Victor,' he said, bitterly, 'and I object very strongly to that.'

When he was shown into the library by the servant, the visitor waited until Ambrose Feltham looked up from his desk.

'You sent for me, sir,' he said.

'Yes, I did. I have some work for you.' He flicked a hand. 'Sit down.'

Richard Satchwell lowered himself into an armchair. He'd removed his uniform and was now wearing a suit. He glanced covetously around the room.

'You have a wonderful library, Mr Feltham.'

'I didn't bring you here to admire my books,' snapped the other. 'I need your help. I seem to have got off on the wrong foot with the detectives. In fact, I spoke incautiously to Sergeant Leeming and we had a heated exchange.'

'You should have put him in his place.'

'I was trying to do the very opposite – reaching out to him by explaining why I was so eager for this investigation to be resolved in as short a time as possible. My temper got the better of me, I'm afraid.'

'What exactly happened, sir?'

'That's neither here nor there,' growled Feltham. 'The point is that I need to – how shall I put it? – recover lost ground.'

'I'll do whatever you tell me, sir.'

'Good man.'

'What are my orders?'

'Firstly, you must keep an eye on the pair of them. After my brush with the sergeant earlier this evening, it's unlikely that he and the inspector will want to keep me abreast of every development. Find out what's going on. As Bedloe's colleague, you have a particular interest in the outcome of this case.'

'I do, Mr Feltham.'

'Secondly – and this may take a degree of diplomacy – I want you to present me to them in a more favourable light. Explain what I've done for the town and how I'm picking up the bill for their stay here out of the goodness of my heart. But, above all else, do it subtly.'

'I understand.'

'You won't lose by it. When I become mayor, I'll remember what you did on my behalf.' Satchwell smiled. 'But you have to earn my gratitude.'

'I will, Mr Feltham. I promise.'

'Then off you go,' said the other, indicating the door. 'And don't come back until you have good news to report.'

Satchwell got to his feet, had a last look around the room then went quickly out.

During the night, there was another false alarm. Because the baby started kicking with more insistence than before, Madeleine feared that something serious was happening. She rang the bell on the bedside table and the nurse who'd been engaged to look after her came swiftly in from the adjoining room. Madeleine was soon reassured. What had happened was perfectly normal. There was no need to summon the doctor. The trouble was that, having woken up, the mother-to-be now had great difficulty in dozing off again. For several weeks now, her sleeping pattern had been disturbed. Madeleine slept best when her husband was beside her but he had moved into a guest bedroom some time ago. At that moment, of course, he was somewhere in Dorset, no doubt thinking about her but unable to offer her any practical support.

It was hours before she finally fell asleep. When the doctor called not long after breakfast, Madeleine was still drowsy. She was, however, heartened by the certainty with which he said the baby was not due for at least a week. As he was leaving the house, Lydia Quayle arrived and was shown straight in. Madeleine was so thrilled to see her friend that she didn't notice how tense and preoccupied Lydia seemed. They went through the ritual exchange about Madeleine's condition then discussed the plans that had been made for the baby. Out of the blue, Madeleine asked a question that had never occurred to her before.

'Does Miss Myler know that you've been coming here?'

Lydia was caught unawares. 'No,' she said, 'as a matter of fact, she doesn't.'

'Why haven't you mentioned it?'

'There's no special reason, Madeleine.'

'Is it because you think she might disapprove?'

'No, not at all.'

'Well, she certainly didn't approve of me when we first met,' recalled Madeleine. 'She made that crystal clear.'

'Beatrice is a wonderful woman, really. She holds no grudges against you.'

'I'm glad to hear it.'

Lydia was plainly discomfited. While Madeleine had not been responsible for the way that Lydia and Beatrice Myler had been forced apart, she was blamed by the older woman. Unwilling to explain why she'd deliberately kept her friend in the dark, Lydia instead shifted the conversation to a development that was causing her great apprehension.

'I had a letter from my solicitor this morning,' she confided.

'What did it say?'

'It's bad news, Madeleine. Mother's will is being contested.'

'Oh dear!'

'After all that we've been through, I thought that the family had closed ranks but that's clearly not the case. Because the terms of the will are very favourable to me, Stanley, my elder brother, has elected to mount a challenge.'

'On what possible grounds is he doing that?'

'I won't bore you with the details. Suffice it to say that there's going to be a protracted legal wrangle and I may not receive in full what Mother intended. But let's forget about my troubles,' she said, squeezing Madeleine's arm, 'and concentrate on you instead. Your situation is far more important than mine. Robert must be so annoyed at being sent away at such a moment. When will he return?'

Madeleine shrugged. 'I wish that I could answer that question.'

Colbeck decided that the only person in whom he could confide was Oliver Keddle. The doctor was a kind, tolerant, understanding man who enjoyed the trust of all his patients. He was habituated to keeping secrets about the medical records of the people who came to his surgery. For that reason, Colbeck felt able to talk to him and to show him the letters that he'd acquired in John Bedloe's house. Keddle read them with an interest tempered with sadness.

'Those poor deluded creatures,' he said. 'While I'd censure them for what they did, I also have some sympathy for them.'

'Do you have any idea who the women might be?' asked Colbeck.

'I can't say that I do.'

The letters were spread out in three piles on a table in his drawing room. As he spoke, he touched each pile in turn.

'This one is a complete mystery,' he complained, 'because there's no signature. Whether out of shame or caution, the woman shielded her identity.'

'What about the second pile?'

'Your guess is as good as mine, Inspector. It looks as if a spider dipped itself into an inkwell before signing the name. It could be Jane, or Jenny, or Jesse, or that "J" might really be an "I" and so she could be Irene, Iris or one of half a dozen other names. I've never seen such appalling calligraphy before.'

'That leaves the last pile – only two letters.'

'Yes,' said Keddle, 'but they're by far the most poignant. This woman, Susan, was prepared to sacrifice everything for him.'

'Does the name mean anything to you?'

'We have several Susans in Wimborne but I don't think that she hails from here. There's a mention of Fordington and that's near Dorchester. In fact . . .' His hand shot up to his forehead. 'Oh, no, it can't be her!' he exclaimed. 'I pray to God that it isn't.'

'Who are you talking about?'

'*Please* let it be an unfortunate coincidence.' He picked up the two letters and read through them. 'And yet, I have a horrible feeling that it's not. Forgive me, Inspector. I do apologise. Something just popped into my mind.'

'I'll be interested to hear what it is.'

'A couple of years ago – it might even be longer – I was at a dinner with some medical colleagues in Dorchester. One of them was telling me the sad tale of a young woman who drowned herself in the River Frome. You can probably guess why.'

'She was with child?' suggested Colbeck.

'Exactly,' said Keddle. 'And her husband was a sailor who'd been at sea for some time. When the child was conceived, he was somewhere in the Atlantic.'

'Do you think that this was the woman in question?'

'It would not surprise me.'

'So she believed all the promises that Bedloe had made to her,' said Colbeck, 'then found out that they were a tissue of lies. Did you say that the suicide occurred two years ago?'

'It was about that length of time.'

'Then it ties in with what Satchwell told my sergeant.'

'What did Dick Satchwell say?'

'He claimed that Bedloe came to Wimborne two years ago. Have we just stumbled on his reason for doing so? Was he keen to move away from Dorchester before the return of this woman's husband?' He took the letters from Keddle and read them once more. 'Thank you, Doctor,' he said. 'I'm so glad that I came to you.'

Because it involved a journey in two separate trains, Victor Leeming was not looking forward to the visit to the estate where Bedloe had once worked. As he sat on a bench on the platform at Wimborne Station, he wished that the wind was not quite so fresh. It was threatening to dislodge his top hat. He also began to have doubts that they would be able to solve the murder as quickly as they'd hoped. As a rule, a couple of suspects tended to surface at the very start of an investigation but they'd had no such luck on this occasion. If the crime was, in fact, as seemed likely, an act of vengeance by a jealous husband, there might be plenty of *potential* suspects but none of them as yet had a name. And while Colbeck believed that the collection of billets-doux provided crucial evidence, all that it did in Leeming's view was to confirm that John Bedloe was a man who specialised in courting and seducing vulnerable wives.

It was only when he heard a familiar voice that the sergeant realised someone had sat down next to him. Back in uniform, Richard Satchwell sounded a friendly note.

'Good morning, Sergeant,' he said. 'I hope that you had a good night.'

'I never have a good night when I'm away from home.'

'Have you seen the local paper today?'

'No,' said Leeming. 'The only thing I've read is the breakfast menu.'

'You're mentioned on the front page. Well,' Satchwell continued, 'it's the inspector whose name is actually given but it did say that he had an assistant. The article also praised Mr Feltham for bringing you here so swiftly to take on the case. In fact, there's quite a bit about Mr Feltham.'

Leeming pursed his lips. 'I had a feeling there might be.'

'You should be very thankful to him.'

'Why?'

'Well, to start with, you're sitting on one of the benches he donated to the station. He's the leading public benefactor in the town and a sort of champion of good causes. People here look up to him.'

'That's their business.'

'Mr Feltham wants to help in the investigation.'

'He can do that best by keeping out of our way,' said Leeming, pointedly. 'When we take on a case, Inspector Colbeck insists on being given a free hand. We don't want anyone peeping over our shoulder all the time. You might care to pass that on to Mr Feltham when you report this conversation to him.'

Satchwell stiffened. 'I don't know what you mean.'

'Oh, I think you do. He told you about our argument, didn't he?'

'What argument?'

'Stop pretending,' Leeming told him. 'We both know why you're here. I had a row with Mr Feltham and, because I objected to what he said, I didn't mince my words. He went off in a huff. I think he sent you to explain what a wonderful man he really is

88

and that the fault was all mine for misunderstanding him. There's just one problem,' he added with a grin. 'I understood him only too well.'

'I simply sat down to have a pleasant chat with you.'

'But who ordered you to do so?'

'Nobody,' claimed Satchwell. 'I've got a stake in this case. John Bedloe and I worked side by side. Doesn't that entitle me to know how the investigation is going?'

'It's going to the Sweetbriar Estate at the moment.'

'That's where John used to work.'

'I know. I need to find out why he left his post.' The sound of an approaching train made him stand to his feet. 'I'll have to leave you now, I'm afraid. You'll have to wait until we meet again before you can ask the rest of the questions Mr Feltham told you to put to me.' Leeming gave him a friendly pat on the shoulder. 'Give him my regards, won't you?'

Something had happened to him. It was as strange as it was disturbing. Rebecca Tullidge didn't know what had come over her husband but, from the moment he'd got up the previous day, his behaviour had been odd and, at times, quite alarming. He'd looked at her with such studied concentration over their meals that she quivered inwardly. Rebecca kept telling herself that he couldn't possibly know the truth, yet it was the death of her lover that had brought about the profound change in Tullidge. There was worse to come. Instead of passing the day in his customary gloom, he somehow shook off his melancholy and became more animated. When they retired to bed that night, he did something he only ever tried to do on a Saturday night when he was rolling drunk. He made love to her.

From her point of view, there was not much love involved.

Without any warning or sign of affection, he simply rolled over on top of her and took his pleasure fiercely with an animal disregard for her. All that she could do was to submit. Though it was over very quickly, he'd managed to inflict several bruises and a bite on her shoulder. While he'd fallen asleep almost immediately, she lay awake for hours in discomfort, wondering what was going on. Of only one thing was she certain. She'd been punished.

There was no mention of the incident the next day. They were up early and he was out on duty. For the first couple of hours, they hardly exchanged a word. But at least he was not glaring at her any more. He seemed much more his usual self, going through his routine by force of habit and, in moments of rest, having the vacant look on his face that she knew so well. Rebecca did her best to avoid him but that was difficult. At one point, she watched him through the window. He was opening the gates after a train had shot past. Tullidge then saw something that obviously upset him. It made him trot back to the house and into the scullery.

'Don't leave here,' he cautioned.

'Why not?'

'I'll take care of him.'

'Who are you talking about, Michael?'

'Stay out of sight. I don't want him to see you.'

'I don't know who you mean?'

'It's that damned detective who called here yesterday.'

'What does he want with us?'

'Leave me to find that out. You hide in here.'

'Yes, Michael.'

'I'll get rid of him as soon as I can.'

He went back outside the lodge in time to see Colbeck pull up in the trap that he'd hired in Wimborne. The inspector was as immaculate as ever and it made Tullidge acutely aware of how rumpled and unkempt he was. Feet apart and arms folded, he waited until his visitor alighted from the vehicle.

'What d'you want?' he asked, inhospitably.

'Good morning, Mr Tullidge. I was hoping for a word with you.'

'I'm too busy. A train's due any minute.'

'Not according to the timetable I consulted,' said Colbeck, suavely. 'You've got all of fifteen minutes before the next one comes. That should be more than enough for me to ask you a few questions.'

'You did that yesterday,' protested Tullidge.

'I did, sir, and I very much enjoyed meeting you and Mrs Tullidge. That's why I came back today. I sensed how eager you both were to be of assistance to me and I'm very grateful.'

Tullidge glowered at him.

CHAPTER SEVEN

When he reached Sherborne Station, Leeming had to hire transport to complete the remaining leg of his journey. The driver of the trap was a shaggy old man who looked as if he'd slept in his clothing over an extended period of time. Climbing up beside him, the sergeant was hit by a compound of unpleasant odours. The driver smelt in equal parts of rancid food, stale beer, foul tobacco and horse dung. When he opened his mouth, bad breath served to intensify the general stink.

'Wheer to, sir?' he asked.

'Sweetbriar Estate.'

'I'll get ye theer in no time at all.'

He cracked his whip and set the horse in motion. Leeming was grateful for the biting wind now. It might have designs on his hat but it helped to dispel the stench beside him. Sherborne was a pleasant town, nestling around a magnificent abbey. It had great charm and a sense of distinction, yet Leeming hardly took any notice of it. His mind was focused on his destination.

'What can you tell me about Sweetbriar?' he asked.

''Tis big, sir, very big.'

'Who owns it?'

'That'd be Lord Barrin'ton.'

'What sort of a man is he?'

'Very rich, sir, very 'igh an' mighty.'

'How much land does he have?'

'Thousands of akers.'

'Do you know anyone who works there?'

'Lots o' people – tenant farmers, mostly.'

'Does Lord Barrington have any deer?'

The old man chuckled. 'Bless ye, sir. They're the best 'erds in Dors't.'

'No wonder he needs a gamekeeper, then. That's why I'm going there. I want to ask some questions about a man who once worked there as a gamekeeper.'

'What were 'is name?'

'John Bedloe.'

'Ah,' said the other, chuckling again, 'ye must be that detective what's come from Lunnun.'

'I'm one of them,' admitted Leeming. 'How do you know about us?'

'Word travels.'

'Then you'll know why we're here.'

'It's that murder in West Moors. Some black-'earted villain killed John.'

Leeming was surprised. 'You knew him?'

'I know most folk round 'ere, sir.'

'How did you come to meet Bedloe?'

The old man seized his cue and talked at length. Though he

was forced to inhale gusts of his companion's bad breath, Leeming didn't mind. He was rewarded with a lot of useful information. During his time at Sweetbriar, it emerged, Bedloe had often come into Sherborne and, on occasion, needed the services of the old man to get back to his cottage late at night. With a series of cackles and nudges, the driver hinted that Bedloe had come in search of female company. Leeming reasoned that even a place as small and apparently respectable as Sherborne would have some prostitutes but, when he suggested that that's what brought Bedloe there, the driver shook his head violently.

'Good Gad!' he exclaimed. 'John'd no need to pay for it. If you'd seed 'im, ye'd know that 'cos 'e were an 'ansome man. No, what 'e liked best, I fancies, was lonely wives – an' I knows why, sir.'

'Do you?'

'Can't ye guess?'

'They were easy to take advantage of.'

'That weren't it, sir,' said the other, scornfully. 'Most men only gets what they wants from wimmin by promisin' to marry 'em. John Bedloe was clever, that's for sure. 'E went after those as was already wed. Can ye see why?'

'Yes,' said Leeming with an expression of disgust. 'It meant that he didn't have to commit himself to any of them in the sight of God. He could take what he wanted then walk away afterwards.'

The driver chortled. 'Lucky ole divil!'

'That's not how I'd describe him.'

'Ye never met John.'

'No,' replied Leeming, 'and I'm very glad that I didn't.'

Colbeck talked inconsequentially with him for a couple of minutes in the hopes of breaking down his reserve. It was a futile effort.

Tullidge remained sullen, watchful and quietly hostile. Colbeck glanced down the track.

'What was John Bedloe doing there two nights ago?'

'I've no idea.'

'You told me you'd never seen him here before.'

'I haven't,' said Tullidge, face motionless.

'Correct me if I'm wrong,' said Colbeck, 'but railway policemen usually have a hut at their disposal, don't they? That must have been the case with Bedloe, surely?'

'So?'

'Where exactly was it?'

'You'd have to ask Dick Satchwell. He'd know.'

'Don't you?'

'No, I don't.'

'It must have been some distance away from here, surely?'

'It must have been,' said the other, dully.

Colbeck pointed. 'So why was his body found near *that* shed down there?'

'You tell me, Inspector,' said Tullidge, almost insolently.

'Let's go back to the night of the murder, shall we?'

'Why?'

'Because it's important to do so,' said Colbeck, sharply. 'You don't seem to be interested in having the killer caught and convicted but I certainly do. When I spoke to your wife yesterday, she told me that you'd got back home around eleven o'clock. Is that right?'

'It could be.' Tullidge gave a crooked smile. 'I'd been drinking.'

'That's what I was told. Mrs Tullidge said you'd been out with friends.'

'True.'

'So I called on two of those friends this morning before I came here. Both of them live here in West Moors. One of them was Elias Rawles and the other was Hugh Delafield.'

Tullidge was annoyed. 'Why did you go bothering them?'

'They drink with you every Saturday night, it seems.'

'No law against that, is there?' challenged the other.

'None at all, Mr Tullidge,' said Colbeck. 'All three of you go to the Waggon and Horses. I know that because I took the trouble to pay it a visit after I'd spoken to Rawles and Delafield. The landlord knows you well.'

'And so he should.'

'He described you as a creature of habit. You always stay at the inn until it's getting towards eleven o'clock but it was different on Saturday, wasn't it? According to the landlord – and to your two friends – you left well over an hour earlier. Why was that?'

'I can't remember.'

'Mrs Tullidge was fairly precise about the time you got back home.'

'She could be mistaken.'

'You were the one who'd been drinking – not your wife.'

'Becky makes mistakes sometimes.'

'Then let's go and speak to her, shall we?' said Colbeck, moving.

Tullidge stepped into his path. 'She's not here.'

'I thought I saw a face at the window.'

'It weren't Becky.'

'Mrs Tullidge can't be far away. Where is she?'

'You come here to make an accusation,' said the other, squaring up to him. 'Why don't you make it?'

Colbeck was polite. 'It's not so much an accusation as a simple question.'

'Go on.'

'The Waggon and Horses is less than ten minutes' walk

97

away. What were you doing on Saturday night in the hour or so between leaving there and coming back to your home?' There was a taut silence. Colbeck's voice hardened. 'I'd like an answer, Mr Tullidge.'

After keeping him waiting, the other man spat onto the ground.

'I told you,' he said, coldly. 'I can't remember.'

When she'd taken her children to school, Estelle Leeming made the effort to go all the way to the house in John Islip Street. Though she had reservations about calling on Madeleine Colbeck, she'd been urged to do so by Caleb Andrews. What would have given his daughter the greatest comfort, of course, was the advice and support of her mother. Since that was impossible, Andrews felt she needed a woman friend who'd been through the rigours of childbirth and who could help to prepare her. Estelle could offer the kind of counsel that a spinster like Lydia Quayle was not qualified to give. For that reason, she'd be especially welcome.

As Andrews had predicted, Madeleine was overjoyed to see Estelle again and was able to talk freely with her about her symptoms. The doctor and the nurse tended to offer bland reassurances but Estelle was able to call on her own experience and talk frankly about it. The visit cheered Madeleine up immensely and she was sorry when Estelle finally had to leave.

'Come again soon, won't you?' she said.

'I'll do my best,' replied Estelle. 'Any word from the inspector?'

'I'm afraid not.'

'I keep wondering how he and Victor are getting on.'

Feeling uncomfortable, Madeleine adjusted her position in the bed. 'I have other things on my mind at the moment,' she said with a pained smile.

'That's only natural.'

Madeleine reached out to squeeze her hand. 'Thank you, Estelle.'

'For what?'

'For being such a wonderful support to me. Lydia Quayle called here earlier and she said the same thing. She described you as a tower of strength.'

Estelle was surprised. 'Did she?'

'You know what's happening to me. You understand the implications of childbirth. They're still a mystery to her. Miss Quayle pointed out that she can only offer friendship whereas you can give practical advice. That's why she's so glad that you come here whenever you can.'

The news delighted Estelle. She looked at Lydia Quayle afresh. She no longer felt that she and the other woman were unable to speak together without unease or embarrassment on her part. Lydia recognised her value and that was important to Estelle. When she walked away from the house, she savoured the comments. She shook off the embarrassment she always felt in Lydia's presence. Each of them was trying to offer Madeleine help during the last stages of pregnancy but it was Estelle's assistance that was of more use. She felt validated. Instead of fearing it, Estelle could now look forward to a chance meeting with Lydia Quayle.

The closer they got to the Sweetbriar Estate, the more notice Leeming took of his surroundings. Rolling fields surrounded him and, in the hedgerows, there was a profusion of early wild flowers. The abiding sense of space and bright colours reminded him how dark London could be and how restrictive its roads and streets were. On his way to Scotland Yard every morning, he passed very few trees and only had a fleeting glimpse of a park. Nature had been subdued and, in some areas of the capital, entirely obliterated. In Dorset, by contrast, it flourished. Notwithstanding the reek from his companion, the sergeant felt that he was breathing an altogether fresher and healthier air. It was invigorating.

Leeming was relieved that he didn't have to approach Lord Barrington himself. Aristocrats always frightened him slightly and, unlike Colbeck, he didn't know how to talk to them without feeling inferior. On the driver's advice, they went straight to the house where the estate manager lived and the sergeant introduced himself to a tall, upright, well-built man in his forties with a military air about him. Leonard Findlay was like a younger version of Superintendent Tallis. He even had the same rasping voice. Leeming found him a trifle unnerving.

Findlay was hearing about the murder for the first time. He was shocked.

'I'd never have expected it of Bedloe,' he said in astonishment. 'He was the sort of man who could look after himself. And what's this about a corkscrew?'

'I wish I knew, sir,' confessed Leeming. 'It's baffling.'

'Do you have any suspects?'

'The investigation is still at a very early stage. I came here because I understand that John Bedloe was employed on the estate for some time.'

'That's true. He was my best keeper.'

'Why did he leave?'

'Well, it wasn't because of the standard of his work,' said Findlay. 'That was exemplary. He kept the local magistrates well supplied with poachers. More to the point, he used his discretion.'

'What do you mean?'

'Well, if he caught a couple of lads snaring rabbits, he didn't bring the full weight of the law down on them. He'd simply clip their ears and give them a stern warning. That was usually enough. Manders is very different.'

'Manders?'

'One of the other keepers – we have three on the estate. There's a huge area to police and, of course, no one man can be on duty twenty-four hours a day. Bill Manders is a martinet. Left to him, he'd set mantraps everywhere if they weren't illegal now. He believes that a one-legged poacher would be the best deterrent to others. And if a child so much as strays by mistake on to our property, he'll be charged with trespass by Manders. I don't hold with that and neither did Bedloe.'

'Why did he leave?'

'The truth is that I don't rightly know,' admitted Findlay.

'Was there some scandal involving a woman?'

'Not that I know of, Sergeant. I don't pry into the private lives of my keepers. As long as they do their job properly, I'm happy. Bedloe seemed quite content to be living by himself.'

'What about the other keepers?'

'They're both married.'

'You must have some idea *why* Bedloe left,' said Leeming. 'We've been told that he enjoyed working here. Why not stay?'

'I think the answer lies in his relationship with Bill Manders. They never really got on. There was always an underlying friction between them. I had to bang their heads together once and issue a warning. They seemed to come to their senses after that. A few months later, Bedloe told me that he was off.'

'Did you give him a reference?'

'Of course – he deserved it. He was quite fearless, you know. When he caught two poachers one night, making off with a couple of our deer, he took on the pair of them single-handed and knocked them both out. That's why I was so surprised to hear that he'd been murdered. Bedloe was a tough man.'

'What happened after he left?'

'I simply engaged a new keeper and that was that. Until you told me,' said Findlay, 'I had no idea that he'd become a railway policeman. That would've suited him, I daresay.'

'He'd still have to look out for trespassers.'

'He'd had plenty of practice at that.'

'Thank you, sir,' said Leeming. 'It's good of you to give me your time. I'm interested in what you say about this other keeper, Manders. Would it be possible for me to speak to him?'

'Is it necessary?'

'I think so, sir. My inspector insists on thoroughness.'

'Well,' said Findlay, guardedly, 'if you promise not to distract him from his work too much, I'll track him down for you. But I hope that you're not even thinking of Bill Manders as a likely suspect. You'll be wasting your time if you do.'

The train journey from Wimborne to Dorchester was over twenty-five miles and involved intermediate stops at Poole, Wareham, Wool and Moreton. Ordinarily, Colbeck would have shown keen interest in everything he could see out of the window but he was too preoccupied on this occasion. Madeleine dominated his thoughts and blocked out everything else. He wished that he was still in London or, at the very least, in possession of the latest bulletin about her condition. Yet, in an uncharacteristic fit of pique, he'd spurned the chance to let someone else take charge of the investigation. As a result, he was now feeling guilty and his wife was missing the one person she most wanted close to her at such a time. While concern for her spurred him on to solve the crime that had taken him to Dorset, he kept reminding himself of the old adage that more haste meant less speed. Urgency had to be kept in check by slow, methodical, meticulous attention to detail.

When the train steamed into the county town, all thoughts of impending fatherhood were put aside. Colbeck was there to broaden his investigation. The station was a quarter of a mile outside the town and the cab ride gave him the opportunity to see something of its environs. Dorchester had a population of almost seven thousand but it was market day and masses of other people had streamed in from surrounding farms and villages to swell the numbers. Penned, tethered or caged, farm animals contributed loudly to the pandemonium and rural aromas invaded Colbeck's nostrils. His driver had great difficulty negotiating the crowds but eventually deposited his passenger outside a fine Regency house in High West Street. The brass plate on the wall confirmed that he'd reached the home of Dr Francis L. Anson.

Colbeck had to wait until Anson had finished his last consultation of the morning. When he heard why the detective was there, he was only too ready to help.

'Keddle sent you, did he?'

'Yes, sir, and I'm to pass on his warmest regards.'

'Please give him mine in return. I like Keddle – splendid fellow, good knowledge of clinical medicine and, more importantly, of human nature.'

'Do you recall the case about which he told me?'

'I do, indeed, Inspector. It was a tragedy in every sense. The woman lost her life, her baby and her reputation. As for the husband . . .'

Anson was a tall, pale, cadaverous man in his sixties with expressive hands. To a full head of luxuriant white hair, he'd added a well-trimmed moustache and a goatee beard. More tufts sprouted from his ears. His voice was deep and measured.

'Susan Elwell,' he said, 'that was her name. Twenty-odd years earlier, I'd helped to bring her into the world. She was Susan Jamieson in those days. Then she met and married Jack Elwell, a sailor from Weymouth.'

'Was it a happy marriage?'

'It was when her husband was here but that was the exception rather than the rule. The call of the sea is a very powerful one. I'm grateful that I never had the misfortune to hear it.'

'So the wife was left alone for long periods.'

'That's what happens if you wed a sailor.'

'Do they have no children of their own?'

'No, Inspector, but both were keen to start a family.'

'Is there no chance that Elwell was the father of her baby?'

'Not the slightest,' said Anson, sadly. 'It was a simple case of mathematics. When Susan came to me, I was able to make a fairly reliable guess at the time when the child must have been conceived. She almost fainted on the spot. It was weeks after her husband had set sail.'

'What did she do?'

'What would any wife do in that position? Susan flew into a panic. At one point, she even begged me to perform an abortion. I was hurt and insulted that she could imagine I would ever do such a thing,' said Anson with righteous indignation. 'As a doctor, I've taken the Hippocratic oath, a vow to *save* lives. Abortion is anathema to me. I gave her a good talking-to and that seemed to calm her down.'

'Did you give her any advice?'

'I told her that she should confide in her mother at once because she needed someone who could stand by her in the crisis.'

'How did Mrs Elwell react?'

'She said that she couldn't possibly do that.'

'Why not?'

'Her mother was more likely to disown her than support her. That's what she claimed, anyway. And the mother would, in any case, demand to know the name of the real father. Susan Elwell refused to reveal his identity to anyone.'

'Had she made him aware of her condition?'

'Yes,' said Anson, hands weaving intricate pictures in the air. 'All he did was to order her to get an abortion. He wanted the problem well and truly out of the way before her husband returned.'

'In other words,' said Colbeck, 'he was thinking about himself as much as about her. A baby conceived out of wedlock would be a grave inconvenience to him. Apart from anything else, it would put an angry husband on his tail.'

'That was what drove her to desperation, in my view. The poor woman had nobody to turn to. The mother would have rejected her, the lover lost interest the moment she told him what the situation was and, in her own fevered mind, she probably blamed me for not agreeing to an abortion. All in all, Susan Elwell must have felt comprehensively let down.'

'When did she commit suicide?'

'The very night after she'd come to see me.'

'How dreadful!' said Colbeck.

'She wore an old overcoat, filled the pockets with stones, chose the deepest part of the river and waded in. I saw her when they dragged her out of the water. It was a pitiable sight.'

Colbeck remembered the packet of letters inside his coat.

'Did Mrs Elwell ever have reason to write to you, Doctor?'

'Good Lord – no! Why should she? In all the years she was my patient, I probably only saw her three or four times. Medical treatment costs money and the Elwells had very little. Besides, she was a woman with little education. I doubt very much if she had a legible hand.'

'Oh, she did,' Colbeck told him. 'I've seen letters that were almost certainly written by her. They were in the possession of John Bedloe.'

Anson frowned. 'Isn't he the victim of that murder in West Moors?'

'He was working in Dorchester at the time when Mrs Elwell came to you.'

'Really? What was he doing here?'

'He was a railway policeman.'

'Are you telling me that . . . ?'

'Yes,' replied Colbeck. 'On the strength of the evidence you've supplied, I believe that he may well have been the father of Mrs Elwell's child. The callous way that he responded to her plea seems very much in character.'

'So *that's* why you came here today,' said Anson, clapping his hands. 'You're in search of a suspect.'

'I may have found one.'

'Jack Elwell?'

'I'm bound to wonder if he finally discovered who'd fathered his wife's child. I'm banking on the fact that you're going to tell me that he's not at sea.'

'He's not, Inspector, he's right here. Elwell has turned his back on voyaging.'

'I had a feeling that he might have done so.'

'He's remarried and is watching the second Mrs Elwell more closely.'

'Where might I find him?'

'He works for a boatbuilder so he hasn't abandoned sailing altogether. And he still lives in the house in Fordington that he shared with his first wife. That puzzles me. It must be filled with bad memories for him. Most men in his position would have moved well away from the place.'

'Perhaps he stayed there for a purpose, Doctor.'

'I can't discern one.'

'That's because you've never been in the position of wanting to wreak your revenge against someone who caused you the most terrible anguish. If Elwell had moved to another town to put the whole thing behind him, his fury would slowly have died down. He may have wanted to keep it simmering away,' argued Colbeck. 'And the best way to do that was to stay in the very house where he was betrayed.'

When her husband's letter arrived, Madeleine was overjoyed. He sent his love, talked about the thrill of becoming a father and assured her that she was constantly in his thoughts. What cast a slight shadow over her pleasure was the fact that Colbeck said nothing at all about the investigation or how long it might last. While it could be that he was shielding her from lurid details of a murder in case they upset her, it could also mean that he and Victor Leeming had made no initial progress. After being involved in so many cases, Colbeck's instincts had been honed. From the outset, he usually had feelings about an investigation that were strangely prescient. There was no hint of them this time. That worried her.

She drew strength from the fact that, while Colbeck was away, she had the support of two kind and caring women. Estelle Leeming understood her predicament only too well because she'd experienced something similar when her first child was born. Wanting her husband to be at hand, she'd been forced to accept that his work took precedence. While she was in labour, Victor Leeming was on the trail of a killer in Northampton and only heard of the birth of his son by telegraph. What Estelle did have, of course, was the help of a loving mother and that was something Madeleine sorely missed.

It was a loss that she shared with another female friend, though the death of Lydia Quayle's mother was far more recent and, it now transpired, was leading to unforeseen complications. There had been a number of times when Madeleine had been involved – albeit surreptitiously – in one of Colbeck's investigations and she'd made the acquaintance of many women along the way. What made Lydia stand out from the rest had been her readiness to call on Madeleine for moral support. The friendship had swiftly deepened and continued well beyond the investigation that had brought them together. It was only in retrospect that Madeleine realised there was another bond between them. Each of their fathers had been the victim of a violent assault. In the case of Vivian Quayle, it had resulted in his death and might very well have done so where Caleb Andrews was concerned. Madeleine's father had been driving a train that was stopped illegally and robbed. Because he'd refused to obey orders, Andrews had been injured so badly that his life had hung in the balance. Madeleine shuddered as she remembered the crisis.

It was ironic. The murder of Vivian Quayle had brought Lydia into her life and the vicious attack on her father had introduced her to Robert Colbeck. Out of two horrific events, therefore, there'd been a positive gain. Reading her husband's letter once more, Madeleine was suffused with love. Her life had changed dramatically since she met Colbeck. When her baby was born, she reflected, it would change even more. Estelle Leeming would become a sort of unofficial aunt and Madeleine found herself wishing that Lydia Quayle would be able to follow Estelle's example.

They met over a cup of tea in a discreet little cafe they'd once patronised. Beatrice Myler was content. It was just like old times. Lydia told her the bad news.

'Your brother has no right to contest the will,' said Beatrice.

'Stanley believes that he has.'

'But he's a rich man, isn't he? And you told me that he's the chief beneficiary of your father's will. Why does he want to prevent you from inheriting what your mother clearly intended you to get?'

'He's not doing it on his own behalf,' explained Lydia. 'Stanley is speaking up for my sister, Agnes. He believes that she should get far more because she was the one who stayed at home and looked after Mother. I recognise the sacrifices that Agnes made. When the will was read, I took her aside and said that I felt duty-bound to pass on some of my inheritance to her as a gift.'

'What did she say to that?'

'She said that she'd have to discuss it with Stanley. This is the result.'

'Oh dear!' sighed Beatrice. 'Families can be so frustrating. There are times when I'm so glad that I was an only child.'

When her parents had died, Beatrice had inherited their house and enough money to lead an extremely comfortable life. Lydia's position was different. In deliberately walking away from her family, she'd had a sufficient income to stay in respectable hotels without having the means to buy a property of her own. Thanks to her mother's will, she'd have been in a position to do just that. Her plans were now thrown into disarray. Stanley Quayle, her elder brother, was a wealthy man who could afford the best legal representation. He would not be threatening to contest the will unless he had a strong chance of success.

Lydia was perplexed and quite unsure how to proceed.

'I'm wondering if I should speak to him face-to-face, Beatrice.'

'No,' said the other with emphasis. 'That's the one thing you must not do. You've told me before that you and your elder brother have always been at daggers drawn. I don't think you'd wrest any concessions from him.'

'I could offer a bigger slice of my inheritance to Agnes.'

'That would be a case of admitting defeat.'

'Litigation could be highly expensive.'

'Have you spoken to a lawyer yet?'

'No, Beatrice, I still haven't decided what to do. It's very worrying.'

'I don't see why it should be. The advantage lies clearly with you. Your mother's wishes are firmly expressed in the will.'

'Not according to Stanley,' said Lydia. 'Mother changed her will only days before she died. Stanley is going to argue that she was not of sound mind at the time and that the will is therefore invalid. Agnes will agree. She'll do exactly what Stanley tells her. In an earlier version of the will, apparently, Mother was not so generous towards me. They are arguing that that version should be reinstated.'

'That's preposterous!'

'My elder brother will stop at nothing.'

'What about the doctor? His medical opinion will be decisive, surely? He will be able to confirm that your mother was of sound mind when she made the changes to her will. There'll be no case to answer. Write to the doctor,' urged Beatrice, 'and get him on your side.'

'I'm too late. Stanley has been working on him.'

'The doctor surely won't lie in court, will he?'

'He may not have to, Beatrice. Mother's behaviour was rather odd towards the end. Even Lucas – my younger brother – admitted that, though he still believes that she knew exactly what she was doing when she changed her will. Oh,' she went on, head dropping, 'I had such high hopes when the will was read to us. I envisaged buying a house on my own here in London. That may not be possible.'

'You never know,' said Beatrice, smiling inwardly. 'Besides, even if you do have to lose most of your inheritance, it's not as if you have nowhere to go. My house is yours whenever you choose to move back into it.' She reached out a consoling hand and touched Lydia's arm. 'Remember that, won't you?'

CHAPTER EIGHT

Under other circumstances, Leeming might have liked the gamekeeper. William Manders was a stringy man in his thirties with a wide stance, rugged features and an obvious commitment to his job. He seemed completely at home in the woods where Leeming and Findlay eventually ran him to ground, and he looked as if he knew how to use the shotgun he was carrying. After introducing the two men to each other, the estate manager took his leave but not before warning the sergeant that the gamekeeper had work to do.

'This won't take me long,' promised Leeming.

'What's going on?' asked Manders.

'I need to ask you a few questions, sir.'

'You've come all the way from London to do that?'

'This is a murder enquiry. We leave no stone unturned.'

'I'm a human being, Sergeant, not a stone.'

Manders was blunt, unapologetic and looked him in the eye.

He was the sort of man with whom Leeming would have liked to walk the beat during his time in uniform because he'd be the type of policeman who'd never shrink from action. There was an impressive solidity about him in every sense.

'Where were you two nights ago, Mr Manders?'

'I was on duty here.'

'Can anyone verify that?'

'Don't you believe me?' demanded the other.

'Corroboration is always welcome.'

'What the hell does that mean?'

'It helps to have a witness.'

'Then find the two little bastards I caught trespassing in the woods,' said Manders, hotly. 'They were too quick for me but I managed to kick one of them up the arse. They're my witnesses that I was on duty that night.'

'Mr Findlay told me that it was your shift.'

'Then why bother me?'

'I'm just checking, sir.' Leeming looked him up and down. 'I understand that you and John Bedloe were not the best of friends.'

'We weren't any kind of friends. I hated him.'

'Why was that?'

'Never you mind.'

'I *do* mind – it's part of my job.'

'That's up to you.'

Leeming tried to needle him. 'Mr Findlay described him as his best gamekeeper.'

'Best at *what*, though?' asked Manders, lip curled. 'Yes, he caught plenty of poachers, I'll give him that, but he also let too many go because he took bribes from them. That's what I think, anyway.'

'Did you have any proof?'

'I never saw him doing it, p'raps, but Bedloe always had more money than he earned. Where else could it come from? I challenged him about it once and we ended up fighting.' He straightened his shoulders. 'I won.'

'Is that why he left the estate?'

'It might've been. He knew I was watching him.'

'Did you pass on your suspicions to Mr Findlay?'

'No point – Bedloe was his favourite.'

'When did you first hear about the murder?'

'It wasn't until just now when the estate manager brought you here.'

'And what's your reaction?'

Manders grinned malignantly. 'I'm very upset.'

'You don't sound it, sir.'

'Bedloe deserved what he got.'

'Nobody deserves to die like that, Mr Manders. It was brutal.'

'He could be a brutal man.'

'Did you ever see him after he left here?'

'Only the once,' said the other, sourly. 'It was in Dorchester. I took my wife there to do some shopping and we saw him on duty in uniform. He was prancing around as if he owned the town. Bedloe ignored me but waved to Nancy, my wife.' The muscles in his cheek twitched. 'That was the other thing, of course. I didn't like the way he looked at her. Are you married, Sergeant?'

'Yes, I am.'

'What do you say to men who ogle Mrs Leeming?'

'I give them a flea in their ear.'

Manders bunched his fists. 'I do my talking with these.'

'Did you hit Mr Bedloe on that occasion in Dorchester?'

'I wanted to – but my wife dragged me away.'

Leeming admired his honesty. He made no excuse for disliking

Bedloe and had shown no remorse over his death. On the other hand, he could not simply be eliminated as a suspect. During a long, dark night, nobody would have known if he'd been on duty where he should have been. It was not impossible that he could have got to West Moors and back without anyone on the estate being aware of it. Manders had the motive and the means to kill his former colleague but, Leeming wondered, did he have the opportunity?

'Was he ever a nuisance to your wife, sir?' he asked.

'Yes,' snapped the other.

'Did Mrs Manders complain?'

'Nancy despised him as much as I did.'

'Why?'

'He got praise for things that I did just as well as him.'

'So you resent Mr Findlay, do you?'

'No,' said Manders, quickly. 'He's a fair man and he knows how to run an estate. It's just that he had a weak spot where Bedloe was concerned.'

'When did you last see your old colleague?'

'I told you – it was in Dorchester.'

'And you've never seen him since then?'

'No, Sergeant, and I'd never want to. He belongs to my past.'

Leeming paused. He'd been up against a brick wall so far. His questions kept bouncing harmlessly off it. After taking a deep breath, he tried again.

'Do you and Mrs Manders ever go to Wimborne?'

The gamekeeper scowled. 'I've not been there for years.'

'So you're never in that part of the county?'

'I didn't say that. We have to go to Blandford quite regular.'

'Oh?'

'My wife's family live there,' replied Manders, swelling with

116

pride, 'and I have another reason to go to the town. I compete in point-to-point races at Blandford. If I win – and I often do – it brings in some extra money, and we can always do with that.'

'Ah, so you're a jockey, are you?'

'It's my hobby.'

'Why do you go all the way to Blandford to compete? Aren't there any races held closer to here?'

'Yes,' said Manders, 'but I'd never win on my own horse. He doesn't have the speed or stamina. When I borrow one from my father-in-law, on the other hand, I'm always in with a good chance.'

'Does your father-in-law have stables?'

'Yes, he's like me. He loves horses. I get the choice of three.'

'Is he a farmer?'

Manders laughed. 'No – that would be too much like hard work for him.'

'What does he do in Blandford?'

'He's a wine merchant,' said the other, blithely.

Leeming felt a corkscrew twisting gently into his brain.

Fordington was a rural village lying cheek by jowl with an urban slum. Six years earlier, cholera had broken out there and it was only prevented from spreading to Dorchester by the tireless efforts of the vicar. When he arrived there, Colbeck noticed that sheep were grazing on the moor and that there were extensive water meadows. Small, compact and unappealing, Fordington itself was home to at least a thousand people packed into what, for the most part, looked like ramshackle dwellings. He'd been warned by Anson that it was a singularly unhealthy place as well as the haunt of beggars, prostitutes and fugitives. There were also many people who led law-abiding lives and who eked out a living in a variety of occupations. When he found the hovel where Jack Elwell lived, he

117

realised that the former sailor didn't earn a large wage. Though the place was spotless inside, it was sparsely furnished and there was a faint smell of decay.

Louisa Elwell was a pretty young woman in a smock. The sight of a well-dressed gentleman at her door threw her into confusion and Colbeck had to reassure her that he merely wished to ask her husband a few questions. Neither Elwell nor she was in any kind of trouble. She remained on edge, however.

'Jack has done nothing wrong, sir,' she bleated.

'I'm sure he hasn't.'

'He's a good husband and works very hard.'

'I don't doubt it. Where might I find him?'

Hands playing nervously with her smock, she gave him directions. Colbeck decided that the second Mrs Elwell was very different to her predecessor. She was a thin, almost waif-like creature with an air of innocence about her and she spoke about her husband as if he were the centre of her universe. He wondered just how much she knew about the suicide of Susan Elwell.

'I can show you the way, if you wish, sir,' she offered.

'I'll find him.'

'It's no trouble.'

'You stay here, Mrs Elwell. Oh,' he continued, 'I do have a question for you, as it happens. Where were you and your husband on Saturday night?'

Her face puckered with concern. 'Why do you want to know that?'

'I'm interested, that's all.'

'Well, I spent the night with my parents in Weymouth.'

'What about your husband?'

'Jack stayed here. He was working late on something and wanted to finish it.'

'So you went to Weymouth on your own?'

She hunched defensively. 'There's nothing wrong with that, is there?'

'Nothing at all, Mrs Elwell,' he said with a comforting smile. 'I hope that you had a very pleasant time with your family.'

After another jolting ride in the trap, Leeming got back to Sherborne Station in time to see the train he should have caught puffing away from the platform. Irritated at first, he soon came to see that there was compensation for the enforced wait. On the wall opposite the ticket office was something he'd been too distracted to see on his arrival in the town. It was a large, beautifully painted map of Dorset and it enabled him to get his bearings. He was able to trace the train journey he'd made and estimate its length in miles. His eye then fell on Blandford and he saw how relatively easy it would be for someone who made regular visits there to get to West Moors on a fast horse. Leeming remembered how proud the gamekeeper had been of his horsemanship and how he'd displayed no sympathy whatsoever over the death of John Bedloe. Resentful at having to visit the Sweetbriar Estate, the sergeant now came to see that it may have yielded a priceless dividend.

'What were you doing on Saturday night?' asked Colbeck.

'I was working here.'

'Were you on your own?'

'Yes, everyone else had somewhere to go.'

'So why did you stay?'

'I promised to have the boat ready for Sunday.'

'How long were you here?'

'Most of the night, I suppose.'

Jack Elwell was quite unlike the person Colbeck had expected.

Given the tragic loss of his first wife and the revelation of her adultery, the sailor had every right to be embittered but, in fact, he was quite the opposite. Elwell was a big, burly man with an open face and a ready grin. He'd been working on the hull of an upturned boat when Colbeck walked down to the river and, though startled by the inspector's appearance, he was willing to answer any questions put to him. Elwell's shirt was open at the neck and the sleeves were rolled up, exposing brawny arms that were covered in tattoos.

'Why do you need to talk to me, Inspector?' he asked.

'I'm speaking to lots of people, sir.'

'But I've never even heard of this man who was murdered. What was his name again – Bedford, Bigelow . . . ?'

'John Bedloe. He used to be a railway policeman in Dorchester.'

'Then I've probably seen him,' said Elwell, cheerfully, 'but I always keep well clear of the law. That's no disrespect to you, sir.'

'No offence taken,' said Colbeck.

He was bound to contrast the man's attitude with that of Michael Tullidge. The crossing-keeper had suffered a serious blow when his wife lost both her first baby and any possibility of having a second one. It had plunged him into a dejection that he seemed quite unable to shake off. Elwell, however, had endured even greater pain when he learnt of his wife's suicide and of her clandestine relationship with another man. Yet he was in no way oppressed by the memory. Colbeck concluded that his buoyancy was in part due to his happy marriage to a young wife. Rebecca Tullidge brought no such joy to her husband. The two of them were locked in a union that was bedevilled by a calamity. While the sailor delighted in his wife, Tullidge simply had one he could blame for their misfortune.

'Do you regret turning your back on the sea?' asked Colbeck.

'Not in the least,' said Elwell. 'I've seen more than enough of the world.'

'Why did you stay in your old house?'

'Why not? It's very easy to get to work from there.'

'I'd have thought it would have . . . unpleasant associations.'

'There's nothing unpleasant about it now, Inspector,' said the other, brightly. 'If you've met Louisa, you'll have seen what a lucky man I am. She's a ray of sunshine to me. We'll raise a family in time. It has its faults, I know, but we like Fordington. We fit in there, Inspector.'

Everything that Elwell said seemed to ring true. It might well have been that, by the time the sailor returned to discover that his first wife had taken her own life, John Bedloe had already left the town as a precaution. Elwell would have had no idea who had seduced Susan in his absence. Had he set out to identify the man, Colbeck reasoned, it would hardly have taken him eighteen months. In any case, would he be reckless enough to put his second marriage at risk by committing a foul murder? It seemed unlikely.

Colbeck had toyed with the notion of showing Elwell two of the letters he'd found in order to get confirmation that they had indeed been written to Bedloe by his first wife. He decided against it. Apart from the fact that they would open old wounds that had patently started to heal, Colbeck chose to believe him. If Elwell claimed that he'd been working in Fordington on Saturday night, then that was the truth.

'Anything else I can tell you, Inspector?' asked Elwell, obligingly.

'No, sir, there isn't. Thank you very much.'

He offered his hand in gratitude and was given a testing handshake. As he glanced down, Colbeck saw something that had escaped his notice before. Though his arms were adorned with an anchor, a coiled serpent, a galleon and all the other familiar tattoos favoured by sailors, there was something on the back of his hand at variance with everything else. It was a crucifix.

Richard Satchwell had just chased a dog off the line when he caught sight of someone standing on the Wimborne Station platform. It was Ambrose Feltham, waiting for a train. Satchwell broke into a trot to reach him in time.

'Ah, Satchwell,' said Feltham as the other man approached. 'Is there anything to report?'

'Yes, sir, but it's not good news.'

'I don't like the sound of that.'

'Sergeant Leeming was here earlier this morning. I did as you told me and explained just how much you'd done for the town.'

'What was his response?'

'He wasn't impressed.'

Feltham was outraged. 'Well, he damn well ought to be!'

'He guessed that you'd deliberately set me on to him.'

'Then you should have gone about it with more guile. I don't know what's got into you, Satchwell. You used to be so reliable.'

'I did my best,' pleaded the other.

'I only pay for good results and you have signally failed to get any.'

'That's unjust, Mr Feltham.'

'What – if anything – have you learnt?'

'Quite a bit,' said Satchwell, eager to regain his trust. 'The sergeant was going to the Sweetbriar Estate not far from Sherborne. It's where John Bedloe worked years ago as a gamekeeper. As for the inspector, I noticed him standing here later on and took the trouble to ask the clerk what ticket he'd bought. It was to Dorchester.'

'Why is he going there?'

'Bedloe worked there before coming to Wimborne. Also, he has a cousin who lives there and is a railwayman.'

'The solution to the mystery lies right here,' insisted Feltham. 'Instead of shooting off to other parts of the county, this is where the pair of them should be looking in every nook and cranny. Wimborne must be *cleansed*.'

'Yes, sir.' He tried to curry favour with a smile. 'That was a good photograph of you in today's newspaper. I drew the sergeant's attention to it.'

The information was partially muffled by the sound of an oncoming train. After belching smoke into the air, it slowed down, shot the length of the platform and came to a sudden halt. Only two passengers alighted. One of them was Leeming.

'Good morning!' called Feltham, beckoning him over. 'You've been to the Sweetbriar Estate, I hear.'

'That's right,' said Leeming, walking towards him. 'Satchwell gave you the correct information.'

'Did you find anything that has a bearing on the crime?'

'I think so, Mr Feltham.'

'May we know what it is?'

'Not until I've discussed it with the inspector. I've learnt from experience that what I sometimes believe are clever deductions often turn out to be nothing of the kind once Inspector Colbeck has examined them.'

'Are the two of you sanguine?'

'We always hope for the best, sir.'

'That's not what I'm asking, man. Have you made any strides forward in this case? I'd like to feel there's been a modicum of progress.'

'Oh, I can promise you that but don't let me hold you up,' he went on, standing back. 'The train is about to leave. If you're not careful, they'll go without you.'

Annoyed at being rebuffed, Feltham boarded the train and sat down heavily. The last thing Leeming saw through the window of the compartment was the snarling expression on the face of the man who'd beamed out from the front page of the day's newspaper. Satchwell chided the newcomer.

'There was no need to be so abrupt with him.'

'I was making an effort to be nice to him.'

'Out of his own pocket, he's offering reward money for information that leads to this murder being solved. You and the inspector have a chance to collect it.'

'Our aim is simply to catch a killer, not to collect a reward.'

'Mr Feltham is the person best placed to *help* you.'

'We both know why.'

'This is nothing to do with the election,' asserted Satchwell. 'It's in everyone's interest to find out who killed John Bedloe. Mr Feltham is a very public-spirited man. In bringing you here, he's doing Wimborne a big favour.'

'And we, in turn,' said Leeming, flatly, 'will be doing *him* a big favour by helping to put the mayor's chain around his neck. Talking of which, he has a rival, doesn't he?' Satchwell nodded. 'Who is it?'

'His name is Godfrey Preece.'

'Is he another local businessman?'

'No, Sergeant. He isn't. Preece is a sheep farmer. The train you just got off brought you right through the middle of his land. He's a wealthy man.'

'Where does Mr Feltham's money come from?'

Satchwell was evasive. 'It comes from a number of sources.'

'In short, he has a finger in a lot of pies.'

'He's a financier, Sergeant, and a very successful one at that. His aim is to invest money in the town and persuade other people to do so. That way, Wimborne can grow into something

124

bigger and more important. Preece wants to keep it the way it is.'

'So it's a case of a financier against a farmer, is it?'

'It's a case of a man with a vision against an old stick-in-the-mud.'

'I've met a lot of people with a vision,' said Leeming, reflectively. 'They always overreach themselves in the end. I've had the pleasure of arresting one or two of them. They get to the point where they have so much power that they think they're beyond the law.' He became conspiratorial. 'Pass that on to Mr Feltham.'

Not for the first time, Colbeck wished that the case didn't keep reminding him of Madeleine's situation. He'd been told of a stillbirth, a child drowned in the womb as a result of a suicide and a sailor's dream of raising a family with his second wife. Each time children came into the conversation, he became acutely conscious of his new life as a father. It served to intensify the pain of separation from his wife and to increase his feelings of guilt. However, there was another kind of separation to take into account. Back at Scotland Yard, the superintendent would be waiting impatiently for news of the investigation. When he reached Dorchester Station, therefore, Colbeck sent him a telegraph with enough abbreviated information to hint at signs of progress without giving any detail. He then stepped out on to the platform and reviewed what he and Leeming had learnt.

His attention was soon diverted. Further down the line was a siding into which some rolling stock had been pulled. Someone was in the act of shunting with the aid of a horse, uncoupling a wagon and tying a thick rope to it. Though the laborious process held some interest for him, it was the railwayman who aroused his curiosity. It was John Bedloe's cousin, Harry Wills. Ignoring the cry of protest from the stationmaster, Colbeck jumped nimbly down on to the track and made his way towards the siding. When he saw the inspector approaching, Wills stopped what he was doing and held the horse by its bridle.

'What are you doing here, Inspector?' he asked.

'I was enjoying the sight of you shunting like that. There's a real art to it.'

'It's hard work, sir, especially with a young horse who can be very wilful. I'm talking about you, Samson,' he said, stroking the animal's neck affectionately.

'I've been making enquiries in the town,' explained Colbeck.

Wills was alert. 'What sort of enquiries?'

'It doesn't matter. They came to nothing, alas.'

'If there's anything *I* can do, just let me know.'

'It looks as if you've got your hands more than full at the moment.'

'Is there any word about the inquest?'

'There's a good chance that it may be very soon, Mr Wills. There's no point in delaying it. The body will then be released for burial.'

'How will I know the time and place?'

'I'll find out the details and tell you what they are.'

'That's so kind of you, Inspector,' said Wills, overcome with gratitude. 'I never dreamt that you'd come all the way back here just to speak to me.'

'I won't,' corrected Colbeck. 'There's a telegraph station at Wimborne. I'll send a message from there to here and someone will pass it on to you.'

'Oh, I see.'

'I take it that you've never had a telegraph before?'

'No, Inspector, there's been no call for one. I rarely get a letter, let alone a telegraph.' The horse jerked its head back. 'Easy, boy,' said Wills, tightening his grasp on the bridle. 'You're very considerate, sir.'

'You don't have to be there. I can tell you now what the verdict will be.'

'It's my duty – if I can get the time off, that is.'

'It's your decision.' Colbeck looked over his shoulder. 'I'd better get back to the platform. The stationmaster is waiting to wag his finger at me.'

'Thank you so much for taking the trouble.'

'What we don't as yet know, of course, is whether or not your cousin has left a will. If he's died intestate – that means there's no will – then his worldly goods should come to you as next of kin.'

'I don't want them, sir. They'd be a horrible reminder.'

'In time, you may change your opinion about that. As for the funeral . . .'

'Yes, I know. I've already discussed it with my wife. Don't worry about that, sir. I know my responsibilities.'

'Then I'll let you get on with your shunting before the stationmaster calls a railway policeman and has me arrested.'

Wills gave a strangled laugh.

Edward Tallis had deployed his men to solve crimes all over London but he always had a special interest in Colbeck's activities, not least because they tended to bring in some much-needed good publicity to the Metropolitan Police. When the inspector's telegraph arrived at Scotland Yard, therefore, he read it avidly. It was short, well phrased and gently optimistic. Tallis was not appeased. Reading between the lines, he sensed that he was being misled.

'What's *really* happening there, Colbeck?' he growled.

The joy of feeling a child growing inside her was offset by the increasing discomfort and by the way that her body no longer conformed to its usual rhythm and routines. Madeleine was also dogged by fatigue. She tried hard to fight it off but it was a sturdy opponent. When she least expected it, she would doze off and wake up in a state of mild bewilderment. Though Colbeck's absence was a source of anxiety, she was aware that there was very little he could do if he was actually there beyond acting as a calming presence. In his stead, Estelle Leeming had taken on that task. Lydia Quayle brought other qualities and her visits were a useful distraction. The news about the contested will had upset Madeleine on her friend's behalf because she'd had some insight into the deep-seated tensions in the Quayle family. She could only hope that Lydia's problems would be satisfactorily resolved.

When she'd first become aware of her pregnancy, she'd assumed that she'd be able to continue her work as an artist, spending the later stages by retiring to bed with her current project. It was several weeks since she'd had the slightest urge to reach for her sketch pad and the notion that she could actually concentrate on a new painting now seemed ridiculous. Maternity excluded everything else.

Madeleine picked up her husband's letter once again and read it as if for the first time, luxuriating in the warmth of his love and concern. It lapped over her. Before she'd got to the end of the first paragraph, however, fatigue sapped her strength and she fell irresistibly asleep. The letter fluttered down to the floor.

Victor Leeming was waiting for him when he returned to the hotel. In the privacy of Colbeck's room, they compared notes. The sergeant described his findings first.

'Manders seemed to have a good alibi,' he said, 'but I'm not accepting it at face value. He admitted that he hated Bedloe and that his wife had to restrain him from hitting the man when they saw him in Dorchester.'

Colbeck was unconvinced. 'It sounds to me as if the gamekeeper is a man with a short temper,' he pointed out. 'His anger flares up then subsides. We're looking for someone who can nurse a grudge for a long time before acting. Michael Tullidge is such a person.'

'Why should he have a grudge against Bedloe?'

'I don't know, Victor. What I can tell you is that Tullidge is definitely lying. He refused to say what he was doing after he left the pub on the night of the murder. And we must never forget that the victim was found only a few hundred yards from the lodge.'

'How did he know that Bedloe was going to be in West Moors that night?'

'I could ask the same question with regard to William Manders. If he works the other side of Sherborne, he'd have no idea of Bedloe's movements.'

'I feel that his link to Blandford could be the key,' decided Leeming. 'It's a lot closer to West Moors than the Sweetbriar Estate is. And there's his passion for fast horses – not to mention the coincidence about his father-in-law being a wine merchant.'

'But is he a wine merchant with a missing corkscrew?'

'Do you want me to find out?'

'In time, perhaps,' said Colbeck. 'I've got something more urgent than that.'

'What is it?'

'I'll tell you in a moment. First, you can hear about my trip to Dorchester.'

Colbeck gave him a succinct account of the visit to Dr Anson, the meeting with Jack and Louisa Elwell and the sighting of Harry Wills. Leeming was amused to hear that the stationmaster had threatened to report Colbeck for trespassing on railway property.

'Why didn't you tell him who you were?'

'That would have spoilt his rant, Victor.'

'He'll have a red face when he learns that he was scolding a Scotland Yard detective in pursuit of a killer.'

'He was only doing his job,' said Colbeck, 'and doing it well.'

When he'd finished his recitation, he used his fingers to count off the names.

'Our first suspect is Tullidge, the second – relying on your instinct – is Manders and the third is Jack Elwell.'

'But you said that he was completely plausible.'

'He was at the time,' said Colbeck, 'but I've been thinking again about him. He didn't seem at all surprised when I accosted him at his work. It was almost as if he'd been expecting me.'

'I thought he was friendly, open and helpful.'

'It's that business about working all Saturday night. It worries me.'

'You told me that you questioned his employer and he confirmed that Elwell often worked late if something needed to be done. *We've* worked through the night if it was an emergency. That's what Elwell was doing.'

'Possibly.'

'He didn't *have* to tell you where he was on Saturday.'

'Yes, he did. He knew that I'd met his wife and guessed that I'd have asked where they both were at the time of the murder. Louisa Elwell couldn't tell a lie if you paid her. I'm no longer quite so certain about her husband. Something keeps nagging away at the back of my mind.'

'What is it, sir?'

'Well,' said Colbeck, 'why take a job in a boatyard on the bank of the river where his first wife committed suicide? That could suggest an unhealthy obsession with the event. He can't drag himself away from the house or the river until he's found the man responsible for Susan Elwell's pregnancy.'

'Found him and taken his revenge.'

'Precisely.'

'So that gives us three possible suspects. Can I add a fourth?'

'Go ahead.'

'I wouldn't dismiss Dick Satchwell from our thoughts,' argued Leeming. 'Of all our potential killers, he's the one closest to the victim. He'd have been aware of his movements and could somehow have found out about the assignation – if that's what it really was – on Saturday night. Satchwell was bullied by Bedloe, that's clear. I think he may have got fed up with being pushed around and struck back.' He sat back in his seat. 'I think we should check his alibi with his wife.'

Colbeck mulled it over. 'No,' he said at length, 'I don't see Satchwell as our man, somehow. What would he hope to gain? Besides, he's the appointed emissary for Mr Feltham, isn't he?'

'Yes, he had another go at me when I got back to Wimborne. According to him, Mr Feltham is the salvation of this town. Oh, by the way, I found out who's standing against him for the position of mayor.'

'Who is it?'

'A rich farmer named Godfrey Preece. Feltham is a financier.'

'Country versus town, eh?' said Colbeck. 'Old money versus new. It's a contest that's being played out all over England. As for Satchwell, I think he's only an outside bet as the killer. In the short term, let's train our fire on the other four.'

'But there are only three without Satchwell, sir.'

'I have a new name to add and I do so with my head held in shame.'

'Who is it?'

'Simon Copsey.'

'Isn't he that drunken old shepherd who found the body?'

131

'He may not have been drunk at the time,' argued Colbeck. 'Did he actually stumble upon the victim or was he the killer? When Feltham pointed the finger at Copsey, I dismissed the idea out of hand but Feltham asked a pertinent question.'

Leeming rolled his eyes. 'Even a fool says a wise thing sometimes.'

'He asked me what Copsey was doing there at that time of night.'

'Did you get an answer from the shepherd?'

'He was too drunk to be of any real use, Victor. He needs to be spoken to when he's sober. That's why you're going to God's Blessing Green.'

'*Where?*' asked the other, eyes bulging.

'There is such a place, I assure you. I found it on the map.'

Leeming groaned. 'Not another couple of train journeys, is it?'

'No, it's way off the beaten track. You'll have to go by horse or trap.'

'That's a relief!'

'Go through his story again with a fine-toothed comb. Above all else, find out why he was very close to the crossing-keeper's lodge in West Moors on Saturday night.'

'What will you be doing, sir?'

'I'll be studying those letters again. They might be hiding a *fifth* suspect.'

'Do you still think the killer could be a woman?'

'Yes, I do.'

'Well, I believe that it was a violent man – someone like Manders.'

'Those letters were written by people who adored John Bedloe and he had no qualms about exploiting that adoration. Consider this,' suggested Colbeck. 'What would *any* married woman feel if the man she trusted wholeheartedly cast her ruthlessly aside in favour of a new lover?'

'She'd be upset.'

'*How* upset?'

'Very upset,' said Leeming. 'She might even go in search of a knife and a corkscrew.'

Because no churchyard would accept it, the grave was hidden behind some bushes in unconsecrated ground. Someone stepped silently forward to place a posy of wild flowers on the mound of earth before reflecting on how sweet vengeance could be.

CHAPTER NINE

Rebecca Tullidge was bemused. Her husband continued to act strangely. He seemed to have shaken off his accustomed torpor and no longer went about his duties as if they were tiresome chores. Something else puzzled her. He spent far more time talking to people who used the crossing and she couldn't understand why. In the past, Tullidge had shown little interest in passing vehicles and pedestrians, exchanging no more than a wave or, at best, a few words with them. Yet he actually seemed to enjoy having a conversation with passers-by now and even rose to an occasional smile. It was almost as if he were trying to make up for the years of unsociable neglect.

Talkative with others, he remained as laconic as ever with his wife. But at least he was no longer exuding a muted hostility towards her. She saw that as a welcome bonus. As for his rough treatment of her in the privacy of their bedroom, he made no reference to it whatsoever and obviously didn't think that an apology was in order. While *he* might pretend that it had never happened, however, Rebecca took a different view. The bruises had not faded and the bite marks were still there. The whole frightening experience was a nasty fire at the back of her mind.

She was upstairs when she heard the front door open. Fearing that her husband had come back to the lodge, she went quickly downstairs so that he couldn't catch her in the bedroom. Her fears were unjustified. Instead of her husband, it was Margaret Vout, her closest friend, who often called in for a chat with Rebecca. A roly-poly woman in her forties with a permanent smile on her red-cheeked face, Margaret was the wife of the publican who ran the Waggon and Horses. She was a garrulous woman but Rebecca didn't mind that. Short of female company, she was always glad to see her friend and she never forgot how supportive the woman had been when her child was stillborn.

'Oh,' she said, 'I was hoping to see you, Maggie.'

'I'm sorry I couldn't come earlier. We've been very busy. But I had to come and tell you about the detective who called on us this morning.'

'Was it Inspector Colbeck?'

'That's him. What a handsome man – and what a perfect gentleman! We don't get many of those at the Waggon. I couldn't believe that he's a policeman with manners like that. The only policeman we ever see is Bert Maycock and he's one of us, if you know what I mean. The inspector is . . . well, he's very special, isn't he?'

'Yes, he is.'

'I'd be happy to serve him with a pint of beer any time,' said Margaret with a flirtatious giggle, 'except that he'd probably want a more refined drink. It's a silly thing to say but he made me feel young again. Did he have that effect on you, Becky?'

'Not really.'

'I know that you met him because he told us. In fact, that's why he came. He wanted to check up on something you'd told him.'

Rebecca was alarmed. 'What was it?'

'It was about what time Michael got home on Saturday night.'

'I told him the truth.'

'I'm sure you did, Becky, and I'm sure he took you for the honest person you are. The inspector is the sort of man who looks deep into your eyes. I wouldn't dare try to tell him a lie. He'd know what it was the moment it left my tongue.'

'Why did he ask about Michael?'

'He said that he was just checking.'

'Didn't he trust me?' asked Rebecca, hurt.

'Of course, he did, but all you could tell him was the time that your husband got back here. We knew when Michael left the Waggon on Saturday.'

'It was the usual time.'

'But that's the thing – it wasn't.'

'He got back here when he always does.'

'Then he must've gone somewhere else in between,' said Margaret, 'because he left us much earlier than usual – an hour, in fact. He was drinking all evening with Elias and Hugh and they stayed till we had to throw them out. But not Michael, because he'd already left. He kept looking up at that old clock of ours until he decided he had to leave.' She jerked a thumb over her shoulder. 'Then off he went. I thought he'd come straight back home.'

'Well, he didn't,' said Rebecca, worriedly.

'It must have been the beer. He does drink heavily on a Saturday. I wouldn't be at all surprised if he lost his way here in the dark or if he sat down somewhere and went straight off to sleep. Hugh Delafield has done that a few times. His wife told me. She

137

found him curled up in a ditch once. He was fast asleep and had wet himself.' She sat down familiarly. 'What sort of a state was Michael in when he got back?'

'He was staggering a bit.'

'There you are, then. He had one pint too many, I expect.'

'Yes,' said the other, trying to reassure herself, 'that must be it.'

'I can't think of any other reason, can you?'

'No, I can't.'

'The inspector was very grateful. He said that I'd been a real help to him. I'm not sure what he meant by that, mind you. As for this terrible murder,' she went on, touching her friend's arm, 'I feel so sorry for you, Becky. It happened just down the track from the lodge. It would've scared me rigid, being so close. I'd never met this John Bedloe – had you?'

'I must have seen him when I went into Wimborne,' replied Rebecca, her mouth suddenly dry, 'because he'd be on duty near the station, but I'd never spoken to him. It's the other one I've met – Dick Satchwell.'

'Oh, yes, *we* know Dick Satchwell. He's been to the Waggon a few times and very welcome he is. Not as welcome as Inspector Colbeck, though,' she added with a throaty laugh. 'The pity of it is that the only chance we get to see him is if someone else is murdered and I hope that never happens again.' She gave a shudder. 'My blood runs cold when I think of it. Who could possibly have stabbed him to death? People round here are friendly. We like each other. Do we *really* have a killer in our midst?'

At that moment, Rebecca had the uncomfortable feeling that she was being watched. Turning around sharply, she saw the unsmiling face of her husband framed in the window. It shook her.

* * *

Given the choice, Leeming opted to hire a trap rather than a horse. When the animal was between the shafts, it always seemed much more obedient than when he was in the saddle. As it trotted ahead of him, he actually felt in control of the horse and he was reminded of his earlier ambition to be a London cab driver. It had always appealed to him as a way of life and, while it lacked the adventure that he routinely enjoyed, it was largely devoid of the concomitant danger. The idea of rolling through the streets of the capital was tempting enough but, he now discovered, driving through beautiful countryside was an even better experience. On the trip to the Sweetbriar Estate, he'd had to endure the malodorous companionship of his driver. There was no such handicap now. Leeming was alone and in charge. Amongst the rough-hewn country people he drove past, he cut an incongruous figure but that didn't trouble him. For the first time since he'd come to Dorset, he felt something akin to happiness.

Frustration soon set in, however. He'd been told that God's Blessing Green was a couple of miles north of Wimborne. All that he had to do, he was assured, was to follow the signs to Holt and he would reach his destination. What nobody warned him was that the road would soon become a winding track and that he'd be faced with a plethora of conflicting signposts that would send him in an ever-decreasing circle. Everyone whose help he sought had a different view of how best to reach the tiny hamlet and it was impossible to decide on whose advice to rely. Leeming became so confused and fretful that he came to believe he'd lost God's Blessing and was under the malign spell of the Devil's Curse.

The horse was increasingly fractious. When they passed the same wayside cottage for the third time, it became mutinous and broke into a canter that made the trap rock violently side to side. Leeming could neither stop the animal nor establish any control over it. All that he could do was to cling on for dear life. Miraculously, they did actually reach God's Blessing Green, but he only had the briefest glimpse of it as the trap hurtled past. Half a mile outside the hamlet, the horse eventually decided that it had had enough strenuous exercise and it reverted to a gentle trot. There was another welcome source of relief. Leeming chanced upon a man repairing hurdles and was, for once, given accurate directions. He was to skirt the forest around Holt and look for Manor Farm. That was where Simon Copsey worked.

By the time he finally got there, Leeming was exhausted and had abandoned his dream of becoming a cab driver. Whether in town or country, horses were a law unto themselves and they were far too unpredictable for comfort. Though Colbeck could be wilful at times, he was much more dependable as a work partner. At Manor Farm, Leeming was greeted by a stroke of luck. The old shepherd was actually there. Attended by his tail-wagging dog, he was acting as midwife to yet another of the spring lambs. He'd just brought one more slippery creature into the world and placed it in the straw beside its mother before wiping his hands on a piece of sacking.

Leeming looked and felt completely out of place in a farmyard. Chickens ran between his legs and he had to be careful not to scuff his shoes or step into any dung. He couldn't decide whether the incessant squawking or the pervading stink was the more offensive. Introducing himself to Copsey, he took him aside. They sat on a rickety bench close to the pens. The shepherd eyed him up and down.

'Another p'liceman, eh?'

'Yes, sir.'

'But uglier than the last one.'

'Inspector Colbeck has already spoken to you, I believe.'

'So 'e did – bought me a drink.'

'Well, you'll not get one from me.'

'Pity.'

'There's something he sent me to ask you, Mr Copsey.'

'Call me Sim, if ye likes,' said the other. 'Everyone else does.'
His dog barked. 'I'm Sim and this is Sam. Some folk gets us
mixed up.'

'This is important, sir.'

'Is it?'

'You may have information that's valuable in a murder enquiry.'

'I told everything to th'inspector.'

'But you'd been drinking at the time,' Leeming reminded him.
'That's not a criticism. After the shock of what you discovered,
anyone would want a pint or two.'

Copsey laughed. 'I 'ad a lot more'n that, Sergeant.'

'Let's go through the details once again, shall we?'

'Why?'

'Because I said so, Mr Copsey,' warned Leeming. 'We can
either do it here or I can take you back to Wimborne to question
you at the police station.'

'Leave me be!' howled the shepherd.

'Do as I tell you or there'll be trouble.'

'I can't leave the farm now. I got lambs comin'.'

'Then answer my questions right here.'

Copsey regarded him with a combined disgust and wariness.
Averse to anyone involved in law enforcement, he was nevertheless
careful not to provoke them. It had led to cold nights in comfortless
cells before. He was getting much too old for that. Against the
background of plaintive bleats from the lambs and clucking from
the hens, he told his story once more. Give or take a few playful
digressions, it was very much the tale that Colbeck had heard.

'That's it,' said the shepherd, getting up. 'I'll go back to work.'

'I haven't finished yet, sir. Sit down again.'

'I'm too busy.'

Leeming pulled him back on to the bench. 'Sit down!' he ordered. 'That's better. And it's no good trying to ignore a murder investigation. There'll be an inquest any day now and you'll be called to give evidence.'

The shepherd gasped. 'I can't take time off from the farm.'

'You'll have to, Mr Copsey. You'll be fetched and brought back here. One word of warning – you'll be under oath before the coroner. He'll want the truth.'

'I *always* tell the truth,' protested the other.

'Then answer me this – what were you doing in West Moors on Saturday?'

'I was going for a walk.'

'At midnight?'

'I couldn't sleep.'

'It must be the best part of three miles away.'

'That's nothing to me, Sergeant.'

'Do you often go to West Moors?'

'No, I don't.'

'So what was special about last Saturday?'

'That'd be tellin',' said the other, baring his few remaining teeth.

'Then tell me,' insisted Leeming. 'I didn't come all this way to be fobbed off. You go somewhere you don't usually go and – lo and behold – you just happen to stumble on a body draped across a railway line. Did you actually *find* John Bedloe or did you help to put him there?'

'I *found* 'im,' yelled Copsey. 'I'll swear it on the 'Oly Book!'

'So what were you doing in such a remote place?'

'I told ye – goin' for a stroll.'

'You went there for a purpose, didn't you?' demanded Leeming, putting more authority into his voice. 'I'm not leaving till I know what that purpose was.'

Simon Copsey drew back with a hunted look in his eye. He'd had many brushes with the law in the past and he'd usually been able to talk his way out of trouble. Local constables were more easily duped. Leeming was very different. He had a tenacity about him that was unsettling. He needed an answer.

'I went to see a friend,' said Copsey. 'Are ye 'appy now, Sergeant?'

'I will be when I know the friend's name.'

'Why'd ye say that?'

'I need to meet him and confirm that you're telling the truth.'

'Ye can't do that,' whispered the other, anxiously.

'Why not?'

Copsey's voice dropped to a whisper. 'It weren't a man I went to see.'

'Then give me the woman's name.'

'And what d'ye think will 'appen when ye roll up to speak to 'er in front of 'er 'usband? It'll be my death warrant,' wailed the shepherd. 'I'll finish up stretched across that friggin' railway line just like Bedloe!'

Alone in his room, Colbeck read the letters over and over again in the hope that they would yield up the telling clue that he needed. Those written by Susan Elwell were set aside. Her romance with John Bedloe had run its full course and ended in a disaster that had an exact date. The other two women, it was clear, belonged to a later stage in the railway policeman's career. Both expressed an ardent desire to see him more often but their freedom of movement was largely curtailed by the presence of a husband. Colbeck got the distinct impression that they lived in or near Wimborne. The one who'd written the most letters had been careful neither to sign nor date them in case they fell into the wrong hands. Her handwriting was more legible and her feelings more fervently expressed. The last of the three women had dashed off her letters so quickly that many of the words were indecipherable as was the signature at the bottom of each letter.

Since both women lacked a name, Colbeck bestowed one upon them in order to give them some definition. The woman who sent the majority of the letters was Alice while the other became Betsy. Aspects of their respective characters came through in what they'd written and it was the same with Susan Elwell. Each of the three had a distinct individuality. What linked them was their susceptibility to the wiles of John Bedloe. Of the trio, Susan had been the most impressionable and the fact that she had an absent husband made her more available. She didn't have to wait patiently to contrive a meeting with her lover. Susan had a freedom that the others lacked. In the end, it was her downfall.

It seemed obvious to Colbeck that the railway policeman had been enjoying the favours of Alice and Betsy alternately. Each laboured under the delusion that she was involved in a romance with someone who loved her devotedly and who spent the time without her yearning and suffering. The two women certainly yearned and suffered. It was agony to be apart from him for lengthy periods. Never having met the man, Colbeck had no idea what his appeal had been but, patently, he offered the two women a love that they couldn't find at home and they responded with the complete submission that he sought.

That could be their weakness. Neither of the women was practiced in the arts of deception. One of them might well have given herself away. In a sense, that was what Susan Elwell had done. When her death was reported in the newspapers, the truth had been exposed. The shock to her husband must have been profound. Had he nursed the pain all this time as he sought to discover who'd led his wife astray? Was that why he lived in the same house and worked beside the river in which she'd drowned herself and her unborn child? In Colbeck's mind, Jack Elwell had to be considered a prime suspect but he was not the only one. The husbands of the other two of Bedloe's victims had to be remembered. Had one of them discovered his wife's betrayal of him? Had he beaten the truth out of her then gone to take revenge?

Who *were* Alice and Betsy? What were their real names? Where did they live and how had Bedloe been able to work on them so cunningly? Colbeck was intrigued by another possibility. He speculated on what would have happened if Alice or Betsy had found out about each other and realised that they'd been cruelly betrayed. Each was in the grip of a passion but, when thwarted, was that passion strong enough to drive them on to murder? Colbeck was ready to accept that it was until he had second thoughts. If Alice or Betsy had discovered the existence of a rival, would their anger move them to stab Bedloe to death or would they instead want to eliminate the rival to his affections? It would certainly be easier to kill another woman than to murder a powerful man.

As he sifted through the letters once more, another idea took root in Colbeck's mind. Each woman had been tricked and exploited to the full by a master of his trade. If one of them had learnt the awful truth about her fake romance, would she really turn on the other woman or might she instead make common cause with her? Should the detectives stop looking for a jealous husband and try to identify two desperate wives bonded together in a murder pact?

* * *

'What's happened, Bert?' asked Satchwell.

'Don't ask me.'

'You're much closer to them than I am.'

'I wish I was.'

'What has Inspector Colbeck said to you?'

'Very little,' said Maycock.

'I would've thought you'd be involved in the hunt.'

'So would I, Dick.'

'Why aren't you?'

Bertram Maycock gave a philosophical shrug. After taking advice from him soon after their arrival, the detectives had been pursuing lines of enquiry on their own, ignoring Maycock along with other members of the local constabulary. He had hoped to learn something of the methods employed by Colbeck and Leeming but they didn't seem to need him. While other policemen might have been upset, he accepted it with a tolerant smile.

'They've caught killers before, Dick,' he said. 'We 'aven't. They've 'ad a police force in Lunnun for thirty years. Dorset's only 'ad a proper one for three or four. We're still learnin'.'

'Has there been any response to the posters advertising a reward?'

'Oh, yes, the usual folk 'ave started rollin' in. Whenever there's a reward, they always claim to 'ave seen somethin' important. They lie their 'eads off, Dick.'

'So you've had no new evidence, then?'

'Not so much as a whisper of it.'

'Mr Feltham will be disappointed.'

The two men were on the platform at Wimborne Station. Seeing him standing there, Satchwell had been quick to swoop down on Maycock in the hope of picking up information about the progress of the investigation. He was upset to learn that there was no new development he could pass on to Feltham.

'I seed 'is picture in the paper again,' said Maycock. 'Mr Feltham is never slow to get 'imself on the front page, is 'e?'

'It was he who summoned Inspector Colbeck. The town needs to know about that. They ought to appreciate what Mr Feltham does for Wimborne.'

'Oh, 'e's appreciated, Dick. It's just that nobody likes 'im.'

'That's not true. He'll be the next mayor.'

'Only if Mr Preece drops down dead, and that's unlikely. Last time I seed 'im, 'e looked as fit as a flea.'

'Godfrey Preece doesn't have Mr Feltham's initiative.'

'Maybe not but 'e 'as a lot more friends round 'ere.'

'Wait till this murder is solved. Who'll get the credit?'

'Well, it won't be me.'

'It will be Mr Feltham. He'll get the recognition he deserves.'

Maycock grinned slyly. 'Oh, I think that folk already recognise 'im for what 'e is, Dick.'

'He has big ambitions for Wimborne.'

'I like it the way it is.' He leant in close. 'Do you miss 'im?'

'Who are you talking about?'

'John Bedloe.'

'Yes, I miss him all right,' said Satchwell with feeling. 'Turning up for work is a real pleasure now. I don't have to put up with his sneers and his bullying. Losing him is the best thing that could have happened to me.'

'Don't say that too loud,' cautioned Maycock.

'Why not?'

'Anyone'd think that *ye'd* killed 'im.'

The return journey to Wimborne went without mishap. Leeming reached the town in half the time it had taken him to get to Manor

Farm. On the way back, he had the chance to review his conversation with Simon Copsey. The old shepherd's claim that he'd come to West Moors in search of a woman seemed improbable. To begin with, there'd be very little choice of female companionship for a man of Copsey's age. According to Colbeck, who'd visited houses in the area, they were scattered in little clusters. In a community as small as that, people tended to know each other's business. There'd be severely limited opportunities for a secret rendezvous. More to the point, what woman would look twice at someone as poor, crude, unsightly and unwholesome as the shepherd? He was no John Bedloe. Copsey would surely have to pay for his pleasures.

Having taken the trap back to its owner, Leeming went in search of Richard Satchwell's house. He'd taken the precaution of making a note of the address when he first met him. It was important to go there when Satchwell was at work and unable to shield his wife from questions about his movements. When he called at the house and explained who he was, Leeming got the expected response. Amy Satchwell was disturbed.

'Why do you want to speak to me?' she asked.

'Actually,' said Leeming, telling a white lie, 'I was hoping to catch your husband. Since he's not here, I wonder if you could help me, Mrs Satchwell?'

'Yes, yes, I suppose so . . .' She opened the door wide. 'Do come in.'

Doffing his hat, the sergeant entered a living room that was remarkably like his own back in London. Small, low-ceilinged and compact, it had the same cosiness and the same amiable clutter. The railway policeman's wife, however, bore no resemblance at all to his own. Where Estelle was confident and forthright, Amy Satchwell was tense and apprehensive. Her hands were clutched tightly together. She was a short, slim, dark-haired woman wearing an apron over her dress. Had she not been so nervous, she would have been attractive. As it was, her face was scrunched up and her eyes fearful.

'What do you want to ask me?' she said.

'I'd like you to tell me what happened on Saturday night, Mrs Satchwell.'

'Richard has already told you, hasn't he?'

'Yes, but I'd like your version of events.'

'I can't tell you anything, Sergeant.'

'Why not?'

'I slept through it,' she told him. 'I'm so used to having a husband who climbs out of bed at all hours that it no longer wakes me up. All I know is that Richard got up in the night because someone was banging on the door.'

'What time would that be?'

'I couldn't say for sure.'

'But he must have told you afterwards.'

'It was very early in the morning, Sergeant. That's all I know.'

Leeming studied her for a moment. Her distress was out of all proportion to the situation. All that he wanted was confirmation of her husband's testimony. Amy was behaving as if she were under suspicion.

'Does your husband like working as a railway policeman?' he asked.

'He used to.'

'What about now?'

'Richard never talks about his work,' she said. 'When he comes home, he likes to forget all about it. Not that he's here all that often, mind,' she confided. 'He usually has things to do in his spare time.'

'Some of them involve Mr Feltham, I understand.'

There was a considered pause. 'Yes, they do sometimes.'

'Is he *employed* by the gentleman?'

'I told you. He never discusses his work with me.'

'That's odd,' he said. 'I always tell my wife what I've been up to at work. If I've been dealing with something gruesome, of course, she doesn't want to hear the gory details. I won't tell her everything about *this* case, for instance. Estelle will guess that there are nasty aspects to it and that's enough for her.' He could see that her teeth were gritted and that her knuckles had turned white. 'Since he was a colleague of your husband's, you obviously knew the victim.'

'I knew *of* him,' she said.

'Did he ever come here?'

'No, he didn't. Richard wouldn't have him in the house.'

'But you must have bumped into him at some point.'

'I'd been warned to keep away from him.'

'Did you know anything about Mr Bedloe?'

'My husband didn't like him, that's all.'

'He must have told you why.'

'Well, he didn't,' she replied with sudden firmness.

'Thank you for your help, Mrs Satchwell,' he said, backing away. 'I'm sorry to burst in on you like this. I'll catch your husband another time.' After moving to the door, he turned to face her again. 'My wife's biggest complaint is that I work long hours. I suppose that you could make the same one. Unfortunately, crime takes place twenty-four hours a day. If you're involved in law enforcement – like me and your husband – you have to work through the night sometimes. Estelle hates that. I daresay that you do as well.'

'I'm here for Richard whenever he wants me,' she said, loyally.

'Then he's a very lucky man.'

Stepping out of the front door, he put on his hat and walked away.

* * *

Rebecca Tullidge had only confronted her husband once before. It had been in the early years of their marriage and she'd soon regretted it. Once roused, he became foul-mouthed and intimidating. It had frightened her so much that she vowed she'd never do it again but the visit of Margaret Vout had made her question that resolve. On the night of the murder, Tullidge had departed from a routine that he'd kept religiously for years. There was an unexplained gap of an hour or so between his leaving the Waggon and Horses and returning to the lodge. Where had he been and what had he been doing?

The questions yapped at her like angry dogs until she was eventually forced to ask them. Knowing the timetable, she'd waited until there was a substantial gap between two trains. Rebecca didn't want their conversation to be interrupted by a dash to the crossing gates. Over a cup of tea, she raised the subject.

'Maggie Vout called earlier.'

'I know. I saw her.'

'She told me something interesting.'

'Oh?'

'It was about Saturday night, Michael.'

'What about it?'

'She said that you left the pub much earlier than usual.'

He stiffened. 'Telling tales on me, is she?'

'Is she right?'

'Maggie makes things up. Don't listen to her.'

'But she sounded so certain of it. And she's not the only one. Elias Rawles and Hugh Delafield were there as usual. You played cards with them. After you'd gone, they were annoyed you'd sneaked off so early.'

'I didn't sneak off,' he asserted, voice rising in volume.

'So what did you do?'

'Shut up!'

'I'd just like to know, Michael.'

'What difference does it make to you?'

'You're my husband.'

'I can do what I like when I like it,' he roared, rising from the table.

'Of course you can,' she said, trying to appease him. 'I shouldn't have asked. What time you get back home is your business. Forget that I asked.'

For a moment, he towered over her and she was afraid that he was about to hit her. Instead, he swung on his heel, left the room and slammed the door after him.

Rebecca was even more troubled now. Her polite enquiry had turned a cold and cheerless husband into a dangerous one.

It was late afternoon when Colbeck and Leeming finally had the opportunity to sit down in the inspector's hotel room and look back over their day. It had been full and productive. The inspector talked about his meditations on the cache of letters from the victim's house and how Bedloe had clearly revelled in the power he had over the three women. He also held an important advantage over them.

'He was able to keep their letters and read them at will,' he said. 'That was a luxury the women could never enjoy. If he wrote to them – and one suspects that he must have at some point – they'd have had to destroy the missives. None of them would have dared to keep them under the mattress in case their husband found them.'

'That's not the only advantage he had, sir,' observed Leeming. 'From what you've told me, he was dallying with two of those women at the same time. That's dreadful. He was not only betraying their husbands, he was betraying them as well. They had no idea that each other existed. It's just as well.'

'I incline to the view that one of them *did* learn the truth.'

'Do you believe that she killed him?'

'It's something to consider.'

'I believe that the murder was a man's work. Someone like Bill Manders fits the bill for me but I wouldn't forget Copsey or Satchwell.'

'What motive would the shepherd possibly have?'

'I don't know,' confessed Leeming. 'But he was in the right place at the right time. And he wasn't there to meet a woman, as he claimed, I'm sure of that. He stinks to high heaven. That would put anyone off.'

'What about Satchwell?'

'He does have a motive and could easily have followed Bedloe one night to see what he was up to. His wife is a heavy sleeper. She never knows if he's lying beside her in bed or not.'

'That can't be conducive to harmony between them.'

'She didn't strike me as being a happy woman, sir.'

'I trust your judgement on that score, Victor. Did you think that the visit to her was worthwhile?'

'Oh, yes,' replied Leeming. 'It proved to me that Satchwell could have slipped out of the house, lain in wait for Bedloe, killed him near the spot where he was expecting to meet someone, then gone straight back to his house. When someone banged on his door, he was in bed with his wife – and with an alibi.'

Colbeck sat back with his hands behind his head. 'I fancy that the killer is either a woman or it's Jack Elwell. Did he really work all night on a boat? I suppose he might have done – unless he had business in West Moors.'

'How could he keep track of Bedloe's movements?'

'There's one obvious way, isn't there?'

'He paid someone to follow him,' said Leeming. 'When he saw there was a pattern to Bedloe's antics at night, he could have moved in to strike.'

'He could have,' said Colbeck, 'but *did* he?' His fingers counted them off again. 'Elwell, Manders, Copsey, Satchwell or a mystery woman – not forgetting Michael Tullidge, of course. If we're talking about being in the right place at the right time, we have to include him.'

'That gives us six suspects.'

'I'd rather have too many than too few, Victor.'

'I prefer too few. There's less travel involved.'

'I thought you were enjoying your sojourn in Dorset. A little earlier, you were telling me what wonderful vistas you saw on your way to God's Blessing Green.'

'That was before the horse bolted.' There was a firm knock on the door. 'I hope that's not Satchwell again, coming to tell us what a marvellous man Feltham is.'

'Let's find out,' said Colbeck, getting to his feet and crossing to the door.

He opened it wide and then stood back in horror. Edward Tallis was standing there like a figure of doom. Leeming gurgled.

'Good evening,' said Tallis, stepping into the room and setting down his valise. 'Since you can't be bothered to send me a full report on this case, I decided to come here in person to find out the details.' He looked from one to the other. 'Have you made an arrest yet?'

'No, Superintendent,' said Colbeck. 'We were just discussing the suspects.'

'Then I've come at the ideal time.' He turned to Leeming. 'Don't goggle at me, man. I'm not a ghost.'

'You were the last person we were expecting, sir,' said the other.

'Surprise gives you an advantage. It was one of the first things I learnt in the army. Strike when the enemy least expects you.'

'Are the sergeant and I being depicted as enemies?' asked Colbeck, drily.

Tallis smiled grimly. 'That remains to be seen.'

CHAPTER TEN

When their visitor had settled into a chair, it was left to Colbeck to give him a detailed account of the investigation. It was concise yet comprehensive. Leeming would have been far more prolix and was always likely to make mistakes with the superintendent sitting so close to him. Tallis listened carefully then gave his judgement.

'My instinct,' he said, 'would be to side with the inspector and single out this sailor, Jack Elwell.'

'Why?' asked Leeming.

'He has the strongest motive to kill.'

'Elwell is just one of three jealous husbands, sir.'

'That may be so, Sergeant, but all that the other two have to worry about is their respective wives' infidelity. Elwell came home to find that his wife had committed suicide and taken with her the unborn child of a different father. That would not just rankle. It would fill him with a burning desire for revenge.'

'Yet I saw no hint of it when I met him,' said Colbeck. 'Elwell seemed a happy-go-lucky character.'

'I'll make a point of meeting him.'

Leeming groaned. 'You're *staying*, sir?'

'Do you have any objection to that?' asked Tallis, warningly.

'No, no, we're . . . delighted to have you here.'

'I flatter myself that I can be of great use. For one thing, I can keep Mr Feltham off your back. I'm not having my detectives treated as if they're the personal property of some local bigwig.'

'That would be helpful, Superintendent.'

'What about the letters I found in Bedloe's house?' asked Colbeck. 'Would you care to see them?'

'No,' said Tallis, wrinkling his nose in disgust, 'I most certainly wouldn't. You've given me an admirable insight into their contents. Somewhere in this town, there are two adulterous women and I roundly condemn what they did.'

Colbeck was relieved. Tallis was a confirmed bachelor with a lifelong suspicion of the opposite sex. He'd be embarrassed to read the intimate thoughts of two infatuated women. The detectives were spared the diatribe against daughters of Eve that would certainly have followed.

'We have a date for the inquest, sir,' said Colbeck. 'It's tomorrow morning.'

Tallis nodded. 'Good.'

'I've sent a telegraph to Harry Wills.'

'He's the deceased's cousin, isn't he?'

'Yes, he's also the likely recipient of Bedloe's worldly goods. While the sergeant was visiting Manor Farm, I had a more thorough search of the man's house. There's no sign of a will. I'll check with every lawyer in Wimborne, of course, but my feeling is that he died intestate.'

'That's what I expected,' said Leeming. 'He felt that he was far too young to die. It's only people of *your* age who need to worry about making a will, sir.'

Tallis glared. 'Are you implying that I'm *old*?'

'Not at all, Superintendent.'

'Do you see any signs of decay?'

Leeming cowered. 'You're very spry for a man of your years.'

'Will you please stop going on about my age!'

'The sergeant is making a reasonable point, sir,' said Colbeck, intervening. 'Bedloe had no cause to expect imminent death. He'd assume that he had decades to live and that he could carry on as he had been doing.'

'Yes,' said Tallis, 'preying on weak-willed females.'

'With respect, sir, I'd hardly call them that. Weak-willed wives would never have the urge to betray their husbands. While we all disapprove of what these women did, we must accept that it took an immense amount of commitment – not to say courage – to follow the path they took.'

'I refuse to accept that infidelity is a courageous act.'

'That's not exactly what I'm saying, sir.'

'Then perhaps you shouldn't have said it,' observed Tallis, crisply. 'Now, Inspector, is there anything else you wish to tell me about this case?'

'I don't think so.'

'Then you have my permission to leave.'

Colbeck was puzzled. 'Where am I going?'

'You're going home, man.'

'But you can't take me off this case. That would be deeply insulting to me.'

'I'm not taking you off anything, Colbeck. I'm merely suggesting that you've done sterling work in a very short time and deserve a slight rest. To be more exact, your presence would be welcomed back in London, if only for the night.'

'Can I go as well, sir?' asked Leeming, hopefully.

'Be quiet, Sergeant.'

'The inspector and I could catch the first train back tomorrow.'

'You're not going anywhere. Well,' said Tallis, switching his gaze to Colbeck, 'don't just stand there, man. There's a train in half an hour. You're not the only person with a copy of Bradshaw, you know. You'll get to London by nine-thirty. Leeming and I will just have finished breakfast when you return to Wimborne on the early train.'

Colbeck was rarely lost for words but his entire vocabulary had deserted him now. He was overwhelmed by Tallis's gesture of kindness. Aware that the inspector was missing his wife – and that Madeleine, in turn, would be missing her husband at a crucial time – Tallis had gone out his way to grant Colbeck what amounted to compassionate leave. When he eventually found his voice, the inspector felt obliged to protest.

'I can't desert my post, sir.'

'That's not what you're doing,' contended Tallis.

'I'm wholly committed to this investigation.'

'Only a fool would doubt that, Inspector. Your dedication is legendary. But you're not deserting us. You know as well as I do that an important element in any murder enquiry is thinking time.'

'That's true, sir.'

'Well, you'll have four hours of uninterrupted thinking time on the journey back to London and another four hours on the way back here tomorrow. Having given that amount of concentrated thought to the case, you'll probably turn up having solved the crime.' He glanced at Leeming. 'Don't you agree, Sergeant?'

'I wouldn't mind some of that thinking time for myself, sir,' said Leeming.

'You'll stay here with me. I can't spare both of you.'

'A trip to London would refresh the two of us.'

'You're not budging an inch until the killer has been caught. You've only been here a day and a half. Besides, your domestic situation is not comparable to that of the inspector.' He snapped his fingers. 'Stop dithering, Colbeck. Do you want to miss that train?'

'No, no,' said Colbeck, leaping up. 'Thank you, sir. Thank you very much.'

'Come along, Sergeant,' said Tallis, moving to the door with his valise. 'We're only detaining the inspector.'

'Yes, sir,' murmured Leeming, following behind him.

After exchanging farewells with Colbeck, the two men went out.

'You could travel back with the inspector, you know,' suggested Leeming.

'Why on earth should I do anything as stupid as that?' asked Tallis, shooting him a look of utter disdain. 'I'm needed here. You can't possibly cope on your own.'

'How long do you intend to stay, sir?'

'I'll be here until the murder is solved.'

Leeming sighed. Tallis had intruded into their investigations before and always managed to hinder them in some way. The fact that he intended to take an active part in the case from now on was a devastating blow. Catching the killer had suddenly become much more difficult.

Fate could be cruel. That was Rebecca Tullidge's opinion. It had at last given her a man she could truly love only to snatch him away from her in the most brutal manner. To compound her anguish, she was unable to mourn him properly. Lest he became suspicious, Rebecca had to hide her feelings from her husband and carry on as if nothing had happened. It was a continuous ordeal. What she really wanted to do was to fling herself on the bed and weep for the searing loss of love and hope. There would never be another John Bedloe in her life. The only man who'd ever get close to her from now on was the one she'd inadvertently married in a fit of sympathy. The future looked bleak. She felt ill.

Since there was nowhere to hide, the only way that she could escape her husband's vigilance was to go for a walk. It allowed her to brood on her lot. Her sense of bereavement was tempered by two other emotions. The first was guilt. Bedloe's murder was, to some extent, her fault. If he hadn't been involved with Rebecca, he'd have been nowhere near West Moors on Saturday night. He'd have been safe and well elsewhere. She felt that she must take some of the blame. The deeper guilt, however, was the one that came from her adultery. Only now that it was all over could she see the enormity of the step she'd taken. She had cast aside solemn vows taken during a wedding ceremony as if they'd never existed. Rebecca couldn't believe that she'd been so wicked and so reckless. What she'd done was unforgivable. Guilt would torment her for the remainder of her life.

A third emotion swelled up inside her. It was fear. Someone knew where John Bedloe would be on Saturday night and what took him there. The secret that Rebecca shared with him was out. She was terrified that the killer would reveal her shame to the whole town. Had that happened, she believed that the Scotland Yard detectives might be investigating a second murder and that she would be the victim. Tullidge would never be able to stomach the knowledge of his wife's infamy and the derision he'd receive from some quarters at his cuckoldry. He'd rather hang than endure that. The cold fear that he'd find out the truth about her adultery gnawed hungrily into Rebecca's entrails.

Loss, guilt and fear. One of them on its own would be enough to torment her yet she had to cope with all three. It was an impossible burden and Rebecca didn't know how long she could carry it before she stumbled and fell.

'Where've you been?'

'I went for a walk.'

'Why?'

'I had a headache.'

'Why didn't you tell me you were going?'

'You were too busy talking to someone.'

'Then you should've waited.'

'I'm sorry, Michael.'

'Don't do it again.'

'If that's what you want, I won't.'

'Stay here. I like to see you.'

Tullidge made it sound like a threat. At a stroke, her brief escape route had been cut off. The only respite she could get from her husband's surveillance was a visit from Margaret Vout and even that was now in danger. He'd been angry at the publican's wife for telling Rebecca what time he'd left the Waggon and Horses on Saturday night. It was more than possible that he'd retaliate by forbidding the friend to visit the lodge. Tullidge wouldn't worry that it would complicate his relationship with the publican. If he needed to patronise another hostelry, then he would. Rebecca hoped that it would not reach that stage. Margaret was her one true friend and she was never more needed.

'What about going to market?' she asked.

'I'll tell you when to do that.'

'I'll have to go into Wimborne one day.'

'Let me decide that.'

When she'd got back from her walk, Tullidge was waiting to pounce on her. He'd never been so controlling in the past. Rebecca wondered why he'd changed. There was one possible explanation and, if correct, it would be like a hammer blow.

He might actually *know*.

Given the unexpected gift of thinking time, Robert Colbeck spent the first few minutes of it looking forward to being at home again. He wanted to see the look of surprise and joy on Madeleine's face when he arrived out of the blue. It would not be the kind of reunion they'd had in the past when he finally returned from a distant part of the country where a murder had occurred. In her condition, that was out of the question. But it would be equally delightful and fulfilling. Of that, he was confident. Putting his wife gently aside, he turned his thoughts once more to the investigation. Tallis had been right. Thinking time was invaluable.

As he sat on the train with his eyes closed, Colbeck ran through the suspects in his mind. All had clear motives to take the life of John Bedloe. Why had the killer chosen that specific location? It was a long way from where Jack Elwell and William Manders lived but that would be no hindrance to them if they were really determined to murder the railway policeman. Those who lived closest to the scene of the crime were Michael Tullidge and Richard Satchwell and it was significant that Simon Copsey had been in West Moors on the night in question. Did he have a corkscrew as well as a knife with him? If he'd committed the murder, why did he raise the alarm? Colbeck had met killers before who'd tried to disguise their villainy in exactly the same way but they'd been more calculating than the old shepherd. After stabbing his victim, he'd have been much more likely to melt away into the night.

That brought Colbeck back to the possibility of a female assassin. It might well be the woman he'd arranged to meet close to the shed where, presumably, they'd consummated their love in the past. Had she discovered that she had a rival? Would she prefer to kill her lover rather than share him, thereby punishing Bedloe for his betrayal and spiting the other woman by removing him forcibly from her life? When he'd met her that night, Bedloe would have been off guard. A man with such power over women would never suspect one of harbouring murderous desires. To be killed by a wife he'd cleverly seduced could be seen as a form of poetic justice.

Colbeck was still cogitating as the train sped into a tunnel. Its clatter took on a harsher tone and everything went dark.

Edward Tallis wasted no time before getting involved in the hunt for the killer. Having absorbed the evidence gathered by his detectives, he dispatched Leeming in one direction while he went off in another. He was eager to meet Jack Elwell.

'What were you doing to the boat?' he asked.

'I was repairing it, sir.'

'And it took you all night?'

'There was a lot to do.'

'What exactly was wrong with it, Mr Elwell?'

'You'll have to ask Tom Younger. It was his boat. He lives in Dorchester. I can give you his address, if you wish.'

Tallis was getting the same reception that Colbeck did. The former sailor was amiable and willing to answer any questions. The two men were standing outside the boathouse and Tallis was studying the tattoos on Elwell's bare forearms closely. The crucifix stood out.

'Are you a true Christian?' he asked.

'I try to be, sir.'

'So you believe in God?'

'Oh, yes,' said Elwell, seriously, 'I've seen what he can do. There've been times at sea when I thought we were done for – a howling tempest with waves as high as a mountain and a wind like a giant hand set to sweep you off the deck. I couldn't believe that any ship could come through that in one piece. And yet she did – thanks to God. Some of my shipmates used to say that we had the luck of the devil but it wasn't luck. It was help from above.'

'Did you enjoy being a sailor?'

'It was the making of me, sir.'

'Yet you gave it up.'

'Yes, I did. When I met Louisa – she's my wife now – I knew that it was time to drop anchor. I only sail on the river these days.'

Tallis sprung the next question on him without warning.

'When were you last in Wimborne?'

Elwell became vague. 'I can't remember.'

'Do you have any reason to go there?'

'No, I don't. We have all we need in Dorchester.'

Tallis glanced over his shoulder. 'Fordington is not the most salubrious place.'

'It's cleaner than it used to be, sir. We have good friends here. Louisa didn't like it at first but she wouldn't live anywhere else now. We've settled in.' He gave a chuckle. 'I don't know what I've done to deserve a visit from a superintendent come all the way from London. I was flattered when that inspector came to see me. Why are you showing interest in someone who builds and repairs boats?'

166

he went on. 'I don't mind it but Louisa was upset when Inspector Colbeck called at the house.'

'I'm sorry if we've troubled your second wife, Mr Elwell,' said Tallis. 'We came here because of what happened to the *first* one.'

'That's all in the past.'

'There are some things you can never forget.'

'Well, I'm doing my best to forget them,' said Elwell with a first hint of aggression. 'I've rebuilt my life here. Everyone is talking about a murder over in West Moors on Saturday night. It's nothing to do with me. I've never heard of this man called Bedloe so I can't help you with your enquiries.'

Tallis regarded him quizzically for a full minute before speaking again.

'What do you think when you look at the river?'

'I see something from which I can make a living.'

'Doesn't the sight of it stir up unpleasant memories?'

'No, it doesn't.'

'Then you must be a very unusual man, Mr Elwell.'

The sailor narrowed one eyelid. 'Do you have a wife, Superintendent?'

'No, I don't,' replied Tallis with indignation. 'Whatever gave you that idea?'

'So you've never known what it's like to have the joys of marriage.'

'My private life is not relevant to this discussion.'

'God has been good to me,' said Elwell. 'Yes, I lost my first wife and I thought at the time that I'd never meet another one I could love in the same way. But I did and it was my salvation. Louisa is the reason I didn't go anywhere but here on Saturday night. When she's away, I think of her all the time. As for wanting to take someone's life, I always remember what the Bible says. "Vengeance is mine, I will repay, saith the Lord." St Paul's letter to the Romans, Chapter twelve, verse nineteen.'

'I prefer a quotation from the Old Testament,' said Tallis.

'Why?'

'It's shorter and just as unequivocal. "Thou shalt not kill." It's from Exodus. Chapter twenty, verse thirteen.'

'Do you think I killed someone?'

'It's a possibility worthy of attention.'

'I'm a suspect, then.'

'You interest us, sir.'

When Elwell spoke, there was a definite note of challenge in his voice.

'Where's your proof, Superintendent?'

'We'll find it, sir,' said Tallis, calmly. 'We always do.'

The shop was just closing when Leeming got there. It stood in the main street directly opposite the imposing church of St Peter and St Paul. Leeming looked at the name etched on to the window – Jeremy Agar, Wine Merchant. The man himself was about to the lock the front door. The sergeant stepped in quickly, explained who he was and asked for a few minutes of Agar's time. They went back into the premises and Agar bolted the door behind them. Light was starting to fade outside but there was still enough illumination for Leeming to appraise the man. Agar was a short, dapper middle-aged individual in a well-cut suit and polished shoes. His face and hands looked as if they'd just been scrubbed. There was a punctiliousness about him reminiscent of Colbeck, though he lacked the inspector's handsome features and sheer presence.

'Why come to Blandford?' asked Agar in surprise.

'I thought it was called Blandford Forum.'

'It is, Sergeant, but to those of us who live here, it's plain Blandford. Forum is a Latin word meaning "market" and that's what we are – a bustling market town.'

'And full of beautiful houses,' observed Leeming with approval.

'Most of them were built in the last century,' explained the other. 'We had a fire in 1731 that almost wiped us off the map. The church was completely destroyed. It was rebuilt by two brothers – both of them architects – William and John Bastard.' He smiled at Leeming's reactions. 'They were Bastards by name, but local heroes by nature. We owe them a great deal.'

Leeming looked around the well-stocked shop. Wine was stored on racks on every wall. There was a pleasing aroma and an air of prosperity about the place. Clearly, there were plenty of residents in Blandford with the money to satisfy their taste for fine wines.

'I prefer beer,' he said.

'I've no quarrel with that, Sergeant. I enjoy a pint myself.'

'You keep horses, I hear.'

Agar went on the defensive. 'Who told you that?'

'It was your son-in-law, sir.'

'Bill Manders?'

'I met him on the estate where he works as a gamekeeper.'

'What were you doing there?'

'I was asking a question about a man who once worked with him – John Bedloe. Does that name mean anything to you?'

'Not really,' said Agar. 'Bill never has much time to talk about his job. As soon as he gets here, he saddles up one of my horses. He's a good jockey.'

'So he told me.'

Since the man obviously hadn't heard about the murder, Leeming told him what had happened in West Moors. The wine merchant was shocked.

'You surely don't think my son-in-law was involved, do you?'

'I'm just making general enquiries, sir.'

'But why pick on Bill?'

'There'd been some animosity between him and Bedloe, it seems.'

'Bill can be awkward with most people,' said the other, ruefully. 'Frankly, I didn't take to him at all when my daughter first brought him here but he improved on acquaintance. And once he realised I kept horses, he changed his tune. We've become good friends.'

'I can't imagine that happening to Mr Manders and me.'

'He looks after my daughter properly – that's all I care about.'

'Where does he come from?'

'He's a Dorset lad who's moved around a bit. Bill was in the army for a while but he never liked taking orders. He wanted a job where he could be on his own and carry a gun. That's his other passion – shooting. It ran in the family,' Agar continued. 'His father used to be a gunsmith in Dorchester.'

'Is he still alive?'

'No, I'm afraid, he became too ill to work and sold the business. That really upset Bill. Whenever he's in Dorchester, he always goes past his father's old shop. He makes a point of it.'

Leeming's ears pricked up. According to the gamekeeper, he hardly ever went to the county town, yet his father-in-law gave the impression that he was a regular visitor there. Because the wine merchant obviously liked his son-in-law, Leeming didn't want to upset him by revealing his suspicions about Manders. Instead, he tried to find out a little more about him.

'When I met him, he talked about point-to-point races.'

'He's won no end of them on my horses.'

'He said that it was a useful source of money.'

'It is – I make wagers for him *and* me.'

'Do you ride yourself, Mr Agar?'

'Oh, I ride whenever I can but I'm too old to race any more.'

Having got him talking on a favourite subject, Leeming prompted him with questions about racing and about the wine trade. He was learning a great deal about Manders, including the fact that the gamekeeper had been in Wimborne recently because he delivered some crates of wine there for his father-in-law.

'He drove a horse and cart that day,' recalled Agar, 'so he wasn't able to go hell for leather. I've offered him a job here but he loves what he's doing and he has no interest in wine. You have to know your stock in this trade. It's the key to success.'

'It sounds as if you see him quite often, sir.'

'Not as often as we'd like, Sergeant. My wife is always complaining.'

'Do you ever go to Sweetbriar?'

'No, we have to wait for them to come here.'

'And when did you last see Mr Manders?'

'It was last Saturday, actually,' replied Agar. 'We weren't expecting him. Bill came by himself. He didn't stay. He just popped in here to say hello.'

Leeming was astounded. 'He was here on *Saturday*?'

'What's so remarkable about that? He's part of the family.'

'Yes, yes, of course.'

'Is there anything else I can tell you, Sergeant?'

Leeming was about to ask a last question when he saw the answer lying on the counter. Neatly placed in a line was an array of corkscrews.

When he reached the house, Colbeck had forgotten all about the case that had absorbed him for the last two days. His heart

171

and mind belonged wholly to Madeleine. The maidservant who admitted him to the house was thrilled to see him but warned him that his wife was fast asleep.

'No matter,' he said, taking off his hat and coat, 'I'll have a word with the nurse then I'll sit with Mrs Colbeck until she wakes up.'

After dining alone yet again, Lydia Quayle went up to her room with the intention of reading a book. She was staying at a small, fashionable hotel. It supplied most of her needs but the one thing it didn't offer was companionship. Whenever she went to the dining room, she felt isolated. What she yearned for was a house of her own with a staff to look after her and, when the details of her mother's will were made known to the family, she felt that the dream was well within her grasp. The letter from her elder brother had destroyed the illusion. Everything on which she'd started to rely had suddenly been thrown into question. Lydia feared that she might end up with virtually nothing and would be condemned to an existence in a series of hotels like the one she inhabited.

There was an easy solution to her loneliness. She could move back in with Beatrice Myler but that decision would bring an unwelcome consequence. Kind and caring, Beatrice was also proprietorial. She'd expect to be the most important person in Lydia's life and so the close relationship with Madeleine Colbeck would, of necessity, wither away. The choice was simple. It was between the doting love of a middle-aged spinster and the friendship of a young woman about to become a mother. Lydia could not have both. When she was with Beatrice, she felt warm, safe and loved but, in Madeleine's company, she was excited and filled with gratitude at being accepted into a family. The day would come when she would have to make the choice and she knew how angry and betrayed Beatrice would feel when she realised that Lydia had been involved in a clandestine friendship with someone else.

While she didn't want to hurt a woman who'd done so much for her, Lydia was frightened by the thought of losing contact with Madeleine and with her baby. Being at the Colbeck house had given her a vision of a new life for herself, one that was brimful with hope and ambition, things that would be smothered to death if she succumbed to the blandishments of Beatrice Myler. There was no easy solution to Lydia's problem. For a time, the generous inheritance from her mother seemed to have provided the answer. It might well disappear now.

Madeleine had only been dozing. Pleasant dreams had soothed her mind and left her feeling refreshed. When she first opened her eyes, she was unable to focus on the figure seated beside the bed. Assuming that it was the nurse, she drifted off for a few minutes. What brought her awake this time was the gentle feel of a hand on her arm. She blinked, rubbed her eyes then recognised the person at the bedside.

'Robert!' she cried.

'Hello, Madeleine,' he said, holding her hand.

'What are you doing here?'

'Do you really have to ask that?'

'I thought you were in Dorset.'

'I came back.'

'Have you solved the case already?'

'Not exactly,' he said, ruefully. 'I had a piece of luck. Superintendent Tallis turned up and suggested that I might come home for the night. I didn't realise that he knew about your situation but he does and . . . that's why I'm here.'

She squeezed his hand. 'I'm so pleased to see you.'

'Make the most of me while I'm here.'

'I've so much to tell you, Robert.'

'Start by telling me what the doctor has said.'

'Everything is as it should be,' she said. 'He thinks that it could be as much as another fortnight.' She tightened her grip. 'You will be back before then, won't you?'

'I don't doubt it for a second. It may well be that, by the time I get back to Wimborne in the morning, Victor and the superintendent may have already solved the case. If they have,' he added with a grin, 'it will be all Victor's doing.'

'How is he?'

'He's very envious of my chance to return to London. He'd dearly love to come back to see Estelle and the boys.'

'Estelle has been a Trojan,' she said. 'She's sat with me for hours. And so has Lydia Quayle, by the way. She's never visited anyone during her confinement before and it's been a revelation to her. Lydia is fascinated by what she's learnt.'

'Well, I've learnt something as well, Mrs Colbeck.'

'What's that?'

'I love you dearly and hate being apart from you.'

'That's good to hear, Robert.'

'No, it's not, it's maddening.'

'I meant that you expressed it so nicely. Oh, this is such a treat,' she went on, gazing lovingly at him. 'I could look at your face all night.'

He laughed. 'I can't guarantee I've the strength to sit here that long.'

'We're under the same roof again. That's what matters. Who would have imagined that the superintendent could be so kind?'

'Perhaps I've misjudged him all these years.'

'It looks as if he has a heart, after all.'

'I wouldn't go as far as that,' he said, smiling, 'but he's obviously responded to a human impulse of some kind. I'm very grateful to him.'

After his meeting with Jack Elwell, the superintendent sought out Dr Anson in Dorchester so that he could hear first-hand about the tragic death of Elwell's first wife and discuss the long-term effect it was likely to have on him. When he left the town, his suspicions of the former sailor had hardened. Tallis's work was not over yet. As soon as he got back to Wimborne Station, he made a point of finding Richard Satchwell so that he could sound out the railway policeman. Tallis found his answers evasive on every subject but that of his attitude to the murder victim. Satchwell was more than ready to admit that he disliked his colleague intensely. The superintendent's final call was on Dr Keddle. He introduced himself, checked a number of details then asked if he could view the cadaver. Like Colbeck, he was repulsed by the sight of the corkscrew.

Tallis's next port of call was the police station to see if anyone there had managed to unearth evidence relating to the murder. He learnt that the promise of a reward had brought in a number of impostors whose claims were swiftly dismissed. No new facts about the case had emerged. Having drawn a blank there, Tallis became aware how late it was and how hungry he'd become. He headed back to the hotel. As he entered the building, he saw Victor Leeming arguing with a man whose identity he guessed at once.

'Good evening, Mr Feltham,' he boomed. 'My name is Superintendent Tallis.'

Feltham turned round to see the burly figure. For his part, the beleaguered Leeming was glad that Tallis had drawn the man's fire away from him.

'I've just discovered that you've taken over the case,' said Feltham, testily, 'and I'm not at all happy. I sent for the Railway Detective.'

'And he duly responded, sir. I haven't replaced him in any way – nobody could do that. I've just come to lend my weight to the investigation.'

'Then perhaps you'll tell me what's going on.'

'The sergeant will have done that, surely.'

'I was trying to do so,' said Leeming, 'but Mr Feltham kept interrupting me. He seems to think that solving a murder is as easy as pulling a rabbit out of a hat.'

'All I seek is *detail*,' asserted Feltham.

'I gave you what little we have, sir.'

'You won't even tell me who your suspects are.'

'That's very wise of the sergeant,' said Tallis. 'It's a policy I advise my detectives to adopt. If you divulge the names of suspects, you can very often frighten the killer away. We don't want him to know that he's under consideration.'

'You could tell me,' said Feltham. 'I have a right to know.'

'And we have a right to hold back the information, Mr Feltham.'

'Why must you all be so stubborn?'

'Perhaps it's because we're members of the Metropolitan Police, sir. A man in your position may be able to browbeat the local constables but your writ does not run to the capital.' Tallis straightened his back. 'You have *no* influence with us, sir.'

'That's what I told him, Superintendent,' said Leeming.

'Damnation!' exclaimed Feltham. 'I was the one who *brought* you here.'

'Calling on our services,' said Tallis, acidly, 'does not entitle you to get in our way. My officers work best when given their head.' His stomach rumbled. 'You'll have to excuse us, sir. The sergeant and I have much to discuss.'

Turning on his heel, he led Leeming off to the dining room and left Feltham frothing impotently behind them. As soon as they'd settled down at a table, the superintendent ordered drinks and reached for the menu.

'Thank you for rescuing me, sir,' said Leeming.

'I despise people like that. The Felthams of this world are an insufferable breed. They think that they can ride roughshod over anyone.'

It occurred to Leeming that Tallis had just described himself but he forbore to point out the fact to his companion. After they'd given their orders to the waiter, the superintendent made sure that nobody could overhear them before he spoke.

'What did you find out?' he asked.

'I discovered that someone told me a string of lies.'

'That's nothing unusual. Did you gather any useful intelligence?'

'Yes, sir – and I may have unmasked the killer.'

'What a strange coincidence!'

'I don't understand.'

'Well, I fancy that I found him as well.'

'My suspect is William Manders.'

'Mine is Jack Elwell.'

'It can't be both of them, sir.'

'Tell me what you learnt in Blandford Forum.'

It took Leeming the entire first course to describe his visit to the wine merchant. During the much longer main course, Tallis slowly recounted his conversations with Elwell, Anson, Satchwell and Keddle. Neither of them would be prised away from the belief that they had discovered the man who'd killed John Bedloe. Leeming swallowed a last potato then offered an opinion.

'I've been thinking very hard about those women, sir,' he said.

Tallis frowned. 'To which women are you referring?'

'The three who got themselves ensnared by Bedloe and wrote him letters.'

'Only two of them are still alive.'

'I know that, sir.'

'So what's your point about the remaining two?'

'Inspector Colbeck was convinced that they lived in or near Wimborne.'

'That's more than likely.'

'How are they going to react to the murder?'

'They'll be shocked, I daresay.'

'Just suppose that *you* were one of them, Superintendent.'

'I'll do nothing of the kind,' snarled Tallis, puce with anger. 'How dare you suggest that I put myself in the place of an adulterous wife! It's monstrous.'

'Well, I know how *I'd* respond, sir.'

'Then you are more closely associated with the dregs of society than you ought to be. I took you for a man who respected his marriage vows.'

'And so I do.'

'Then why make such an obscene proposal?'

'We have to wonder how *they* would think,' argued Leeming. 'Yes, they'll be shocked and in despair at what happened but they'll also be terrified.'

'Why?'

'They wrote letters to Bedloe, sir. They'll know that the likelihood is that he might keep them as love tokens. In other words, they'll be somewhere in that house of his. They'll be terrified of what would happen if those letters fell into the wrong hands. That being the case,' concluded Leeming, 'what would they do?'

Tallis sat back and used his napkin to wipe some gravy off his moustache.

'They'd try to get the letters back.'

It was pitch-dark when she turned into the street but she'd been there enough times to know exactly where the house was. Trotting silently along, she came to Bedloe's front door, used a key to open it, then stepped inside the building. The frantic search began.

CHAPTER ELEVEN

Robert Colbeck was as good as his word. He caught the earliest train back to Dorset. After a night back in his own home, he was both refreshed and reassured. Madeleine was in good health and good spirits. His surprise visit had given her a tremendous boost and he was quick to acknowledge that it came as a result of an order from Edward Tallis. Over the years, the superintendent's orders had usually taken him away from Madeleine and he'd never expected to be sent back to her. It was proof that there was – notwithstanding his multiple defects – a glimmer of sympathy somewhere deep inside Tallis. Wanting to reflect at leisure on the joy of his reunion, Colbeck steeled himself to forget it for a while. Rail travel was thinking time. To all intents and purposes, Madeleine didn't exist. His brain was occupied by a series of murder suspects, each one waiting in line for closer examination.

When the train eventually reached the stretch of the line known jocularly as Castleman's Corkscrew, he realised that it was an appropriate description of the case. During the two days he and Leeming had been in Dorset, they had gone in a series of bewildering circles that burrowed deeper and deeper into the mystery. Colbeck wondered how long it would be before the corkscrew had been turned to its fullest extent and could finally be withdrawn by force. Which of the names they'd identified as suspects would pop out of the bottle?

For the most part, he ignored the landscape that scudded past him. When the train reached Leonard's Bridge, however, he began to look out of the window properly. Though the next scheduled stop was Wimborne, his primary interest was in West Moors. He expected to see Michael Tullidge standing beside one of the crossing gates and to catch a glimpse of the actual spot where the corpse was discovered. In fact, he saw rather more than he'd anticipated. Tullidge was there but so was Edward Tallis and they were deep in conversation.

'What the devil are you playing at, Sergeant?' he demanded.

'I was just following my instincts.'

'You had no call to bother my wife.'

'I didn't bother her. I simply asked her a few questions.'

'You were checking up on me.'

'I always like to verify the facts.'

'Wasn't my word good enough for you?'

Sooner or later, Victor Leeming knew, there'd be a confrontation with Richard Satchwell. The railway policeman took exception to the fact that the sergeant had questioned his wife. The moment that Leeming appeared on the platform at Wimborne Station, therefore, Satchwell hurried across to him. He was incandescent.

'You didn't even ask my permission,' he protested.

'Why should I need it?'

'Amy was very alarmed when you turned up on the doorstep.'

'I thought we had a polite conversation.'

'You upset my wife.'

'It was not intentional,' said Leeming. 'Mrs Satchwell was very helpful.'

'Amy was horrified to think that you didn't trust me.'

'I don't trust anybody.'

'Why not? I'm a railway policeman. Doesn't that mean anything to you?'

'Unfortunately, it does,' replied the other. 'Inspector Colbeck and I spend most of our time clashing with people like you. They always manage to get under our feet. For some reason, they seem to think that they are on an equal footing with us instead of being mere railway employees with a limited sphere of authority. In your case,' Leeming added, 'there's an additional reason for distrust.'

'What is it?'

'You're in Mr Feltham's pocket.'

'That's not true!'

'I think it is. If he threw a stick, you'd be the one to retrieve it.'

Satchwell coloured. 'Take that back,' he ordered.

'I've no reason to do so.'

'Take it back, I say.'

He tried to reinforce the demand by grabbing Leeming by the collar. It was a mistake. The sergeant not only detached himself with ease, he pushed Satchwell hard enough against the side of the ticket office to take the breath out of him. A tense moment was broken by the sound of an approaching train. Leeming stood back.

'If you have a complaint to make against me,' he said, 'make it

183

to Inspector Colbeck. He'll be on this train. And if you dare to lay a finger on me again, I'll have the pleasure of beating you black and blue before I arrest you for assaulting a police officer. What would your wife say to that?'

Satchwell was shamefaced. 'I'm sorry . . .'

'And so you should be. Now go off and do the job you're paid to do.'

As the railway policeman slunk away, the train powered its way into the station and slowed to a halt. Doors began to open. When he saw Colbeck alighting, Leeming went across to greet him.

'Welcome back, sir!'

'Good morning, Victor.'

'The superintendent has gone to West Moors.'

'I know. I spotted him through the window of my compartment. He was talking to Michael Tullidge.'

'How was your visit home?'

'It was idyllic,' said Colbeck. 'Madeleine was thrilled to see me and my mind was put at rest. The baby is not likely to come for some time yet. Madeleine made a point of telling me that Estelle had been a great help to her.'

'Thank you for passing that on, sir.'

'What's been happening here?'

'Oh,' said Leeming with a chuckle, 'a great deal has been happening. The superintendent believes that Jack Elwell is the killer and – until today – I was shifting to and fro between Simon Copsey and William Manders.'

'You've had second thoughts?'

'Yes, they came to me only a moment ago.'

'Has someone displaced Copsey and Manders?'

'Richard Satchwell – he just accosted me.'

'On what grounds?'

'He was upset because I questioned his wife. When I accused him of being Mr Feltham's lackey, he grabbed hold of me in a fit of temper. If the train hadn't come in, I'd have made him wish that he hadn't touched me. He needed to be taught a sharp lesson, sir.'

'So he's capable of violence, is he?'

'Yes,' said Leeming. 'All that I did to provoke him was to point out that his first allegiance is to Feltham. I think that Bedloe would have given him a lot more provocation than that.'

'But the argument started over his wife, you say?'

'He said that I had no reason to speak to Mrs Satchwell.'

'Was he simply being protective towards her?'

'No, sir, he was being downright aggressive.'

'Did he feel that she might have given him away?'

'It was partly that, I fancy.'

'You told me that his wife was an attractive woman.'

'I thought she was very pretty, sir.'

'Then I don't think the fact would have gone unnoticed by John Bedloe,' said Colbeck, thoughtfully. 'By all accounts, he would have noticed every pretty face in Wimborne. If his colleague had shown interest in Mrs Satchwell, as was highly likely, what do you think her husband would have done?'

Leeming recalled the look of blind rage in Satchwell's eyes.

'I think he'd have gone in search of a corkscrew.'

Michael Tullidge had to be careful. He knew that he couldn't be too argumentative with his visitor. A superintendent from Scotland Yard, he reasoned, would have influence. If he offended Tallis, he might be reported to the railway company and lose his job. With all its faults, the life of a crossing-keeper was something he very much wanted to keep, not least because of the lodge that came with his post. When Tallis asked to speak to his wife, therefore,

Tullidge couldn't refuse. Much against his will, he led his visitor into the lodge and performed a grudging introduction.

'I'm pleased to meet you, Mrs Tullidge,' said Tallis, removing his hat. 'I just wish to confirm something that you told Inspector Colbeck.'

'I told him the truth, sir,' she said, nervously.

'I'm sure that you did. Could you please repeat it for me?'

'What is it that you want to know, sir?'

She glanced at her husband who was watching her intently and imparting a silent warning. Her eyes flicked back to Tallis.

'Tell me what time Mr Tullidge returned home on Saturday night.'

'It must have been around ten-thirty, sir.'

'You told the inspector that it was eleven o'clock.'

'I must have made a mistake about that. It was earlier than usual, I know that.'

'Ten-thirty would still leave a gap of up to half an hour for your husband to walk the relatively short distance from the Waggon and Horses to here.' He turned to Tullidge. 'What delayed you?'

'I lost my way,' replied the other.

'I find that hard to believe, sir.'

'They serves a strong pint of beer at the Waggon.'

'Are you saying that you were too drunk to know your way home?'

'Yes.'

'My husband deserves a drink at the end of the week,' said Rebecca, quickly. 'He never touches it when he's on duty, of course, or on weekdays. On Saturday, he always goes to the Waggon with Elias Rawles and Hugh Delafield. They live nearby, sir. Sometimes they celebrate too much.'

'Hugh *always* does,' said Tullidge, taking up her theme. 'Elias and me have had to carry him home more than once. I must have done the same thing on Saturday and had more than I could handle. I remember leaving the pub and getting back home but I can't recall a thing about what happened in between.'

'That's rather convenient for you, isn't it?' said Tallis, ironically.

'It's what happened.'

'Perhaps it was, Mr Tullidge, but you can't prove it, can you? It's strange. Whenever we question anybody, we find that a lot of people have suffered from a sudden loss of memory. They recall everything to their advantage very clearly. If they wish to hide something, a heavy mist somehow descends on their mind.'

'My husband is an honest man,' said Rebecca, staunchly.

'Would you consider yourself to be an honest woman, Mrs Tullidge?'

She almost blushed. 'Yes, I would.'

'And do you have a good memory?'

'I like to think so.'

'Then how can you confuse eleven o'clock with ten-thirty? Inspector Colbeck hears one tale from you and I hear another.'

'Does it matter?' asked Tullidge. 'I had nothing to do with the murder. I don't really see why you're bothering to ask us any questions.'

'You live three hundred yards from the scene of the crime, sir.'

'I can't help that.'

'In all probability,' said Tallis, 'a man was stabbed to death during the time between your departure from the Waggon and Horses and your return here. That's why I took the trouble to come here today.'

'I've nothing to add to what I told the inspector.'

'Like me, he feels that you're not telling the full truth.'

'Yes, we are.'

'We'd never lie to the police,' said Rebecca.

Tallis scrutinised the other man's face. 'Have you ever fallen foul of the law?'

'No, I haven't.'

'Well, you're on the verge of doing so now.'

Tullidge bristled with injured innocence. 'What have I done wrong?'

'Withholding evidence from the police is a crime.'

'I don't *have* any evidence.'

'What about you, Mrs Tullidge?' asked Tallis, moving his attention to her. 'Are you holding anything back from me?'

This time she did blush. 'No, no, I'm not.'

'Can you swear to that?'

'I was in bed with my husband.'

'What Becky says is right,' confirmed Tullidge.

'How do you know?' asked Tallis with asperity. 'You were too drunk to find your way home. Your wife probably had to put you to bed.'

'I did,' she said. 'I always do that on a Saturday night.'

Tallis gave her the full force of his concentration and she quailed beneath it. He seemed to be looking into her soul. When Tullidge was subjected to the same treatment, he responded with his customary vacant stare.

'One or both of you is lying,' decided Tallis.

'We don't have any reason to lie, sir,' said Rebecca.

'I'm not sure that either of you *need* a reason, Mrs Tullidge.'

'Michael and I try to tell the truth.'

'Well, I've heard precious little of it since I stepped into this lodge. It's not just my opinion,' said Tallis. 'Inspector Colbeck had the same feeling. Now why do you think that was?'

* * *

188

Lydia Quayle was beginning to feel that she was intruding at the Colbeck house. Much as she wished to see Madeleine, she was conscious of the physical changes in the other woman and had the sense that it was not her place to be there. While she had two sisters-in-law who'd brought children into the world, she'd not spent time with either of them in the closing stages of pregnancy. The truth was that she knew and understood very little about the practical implications of maternity. As for Madeleine, she decided, it was best to draw back for a while. The friendship could be renewed once the child was born. Rather than spend another lonely hour in the hotel dining room, she'd agreed to have luncheon at a restaurant with Beatrice Myler. No sooner had they taken their seats at the table than the interrogation began.

'You're looking pale, dear,' said Beatrice. 'Are you feeling unwell?'

'No, I'm not.'

'And you're so thin. Are you eating enough?'

'I'm probably eating more than I need, Beatrice.'

'What sort of meals do they serve at the hotel?'

'They're very tasty.'

'You need looking after.'

'I'm fine on my own.'

'Yes, but how long can you keep this up?'

'Keep what up?' asked Lydia.

'This bravado,' said Beatrice. 'Anyone can see that the kind of life you're leading is not entirely healthy. The problems you're having with the family must be pressing down on you all the time.'

'That's true. They're like a ton weight.'

'Let someone else help you to bear it.'

'No thank you, Beatrice. It's my battle. I'll fight it my way.'

'But you're up against impossible odds.'

'That's not entirely true,' said Lydia. 'I have two brothers, remember. Lucas is sure to be on my side. Anyway,' she went on, 'let's not spoil our time together by going on about my troubles. I want to forget them for a while.'

'Then we'll put them aside,' agreed Beatrice.

It was a delicious meal and it enabled Lydia to shrug off her worries for an hour or so. Beatrice was attentive without being inquisitive and had a fund of amusing anecdotes to pass on. The time passed quickly and pleasantly. It was only when the meal was over that the mood changed.

'You won't forget my invitation, will you?' said Beatrice. 'You can move back into the house any time you choose.'

'That's a very kind offer, Beatrice.'

'It doesn't have to be permanent. You can stay for as long or as little as you wish. I just feel that you need a place of sanctuary at the moment.'

'I'm happy at the hotel.'

'You'd get more comfort and better meals with me.'

'I daresay that I would.'

'Think it over, Lydia.'

'I will.'

'Just come for a week or two in the first instance,' suggested Beatrice. 'If the will is contested, my home will be a place of refuge.'

'Litigation will take more than a week or two, I'm afraid. It could go on for months – if I decide to go to court, that is.'

'You'd spare yourself a lot of heartache if you didn't.'

'Part of me thinks that,' admitted Lydia, 'but another part urges me to fight tooth and nail for what's rightly mine. I don't know that I could look myself in the mirror if I didn't put up some kind of resistance.'

'Then you must do just that,' said Beatrice, soothingly. 'Win or lose, you're always welcome to come back to me.'

Lydia was not tempted to accept the offer. Having secured her independence, she didn't want to surrender it easily. Besides, she knew Beatrice of old. There was no such thing as a temporary stay at the house. If she agreed to move back, Lydia would almost certainly be stuck there inescapably and her life would suddenly have become as narrow and predictable as it had been in the past.

'Who will be there?' asked Tallis.

'It will be poorly attended, sir,' replied Colbeck. 'At least, that's my feeling. Apart from Dr Keddle, the only people certain to be at the inquest are Simon Copsey and Harry Wills. I sent Wills a telegraph yesterday. He won't give evidence, of course, but as an interested party, he ought to be present.'

'Don't forget Satchwell, sir,' said Leeming.

'Yes, he should be there as a witness. He was called to the scene of the crime on Saturday night.'

'It's not impossible that he *created* that scene, sir.'

'He's a suspect, I grant you.'

'So is Jack Elwell,' Tallis reminded them. 'He may not be there but I'll wager that he'll be very interested to read the report of the inquest in the newspaper.'

'I could say the same of Manders, sir,' observed Leeming. 'Instead of being on duty at Sweetbriar on Saturday night, he was calling in to see his father-in-law in Blandford. That's a lot closer to West Moors.'

'If we're talking about being close to West Moors, it brings Tullidge and his wife to the fore. They actually *live* there.'

'So do lots of other people, sir,' said Colbeck.

'They *lied* to me,' recalled Tallis. 'Why did they do that?'

'I don't know. I must say that they're an ill-assorted pair.'

'I felt sorry for Mrs Tullidge, having to share her life with someone as grim and humourless as that fellow. Having to look at that forbidding face of his every day must be a real trial for her.'

Colbeck and Leeming fought hard not to trade an amused glance.

'You've met them both, sir,' said Colbeck, 'but you still favour Elwell. Until we have more evidence, he would be my choice. What about you, Sergeant?'

'It has to be Manders,' affirmed Leeming before scratching his head. 'Yet it could equally well be Copsey or Satchwell. If I had to make a guess . . .'

'We don't rely on guesses,' said Tallis. 'You must *feel* someone is guilty.'

'Then I'll stand by Manders, sir. Everything his father-in-law told me about him seemed to fit. He's strong, determined and rides a horse very fast. He could well have been in West Moors at the time of the murder. I believe he's vengeful.'

'Then I think you should arrest him at once.'

'What about the inquest?'

'The inspector and I will be there. That's more than enough. You get off to Sweetbriar to bring Manders here. Back your judgement, Leeming.'

'Yes, sir.'

'Then don't waste any more time.'

After a flurry of farewells, Leeming went out with the confident tread of a man about to make a significant arrest. The others were in Colbeck's hotel room. All three of them had been pooling information and discussing their instincts.

'It could be a wasted journey,' decided Tallis.

'Sergeant Leeming always enjoys making an arrest, sir, and we have to remember that he's met Manders. We haven't. He's always had good instincts in the past. He may yet be right.'

Tallis extracted a gold watch from his waistcoat pocket and looked at it.

'Time to go, I think. We ought to get there early.'

'I agree, sir,' said Colbeck, rising to his feet.

Tallis also got up. 'Oh,' he said, stiffly, 'I forgot to ask you about your visit to Mrs Colbeck.'

'My wife was very pleased to see me, sir. She sends her profound thanks.'

'And your good lady is . . . well?'

'She's very well, sir.'

'Good.'

Tallis dismissed what had obviously been a rather awkward subject for him. As they were coming down the staircase, he reverted to a question about the inquest.

'Who else might turn up today?'

'We can certainly expect one person, sir.'

'And who might that be?'

'It's the man hoping to be the next mayor – Ambrose Feltham.'

As they walked together towards the court, Feltham was scandalised.

'Sergeant Leeming did *what*?' he cried.

'He spoke to my wife behind my back.'

'That's unpardonable.'

'He caught Amy unawares. He gave her a shock, turning up like that.'

'I'm not surprised, Satchwell. The sergeant is not the most prepossessing man. That ugly face of his would not be out of place on the head of a fairground ruffian. Why did he have to bother your wife?'

'He was checking up on me, sir.'

'Why on earth should he do that?'

'That's what I demanded to know, Mr Feltham.'

'You challenged him about it, did you?'

'Yes, sir,' said Satchwell. 'He turned up at the station to await the inspector's train. I seized my chance. Unfortunately, my temper got the better of me and I jostled him. It was his fault. He provoked me.'

'What did he say about you?'

'It was what he insinuated about *you* that annoyed me.'

Feltham was roused. 'How did I come into it?'

'He showed you disrespect, sir.'

Satchwell embellished the conversation he'd had with Leeming so that the latter appeared to be denigrating Feltham. The older man was furious and vowed to complain to the superintendent.

'I won't be treated in this way,' he said, angrily, 'and I won't have your word questioned by the sergeant. I sent for them in order to help us not to cause so much upset. If any of our local constables dared to speak to me the way that they did, I'd have them dismissed on the spot.'

'You can't dismiss a detective superintendent.'

'Perhaps not, but I can go over his head to the commissioner. If they don't buck up their ideas, Tallis and his men will have their ears boxed when they get back to Scotland Yard.' They walked on in silence until Feltham remembered something. 'Do we have any idea who their suspects are?'

'I found out the name of one of them, sir.'

'Good man.'

'I bribed a waiter at the King's Head to pick up what he could.'

'What did he tell you?'

'They think that the killer is a man named Jack Elwell.'

Presided over by an elderly coroner with a high-pitched voice, the inquest was short, inconclusive and poorly attended. Apart from Colbeck and Tallis, the only people who'd come to watch proceedings were Harry Wills, Ambrose Feltham, one old man, two old ladies, and a young reporter from the local newspaper. Three witnesses were called – Simon Copsey, Oliver Keddle and Richard Satchwell. The shepherd spent most of the time protesting about the fact that he'd been hauled away from his work at a time when he was most needed. When asked what he was doing in West Moors at the time he found the body, he was ingeniously obscure. Keddle and Satchwell gave their statements, then the inquest was over. John Bedloe, it was declared, had been killed by a person or persons unknown.

As soon as they came out into the street, Feltham cornered Tallis to make a complaint on Satchwell's behalf. Colbeck was left free to speak to Harry Wills. The railwayman had sat on the edge of his seat throughout the proceedings, not quite sure that he had the right to be there.

'You managed to get the time off, then?' asked Colbeck.

'Yes, Inspector, that was thanks to you. I showed them your telegraph.'

'It wasn't exactly a royal summons, Mr Wills.'

'It was to me, sir.'

'I'm sorry you had to listen to Dr Keddle giving details of the post-mortem,' said Colbeck. 'I saw you wince at one point.'

'To be honest, Inspector, I felt sick.'

'The worst is over now. The body will soon be released for burial.'

'I've already spoken to an undertaker,' said Wills, sadly, 'and to the vicar of our church. I think that John would prefer to be buried in Dorchester. He lived there longer than here and I'd rather get him away from Wimborne. It holds too many bad memories.'

'The decision is yours, sir. I endorse it.'

'What will happen next?'

'Your cousin's house and worldly goods will be—'

'I didn't mean that,' said Wills, interrupting. 'I'm still not sure that I'm entitled to have anything of John's. My wife feels the same. We don't deserve it. No, what I want to know is when you're going to catch the man who did those dreadful things to my cousin.'

'We're doing our utmost, Mr Wills.'

'Are you likely to make an arrest soon?'

'As a matter of fact, one will take place today.'

'That's good news,' said Wills, brightening.

'Not necessarily,' explained Colbeck. 'We're going to hold this person in custody so that we can question him properly. He may or may not be the killer.'

'I hope that he is, Inspector. My wife is frightened at the thought that the man is still on the loose. She'll be so pleased when I tell her that an arrest has been made.'

'Strictly speaking, it hasn't.'

'Why not?'

'Sergeant Leeming, my colleague, is on his way to find the man in question. That may take time. The suspect is a gamekeeper on a large estate. Tracking him down could be a problem.'

Leeming spent the journey to Sherborne hoping that he wouldn't have the same driver as on his earlier trip to the Sweetbriar Estate. It had been an ordeal to sit beside him. In the event, he was able to hire the services of a much younger man with some insight into the value of personal hygiene. His driver was also less talkative and more intent on getting his passenger quickly to his destination. The long periods of silence suited Leeming. He was able to rehearse what he was going to say to Manders. There was one potential problem. Manders had a gun. If he really was the killer of John Bedloe, he wouldn't scruple to use it on the detective who tried to take him into custody. Leeming needed guile as well as common sense.

As before, his search for the gamekeeper began with the estate manager. Leonard Findlay was surprised to see him again and blinked in disbelief when he heard the sergeant's reason for being there.

'Is an arrest *justified*?'

'We believe so, sir.'

'Bill Manders is no killer,' insisted Findlay.

'He's yet to convince us of his innocence, sir.'

'But you questioned him last time.'

'New evidence has come to light.'

'What does it concern?'

'His ability to tell me outrageous lies.'

'Manders is no liar, He's a man of integrity.'

'You'd be amazed how many men of integrity we've put behind bars, sir. One of them was a vicar with a devoted flock. They'd have done anything for him. That was before they learnt how much money he'd stolen from the parish.'

'You're making a hideous mistake, Sergeant.'

'Oddly enough, the vicar said exactly the same thing to me.'

'As you wish,' said Findlay, petulantly, 'go ahead and arrest him. You'll be forced to release him before too long. I'll give you my word on that.'

'What I'd prefer is some idea where I might find Manders.'

'Step this way.'

Visibly upset, the estate manager took him into his office and pointed to the map of the estate on the wall. He explained where the gamekeeper was likely to be, tracing a wide circle with the palm of his hand.

'He could be anywhere within this area, Sergeant.'

'He must do a lot of walking in a normal day.'

'Fitness is essential for a gamekeeper.'

'Then I won't pretend that I could ever be one, sir. My driver will take me as far as that wood then I'll go on foot from there.' He shook hands with Findlay. 'Thank you for your help. I'm sorry to bring bad news.'

'There'll be good news to follow,' said the other, confidently, 'because you'll be forced to let him go and offer him an abject apology.'

'I admire your loyalty, Mr Findlay.'

Leeming returned to the trap and asked the driver to take him off in an easterly direction. After half a mile, they came to a wide expanse of grass that swept down to some woodland. Their appearance disturbed some deer grazing in the middle distance. The animals fled at once into the trees. On Leeming's instructions, the driver took the trap carefully down the incline. When they reached the wood, Leeming called a halt and clambered down from the vehicle.

'You wait here for me,' he ordered.

'Yes, sir,' said the driver.

'I won't be long.'

Leeming cupped his hands to call. 'Mr Manders!'

There was no answer. He plunged into the trees and followed a path that took a serpentine route. The deeper he went into the wood, the more deer he put to flight. It also became slightly darker as closely packed trees blocked out some of the light. He pushed on regardless because Findlay had told him it was the most likely place to find the gamekeeper. To his dismay, Leeming soon realised that he had no idea where he was or how he could find a way back to the waiting trap. It was worrying. He was also hearing strange noises and was startled when small animals darted past him through the undergrowth.

The worst was yet to come. Short of breath and needing a rest, he lowered himself down on to a fallen log. The moment he moved, a shotgun was fired and his top hat was knocked from his head. He was incensed. Jumping up, he yelled angrily.

'It's me – Sergeant Leeming!'

There was no reply.

Rebecca Tullidge's fears were allayed. When her friend called on her that afternoon, her husband made no objection. In fact, he exchanged a few words with Margaret Vout before going out of the lodge. Over a cup of tea, the women talked freely.

'The inquest is being held today,' said Margaret.

'What happens after that?'

'There'll be a decision by the coroner, then the body will be released for burial. That's what happened in Ted Rowland's case, anyway. Because he was hit by that train, it was an unnatural death so they held an inquest. He was buried not long after. His wife has still not got over it. I wonder if John Bedloe was married.'

'No, he wasn't,' said Rebecca, blurting out the words.

'How do you know?'

'The detectives told us, Maggie.'

'I thought you'd only seen one of them – that Inspector Colbeck.'

'A Superintendent Tallis came to see us this morning.'

'Why was that?'

'He wanted to ask some questions and see . . . exactly where it happened.' She pulled a face. 'He's not the only one.'

'What do you mean, Becky?'

'Lots of other people have come to take a look – children, mostly. Michael chases them away. It's not right, staring at a place where someone was murdered. I washed the bloodstains off the line but they still turn up to stare.'

'I hope they catch the killer soon.'

'So do I, Maggie.'

'If he can kill once, he can kill again. That's what I say. I don't envy you, being so isolated out here.'

'We can look after ourselves.'

'Yes,' said the other woman. 'You'd have to be rash or stupid to take on someone as strong as Michael.'

It was a sobering thought. Most of the time, Rebecca dwelt on her husband's manifold faults yet he did possess virtues. One of them was that he protected her. If someone could kill her lover, she was bound to feel vulnerable. It was good to be reminded that she had a robust line of defence in the person of her husband.

'What was he *doing* here?' asked Margaret. 'That's what we all keep asking. Why was he anywhere near West Moors?'

'We may never know,' said Rebecca, quietly.

'Hugh Delafield thinks he was killed somewhere else and dumped here.'

'Yes, that could be the answer.'

'But why would anyone do that?'

They chatted away until it was time for Margaret to leave. Rebecca opened the front door for her. As her visitor went out, Tullidge was approaching the lodge. He waved her off then looked after her.

'What did Maggie have to say?' he asked.

'Oh, it was just the usual gossip.'

'Did you tell her about that superintendent coming here?'

'No,' she lied, 'you told me not to.'

'Then you did the right thing,' he said with a grunt of approval.

Since the moment when Tallis had left that morning, Tullidge had been unusually civil to her. He was pleased with the way that she'd supported him in the face of more police questioning. It deserved a reward.

'If you want to go into Wimborne,' he said, 'then you can.'

Leeming was acutely aware of the danger he was in. Unarmed and lost in the middle of a wood, he'd already been shot at once. Someone was stalking him. Whatever he did, he must not present a sitting target. He'd therefore retrieved his top hat, noted the hole in it then crept away into the undergrowth. He was now crouching down low as he moved past a clump of bushes. Every so often, he'd stop and listen. He could hear the wind rustling the foliage but little else. Keeping on the move, he swivelled his head constantly from side to side but he saw nobody. Had his attacker fled or was he just biding his time? There was no way of telling.

What he needed was a weapon. He looked around desperately for a stout stick or a fallen branch but none were at hand. In any case, they would have been no match for a shotgun. Leeming kept going, hoping that he could reach the edge of the wood and somehow make his way back to his driver. He'd have a witness then. Among the trees, he was in jeopardy. The gamekeeper – if, indeed, it *was* Manders – would not miss with his second shot. As the son of a gunsmith, handling his weapon would be second nature to him. All that Leeming could do was to keep out of his sight line.

The trees eventually began to thin out and he realised that he was near the margin of the wood. As more light guided his way, he dared to think that he'd escaped from his stalker. Hat in one hand, he broke into a run and built up speed. Leeming was only a dozen yards short of the last stand of trees when he tripped over something and fell headlong to the ground. Before he could move, he felt cold steel pressing against the back of his head.

'Don't move,' ordered Manders. 'Oh, it's you, Sergeant,' he added in surprise.

'Of course, it's me,' said Leeming, 'and you knew it.'

The gamekeeper lowered his gun. 'I thought you were trespassing.'

'Is that what you do with trespassers – try to kill them?'

Leeming got to his feet to confront him and waved the hat under his nose.

'I'm sorry about that,' said Manders, flatly.

'It was deliberate.'

'You could have been a poacher.'

'How many poachers wear a top hat?'

'All I saw was a shape in the gloom, moving stealthily towards the deer.'

'I called out your name. You recognised my voice.'

Manders' face was inscrutable. Leeming was still at a disadvantage. The gamekeeper was armed and he was not. It was time to turn the tables. Pretending to examine the hole in his hat, Leeming suddenly flung it into the other man's face, punched him hard in the stomach, then grabbed the shotgun. There was a violent struggle and they fell to the ground. As they threshed around, Leeming heard an ominous noise and realised that his frock coat had just been ripped apart. It put fresh strength into him. After pummelling away with his free hand, he caught

Manders a fearsome blow on the chin. Momentarily stunned, the gamekeeper was unable to stop the sergeant from wresting the weapon from him.

Leeming got to his feet. When he began to recover from the blow, Manders looked up to find that the shotgun was now being aimed at him. The harsh tone of the sergeant's voice suggested that he was more than ready to pull the trigger.

'You're under arrest,' he shouted.

CHAPTER TWELVE

As he turned the corner, Caleb Andrews recognised the woman crossing the road ahead of him. He lengthened his stride in order to intercept her, dodging a cab to reach the other pavement. It was Estelle Leeming, on her way back from the Colbeck house. Andrews hailed her.

'Oh, good afternoon,' she said, pleased to see him.

'How are you, Estelle?'

'I'm very well, Mr Andrews. What about you?'

'I'm getting restless,' he confessed. 'All this waiting will be the death of me. I'm beginning to wish that I was back at work again. I'd have no chance to brood or to worry about Maddy then.'

'I'm sure that everything will be all right.'

'Have you seen her?'

'Yes, but I didn't stay long. She's very tired. It's only to be expected.'

'You know more about these things than I do.'

'What tired your daughter out was all the excitement. I'd have been the same.'

'Excitement?' He was mystified. 'Why was Maddy excited?'

'It was because her husband came back to see her.'

'When?'

'Yesterday evening. He stayed the night.'

'Robert was *here*?' he said. 'Why wasn't I told? Why wasn't I sent for?'

'I think that he just wanted to be alone with his wife.'

'I'm his father-in-law. Apart from anything else, there are a few things I could tell him about the LSWR. It's a dreadful railway. I can't believe that he came home without asking my advice about it.'

'I'm afraid that it was only a flying visit.'

'What did he say about the case?'

'Nothing at all, as far as I know. He didn't arrive until late.'

'Well,' said Andrews, 'it was very good of him to come, I suppose – though he should never have gone to Dorset in the first place. How is Maddy?'

'You'll be able to find out for yourself.'

'No, Estelle, I didn't mean to bother her. There comes a time when I ought to leave her to . . . you know. I was just going to ask the nurse how Maddy was faring.'

'After the inspector's visit, she's blooming.'

'Has she had any other visitors?'

'None that I know of,' said Estelle.

'What about that friend of hers?'

'Miss Quayle hasn't called today. Madeleine was disappointed about that. Visitors help to break up the day for her.'

'Other women might do that. I'd just be in the way.'

'That's not true at all, Mr Andrews.'

'How did Robert manage to take the time off from the investigation?'

'It was the superintendent's idea,' replied Estelle. 'That's what I heard. It was a pity he couldn't send Victor home for the night as well. I'd have loved that.'

'Giving one of his detectives leave?' said Andrews, clicking his tongue. 'That doesn't sound like Superintendent Tallis to me. He likes to keep their noses to the grindstone.'

'He made an exception because of Madeleine's situation.'

'Then he deserves a pat on the back.'

'Have you ever met the superintendent?'

'Yes, I have. I didn't like him one bit. He looked down his nose at me.'

'Victor is terrified of him.'

'Robert isn't. Nobody frightens him.'

'The superintendent seems to keep picking on my husband. Victor can't do anything right in his eyes. It must be very wearing. Victor is determined to impress him one day.'

'Look at the state of you, man!' exclaimed Tallis. 'You're supposed to be a detective sergeant and not a tramp. However did you get like that?'

'He resisted arrest, sir,' said Leeming.

'Where is he now?'

'He's cooling his heels in a cell at the police station.'

'How did you get that hole in your hat?' asked Colbeck.

'It's a long story, sir.'

'Then sit down and tell it to us.'

Victor Leeming had never been so glad to lower himself into a comfortable chair. All three of them were in Colbeck's room. Having just returned from his adventure, the sergeant was in a sorry state. His frock coat was torn, his trousers were covered in grass stains and his cravat had been yanked from its moorings. There was a nasty bruise on his temple and his hair had the look of an abandoned bird's nest. He was clearly fatigued.

'Well,' prompted Tallis, 'what happened? Tell us before you fall asleep.'

Leeming cleared his throat. 'It was like this, sir . . .'

He gave a long-winded account of the pursuit and arrest of William Manders, stressing that the gamekeeper had fired at him and fought hard to escape. Had the prisoner not been handcuffed, Leeming might never have got himself safely back to Wimborne. Colbeck was complimentary.

'Well done, Sergeant!' he said. 'You acted with bravery and resourcefulness.'

'He's our man, sir,' declared Leeming. 'I'm certain of it.'

'Did you get a confession out of him?'

'Trying to kill me was a confession in itself.'

'I won't have my detectives shot at,' said Tallis, rancorously. 'I'll make that point when I question Manders.'

'The inspector should do that, sir.'

'I can manage quite well.'

'He has a way of getting under the skin of suspects,' said Leeming. 'I've seen him do it a hundred times. It comes from having been a barrister before he joined the police force. He knows how to cross-examine people.'

'Thank you, Sergeant,' said Colbeck.

'I know how to shake the truth out of someone just as well,' asserted Tallis. 'I spent thirty years in the army having to discipline recalcitrant soldiers. Nobody dared to tell me a lie.'

'Manders will,' said Leeming.

'I doubt it.'

'Perhaps you should take the sergeant with you,' suggested Colbeck. 'After all, he actually identified Manders as a suspect and took the trouble to visit the man's father-in-law. Sergeant Leeming is in possession of all the relevant facts.'

'That's true,' conceded Tallis. 'Very well, Leeming, you can join me.'

The sergeant beamed. 'Thank you, sir.'

'As long as you hold your peace and let me do the talking.'

'Yes, Superintendent.'

'What will *you* do, Inspector?'

'I'd like to take another look at Bedloe's house,' replied Colbeck. 'My first visit produced the letters and they were instrumental in setting me on the trail that led to Jack Elwell. On my second visit, I was simply searching for a will. Let's see if a third, more painstaking hunt turns up something new.'

'That's a good idea.'

'We can meet up here later on, sir.'

'Agreed.' Unable to stifle it, Leeming gave a spectacular yawn. 'Stay awake, man,' scolded Tallis, 'and change into something less befitting a scarecrow. We have a suspect to interrogate.'

'He's not merely a suspect, sir,' said Leeming. 'Manders is the killer.'

'William Manders?' said Feltham. 'I've never heard of the fellow.'

'He was arrested this afternoon by that sergeant.'

'I thought that their main suspect was someone called Jack Elwell.'

'It is, sir,' said Satchwell, 'but they obviously have more than one. Bert Maycock was at the police station when Manders was brought in.'

'What do you know about him?'

'He's a gamekeeper somewhere and he's a real handful. It took two of them to get him into the cell. Manders used to work with Bedloe. They never got on.'

'Did you ever meet anyone who *did* get on with John Bedloe?' asked Feltham, pointedly. 'Apart from women, that is.'

'No, sir, I didn't.'

'What about that cousin of his, the one at the inquest?'

'I think he was embarrassed to be related to Bedloe.'

'Who wouldn't be?'

'Harry Wills was responsible for getting his cousin a job as a railway policeman in Dorchester. He was probably glad when Bedloe moved here.' Satchwell curled his lip. 'I can't say that I was.'

'Well, at least we've had an arrest.'

'True, sir.'

'They seem to be making progress at last.'

'Yes,' said Satchwell. 'It's a promising sign. Maycock will pass on any developments at the police station.' He remembered his confrontation earlier in the day. 'Did you have a chance to speak to the superintendent, sir?'

Feltham scowled. 'Yes, I did.'

'What did he say?'

'He said that he always supports his detectives.'

'There was no need whatsoever to harass my wife.'

'I made that point, Satchwell – forcefully. The superintendent replied that Sergeant Leeming was showing admirable initiative.'

'That's not what I'd call it!' howled the other.

'Calm down, man.'

'How would you react if they questioned Mrs Feltham?'

'In the present circumstances, I might feel grateful. It would at least prove that they were aware of my existence,' said the older man, gloomily. 'I'm poised to become the next mayor and they treat me with something akin to contempt. I won't have it, I tell you. There was a time when policemen knew their place and always went to the servants' entrance at one's house. The superintendent and his men should behave with due deference.'

'I couldn't agree more, sir,' said Satchwell.

'Tell Maycock that I want regular reports.'

'He knows that.'

'I want to hear everything he can tell me about . . . What was his name?'

'Manders, sir. It's William Manders from the Sweetbriar Estate. He put shotgun pellets through the sergeant's top hat. Mind you,' he added, 'after the way he upset my wife, I'd be happy to do exactly the same.'

Because they were having difficulty controlling Manders, they had left his handcuffs on and threatened him with leg irons in the event of further trouble. The gamekeeper stopped yelling at the top of his voice and demanding that his employer be told where he was. When Leeming arrived in the company of Edward Tallis, the prisoner gave him a look of sheer hatred. It was an expression that Leeming had put on many faces over the years and he ignored it. Tallis ordered that Manders be taken from his cell and put in a small, featureless room at the rear of the police station. The prisoner was made to sit at a table with his back to the wall. Seated opposite, the detectives were between him and the door. Leeming had a pencil and pad ready to take notes. Manders glowered at them mutinously.

After introducing himself, Tallis issued a dire warning.

'Behave yourself,' he said, sternly, 'or you'll be put in chains. You're already charged with two offences – aggravated assault and the attempted murder of a Scotland Yard detective.'

'I didn't try to murder him,' said Manders, vehemently. 'I just wanted to scare him a bit.'

'You certainly did that,' confirmed Leeming.

'If I'd wanted to kill him, he wouldn't be sitting there now. When I've got a shotgun in my hands, I never miss.'

'You fired at Sergeant Leeming,' said Tallis. 'That's all I need to know.'

'Did he tell you that he attacked me?'

'He explained that he made an arrest.'

'He punched me in the stomach before he did that.'

'I had to disarm you,' said Leeming. 'The only way to do that was to use some force. Once I'd done that, I arrested you for the murder of John Bedloe.'

'I never touched the bastard.'

'Yes, you did. The first time we met, you boasted about a fight you had with him. You won. But it wasn't enough to give him a hiding, was it? You wanted him out of the way for good.'

'Let me ask the questions,' said Tallis, quelling him with a look.

'I'm sorry, sir.'

'What have you to say for yourself, Manders?'

'I didn't commit a murder,' retorted the other.

'Where were you last Saturday night?'

'I told the sergeant – I was on duty at Sweetbriar.'

'Then how did you manage to turn up at your father-in-law's shop in Blandford Forum?'

Manders gulped but recovered quickly. His tone was defiant.

'Who says I went there?'

'Mr Agar, the wine merchant.'

'His shop is in the main street,' said Leeming, flinching as Tallis shot him another look. 'I'm sorry, sir.'

'The reason the sergeant knows that,' explained Tallis, 'is that he took the trouble to go to the town in order to check your alibi. When he met you for the first time, you aroused his suspicions.'

'There's nothing illegal in speaking to my father-in-law, is there?' asked Manders. 'I was only in the shop for a few minutes.'

'You shouldn't have been there at all. You were on duty that night.'

'I had an arrangement.'

'What sort of arrangement?'

'That's private.'

'There's no privacy for someone in your position. Don't you realise what's at stake here? You're a prime suspect in a murder enquiry.'

'That's ridiculous. I haven't seen Bedloe for ages.'

'We don't believe you.'

'It's the truth,' asserted Manders.

'You went to Blandford Forum on Saturday so that you could get to West Moors more easily that night. Why not admit it?'

'That's a downright lie.'

'And what's this about an arrangement? Is the estate manager aware of it?'

'No,' said Manders, 'and there's no need to tell him. It's an agreement I have with one of the other keepers. If one of us has somewhere to go, we change shifts. That's what happened on Saturday. Somebody covered for me.'

'So that you could murder John Bedloe,' said Leeming, accusingly.

'No!'

'Then what were you doing in Blandford?'

'Leave this to me,' said Tallis with a restraining hand on the sergeant's arm. 'You heard the question, Manders. What were you doing so far from the Sweetbriar Estate?'

The gamekeeper looked uneasy. 'It was a business matter.'

'What kind of business matter?'

'I'd rather not say.'

'I'm afraid that you'll have to,' said Tallis, leaning forward and thrusting out his chin. 'We'll not let you hide behind these so-called "arrangements" and "business matters". Unless you wish to be charged with the murder of John Bedloe, stop trying to keep us at arm's length.' When the prisoner remained silent, Tallis applied more pressure. 'What would your employer say if he knew that you sneaked off the estate when you were supposed to be on duty?'

'I'd rather he didn't know.'

'He's going to know *everything* when the truth comes out.'

'I saw them,' said Leeming, unable to keep out of the interrogation. 'I saw that collection of corkscrews on the counter. Is that why you went to Mr Agar's shop?'

'I haven't a clue what you're talking about,' said Manders, frowning.

'Let's go back to this business matter of yours,' suggested Tallis. 'No more prevarication – we want the truth.'

'It's . . . a bit awkward.'

'We can cope with awkwardness.'

'My father-in-law doesn't know about it yet.'

'Why did you go to see him?'

'I didn't,' replied Manders. 'I went for another reason. While I was there, I had to call at the shop. I'm known in Blandford. Somebody would have told him that I'd been there. That's why I had to show my face.'

'Did you tell him what brought you to the town?'

The prisoner shook his head. 'I couldn't do that.'

'You must have told him something.'

'I said that I was delivering a package from Sweetbriar to a nearby farm.'

'In short, you lied to him.'

'Yes and no,' said the other. 'I did visit a nearby farm so that bit was true. But I didn't deliver anything.'

'So what were you doing there?'

Manders licked his lips and glanced towards the door. For a moment, Leeming thought he was going to try to escape and he readied himself to respond. As it was, the gamekeeper decided that there was no purpose in hiding the truth from them.

'I went to see some horses,' he told them. 'As the sergeant knows, I ride in point-to-point races in Blandford and I use my father-in-law's horses. But two of them are getting old and the third is so badly injured that he won't be racing for months. I don't ride to lose,' he went on, sitting up. 'If I have a decent mount, I can beat almost anybody. That's what I need to do.'

'Is that so that you can earn money?' asked Tallis.

'Pride is more important than any winnings. At the last meeting, someone had a quiet word with me. He's a farmer with a string of thoroughbred horses. His jockey is nowhere near as good as me so he made me a very tempting offer.' He lowered his head. 'I agreed to it. My father-in-law isn't going to be pleased when I tell him. I'll be riding for someone else from now on.'

Leeming was deflated. His face crumpled.

'It's not him, Superintendent,' he said.

Since he still had the key in his possession, Colbeck let himself into Bedloe's cottage and looked around. He knew at once that someone else had been there. The furniture had been moved and the drawers of a little sideboard had been pulled out. In the scullery, too, there was evidence of a thorough search. When he went upstairs, he found that cupboard doors were left wide open and that someone had even turned the threadbare carpets back in the course of their search. In the main bedroom, bed sheets and pillows had been tossed to the floor. Evidently, the mattress had been lifted and left hanging over one side of the bed. Whoever had been there had looked in almost every possible place.

His first thought was that a burglar had somehow got into the cottage but he soon dismissed that theory. Nothing seemed to have been stolen. There were several items of moderate value that would have interested a burglar. All were still intact. Whoever had been there, Colbeck surmised, was hunting for the letters she'd sent to Bedloe. Knowing that he'd keep them, the woman was desperate to retrieve them before someone else found them and identified her. As it could not have been Susan Elwell, it had to be one of the two anonymous correspondents, christened by him as Alice and Betsy. Which had it been?

Colbeck took a closer look at the door and all the windows. None had been tampered with so it could be safely assumed that nobody had broken into the property. That meant that the visitor had a key, allowing her to come and go as she pleased. The woman had to be the one he called Betsy, he concluded, because her scrawled letters thanked Bedloe for the times they'd spent together. Though it had been difficult to read every word, enough of them were legible to give Colbeck the impression that the relationship was a happy one, held together by regular encounters. Betsy, therefore, lived in Wimborne within easy reach of the cottage.

Alice was different. She wrote more often than the other woman and there was an underlying frustration in her letters. While she expressed her love and devotion more touchingly than Betsy, she complained about the domestic constraints that kept her apart from John Bedloe. Had they met more frequently, her letters would not have been so filled with regret. Colbeck deduced two things. First, while Betsy lived locally, Alice was some distance away, allowing the man they both adored to enjoy their favours alternately because they were quite unaware of each other's existence. Second, on Saturday night, Bedloe had had an assignation with Alice. Before they could meet, the railway policeman was murdered.

Insofar as he had any sympathy – and it was impossible to keep it entirely at bay – Colbeck bestowed it on Alice. She was getting far less out of her romance. Betsy was the preferred lover, trusted enough to be given the key to the cottage. In stolen moments there, the couple would be together in a warm, comfortable bed. Alice, by contrast, had to settle for a mattress in a draughty shed beside a railway line. Only someone completely infatuated by Bedloe would endure that.

As he conducted a search of his own, Colbeck tidied the place up, closing drawers and cupboard doors and rolling back carpets. In the tiny back bedroom, he found something that had eluded Betsy. Noticing the specks of soot on the hearth, he put his hand up the chimney until it closed on something square and metallic. As he brought it out, he dislodged a little more soot. What he was holding was a cash box with a tiny key in the lock. When he opened it, he saw a substantial amount of money, much more than he'd expect a railway policeman to possess. He recalled something that Leeming had learnt on his first visit to Sweetbriar. William Manders had accused his former colleague of taking bribes when he worked there as a gamekeeper. Had Bedloe been doing the same thing in his new occupation? It would be an easy way to supplement a modest wage.

After counting out the money, Colbeck tore a page from his notebook and wrote the amount down on it. He put the piece of paper inside the cash box and locked it, intending to take it to the police station for safekeeping. In time, it would go to Harry Wills as part of his inheritance. After a final look around the cottage, Colbeck left and locked the front door behind him. He was too preoccupied with what he'd found to see the figure crouched in a doorway nearby. As he strode past her, the woman waited a few seconds then stepped out to look after him.

'I was hoping you'd come, Lydia.'

'I wasn't sure that I should.'

'Why did you think that?'

'Well,' said Lydia, 'I was starting to feel that I shouldn't be here.'

'But I told you how much I value your visits,' said Madeleine. 'And, as it happens, I've got so much to tell you.'

Lydia Quayle was glad that she'd changed her mind about going there. Having spent the best part of two hours in the company of Beatrice Myler, she felt that she needed to see Madeleine by way of an antidote to the older woman's attempt to woo her back into living with her. She therefore forgot her earlier resolve and made her way to the Colbeck house where she was given a cordial welcome.

'Has something happened, Madeleine?' she asked.

'Yes, it was the most wonderful surprise.'

'Go on.'

'I opened my eyes and Robert was sitting right next to the bed.'

'I don't believe it!' exclaimed Lydia.

'I didn't believe it myself at first. I thought he was miles away but the superintendent turned up in Dorset and sent him home – just for the night.'

'You must have been overjoyed.'

'It was the perfect tonic,' said Madeleine. 'I've been in a state of high excitement all day. It's probably not good for the baby but it's made me feel wonderful.'

'Oh, I'm so pleased for you.'

'Robert is the best husband in the whole world.'

'Yes,' said Lydia, wistfully, 'I expect that he is.'

'However, I'm not going to boast about it. That would be selfish. Tell me your news, Lydia. Have you heard any more about the will?'

'No, I haven't. When I do, I'll need legal advice.'

'What your brother is trying to do is wicked. Your mother loved you enough to bequeath what she did to you. Everyone in the family should respect that.'

'I did walk away from them, Madeleine.'

'No, you didn't. You were driven away by your father. He deliberately broke up your romance and sent you off abroad. I don't blame you for striking out on your own. It was the right thing to do and your mother obviously accepted that. Then again,' said Madeleine, 'you didn't cut yourself off from the whole family, did you? You kept in touch with your younger brother.'

'It was more a case of Lucas keeping in touch with me.'

'Isn't that what you wanted?'

'Yes, it was. Unfortunately . . .'

Madeleine knew what she'd been about to say. The murder of Lydia's father had led to her rejoining the family for a while, thereby alienating Beatrice. It had been a fraught period in Lydia's life, relieved only by the burgeoning friendship with Madeleine Colbeck. The latter made no demands on her. She was simply there to offer immediate and uncritical support.

'Have you seen Beatrice recently?' asked Madeleine.

'We had luncheon together earlier today.'

'How is she?'

'Beatrice is fit and well.'

'Is she still hoping that you'll . . . ?'

'Yes, Madeleine. I'm afraid that she is.'

'And how do you feel about that?'

Lydia gave a wan smile and glanced down at the swollen contours of her friend's body. She was in a different world now, a place of domestic harmony and joy. In bringing a new child into the world, Madeleine would have an experience that would change her life for ever. A family would be created and Lydia wanted to be part of it, if only intermittently. That wouldn't happen if she moved back in with Beatrice Myler. It was time to be realistic.

'I feel that it would be a big mistake,' she said.

They conferred in the bar at the King's Head. Having been so convinced that Manders was the killer, Leeming was downcast. All his efforts had been in vain. The fact that the gamekeeper would be charged with other offences was little consolation to him.

He turned to Colbeck. 'What did *you* find, sir?' he asked.

'I found that someone else had got to Bedloe's cottage before me.'

'I thought they might. It will have been one of his women.'

'Yes,' said Colbeck, 'it was Betsy.'

'Betsy?' echoed Tallis. 'That's a new name to me. Who is this Betsy?'

'I don't know what she's really called, sir.'

'Then why confuse matters by calling her Betsy?'

'It brings her into focus in my mind that way.'

Tallis snorted. 'You have weird methods sometimes, Colbeck.'

'It helps me to separate her from Alice.'

'Alice *who*?'

'I can't tell you, sir. I invented that name, too.'

'Dear God! This gets worse and worse.'

'You were going to tell us what happened, sir,' prompted Leeming. 'How did you know that someone had been there?'

In the interests of lowering Tallis's blood pressure, Colbeck cut his account to the bone. Having jettisoned Alice and Betsy, he talked only of the first woman and the second. Tallis expressed the hope that both could be identified and exposed to all and sundry for their adultery.

'I'm not sure what purpose that would serve,' said Colbeck.

Tallis was merciless. 'They deserve to *suffer* in public.'

'Are you suggesting they should be stoned to death?'

'Of course not – I'm talking about humiliation.'

'Which one is the worst?' asked Leeming, unwisely. 'Alice or Betsy?'

'Don't you dare mention those confounded names!' hissed Tallis.

'No, sir. I'm sorry, sir.'

'We must move on,' said Colbeck. 'It's a question of eliminating the suspects one by one. Manders has been the first to go. The next one is Jack Elwell.'

'He was my choice from the start,' said Tallis.

'Then we should pay him another visit.'

'You and I will go together, Inspector.'

'With respect,' said Colbeck, 'it might be more sensible if the sergeant comes with me. You and I have already met Elwell. It will be interesting to see what a fresh pair of eyes detects about him.' He could see Tallis hovering. 'In addition to that, sir, may I remind you that this is our investigation. You promised that your main role would be to keep Mr Feltham from getting under our feet.'

'That's what I've endeavoured to do,' said Tallis.

'Your intervention has not been effective.'

'I told the man to keep out of our way.'

'Then why is he still spying on us, Superintendent?'

'*Spying?*'

'Since you don't have eyes in the back of your head, you haven't noticed the waiter who's walked slowly past you on five separate occasions. My guess is that he's there to gather any titbits from us. They will doubtless find their way back to Mr Feltham.' He looked up as the waiter reappeared. 'Here he comes again.'

Tallis turned round to see a tall, skinny, young man bearing down on them in the attire of a waiter. Moving at a gentle pace, he was carrying two drinks on a tray and had a distracted air. Colbeck got up to intercept him.

'Who is paying you?' he demanded.

'I don't know what you mean, sir,' said the man, nervously.

'If you value your job, tell me the truth or I'll have you kicked out of here by the manager. Better still,' added Colbeck, 'I'll kick you out of here myself. Who is bribing you to listen to our conversations?'

'Nobody, sir – I'm just doing what I'm asked.' Colbeck grabbed him by his free arm and started to move him away. 'Wait!' pleaded the other.

'Who was it?'

'I didn't think there was any harm in it.'

'Who *was* it?' demanded Colbeck.

'Mr Satchwell, the railway policeman.'

'As of now, you stop working for him. Is that understood?'

'Yes,' said the waiter, trembling with fear.

'Now get out of my sight.'

As the young man scurried away, Colbeck went over to Tallis and Leeming.

'He was taking orders from Satchwell,' he said.

'That means they came from Mr Feltham,' decided Leeming. 'The inspector is right, sir. We do need your help. Feltham will only hamper us.'

Tallis took a few moments to think it over. He then waved a peremptory hand.

'Off you go,' he instructed. 'I'll deal with Feltham.'

It was as if nothing had ever happened. Michael and Rebecca Tullidge had fallen back into their normal routine. The old equilibrium had been restored. Tullidge was completely disengaged as he went about his work and his wife had to keep watch so that he didn't forget something. Twice that afternoon she'd had to remind him that a train was due. When he forgot to reopen the gates on one occasion, she went out and did the job for him. Rebecca was happy to do so. If her husband had lapsed back into his old ways, he was not brooding about her. Outwardly, she was calm and practical; inwardly, there was a raging torrent of guilt and fear. Whenever he glanced at her, there was the usual look of stoicism on her face. Only when he left the lodge could Rebecca mourn her loss.

It was momentous. The murder of John Bedloe had deprived her of something she could never have again. News of the crime had sent tremors through her. Now that she'd had time to get used to it, she worried on her own account. Bedloe had been stabbed to death within sight of the place where she lived. The killer must have known that he'd be there at that time of night. It was likely that he also knew with whom Bedloe had arranged the tryst. That meant he had a power over Rebecca. He could reveal her treachery at a time of his choosing. Tullidge might seem slow and ponderous once more but he'd burst into action if someone whispered the truth about his wife in his ear. She could never feel safe.

Names flashed through her mind. She recalled men who'd smiled at her and others who'd paid her attention when she was in charge of the gates. Had one of them discovered her secret and murdered Bedloe because he was a rival? Or was the killer someone she'd never even met before, some phantom figure who'd trailed Bedloe and picked a lonely spot as the moment to strike? She knew that the railway policeman had few male friends and made no effort to acquire any. She tried to remember some of the people he'd described as enemies or detractors. Though he rattled off a long list, she'd paid no attention at the time. All she'd ever wanted to do was to relish the delight of his company and do his bidding.

Alone in the lodge, she walked over to the mirror and stared into it. The story it told her was frightening. She was looking into the face of a desperate woman, someone who was grieving, haunted and years older than her real age. How long could she keep up the pretence? How long would it be before other people began to see the face that stared balefully back at her from the mirror? Her husband might not notice but Margaret Vout would do so in time. She was a sharp-eyed woman, used to making judgements at short notice about her customers. Surely, she would be the first to know that something was festering away inside her friend's mind. Rebecca had to be brutally honest. The days of remaining in the shadows were numbered.

Hearing a noise outside, she went to the window and looked out. Her husband was closing one of the gates before the next train was due. He then plodded across the lines to close the gate opposite and leant against it. He was in an attitude she knew well. What was different was the evil smile. Tullidge rarely managed a smile of any kind, still less any laughter. Nothing amused him enough. Yet it was doing so now. He seemed to be savouring a memory and the smile broadened into a wicked grin. A thought that had troubled Rebecca once before suddenly took on more force. Could her husband actually be the killer? Had he discovered her infidelity and taken revenge on her lover? Was that what he was doing in the time between leaving the Waggon and Horses on Saturday night and coming back into the lodge? Had *he* committed the murder?

It was too much to comprehend. In her febrile review of what had happened since Saturday night, little things took on great importance. Instead of being horrified by the terrible crime committed near their home, he'd been phlegmatic at first and then, later on, almost pleased. There was the interest he'd begun to show in other people and the glimmerings of enthusiasm for his job. There'd been the way he looked at her and sought to control her movements. Most of all, there was the crude and painful intercourse he'd forced upon her. Put together, they painted a hideous portrait of the man with whom she was doomed to spend her life.

Gritting her teeth, she brought both hands up to her face. Her heart was pounding and her brain was racing. All that she could think about was a way out of her despair. In a couple of minutes, she was given the answer.

A train approached, sounded its whistle then steamed past at full speed, making the lodge tremble for several seconds. Rebecca felt some relief at last.

There was a way out.

'I could have sworn that Manders was our man,' said Leeming, sadly.

'He was a plausible suspect, Victor.'

'When he shot at me, I felt certain he was the killer.'

'He'd say that he did it in fun.'

'What's funny about having your top hat shot off?'

'Manders wanted to give you a fright,' said Colbeck, reasonably. 'That much I do believe. He knows the penalty for attempted murder. If I were his lawyer, I'd argue that he was only guilty of assault and resisting arrest.'

'What about that hole in my hat?'

'He'll be ordered to pay the cost of a new one.'

Leeming was pessimistic. 'We failed, Inspector.'

'There's nothing new in that. Our job is nine-tenths failure and one-tenth success. When all's said and done, that's not a bad proportion.'

'Do you really think that Jack Elwell will be our success in this case?'

'I hope so.'

'The superintendent had the same feeling about him as you, sir.'

'He noticed that crucifix tattooed on Elwell's arm.'

'That doesn't mean anything,' said Leeming. 'I've got a friend who was a sailor. He has tattoos everywhere and didn't choose one of them. Whenever they put into port, his shipmates got him hopelessly drunk then took him off to a tattoo parlour. They chose all sorts of things for him. My friend has a naked woman on his chest. He showed it to me. I don't think Estelle would like *me* to have anything like that.'

'Sailors might well choose a naked woman,' said Colbeck, tolerantly, 'but how many of them would choose a crucifix?'

'Very few, I'd say.'

'Elwell did.'

'Then he must be a devout Christian.'

'I think that his Christianity may have turned sour. When I first spoke to Copsey, he told me that the body of John Bedloe had been across the line. I did some drawings of the position he might have been in. Copsey picked out the one where the corpse lay with his arms outstretched as if he were on a cross.'

'I remember you telling me about it, sir. You said he was like a sacrifice.'

'He could simply have been killed and left beside the line.'

'So why was he draped across it?'

'Someone wanted him sliced into three pieces.'

'Jack Elwell?'

'I think so. Since he had that tattoo, his religion might have become warped.'

On arrival in Dorchester, they hired transport and were driven straight to the boathouse. Elwell was not there. They were told that he'd left abruptly earlier that afternoon and hadn't been seen since. Getting back into the trap, they were taken off in the direction of the man's house.

'Do you think he's made a run for it?' asked Leeming.

'He'd only do that if he felt he was in danger of arrest.'

'The superintendent might have given him that feeling. He had a sense that Elwell was not as friendly as he appeared to be.'

'It's a false geniality,' said Colbeck. 'He conceals his feelings very cleverly.'

'Then where is he?'

'I'm hoping that his wife will be able to tell us.'

'What if he's taken her with him?'

'I doubt if that's the case, Victor.'

When they got to the house, they alighted from the trap. Colbeck rang the bell that hung beside the front door. It swung open almost immediately and an anxious Louisa Elwell stood there.

'Oh,' she said, face clouding, 'I thought it might be Jack.'

'I'm afraid not, Mrs Elwell,' said Colbeck.

'You haven't come to arrest him, have you?'

'We just need to speak to him, that's all.'

'Jack hasn't done anything wrong. He wouldn't.'

'Do you have any idea where he is?'

'No, Inspector,' she replied. 'He came home from work in a

temper about an hour ago and grabbed a few things before going off. He said that he had something important to do.'

'Did he say how long he'd be?' asked Leeming.

'No – Jack was only here for a minute or so.'

'You said that he grabbed a few things,' noted Colbeck. 'What were they?'

'I'm not sure. He went into the kitchen to get them. When he came out again, I did see one thing he was carrying.'

'What was it, Mrs Elwell?'

'It was a knife.'

CHAPTER THIRTEEN

By comparison with his own abode, Edward Tallis found the house palatial. It oozed prosperity. Tallis rented some well-appointed rooms in an apartment block and, while they were ideal for a bachelor like himself, he still felt a surge of envy at the luxury enjoyed by Feltham. The visitor was ushered into the drawing room. As soon as they were seated, the would-be mayor fired his first salvo.

'I demand to be more involved in this case,' he said. 'I have local knowledge that's invaluable and, as the person who summoned Inspector Colbeck, I have a right to be at his shoulder throughout.'

'Is that what sending a telegraph entitles you to, sir?'

'I think so.'

'Then I must disillusion you. Detective work is something best left to those trained to do it properly. The presence of amateurs like you is always intrusive and usually detrimental to the investigation.'

Feltham reddened. 'I find that insulting.'

'It's a plain fact, sir. Not to put too fine a point upon it, you're in the way.'

'I'll not brook this appalling lack of respect,' said Feltham, pompously. 'I'll be writing to the commissioner this very day.'

'I'd encourage you to do so, Mr Feltham.'

The other man gaped. 'You *would*?'

'Yes,' said Tallis, 'it will give you a measure of satisfaction and, as for the commissioner, it will be one more complaint to add to his collection. It's a very large one, you see. You're not the only person who wilfully misunderstands the operation of the Detective Department at Scotland Yard. We've met countless malcontents. Like you, they expect to gain local fame by assisting – as they foolishly see it – in the investigation. When we brush them aside in order to do the job properly, the pen is in their hands within seconds.' He stood up. 'I'll leave you to get on with your correspondence, sir.'

'Wait!' exclaimed Feltham, leaping from his chair. 'I haven't finished yet.'

'Well, we have. Since you feel we are giving poor service, we will shake the dust of Wimborne from our feet and leave the search for the killer to those bumbling yokels in ill-fitting uniforms that pass for policemen out here in the country.'

Feltham was aghast. 'You're *leaving*?'

'We're not going to stay and be the target of unremitting criticism.'

'But we need Inspector Colbeck.'

'A moment ago, you were berating him.'

'I may disapprove of his manner but I admire his expertise. I understand that he has a suspect in custody already – a William Manders.'

'That's the other thing, sir.'

'What is?'

'We resent this little spy ring you operate,' said Tallis, sharply. 'I believe that the man at the centre of it is one Richard Satchwell. He is clearly getting information from the police station. We've stopped his supply at the King's Head, by the way. He was paying a waiter to eavesdrop on our discussions. Well, you can tell Satchwell this. He should concentrate on his job as a railway policeman. If he'd been doing it properly, his colleague might not have been murdered.'

Tallis turned away and walked out into the hall. Feltham ran after him and plucked at his sleeve until the superintendent came to a halt. He pushed the other man's hand away.

'Don't touch me,' he snapped.

'I'm sorry, Superintendent. I just want to get something clear. Can you confirm that the man in custody is the person who killed John Bedloe?'

'No, I can't.'

'Why not?'

'He has an alibi.'

'So he was arrested by mistake?'

'I didn't say that, sir. Manders will face charges in due course. I regret to tell you that murder will not be one of them.'

'So the killer is still at liberty?'

'Unhappily, he is.'

'In that case, you can't possibly walk away from us.'

'I'm not asking my men to work under hostile conditions,' said Tallis, levelly. 'From the moment they got here, you have been harrying them and, when they escape your clutches, they have to put up with that loathsome creature of yours, Satchwell.'

'He's not my creature.'

'Call him what you will. He's odious. One last thing . . .'

'Yes?'

'We'll catch a train this evening. If you care to draft that letter of complaint to the commissioner, I'll be happy to deliver it by hand for you. Good day, sir.'

Tallis was about to move off when he saw Feltham groping for an apology. The superintendent's bluff had worked. He'd had no intention of pulling out his detectives. He'd simply wanted to scare the other man by forcing him to imagine an investigation led by the inexperienced local police. It had brought Ambrose Feltham to heel. The financier had not only shuddered at the prospective loss of Robert Colbeck, he'd been afraid of the newspaper headlines it would attract. Feltham would inevitably be blamed for driving away the celebrated Railway Detective and leaving the killer at liberty. As an advertisement for his campaign to be the mayor, it would be a disaster.

'Could I invite you to take a glass of brandy?' he asked, softly.

'No, you can't,' replied Tallis, shunning the peace offering.

'I urge you not to make hasty decisions.'

'You force them upon us, sir.'

'What would it take to keep Inspector Colbeck here?'

'It would require a firm promise that he and the sergeant will henceforth have a free hand.'

'I can guarantee it,' said Feltham.

'There's to be no more spying.'

'I can promise you that as well.'

'If we so much as see a hint of someone listening outside a door or peeping through a keyhole, we will leave Wimborne within the hour.'

'You can't do that, Superintendent. I beg you.'

'I'll need to discuss your offer with my detectives,' said Tallis, feeling that the other man had been completely routed. 'And on reflection, perhaps I *could* force down a glass of brandy.'

Edmund Rickwood was not pleased to be hauled out of the comfort of his armchair. As editor of the *Dorset County Chronicle*, he'd spent a long, hard day at his desk and simply wanted to be able to relax at home. The appearance of two detectives made that impossible. Annoyed at first, he quickly came to see that he might well be getting an exclusive story and shook off his fatigue in an instant. He conducted them to the newspaper's offices and unlocked the door.

'Yes, Inspector,' he said, 'we do keep copies of every edition. We have a complete archive. Historians will one day be able to trawl through it and get a feel of what it was like to live in Dorset in the blessed reign of Queen Victoria.'

'Her Majesty is not the person in whom we're interested at the moment,' said Colbeck. 'It's a woman from a much lower station in life.'

'What was the name again?'

'Elwell, sir – Susan Elwell.'

'Oh, yes, I remember that sad business.'

'It would be something like eighteen months or two years ago.'

'Leave it to me, Inspector.'

Rickwood was a short, rotund man in his fifties with an academic's hunched shoulders and staring eyes. A nervous twitch animated his face. He took them into the room where past copies of the periodical were kept in chronological order in a series of wide, flat drawers. When he lifted out the first sheaf, he did so with great care, placing them on the desk then turning up the light. Bent over the newspapers, he flicked gently through them until he came to the one he sought. He extracted it and put it down in front of his visitors.

'The story is on the front page,' observed Leeming.

'It fully deserved its prominence,' argued Rickwood.

'When was this photograph of her taken?'

'It was at her wedding. As you can see, we cut her husband out of the picture. Some photographs were taken when the body was pulled out of the river but I felt that they were too sensational to print. We like to inform our readers, not to excite their ghoulish tendencies with gruesome material.'

'How long did the story run, Mr Rickwood?' asked Colbeck.

'Oh, it went on for a number of editions. People kept writing in to express their condolences or – in some cases, alas – their frank disapproval of what Susan Elwell had patently done. It's not for us to condemn the poor woman. Anyone driven to such lengths deserves sympathy.'

'I couldn't agree more,' said Colbeck.

'Nor could I,' added Leeming.

They took it in turns to read all the coverage of the suicide. The story had been tastefully handled. Details of the inquest were also printed as was a short obituary. The editor watched them until they'd finished.

'Fortunately,' he said, 'the husband was not here at the time. Had he been at home, of course, none of this would have happened. As it was, Jack Elwell was at sea and it was some time before he returned to learn the full horror of what had happened in his absence. One can only hazard a guess at his initial feelings.'

'He must have felt betrayed,' said Leeming, 'and deeply hurt.'

'The only thing that I saw was his towering rage,' said Rickwood. 'He stormed in here and demanded to see our coverage of the tragedy. One moment he was using foul language to describe his dead wife, the next he was insisting that her memory be preserved with respect. He offered to pay for an elegy to be written – it's the one you've both seen.'

'It's very touching, sir,' said Colbeck.

'Thank you, Inspector, I laboured over it for hours. Needless to say, I didn't charge Mr Elwell. I hoped it would calm him down. He was like a powder keg when he came in here and could have exploded if we'd said the wrong thing.'

'What happened afterwards?'

'I lost track of him. Someone told me that he'd given up the sea but I had no idea what he was doing instead. Then, all of a sudden, he popped up – if you'll forgive a disgraceful pun – like a jack-in-the-box. It was almost exactly a year since the death of his wife. He wanted the occasion marked by an article about her.'

'I daresay that you obliged.'

'I most certainly did.' He went burrowing again. 'I'll find the edition.'

'What sort of mood was he in this time?'

'Oh, he'd mellowed a great deal, Inspector. There were no melodramatics. He asked – politely – if there could be something in the *Chronicle* to coincide with the anniversary of Susan Elwell's death. Naturally, I agreed. There was something I spotted,' he went on, pulling another edition gingerly from its sheaf. 'The first time I met him, he had no wedding ring on. The second time, he did. I thought it was clever of me to spot that.' His laugh was like the tinkle of a small bell. 'A journalist has to be something of a detective, you see. We're in allied trades.'

Colbeck took the newspaper from him and turned to the article about the suicide of Susan Elwell. It was substantially a repeat of the earlier coverage and it was much reduced in length. There was no photograph of the deceased.

'Jack Elwell asked us not to use it again,' explained Rickwood.

He looked as if he expected a round of applause. 'Has that been of any use, Inspector?'

'You've been extremely helpful, sir,' said Colbeck. 'We know the sort of man we're dealing with now.'

'Has that made you change your opinion of him, sir?' asked Leeming.

'Yes, it has. Elwell is a more complex person than I thought.'

'He puzzles me.'

'Why is that, Victor?'

'I thought that he'd married the second wife in order to forget the first one but he's obviously keen to preserve the memory of the first Mrs Elwell, even though she caused him such grief.'

'I don't think it was done out of love,' said Colbeck. He handed the last newspaper back to the editor. 'Thank you so much for taking the trouble to let us peep into your archive, sir. It's an invaluable resource.'

Rickwood smiled. 'Old newspapers are living history.'

'The ones we've just seen may help to solve a murder.'

'Does that mean you're going to arrest Jack Elwell?'

Colbeck sighed. 'We have to find him first, sir.'

Night was starting to hunt the last vestiges of light from the sky. Michael Tullidge had to work with the aid of a lantern. After waving at another train as it shot past and created a blast of wind, he opened the gates in turn then went back into the lodge. Rebecca had just lit a fire and was seated beside it as she knitted. Seeing her husband, she moved to get up.

'Stay where you are, Becky,' he said.

'You like to sit here of an evening.'

'Well, I won't be staying for long.'

'Oh?'

'I thought I might walk along to the Waggon.'

'But you never drink on a weekday,' she said in surprise.

'Tonight is different – and don't ask me why.'

She wouldn't dare to question his decision when he was in such a surly mood, even though it represented a major change in their daily round. Rebecca didn't mind the fact that his duties would now fall fairly and squarely on to her shoulders. It would give her something to do. She was bound to wonder what lay behind her husband's declaration and hoped that the publican's wife would call in on the following day. Margaret Vout would be able to tell her with whom Tullidge spent the evening.

'What are you knitting?' he asked, absently.

'It's a cardigan for you.'

'I won't need it when the warmer days come.'

'It can get cold in April, Michael. You need wrapping up.'

'Don't mollycoddle me, woman.'

'Someone has to,' she murmured to herself.

He went off into the kitchen and she heard the tap running. Tullidge was washing himself before going out. How long he'd be at the pub she didn't know but it would give her priceless freedom from his lowering companionship. Only when he was out of the way could she sift through her memories of John Bedloe. After she'd watched a train go through, she might even walk down to the little shed where they'd had their brief rendezvous. That phase of her life was definitively over now. She wondered how long it would be before happy memories faded entirely and she lapsed back into her former misery.

'I'll only be an hour or so,' said Tullidge, coming back into the room.

'Take as long as you like, Michael.'

'I will.'

'I've got plenty to keep me occupied.'

'Don't forget to keep to the timetable.'

Angering slightly, she said nothing. Her husband was the only person found wanting on occasion. Had she not stepped in to do his work, trains would have smashed into the gates across the line and perhaps been derailed. Because of Rebecca, catastrophe had been averted time and again. Drivers and fireman had grown used to the sight of her outside the lodge. She'd always collected friendly waves from them. What she never got was gratitude from her husband. The more Rebecca did, the more he relied on her.

'They've arrested the killer,' he said, tossing the information to her as if throwing food to an animal. 'Hugh told me.'

'When?'

'It was an hour or so ago. He'd just come from Wimborne and heard the gossip there.'

'Why didn't you tell me?'

'I just did.'

'It was important for me to know,' she complained.

'Was it?' he asked, standing in front of her. 'I don't see why.'

'As long as he was on the loose, I was bound to worry. Everyone was. Maggie Vout said she wouldn't sleep proper until he was behind bars. We're cut off out here, Michael. It makes me feel unsafe. That's why I'm glad,' she continued. 'It's good news that he's caught.'

'Yes, it is,' he said, watching her intently.

'Did Hugh tell you his name?'

'Manders.'

'Where's he from?'

'I've no idea.' After staring at her for a moment, he headed for the door. 'I'm off. Lock up when you go out to close the gates.'

'I always do, Michael.'

'You never know who's lurking in the dark.'

'Goodbye.'

Tullidge made no reply. He opened the door and left in silence. She could hear his boots scrunching on the gravel path outside. Rebecca waited until the sound faded completely. The tension vanished from her body and she smiled with relief. Her curiosity as to why her husband had broken the standard pattern of his day was more than outweighed by the gratitude she felt to be on her own at last. It left her mind free to address the news that he'd passed on to her. The killer had been caught. The man who'd murdered her lover was in custody and therefore of no threat to her. It never occurred to her to question whether or not the prisoner was guilty of the crime. If his arrest was common knowledge in Wimborne, it meant that he was definitely the man who'd ended the life of John Bedloe.

Why had he done it? That's what she wanted to know. Why had someone hated Bedloe enough to kill him on a deserted railway line not long before he was due to meet her for an assignation? What most people would see as a rickety shed was to Rebecca a place to rival the most sumptuous bedroom. The passion she shared with her lover made light of its obvious shortcomings. Until Saturday night, she couldn't look at the shed without feeling a glow deep inside her. It ignited different feelings now. The structure symbolised the empty shell of her romance.

When the time came, she put her knitting aside, put on her coat and went out of the lodge with a lantern. After locking the front door, she crossed to the first of the gates and swung it back from the line on its hinges. Rebecca did the same for the other gate then leant against it. Minutes later, she heard the train puffing with its usual ferocity. Temptation beckoned. In losing Bedloe, she was destined for the same joyless existence she suffered before the railway policeman had come into her life. Tullidge would never improve. He could only get worse. Did she want to undergo the ordeal of marriage indefinitely or join her lover in the grave? The oncoming train was there to provoke a decision. All that she had to do was to step in front of it and her desolation would be over.

Closing her eyes, Rebecca tried to summon up her courage.

'Where is he?'

'We don't know, sir.'

'What did his wife say?'

'Mrs Elwell is as baffled as we are,' said Colbeck. 'Her husband came back from work, took some things from the kitchen and told her that he had somewhere to go. He left without any explanation.'

'He tried to convince me that he doted on his wife.'

'I think she's been supplanted in his mind by her predecessor.'

'Is he still so obsessed with the first Mrs Elwell?'

'I believe so.'

Colbeck had returned to Wimborne and was sitting with Tallis in the latter's hotel room. He explained how they'd been to the boathouse and on to Elwell's home before calling on the editor of the *Chronicle*. When he revealed what they'd learnt from the newspaper archives, he drew a grunt of appreciation from the superintendent. Having lost Manders as their prime suspect, they'd installed Elwell as his replacement and the evidence was pointing to the wisdom of their choice.

'Where's the sergeant?' asked Tallis.

'He's trying to pick up a scent in Dorchester.'

'It sounds as if Elwell has taken to his heels.'

'I'm not so sure, sir.'

'He knows that we're closing in so he's bolted.'

'Then why did he take a weapon with him?' asked Colbeck. 'The knife was the one thing that Mrs Elwell saw. If he was simply trying to get away, he'd have taken some clothing and any valuables he had. More to the point, he'd have taken his wife. I've got a feeling that he's not all that far away.'

'I disagree.'

'Where do you think he is, sir?'

'I believe he's decided to cut and run,' said Tallis. 'He's a sailor by instinct. He'll head for the coast and find a ship to take him out of our reach. Elwell is a man of impulsive action. That's what I discerned when I questioned him.'

Though Colbeck rejected the superintendent's opinion, he saw no purpose in arguing with him. Elwell had disappeared. Only by catching him could they find out the man's true motives. The inspector manoeuvred the conversation elsewhere.

'Have you spoken to Mr Feltham?'

'Yes,' replied Tallis. 'Figuratively speaking, I flayed him alive.'

'That must have been an interesting exercise, sir.'

'I reduced him to a dithering wreck.'

'And how did you contrive that, sir?'

'I told him that you, I and Leeming would leave the town forthwith.'

Colbeck was astonished. 'We can't abandon an investigation, sir.'

'I never intended that we should, Inspector. I simply wanted Feltham to *believe* that we would.' He grinned. 'You don't spend as many years in the army as I did without mastering the art of rattling a sabre.'

'Has he promised to stop hindering us?'

'He was more or less on his knees.'

'Thank you, sir.'

'And he's calling off his spies as well.'

'That's a relief,' said Colbeck. 'I hate the feeling of being watched.'

'It won't happen again, Inspector. I can assure you of that.'

Richard Satchwell had been reprimanded by him before but never to such scorching effect. As he stood in the drawing room at the Feltham residence, he felt as if he were being flogged in public. Strutting up and down, the older man worked himself up into a fury.

'You're an imbecile,' he shouted, 'a blithering, mindless, useless imbecile.'

'What have I done, sir?'

'What *haven't* you done? For a start, you exposed me to humiliation.'

'How did I do that?'

'You employed some dolt at the King's Head to gather information.'

'That's what you wanted,' said Satchwell.

'I wanted secrecy, man. I wanted discretion.'

'It's what I paid him for, sir.'

'Then you must get every penny back because he gave himself away and, in doing so, he put me in an impossible position. I've had Superintendent Tallis in here, threatening to call off the investigation and take his men back to London.'

Still on the move, Feltham described how he'd been exposed to a withering attack for trying to keep abreast of the murder enquiry. Satchwell was duly abashed but one piece of news startled him.

'Manders is *not* the killer?' he asked.

'I should have thought that Maycock would have told you that.'

'I've not had the chance to speak to him, sir. I've been on duty all day.'

'Well, it seems that they're holding the gamekeeper on other charges but he did not, after all, commit the murder.'

'Where does that leave Inspector Colbeck?' asked Satchwell.

'What do you mean?'

'Perhaps his reputation has misled you, sir.'

'It's beyond compare, man.'

'Well, I haven't seen any signs of progress so far. All they've done is to run round in circles and arrest the wrong man. Would it be such a loss if they *did* go back to London?'

'Have you taken leave of your senses?' cried Feltham.

'*We* could solve this murder, sir.'

'Don't talk nonsense.'

'We could, Mr Feltham. We know this area and we know its people. It's only a question of ferreting away and we can amass enough evidence to lead us to the killer. I was closer to Bedloe than anyone so I should play a part in the investigation.'

'And who is supposed to help you?' asked Feltham with contempt. 'Bert Maycock and his like? All they can do is to round up drunks. Who else would you call upon – that lunatic waiter at the King's Head who was supposed to keep his ears pricked? No, it's an absurd suggestion.'

'We couldn't do any worse than Inspector Colbeck.'

'I need him here, man, and I need him to solve the crime. Only then can I get the plaudits that are my due. Have faith in Colbeck. He's working hard on the case.'

'He and the sergeant went off to Dorchester earlier on.'

'How do you know?'

'I saw them buying tickets at the station, sir. Later on, I watched the inspector coming back to Wimborne. He was on his own.'

'So where is Sergeant Leeming?'

'He must still be there for some reason.'

Victor Leeming was undaunted. Though he was in a strange town, looking for a man he'd never seen before, he was not disheartened. It was a position he'd been in many times. He'd been given a good description of Jack Elwell by Colbeck and felt that he would be able to recognise him by his distinctive voice, build and apparel. The first places he checked were the two railway stations in Dorchester. He reasoned that if Elwell were fleeing the town, he'd take the fastest route out of it. Yet the clerks in both ticket offices were certain that they hadn't dealt with anyone who answered the description given to them by Leeming. That raised the question of whether or not Elwell was still in Dorchester. If so, where was he?

The most likely place to find an answer, he believed, was in Fordington. There was no point in going to the boathouse again because it would be closed and, in any case, all that Elwell's workmates could tell him was that he'd left at short notice. Leeming was also careful not to trouble the man's wife again. Louisa Elwell was clearly distressed by her husband's behaviour and was best left in peace. When he got to Fordington, therefore, the sergeant fell back on the time-honoured formula of detective work. He started to knock on doors.

Fordington Village was not the most inviting place even in daylight. After dark, it took on a more sinister aspect. Its mill, churches, glebe, pound, cross and other landmarks became ghostly silhouettes. The streets now seemed narrower, meaner and more pungent. Elwell's neighbours were wary of any kind of policeman and simply wanted to send him on his way without even trying to help him. While nobody admitted knowing where Elwell was, he got the clear impression that the man was very popular. They'd closed ranks to defend him. On the point of giving up the search, Leeming remembered the tattoo of a crucifix. It took him straight to the vicarage where he made the acquaintance of the Reverend Henry Moule.

'Yes, I know Jack Elwell,' said the vicar.

'Do you have any idea where he might be?'

'No, I don't, but I can save you the trouble of searching in one place.'

'And where's that, sir?'

'Right here in my church.'

'I thought that Elwell was religious.'

'Wild horses couldn't drag him to one of my services.'

'Is that because he had some kind of grudge against *you*?'

Moule glanced upwards. 'His grudge was against someone rather more exalted than a parish priest, I'm sad to say.'

The moment they met, Leeming realised that he was in the presence of a remarkable man and he was reminded of the first time he'd seen Robert Colbeck. Both men were tall, handsome and striking in appearance. They gleamed with intelligence. Now almost sixty, Moule had an open face and a large forehead topped with wavy hair that had retained much of its original colour. He wore a dark suit and white clerical bands over the top. Though he was only the son of a solicitor, there was a faintly patrician air about Henry Moule.

Leeming recalled what Colbeck had told him and he was curious.

'Is it true that you fought off an outbreak of cholera?' he asked.

'Not exactly,' replied the other, 'but I can lay claim to keeping the disease from spreading to Dorchester.'

'I heard that you risked your life, caring for the sick.'

'That was my Christian duty, Sergeant. I also instituted some basic changes to the local sanitation. It may seem an unlikely thing for a man of the cloth to do but, with the help of a partner, I invented and patented a dry earth closet that is an important step towards removing diseases like cholera. In practical terms, cleanliness is indeed next to godliness. Some of my other initiatives,' he admitted, 'did not meet with quite the same approval. For instance, I got the Dorchester races banned.'

'On what grounds did you do that?'

'The combination of large gatherings and cheap alcohol encourages vice.'

'I know,' said Leeming, 'I've been on duty at the Derby.'

'It caused a great deal of public anger. I was turned into a figure of derision. However,' he went on, 'I stuck to my principles.'

Moule talked with such passion that Leeming could have listened to him all day but he was not there to do that. He was hunting a potential killer and he explained why suspicion had fallen on Elwell.

'How well did you know him, sir?'

'He and his first wife were my parishioners,' said Moule. 'I married Jack Elwell and Susan Jamieson, as she then was, in my church. They were the sort of couple who seemed set for a life of connubial bliss – and that's what they enjoyed in the earlier stages. Elwell then went off on a long voyage.'

'We're aware of what happened.'

'What you don't know is the transformation that he suffered. Having set sail as a happy man with a pretty wife, he came back to discover that she'd been unfaithful and had conceived a child. Susan's death turned him into a bitter and volatile human being. He renounced the Church's teaching and used the most scathing language when I tried to reason with him. It was hopeless,' said

Moule, rubbing his hands slowly together. 'We lost him.'

'Didn't he quieten down a little when he met his second wife?'

'She had a calming effect on him, that's true, but his anger was still bubbling away below the surface. On the anniversary of Susan's death, he had an article written about her in the *Chronicle*.'

'We saw it,' said Leeming.

'Then you'll have some idea of what a tortured soul he is. Elwell is desperate to put the tragedy behind him yet he's still shackled to macabre memories of it. I told him that it was unhealthy to brood,' said Moule, eyebrows meeting like the twin arches of a bridge. 'I can't bring myself to utter the obscenities that came from his lips.'

'Yet he's built himself a new life here in Fordington.'

'It's a hollow existence, Sergeant.'

They were in the vicar's study, a large, low room lit by flickering gaslight and filled with books and religious tracts. On the wall behind Moule's head, Leeming could see a large crucifix.

'Did you know John Bedloe?' asked the sergeant.

'I knew all the railway policemen in Dorchester by sight, if not by name. When I read the newspaper report of his death, I realised that Bedloe was the rather good-looking individual who stood out from the others.'

'He left the town before Elwell returned to it.'

'I was unaware of that coincidence.'

'We feel that it may have been more a case of necessity.'

'Are you certain that . . . ?'

'Yes, sir. We're convinced of it.'

'So *that's* why you're so interested in Elwell.'

'We believe that he finally tracked down his first wife's . . . friend, for want of a better word. You've met Elwell, before and after the event, so to speak. Is he, in your opinion, capable of murder?'

Moule fell silent and clasped his hands together. Not given

247

to instant judgements, he took time to consider all the facts. He inhaled deeply before speaking.

'There was an essential goodness in that man when I first met him,' he said. 'He was only a lad in those days, a carefree youth with a love of the sea. Unlike most of the others, he actually seemed to *listen* to my sermons.' He puffed his cheeks. 'That goodness has gone, Sergeant. It's been corrupted into something else.'

'Are you saying that he could kill another man?'

'Yes, I am – given enough provocation.'

'He didn't lack that, sir.'

'No, I suppose not.'

'Where might I find him?' asked Leeming. 'His wife doesn't know, his workmates have no idea and his neighbours refused to tell me anything at all about him. If he thought he was facing arrest, what do you think he'd do?'

'He might well seek sanctuary – though not in a church, I may add.'

'Where would he turn?'

'He'd choose a trusted friend, I should imagine.'

'And does he have one of those, sir?'

'Oh, yes. His name is Allan Trego. He lives in Mill Street.'

'What does he do for a living?'

'He's a carrier.'

Rebecca Tullidge's husband was away much longer than she'd expected. Almost two hours had slipped by and she'd lost count of the number of trains she'd seen pass by. Each one had been a potential means of suicide and she'd taken a preliminary step towards them. It was as far as she was able to go. Grief-stricken as she was, Rebecca was still not ready to yield to complete despair and step in front of a train. After opening the gates to traffic yet again, she looked down the track. The shed where she'd agreed to meet John Bedloe was invisible in the gloom but it nevertheless exerted an attraction for her. After checking that nobody was about, she walked along the sleepers exactly as she'd done on Saturday night. But there was no exhilaration this time. She moved with a sense of foreboding.

When she drew level with the shed, she raised her lantern so that it illumined the railway lines. Until she'd cleaned it off, they'd been stained by Bedloe's blood. It bothered her that she couldn't find the exact place. After changing her mind time and again, she settled for what she believed was the spot where her lover had been murdered. Rebecca knelt down and kissed the cold rail. She stayed there for several minutes then heard the distant sound of voices. Getting to her feet, she made her way back towards the lodge. One of the voices was clear now. It belonged to Tullidge.

Conjured out of the darkness at last, he was now standing there on his own.

'Hello, Michael,' she said. 'You're late.'

'Is that a complaint?' he challenged.

'No, no, it isn't.'

'It had better not be.'

'Who were you talking to?'

'Nobody.'

'I thought I heard voices.'

'Then you thought wrong, Becky. I came back on my own.'

'I see.'

'Where've you been, anyway?'

'I heard noises farther down the line,' she said, pointing. 'It was only a dog. He ran away as soon as he saw me.' She went over to the lodge and unlocked the door. 'Do you want something to eat?'

'I might.'

'There's not much in the larder. I'll need to go to market tomorrow.'

They went inside and she put the lantern down. She waited for him to give her permission to go into Wimborne on the following day but he said nothing. After a while, she asked him directly.

'Are you happy with that, Michael?'

'With what?'

'You said that I could go to market. There are things we need.'

'Then you'd better get them.'

'Thank you.'

'But don't be long. I'll want your help here.'

'Yes, of course. It won't take me all morning.'

He'd been drinking at the Waggon and Horses, she decided, even though there was no smell of beer on his breath. It was another break in routine and a worrying one. If he was caught drunk on duty, it would cost him his livelihood. Rebecca preferred him sober even if it made him churlish. Tullidge looked as if he was about to speak to her. Instead, he went into the kitchen and left her to wonder with whom he'd been speaking earlier. They had never wasted much time on conversation in the past. Tullidge chose to communicate primarily with glances and gestures. When he did speak to her, however, he'd usually told her the truth in the past. Since the previous Saturday, however, he'd started to lie to her about his movements. In more ways than one, that fateful night had been a significant turning point in her life.

Leeming got back to Wimborne in time to see Colbeck coming down the stairs at the hotel. The inspector's face was solemn.

'I've got some sad news for you, Victor,' he said.

Leeming started. 'Nothing's happened to Estelle or the boys, has it?'

'No, they're perfectly safe. But the sad news *is* from London.'

'Oh dear! It's not . . .'

'No,' said Colbeck, 'it's nothing to do with my dear wife, either.'

'Then what is it, sir?'

'A telegraph arrived from the commissioner. There's some problem at Scotland Yard that merits the immediate recall of Superintendent Tallis.'

Leeming burst out laughing. 'You mean that he's *gone*?'

'Yes – do you think you can bear the disappointment?'

'It will be a hard task, sir.'

Colbeck grinned. 'Tell me why over a drink.'

Going into the bar, they chose a table in the corner from which they could see the whole room. Nobody could creep up behind them to eavesdrop this time. Colbeck ordered a glass of wine and Leeming had a tankard of beer.

'I can see that you didn't manage to find him,' said Colbeck.

'No, sir, Elwell is not in Dorchester.'

'The superintendent thought he'd head for the coast. My feeling is that he's simply gone to ground somewhere. Am I right?'

'Possibly,' said Leeming.

Having spent so much effort on the search, he didn't wish to be robbed of any part of his story. When he'd quenched his thirst, he told Colbeck at length about the vain attempt to get help from Elwell's neighbours and how the man's tattoo had impelled him to call at the vicarage.

'That was an inspiration, Victor.'

'Reverend Moule is very much like you, sir.'

Colbeck spluttered. 'I'm not sure that I'm flattered by that,' he said. 'Are you implying that I'm stuffy, sententious and pious?'

'No, Inspector, you're none of those things – and neither is he.'

'So where's the similarity between us?'

'It's difficult to explain,' said Leeming. 'It's just that the vicar couldn't be anything but what he is and you're the same.'

'Do you mean that we've both followed our destinies?'

'Yes, that's it. You're both doing something for which you're very suited.'

'Oh, I don't think I could compete with the Reverend Moule,' said Colbeck. 'His achievements are amazing. Dr Keddle told me about him. When he became vicar here, he was also chaplain to the barracks in Dorchester. His sermons were so uplifting that he had them published. They sold extremely well, it seems. The royalties were large and he used them to build another church in Fordington. I can't claim to have done anything as impressive as that.'

'You catch dangerous criminals, sir. That's impressive to me.'

'Is Jack Elwell the latest in a long line?'

'I believe so.'

'I'm in two minds about that, Victor. Convince me.'

'Let me go back to the vicar. He told me that Elwell had a close friend, one Allan Trego. He lives in Mill Street so I went straight there. His wife said that he was away on business – he's a carrier. Mrs Trego said that he was taking a delivery to a place named Corfe Mullen.'

'And was Elwell travelling with him, by any chance?'

'Yes, he was.'

'At least we've got some idea where he is now.'

'Corfe Mullen is not all that far from Wimborne, sir.'

'I know that,' said Colbeck. 'I've become very familiar with the map of Dorset now. My memory is that Corfe Mullen is no great distance from Poole, either. If he really is intending to take ship, it could be his destination.'

'You're wrong, sir.'

'What makes you think that?'

'It was the way that Mrs Trego spoke about him,' said Leeming. 'She wasn't at all surprised when Elwell turned up to go off with her husband. It's not the first time. He's helped Trego in the past. Working for his friend is a way of making a bit of extra money. Besides,' he went on, 'he could get to Poole much quicker by train.'

'Where is his destination, then?'

'It's here. After leaving Corfe Mullen, Trego had to come to Wimborne to pick up a load to be transported back to Dorchester. Elwell knew that. He and his friend speak to each other every day. In other words, Elwell would be well aware that Trego could get him here this evening.'

'So could a train from Dorchester West.'

'I thought about that, sir.'

'Keep going, Victor. You have me interested.'

'You and the superintendent had the same feeling about him,' said Leeming. 'Both of you sensed that Elwell wasn't the jolly sailor he pretended to be. He's got sharp instincts – the vicar told me that. I think Elwell realised that he was under suspicion and decided to go into hiding. If he'd travelled by train, we'd be able to learn his destination very easily. Whereas we'd never be able to track him if he went off quietly on his friend's cart.'

'Yet you did track him.'

'The vicar deserves the thanks for that. He put me on to Trego.'

'Well,' said Colbeck, sampling his wine, 'I admire the way you've thought it through but two things trouble me slightly.'

'What are they, sir?'

'First, there's no actual proof that Wimborne is Elwell's chosen destination.'

'That's true,' conceded Leeming. 'What's the second thing?'

'If, as you suggest, he knows that we've identified him as the possible killer of John Bedloe, why should he come to the very place where we happen to be? I don't think he has a confession in mind, Victor. So what would bring Jack Elwell here?'

Having broken into the cottage, he blundered about in the dark until he found a candle. Once he'd lit it, the little flame was all he needed to guide his footsteps upstairs. When he entered the bedroom, he had a feeling of grim satisfaction. Setting the candle down, he looked at the bed with rising hatred. It was a potent symbol of debauchery. Taking out a knife, he used it to shred the bed sheets, then he attacked the mattress with manic energy until it lay in pieces all over the floor. As a valedictory gesture, he thrust the knife deep into a pillow and twisted it like a corkscrew.

CHAPTER FOURTEEN

Even though she was feeling drowsy, Madeleine Colbeck was pleased when Lydia called in again that evening. It was only a brief visit. Lydia had returned with a book she'd recommended, promising that it would be able to hold her friend's attention.

'I know that you find it difficult to read for long,' she said, 'but this story will captivate you. It kept me awake all night, Madeleine.'

'It certainly won't do that to me.'

'I just had to finish it.'

'Thank you for bringing it.'

'I thought it might divert you – unless, of course, your husband comes home again tonight, that is.'

Madeleine laughed. 'Oh, I don't think that will happen again,' she said. 'I exhausted my supply of good fortune yesterday. Waking up to find Robert sitting where you are was like a gift from God.'

Lydia stood up. 'I can't compete with that.'

'Please don't leave.'

'I promised the nurse I wouldn't stay. She said that you needed your sleep.'

'Will you come again tomorrow?'

'If you want me to,' said Lydia.

'I may have read a chapter or two of the book by then.'

'If you read one, you'll want to read them all.'

'I hope that's true.' She stifled a yawn. 'Oh, I do beg your pardon.'

'That's my signal to go.'

Lydia bent forward to plant a gentle kiss on her cheek then bade her farewell. She let herself out. As soon as her friend had gone, Madeleine wanted to call her back. Whenever she was there, Lydia cheered her up in a way that her father could not. The bond between the two women strengthened every time they met. Though she had problems of her own, Lydia didn't try to unload them on Madeleine. She simply wanted to offer love and support at a trying time.

Madeleine picked up the book and opened it to the title page but she didn't have the urge or the concentration to read it. As she put it down again, she heard the doorbell being rung and rallied, hoping that Lydia had forgotten something and returned. Even a few more minutes in her company would be a tonic. But it was not her friend after all. She had to wait some time before she learnt who the caller had been. At the nurse's behest, the maidservant brought up some refreshment.

'Someone called earlier on,' said Madeleine.

'That's right, Mrs Colbeck.'

'Who was it?'

'It was a gentleman,' said the servant. 'He wanted to know who lived here.'

* * *

256

They were still enjoying their drinks when Bertram Maycock came in search of them.

'I'm sorry to disturb ye, Inspector,' he said.

'You look worried,' said Colbeck.

'We've had a report of someone breaking into a house.'

'We're here to solve a murder,' said Leeming, tartly. 'You'll have to deal with lesser crimes yourself, Constable.'

'It's the place where John Bedloe lived.'

'Then we *do* have an interest,' said Colbeck, draining his glass before getting up. 'On the way there, you can tell us what happened.'

Embarrassed by his earlier rebuff, Leeming hastily finished his own drink.

'Is your prisoner behaving himself?' he asked.

'Yes, sir. Manders has stopped bawlin' at us.'

'That's an improvement.'

'The estate manager's turned up – a Mr Fin'lay.'

'I daresay he'll come looking for me sooner or later.'

They left the hotel and made their way through the streets. Maycock explained that a neighbour of Bedloe's had reported seeing a window smashed and left open. Somebody had come rushing out of the cottage, pushed the man aside and vanished into the darkness. The neighbour had gone straight to the police station and Maycock had been sent to investigate.

'Has anything been taken?' asked Colbeck.

'Who can say, sir?'

'What did you find there?'

'Somethin' very strange, Inspector.'

'Oh?'

'Ye wait and see.'

They got to the cottage and found a uniformed policeman

standing outside. He moved out of their way so that they could go in through the unlocked door. Candles had been lit but Maycock picked up the oil lamp instead. He led the way upstairs then took them into the bedroom. It was a scene of utter destruction. The mattress had been hacked to pieces and a knife protruded from the pillow.

Leeming was shocked. 'Why would anyone do such a thing?'

'It's the work of somebody with a lot of anger inside him,' said Colbeck.

'Then it has to be Elwell.'

'We can't be certain of that.'

'We know that he was due to arrive in Wimborne this evening, sir.'

'So were lots of other people.'

'Yes, but he has a strong motive to wreak his revenge.'

Colbeck gazed around. 'Is that what we're looking at?'

'What else could it be?'

'Well, it could be the reaction of a woman, for instance. They, too, can nurse vengeful feelings. Do you remember Alice and Betsy?'

'Who are *they*?' muttered Maycock.

'I remember them well,' said Leeming. 'Betsy was the one who lives in Wimborne and probably came here from time to time to see him.'

'Supposing her rival found out about that,' said Colbeck, pensively. 'She'd be furious. This might have been her response. A woman could do all this damage.'

'I say it was Elwell. We know he left home with a knife.'

'Every home has a knife in it, Sergeant.'

'It's crystal clear to me, sir. Elwell set out from Dorchester with the intention of coming here to do this.'

'Why?'

'It's because his first wife was seduced by Bedloe.'

'That took place in Dorchester,' argued Colbeck. 'He and Susan Elwell had their assignations there. It was only after her death that Bedloe moved here. This place has no association at all with Elwell's first wife.'

Leeming was puzzled. 'That's true.'

'If he'd already got his revenge by killing Bedloe, why would he need to come here and do this?'

'I see your point.'

'Something about this incident worries me.'

'Do you believe that it's *not* Elwell, sir?'

'I've yet to be persuaded that it is. Yes, it's possible that he came here in the kind of rage that blocks out everything else. Once inside the place, he simply went berserk. We've seen people before who've lost all control like that. Jack Elwell could be one of them.'

'He just wanted to vent his spleen.'

'He or *she* might have wanted that. Don't rule out Alice.'

'We don't know that one of Bedloe's mistresses found out about the other.'

'It's only a hypothesis, I grant you,' said Colbeck, 'but it's one we should consider before settling on a single possible version of events.'

'Could juss be a burglar,' said Maycock.

'It could indeed. However, burglars have a habit of taking property rather than destroying it so comprehensively. You told us you didn't know if anything had been stolen. Is that right?'

'Yes, sir.'

'Let's be sure, shall we?'

Using the light from the lamp, he searched in every drawer and cupboard on the first floor. They went downstairs and saw that nothing appeared to have been taken. Items of some value had been left untouched. Colbeck's eye then fell on the wall above the fireplace.

'Something *was* stolen,' he said.

'What was it, sir?' asked Leeming.

'There was a shotgun over the fireplace. It's gone.'

'So Elwell now has a firearm, does he? I don't like the sound of that. I had enough trouble with Manders and his shotgun. I don't want someone pulling the trigger on me again.'

'Let's take one last look upstairs,' suggested Colbeck.

All three of them went back to the bedroom and surveyed the devastation.

'He didn't come for the shotgun. That was just a souvenir. This is what brought him here – if indeed it was a man. It was a chance to make a protest against Bedloe's lechery.'

'I think he wanted to sink this into Bedloe's heart,' said Leeming, pulling the knife out of the pillow. 'Unable to do that, he turned his anger on the bed.' He examined the weapon. 'It's an ordinary kitchen knife, sir.'

'Keep it with you. It's evidence.'

'Yes, Inspector.'

'We might as well go now. I've got a key to lock up. You can stand your man down, Constable. He won't need to stay outside any more.'

'Whose knife is this?' asked Leeming, turning it over so that its blade glinted in the light. 'That's what I'd like to know.'

'And me.'

'I'd like t'know who Alice and Betsy is,' murmured Maycock.

* * *

It was both frustrating and alarming. There were many questions that Rebecca Tullidge wanted to put to her husband but he simply wouldn't allow them. He sat in silence opposite her and went off into a reverie. What he was thinking, she could only guess. It was what he was hiding that worried her. She still had no idea what Tullidge had been doing during the hour after he left the Waggon and Horses on Saturday night. His refusal to tell her was bound to raise the terrifying possibility that he might have been the killer. There were times when the notion seemed ridiculous. In the weeks preceding the murder, he'd given no indication that he was aware of her friendship with John Bedloe. Apart from anything else, he took little interest in his wife. He only seemed to notice her when he wanted her to do something for him. Most of the time, he studiously ignored her.

And yet there'd been other occasions recently when he'd looked at her in the most unsettling way. It was almost as if he were gloating over the fact that he knew something she didn't, something that was very much to her disadvantage. Dying to challenge him, she lacked the spirit to do so. His changes of mood were disturbing and she was still bruised and sore after his assault on her in the bedroom. That had been so out of character that she wondered if it was really him. Now, at least, he was sedate and unthreatening. She felt relatively safe.

Without warning, he sat bolt upright. 'There's a train due in ten minutes.'

'I know, Michael. I'll close the gates.'

'It's my job, woman.'

'I'm happy to help.'

'Leave it to me,' he snarled. 'Do as you're told for once.'

The stinging rebuke was unfair. Rebecca spent the greater

261

part of her life obeying his orders. She had little free time of her own and could never do what she wished. In Bedloe's company, by contrast, she'd been able to breathe. When she was alone with him, she felt an extraordinary sense of freedom, throwing aside the shackles of marriage to experience true love for the first time in her life. Where her husband was clumsy and inexpert, Bedloe had been gentle and sensitive. As a lover, Tullidge could only take. Bedloe had known how to give and share.

'Why aren't you knitting?' he asked.

'I was expecting to go on duty.'

'I told you. That's my job.'

'Yes, Michael.'

'I don't want you getting above yourself.'

'I'll do as you say.'

'You'd better.'

He got up, looked at the clock on the wall then checked it against his pocket watch. After putting on his hat and coat, he unlocked the door and went out. Rebecca watched him through the window, going through the routine he'd followed hundreds of times. At one point, he stood inches away from the railway line and a thought suddenly flashed through her mind. Suicide was not the only escape, after all. Instead of flinging herself in front of an oncoming train, there was an alternative.

She could push her husband into its path.

In spite of his age, his obsession with work and his fondness for alcohol, Ambrose Feltham was in extremely good health. When he called on Oliver Keddle, therefore, it was not in search of a consultation. He simply had a request to pass on.

'I've always thought of you as a good friend, Oliver,' he began.

'That sounds ominous. You're after money.'

'No, I'm not. I have all that any man could desire.'

'In that case, you'll be in a position to help *me*,' said Keddle, jovially.

'I need your advice.'

'Then it's simple – eat frugally, drink less and have regular exercise.'

'I'm talking about the election of the mayor.'

'Well, don't turn to me. I don't have a vote.'

They were in the drawing room of Keddle's house and the visitor had – for the first time ever – refused the offer of a drink. Feltham was edgy and preoccupied. His usual buoyancy had deserted him.

'I won't beat about the bush,' he said. 'I've been putting out feelers.'

'I expected no less of you, Ambrose,' said the other with light sarcasm.

'This is important to me.'

'It's important to everyone in Wimborne, me included. Whoever becomes mayor is in a position to do a lot of good for the town – or, conversely, a great deal of harm.'

'You know where I stand on the matter.'

'So why have you come in search of my counsel?'

Feltham swallowed hard. 'I may not win, after all.'

'There was always that possibility.'

'No, there wasn't. Ten days ago, I thought I had the whole thing sewn up nicely. I had verbal commitments from the people who matter. Godfrey Preece has his hangers-on, of course, so I didn't bother them. Even allowing for their opposition, I still believed I'd romp home.'

'Have there been defections?'

'Yes, Oliver. Nobody has spoken to me directly but I'm very conscious that there's been a change of heart in some quarters.'

'Then you'll have to win people back.'

'How do I do that?'

'To start with,' said Keddle, 'you must stop being so overbearing. I know you have wonderful schemes in mind for the town. Don't ram them down people's throats. Discover the meaning of the word "compromise". You must learn to adjust your ideas to the views of others. At the moment, you've slapped a list of plans in front of them and said, in effect, take them or leave them.'

'Well, at least I *have* plans. You can't say that of Godfrey Preece.'

'Godfrey is an institution.'

'I rather hoped that that was what I'd become.'

'I'm afraid not. Dorset folk are very conservative.'

'So?'

'You're still seen as a relative newcomer.'

'I've been here for years and years,' protested Feltham.

'The Preeces have been in Dorset for centuries.'

'That doesn't explain why people are turning against me.'

'You've had my advice – be more amenable to discussion, Ambrose. And don't keep waving Inspector Colbeck at everyone like a flag. He works for Scotland Yard and not for you.' His eyes twinkled. 'He made that point eloquently.'

'Colbeck is my trump card.'

'Don't let him hear you say that.'

'If only he'd solve this murder!'

'Give him time and give him leeway.'

'It would make such a difference to my hopes of election.'

'There you go again,' said Keddle. 'You see everything in personal terms and judge people by what you can get out of them. Colbeck will find his man – but he won't do it in order for you to be our next mayor.'

Leeming's prediction was accurate. Arriving back at the hotel, the detectives found that Leonard Findlay was waiting for them. After being introduced to Colbeck, he adjourned with them to the lounge. They sat in a triangle.

'I've just been to the police station,' said Findlay. 'My gamekeeper is there.'

'How is he, sir?' asked Leeming.

'He's hopping mad and so am I.'

'Then you're both in good company,' said Colbeck, smoothly. 'The sergeant is mad because he was fired at and I am even madder on his behalf. Experienced gamekeepers may be difficult to replace but there's not a detective in the whole of the country who could adequately fill the sergeant's shoes.'

Leeming was touched. 'Do you really mean that, sir?'

'Yes, I do. You are incomparable.'

'Thank you.'

'Bill Manders is the best man I have,' said Findlay. 'I need him back.'

'Then he shouldn't have tried to kill my sergeant,' said Colbeck, 'or to put a large hole in his top hat.'

'Manders explained that. It was a prank.'

'Then it was a very dangerous prank, sir.'

'He is not a killer.'

'Agreed – we've already reached the same conclusion.'

'Then what's to stop him being released?'

'It's something known as the rule of law,' said Colbeck. 'It means that you can't assault a policeman or resist arrest with impunity. Manders did both.'

'That's not how he sees it, Inspector.'

'I was *there*,' Leeming put in. 'Don't listen to him. Your gamekeeper fought tooth and nail with me.'

'He felt he was being unjustly accused.'

'All criminals feel that, Mr Findlay.'

'He's not a criminal. That's the point. And he's not naturally violent.'

'John Bedloe might disagree with you there,' said Leeming. 'Manders boasted to me how he once got the better of him in a fight. Bedloe left the estate because he couldn't work with Manders any more.'

'That's beside the point,' said Findlay, making an effort to sound more reasonable. 'The facts are these. Bill Manders made a mistake in shooting at you and he apologises. He does have a bizarre idea of fun at times. As for resisting arrest, he claims that he was simply trying to defend himself.' He turned to Colbeck. 'Can't we come to some sort of arrangement, Inspector?'

'What did you have in mind?' asked Colbeck.

'Release my gamekeeper and I'll not only give the sergeant the price of a new top hat of his choice, I'll pay whatever fine is due for Manders.'

'You obviously set a high price on his services.'

'He's worth it.'

'Then my answer is this,' said Colbeck. 'The prisoner can spend a sobering night in his cell while the sergeant and I consider what charges to bring. If we decide that they are serious, bail may be denied. If,' he went on, turning to Leeming, 'the sergeant can bring himself to accept Manders' explanation of why he fired the shotgun, a lesser penalty may be incurred.'

Findlay was hopeful. 'I can have him back?'

'The decision will be made tomorrow.'

'Thank you.'

The estate manager nodded. Realising that he could neither bully nor cajole Colbeck, he backed away. Something in the inspector's manner indicated that the gamekeeper might be shown some leniency and Findlay was ready to accept that. He traded farewells with them and left.

'I'm hungry, sir,' said Leeming.

'Business comes before pleasure, Victor.'

'What sort of business?'

'You still have that knife in your possession,' said Colbeck, 'and you still believe that Jack Elwell stuck it in that pillow.'

'I do, sir.'

'Let's find out if that's the case.'

Madeleine Colbeck surprised herself. Intending to read only a page or two of the novel, she was instead caught up in its magic. Chapter after chapter went by. Lydia Quayle had not only given her a story that dealt with serious themes in a light and often comic way, she'd also provided an antidote to the long periods of boredom and the increasing discomfort. It was the first time that Madeleine had been able to read anything of such length and it was visible proof of the value of Lydia's friendship. Fatigue eventually came and she tried hard to resist its pull. When she finally dozed off, the book lay open across her lap.

Using a lantern to guide his footsteps, he followed the line until it took him to West Moors. He came to a halt beside the shed and studied it thoughtfully for a moment. Then he went to the rear of the structure, felt around for the key and soon located it. Opening the shed, he let the light fall on the collection of implements used in routine maintenance. Expecting to see the mattress on the floor, he was astonished to find that it had been hacked to pieces. Someone had destroyed it completely.

Richard Satchwell was at once shocked and intrigued.

'We're sorry to descend on you again, Mrs Elwell,' said Colbeck, tipping his hat to her, 'but we need to speak to you.'

Louisa was startled. 'Has something happened to Jack?'

'We don't know. Our information is that he's with a Mr Trego.'

'Oh, yes. Allan Trego is his friend.'

'Your husband went off with him,' explained Leeming. 'According to Mrs Trego, they had to deliver something to a house in Corfe Mullen before going on to Wimborne. I'm surprised that Mr Elwell didn't tell you that.'

'Jack doesn't always tell me things. And he was in a rush earlier on.' She stepped back to admit them. 'You'd better come in.'

They were back in Fordington again. As they stepped into the house, the detectives had both reached the same conclusion. Elwell had wanted to keep his wife ignorant of where he was going in case they came in search of him. Put in an awkward position, Louisa didn't know what to do or say. She looked pathetically vulnerable.

'We need to ask you a question, Mrs Elwell,' said Colbeck. 'When your husband left earlier on today, you told us that he'd grabbed a few things from the kitchen. One of them was a knife.'

'That's right,' she replied.

'The sergeant is going to show you a knife that we recovered.

We'd be very grateful if you could tell us if it belongs to you.'

'Where did you get it?'

'That doesn't matter.'

'Did you take it off Jack?'

'No, we didn't. We're not even sure that it was the one he took from here.' He nodded to Leeming. 'You should know, Mrs Elwell.'

Opening his coat, the sergeant brought out the knife concealed beneath it.

'That's not ours,' said Louisa, shaking her head.

'Are you absolutely certain?'

'Yes, Inspector – the one that Jack took was much bigger.'

Leeming was disappointed. 'I could've sworn it came from here.'

'Apparently not,' said Colbeck, unsurprised.

'What happens now, sir?'

'I think that we must prevail upon Mrs Elwell's hospitality. If, as we believe, her husband will be back before too long, you should stay here, Sergeant.' He turned to Louisa. 'Is that possible?'

'Well . . . I suppose so.'

'Thank you.'

She was fearful. 'You're not going to arrest Jack, are you?'

'We just need to talk to him at this stage.'

'What about you, sir?' asked Leeming. 'If I'm to stay here till he gets back, where will you be?'

'I thought I might call at the vicarage,' said Colbeck, cheerfully.

The train had gone past several minutes earlier but there was no sign of Tullidge. Once he'd opened the gates, he didn't usually linger. The cold wind should have driven him back into the house. Rebecca went out to find him and saw a lantern flickering in the

269

distance. It got closer and closer until her husband finally emerged from the darkness.

'Where've you been, Michael?'

'I thought I saw a light.'

'Where?'

'Down by that shed.'

'Did you find anybody?'

'No, but I heard them running away.'

'Who could it have been?'

'I don't know. I'll take another look in daylight.'

'Why should anyone be out here at this time of night?'

'Somebody was here on Saturday,' he said, meaningfully. 'The lantern I saw must have been close to where the body was found.'

Rebecca's cheeks burnt and she was grateful that it was so dark. Had the killer returned to the scene of the crime for some reason? Would he continue to haunt the place? It was more than likely that she'd be on duty at that time another night. If she caught sight of a lantern close to the shed, what would she do? Tullidge had been ready to confront the trespasser. If she tried to do that, would the man flee or would he simply wait? Is that why he'd come? Aware of her assignations with Bedloe, was he trying to make contact with her? To what end would he do that? Did he hope to blackmail her in some way? She trembled at the thought. Having no money, there was only one thing she had to offer. Is that what the killer was after? Did he want to replace John Bedloe? It was a terrifying thought.

'Get inside,' said Tullidge.

'What?'

Coming out of her daydream, she looked at her husband. The lantern illumined a malevolent grin. It was almost as if he was taunting her. Rebecca's cheeks and mind were ablaze now. She only had Tullidge's word that he'd seen a light in the distance. What if nobody had been there but himself? She had the queasy feeling that he was starting to play cruel games with her. It was a new threat.

'What have you been doing since you've been here?'

'We've been gathering evidence,' said Colbeck.

'Have you had time to appreciate the scenery?'

'I'm afraid not.'

'Dorset is a remarkable county.'

'We've found that out.'

'Look around you, Inspector.'

'I can't afford distractions, I'm afraid.'

Henry Moule had not been in any way discomfited by the late visit. Habitually working long hours, he was glad to welcome Colbeck into the vicarage and to take him into the study. They sat opposite each other in leather armchairs.

'May I offer you some refreshment?' asked Moule.

'That's very kind of you, Vicar, but I'll have to decline the invitation.'

He looked around the room and noticed the profusion of framed photographs. They stood on the mantelpiece, on the bookcases and on other available surfaces. Moule and his wife featured in many of them. One photograph showed a group of children with a fairly wide age range. Moule noted his visitor's interest.

'We're the proud parents of eight sons,' he explained. 'Unhappily, only seven of them appear in that photograph. Christopher – God bless him – died in infancy. Childhood is such a fragile blossom,' he went on, sadly. 'It can so easily crumble. Do you have children, Inspector?'

'No,' replied Colbeck, 'but my wife and I expect our first child very soon.'

'May good fortune attend all of you!'

'Thank you, Vicar.'

'Fatherhood is a divine gift. Cherish it.'

Colbeck wished that he could. Until the baby was actually born, however, he couldn't feel that he was a parent. An expectant father was, he'd discovered, prone to all kinds of fears. The vicar had been in that position on eight occasions. Seven had been occasions of joy but one must have brought anguish in its wake. Looking at the crucifix, he offered up a silent prayer for the safety of Madeleine and their baby.

'What do you think of Fordington?' asked Moule.

'Parts of it have great charm,' replied Colbeck, 'but too many dwellings have been crammed into too small a space. People are living on top of each other in squalid conditions. I hardly need tell you that it's hazardous to their health. You've tried to address that problem and I admire the way you've done it.'

'It's been a constant struggle, Inspector. The floors of some cottages are below the level of the pond. Waste was being cast into drains or – at one point – into the streets themselves. The stench was unbearable. I wrote a strong letter of complaint to the officials of the Duchy of Cornwall.'

'Is the Duchy your landlord?'

'Unhappily, it is. Not an ounce of compassion has been shown. I demanded action but it was never forthcoming. They were content to let the place rot.'

'That's reprehensible.'

'Don't get me talking about the Duchy of Cornwall or I'll give you a whole sermon.' He appraised Colbeck, aware how strikingly different he was from his other visitor from Scotland Yard. 'Sergeant Leeming described the desperate search for Jack Elwell. Did you manage to find him?'

'Acting on your advice, we've at least established his whereabouts.'

Colbeck told him about the latest developments and why they'd returned. The vicar was fascinated by the information. Though Jack Elwell now reviled the church, he was still nominally a parishioner. The vicar patently cared about him.

'He's obviously been through some spiritual upheaval,' said Colbeck.

'Yes, Inspector, and it's left the poor man hopelessly confused.'

'He tried to make me believe that his second marriage had obliterated all memory of the first one but I thought otherwise – especially after we looked through the archives of the local newspaper.'

'He'll never be able to forget poor, dear, tortured Susan,' said Moule, pursing his lips. 'His first wife has stayed alive in his heart. Actions speak louder than words.'

'I don't follow.'

'Well, he may still shudder at her betrayal but there's a strong element of forgiveness in him as well.'

'How do you know that?'

'He still tends Susan Elwell's grave.'

The lantern stood nearby, casting enough light for him to see what he was doing. After piling the earth gently in place, he used the flat of the spade to tamp it down. He then stood back and removed his hat in respect.

* * *

Ambrose Feltham had just finished his meal when the visitor called. Annoyed at being hailed out of the dining room, he was even more irritated to see Richard Satchwell waiting for him in the hall.

'What, in the name of all that's holy, are *you* doing here?' he demanded.

'I've brought some information, sir.'

'It had better be news of an arrest. That's what I need most.'

'They're on their way to make that, Mr Feltham.'

'How do you know that? Is this some tittle-tattle from one of your spies?'

'No, sir,' said Satchwell. 'I relied on my own eyes and ears. When I was at the station earlier, Inspector Colbeck and the sergeant arrived with some urgency. They bought tickets to Dorchester. When I asked if there was an arrest in the offing, they said that they were more than hopeful.'

'More than hopeful, eh?' said Feltham. 'That's no use to me. They were more than hopeful that Manders was the killer. I need certainty. I need a name pinned on to the man who murdered John Bedloe.'

'He's been back, sir.'

'What are you talking about?'

'The killer returned to the spot where the crime took place.'

'How do you know that?'

'I've just been there myself,' explained Satchwell. 'Yes, I know that you think I don't have the skill to solve a murder but, acting on my own instincts, I did something that neither the inspector or the sergeant thought of. I went back there.'

'What did you find?'

'I found that it's a cold and lonely place in this weather.'

'Was anyone there?'

'No, sir, but someone *had* been.'

Satchwell told him about his discovery and elicited a gasp of surprise.

'That *is* interesting,' he conceded. 'I'll enjoy passing that on to Superintendent Tallis and asking why his detectives failed to take a second look at that shed.'

'I have more news for you, Mr Feltham. The superintendent is no longer here.'

'Why not?'

'He's been summoned back to London.' He smirked. 'Working near the station has its benefits. I can see who comes and who goes.'

'You've done well,' said the other. 'Thank you for coming to tell me. With the superintendent out of the way, I can feel at ease again. As for Inspector Colbeck, let's see if his hopes are justified.'

'He had a spring in his step, sir. That's encouraging.'

'This crime has cast a pall over the town. In killing Bedloe, the villain created havoc here. I want it removed forthwith and I want the killer in custody, waiting for an appointment with the hangman.' He tapped his chest. 'An early arrest is vital for me. It's the only thing that will bring in the votes I need.'

'You'll be a good mayor, sir,' said Satchwell, sycophantically.

Feltham straightened his back. 'I intend to be a great one.'

Victor Leeming was cold, bored and hungry. He was now stationed outside Elwell's house in case the man took to his heels. Having returned from the vicarage, Colbeck was inside with Louisa Elwell while the sergeant was relegated to a street corner. It was galling and it reminded him of his time in uniform, patrolling dark corners of the capital and listening to his stomach rumbling. What made it worse was that he could hear sounds of jollity from inside the tavern nearby. He longed to be there to enjoy its warmth, to taste its beer and to eat as much of its food as he could. Duty, however, came first. Leeming was stuck. His only companions were drunken revellers who staggered by on their way home and a persistent mongrel dog that kept sniffing his feet no matter how many times he kicked it away.

By the time that he heard the chimes of midnight booming out from distant Dorchester, he was half asleep. He'd given up all hope that Jack Elwell would return that night and decided that the man had fled justice, after all. Leeming had the horrible feeling that he might be there until dawn. He'd already accepted that they'd never get back to the seductive comforts of their beds at the King's Head in Wimborne. The last train had long gone. They were stranded. Even the dog had given up and slunk away in search of cover. It started to rain.

Tempted to knock on the door and ask to be let in by Colbeck, he was stopped by the sound of footsteps heading in his direction. Withdrawing into the shadows, he bided his time. A burly figure soon appeared and rapped on the door of his house. It was opened by Robert Colbeck who bore a welcoming smile.

'Come on in, Mr Elwell,' he said.

'What, in Christ's name, are *you* doing here?' demanded Elwell.

'We need to talk, sir.'

'I've nothing to say.'

'Oh, I fancy that we'll find one subject to interest you.'

'Get out of my house!'

'I'm afraid that I can't do that.'

'Where's Louisa?'

'She's waiting inside,' said Colbeck. 'Because you're so late, she's fast asleep.' He stepped back. 'Now why don't you come on in?'

Elwell needed a moment to size up the situation. Deciding to run, he swung round and tried to dash off in the direction from which he'd just come. Leeming was waiting for him. He grabbed the former sailor and marched him unceremoniously back to the house. Pushing him in, he went after him and shut the door, standing against it to cut off any further attempts at escape. Elwell rounded on him.

'Who the devil are you?' he shouted.

'My name is Sergeant Leeming, sir.'

'You've no right to be in my house.'

'I think that we have every right, Mr Elwell.'

Roused by the noise, Louisa ran into the room and threw herself into her husband's arms. He hugged her protectively and scowled at the detectives.

'Did they frighten you?' he asked.

'Yes, Jack. I'm afraid they're going to arrest you.'

'They can't do that, Louisa.'

'I didn't know where you were.'

'I've been helping Allan deliver things,' said Elwell. 'I only remembered my promise at the last moment. That's why I left in such a rush.' He squeezed her tight. 'Look at you, shivering with fear. Did you have to come here at this hour, Inspector?'

'Oh, we've been in here a very long time.'

'Some of us have been outside a very long time,' complained Leeming.

'We understand that you went to Wimborne.'

Elwell glared at him. 'I might have done.'

'You went to John Bedloe's house,' said Leeming. 'I still think it was you who stabbed that pillow with a knife.' He took the weapon out again. 'Do you recognise this, sir?'

'No, I don't.'

'You're not even looking at it, sir.'

'I don't need to.'

'Your wife told us that you took a knife with you. In order to protect you, she denied that this was the one but I think she was trying to mislead us.'

'No, I wasn't,' cried Louisa. 'It was the truth.'

'Neither of us have seen that knife before,' insisted Elwell.

'Then what happened to the one you took from here?' asked Leeming with a note of triumph in his voice. 'You can't answer that question, can you?'

'Yes, I can. I have it here.'

Elwell pulled back his coat and took out the knife that was stuck in his belt. It was much bigger than the one they'd found in Bedloe's house. Leeming shot a look of mild panic at Colbeck. Another theory had just exploded in the sergeant's face.

'May I ask why you carry such a dangerous weapon?' asked Colbeck.

'Have you ever ridden along Dorset roads at night, Inspector?' said Elwell.

'That's a delight I've yet to experience.'

'You have to be on your guard. Allan Trego, my friend, always has a pistol. I prefer a knife. We were carrying hundreds of pounds worth of merchandise on the cart tonight. That could have made us a target.'

'And were you attacked?'

'No, we were lucky this time. Two weeks ago when I helped my friend to take two hundred chickens to Poole, someone did think that he could sneak a few cages off the back of the cart.' He brandished the knife. 'This changed his mind.'

'You never told me it was so dangerous,' said Louisa, clinging to him.

'It's best that you don't know certain things, my love. You go on up to bed,' he urged. 'I'll answer their questions then send them on their way.'

'I'd rather stay, Jack.'

He whispered something in her ear, gave her a kiss then took her across to the staircase. Reluctant to go, she went slowly up the steps. Once she'd disappeared, her husband confronted the detectives, hand on hips.

'What's going on?' he growled.

'Why don't you sit down?' suggested Colbeck. 'We'll do the same.'

He signalled to Leeming who sank gratefully on to a chair at the table. Colbeck sat next to him. After long consideration, Elwell eventually sat down as well. Still holding the knife, he realised that it might look as if he was keeping them at bay so he put the weapon on the table.

'Ask your questions,' he snapped.

'I spoke to the vicar earlier on,' said Colbeck.

'What's the old fool been saying?'

'The Reverend Moule is far from foolish, sir. He's a very wise man.'

'I've got no time for him.'

'But you used to have,' said Leeming. 'You liked going to church then.'

'Those days are past.'

'You can't blame the vicar for what happened.'

'I can do what I damn well like,' said Elwell, pugnaciously.

'Within the limits of the law,' added Colbeck. 'I learnt something rather interesting at the vicarage, sir, and I'd like you to tell me if it's true.'

'Knowing him, it was probably a lie.'

'That's unkind. He spoke well of you. He's known you for a very long time, after all. His sympathy is genuine.'

'What did the vicar tell you?'

'He said that you still tend the grave of your first wife.'

'Then he should mind his own bleeding business!' yelled Elwell so loudly that his wife came to the top of the stairs. He waved her brusquely away. 'Why did you have to bring that up?' he hissed.

'It's true, then,' said Colbeck.

'It's a private matter.'

'But it happens to be very relevant to our investigation, sir. If a man is trying to outlive his past, as you are claiming to do, it is just conceivable that he might live in the same house as the one he shared with his first wife and he might even work beside the river in which she drowned herself with her unborn child. What is impossible to accept, however,' the inspector continued, 'is that he should keep the memory of the tragedy fresh in his mind by tending the woman's grave. That's bound to stoke feelings of revenge, is it not?'

'It might do.'

'Is that why you do it, Mr Elwell?'

'Is that why you had something put in the newspaper on the anniversary of her death?' asked Leeming. 'The editor showed us the article.'

'Oh,' sneered Elwell, 'so you've got Rickwood on your side as well as the vicar, have you?'

'They've both been very helpful.'

'Evidence has been mounting against you,' said Colbeck, quietly. 'That's why the sergeant and I are here at this ungodly hour. We're starting to believe that on Saturday night – when

Mrs Elwell was conveniently absent – you made your way to West Moors and stabbed John Bedloe to death.'

Jack Elwell folded his arms and stared insolently at them in turn.

'I'm saying nothing,' he asserted.

CHAPTER FIFTEEN

There was a prolonged silence. Elwell exuded defiance, Colbeck was watchful and Leeming was suffering pangs of hunger. Upstairs in the bedroom, a tearful Louisa Elwell was wondering what was going on yet was too afraid to come down and ask. On the table was the large knife, gleaming invitingly. In Elwell's hands, it would be a fearsome weapon and he was eyeing it with interest. Leeming braced himself, ready to disarm him if he made a grab for the knife. In the end, it was Colbeck who reached out for it, inspecting it carefully and testing its sharp blade.

'This would have killed Bedloe instantly,' he decided. 'Slipped between his ribs and into his heart, it would have been very effective. What was the point of using the corkscrew as well?' Elwell was dumb. 'I don't need to ask you if you love your wife, sir – the second Mrs Elwell, that is. It's obvious that you do and it's abundantly clear that you mean everything in the world to her. That being the case, do you really wish her to see you arrested, handcuffed and taken into custody? Is that the image you would like her to hold in her mind as we drag you away?' When Elwell maintained his silence, Colbeck got up and walked to the bottom of the stairs. 'Since you don't mind her witnessing your humiliation, I'll call her down.'

'Wait!' shouted Elwell.

'I thought you'd lost your tongue.'

'There's no need to involve Louisa in this.'

'It's between you and your *first* wife, isn't it?'

Elwell had to force the word out. 'Yes.'

'It still rankles.'

'It's always there,' admitted the other.

'When did you identify Bedloe as the man you wanted?'

'It was weeks ago. I finally worked out who'd driven Susan to kill herself.'

'How did you do that?' asked Leeming.

'I kept searching. I knew I'd find him one day and I knew he'd be doing the same thing to another misguided young woman. He'd find her weakness and work on that. Susan was very lonely. That was my fault, not hers. She had no defence against Bedloe. He was too cunning.'

'Did you ever meet him?'

'I saw him once. He looked exactly as I'd expected.'

'He lived in Wimborne. Why kill him in West Moors?'

'I didn't, Inspector.'

Colbeck was taken aback. 'I thought we were listening to a confession.'

'So did I,' said Leeming in frustration.

'What I'm confessing to is the desire,' said Elwell, grinding his teeth. 'I *wanted* to kill him. I'd spent ages working out how to do it and it wouldn't have been with a knife between the ribs.

That would have been a quick death. He deserved pain. I'd have taken hours over it. I'd have made the bastard *suffer*.' He gave a wolfish grin. 'That would have been my way. But somebody got there before me.'

'Why should we believe that?' asked Colbeck.

'I've no reason to lie.'

'A jury would find the evidence against you compelling, sir.'

'Then put me before one,' said Elwell, offering both wrists. 'Get the handcuffs ready, Sergeant, only give me a few minutes to speak to my wife before you take me off. Louisa will believe me, even if you don't.'

Colbeck needed only a mater of seconds to reach his decision.

'There's no need for handcuffs,' he said. 'We've already arrested the wrong man once. If we do so again, it will be viewed as an unfortunate habit. I'm giving you the benefit of the doubt, sir.'

'I can't say that I would,' opined Leeming.

'We must beg to differ, Sergeant.'

'I think he's bluffing.'

'No, I'm not,' said Elwell, seriously. 'I've told you the truth. It all comes back to what happened between Bedloe and Susan. When I first heard about it, I hated her as if she was my worst enemy. Then I came to see that she was really at his mercy. It wasn't her I should blame.' After glancing upwards, he lowered his voice. 'My wife and I are very happy together but I couldn't forget Susan. There were moments when I felt I still loved her, somehow. Can you understand that? Is it possible to love and hate someone at the same time?'

'Oh, yes,' said Leeming, thinking of Tallis, 'it certainly is.'

'I tried to kill Susan off in my mind but I can't do it somehow.'

'Does your second wife realise that?' asked Colbeck.

Elwell nodded. 'Louisa is a saint.'

'We're sorry to have given her an unnecessary fright, sir. Please apologise on our behalf. The sergeant and I will take our leave.'

'Where are we going?' asked Leeming. 'We're both starving and we can't get back to Wimborne tonight.'

'I have an idea where we can stay,' said Colbeck, moving to the door.

'Wait,' said Elwell. 'We've bread and cheese, if that's any use.'

Rebecca Tullidge was up early so that she could go off to market. Before she headed for Wimborne, however, she paid a call on the Waggon and Horses and sought out her friend. Margaret Vout was cleaning the mirror behind the bar. She saw Rebecca's face reflected in it and turned round to greet her.

'We're not open yet, Becky,' she said.

'I know that.'

'You'll have to come back later.'

'I don't drink, Maggie, as you well know.'

'I'm sure you could manage a cup of tea, couldn't you?'

'No, thank you. I'm on my way to Wimborne. I just wanted a word.'

Her friend put down her duster and beamed amicably at her.

'Here I am.'

'What time did Michael come in here yesterday evening?'

Margaret shrugged. 'He didn't come in here at all.'

'But he told me that he was on his way here.'

'Then he must have changed his mind. I wouldn't have missed him if he'd been here because the place was half empty. Are you *sure* he said he was coming?'

'Yes,' said Rebecca, worriedly. 'Why did he lie to me?'

'You know what husbands are like,' said the other, nudging her. 'He was just teasing you, I expect.'

'Michael would never do that.'

'Maybe he had somewhere else to go and didn't want you to know about it.'

'That's what I'm thinking. The question is – where was it?'

'Ask him, Becky.'

'Oh, no, I couldn't possibly do that.'

'I'd ask *my* husband if I caught him telling a lie,' said Margaret, firmly. 'And I'd make sure that I got an honest answer out of him.'

'Michael would go wild if I did that.'

'Is he in the habit of deceiving you?'

'No, that's what upsets me. He never used to tell me lies. And he never went out during the week. It was just him and me at the lodge. Yesterday was different. Michael was behaving oddly. The next minute, he says that he's coming here.'

'Well, he never arrived. He must have gone somewhere else.'

'He'd been drinking.'

'It's a long walk to the next pub.'

'That's what I've been thinking.'

Margaret looked at her shrewdly. 'What's going on, Becky?'

'Nothing – I'm sorry to trouble you.'

'You wouldn't have bothered to come if you hadn't suspected that he might be lying. It's not like you to check up on Michael. If you really want to know where he was yesterday evening,' she volunteered, 'I'll ask him for you.'

'No, no!' cried Rebecca in alarm. 'Please don't do that.'

'*You* may be afraid of him but I'm certainly not.'

'Just pretend that I never even asked you. Forget the whole thing.'

'What about you, Becky?' asked the other, pointedly. 'Are *you* going to forget the whole thing?'

They'd never spent a night in a church before. While it had had its drawbacks, the experience did mean that they'd had a roof over their heads on a rainswept night. It had been cold and uncomfortable on hard pews in the nave. The only light they permitted themselves was the dancing flame of a small candle. Leeming had slept at an awkward angle and awoken with severe aches and pains.

'Next time the Reverend Moule builds a new church,' he said, 'ask him to put a proper bed in it. A warm fire wouldn't come amiss, either.'

'It was better than nothing, Victor. We should be grateful.'

'My neck hurts and I've got cramp in both legs.'

'I'm more concerned about my appearance,' said Colbeck, brushing his frock coat. 'Everything is creased and we've no means of shaving.'

'The superintendent will not be happy about this, sir.'

'He'll be very unhappy.'

'We came to Fordington to arrest a dangerous killer and all we got was some bread and cheese.'

'Don't forget the pickled onions. They were delicious.'

'He'll make us suffer.'

'No, he won't. I'll omit those details from my report.'

'Will you tell him about Elwell looking after the grave of his first wife?'

'That, too, is probably best kept from him. He'd find it difficult to understand, but then, he finds the whole concept of marriage somewhat baffling.'

'I feel sorry for the second wife.'

'I think she's contented with her lot, Victor, and since Bedloe is dead, her husband won't have to keep on stalking him. Their life together will be a lot less fraught from now on, I fancy.'

'So we don't charge Elwell?'

'He committed no crime.'

'He tried to run away when he first saw you last night.'

'I put that down to a natural reaction,' said Colbeck. 'It must have been a shock to get back home after midnight and find a detective inspector waiting for him in the house. To his obvious chagrin, Elwell is innocent of the murder. That annoyed him. For the sake of his second wife, I'm glad that it turned out that way.'

'I don't like the idea of letting him go scot-free, sir.'

'Show a little gratitude, Victor. He provided our supper.'

After blowing out the candle, Colbeck opened the church door and led the sergeant out into a bright new day. Both of them blinked in the sunshine. As they began the long walk to the railway station, Leeming remembered someone else.

'What do we do about Manders, sir?'

'We exercise discretion.'

'Could you be more exact?'

'The gamekeeper's fate is in your hands,' said Colbeck. 'You arrested him on what turned out to be misleading evidence. No blame attaches to you for that. Any other detective would have done the same.'

'He shot at me, sir.'

'That's where your judgement comes into play, Victor. Even the most zealous gamekeeper would think twice about killing a poacher or trespasser. He'd simply give him a fright.'

'That's what Manders did to me.'

'Then he wasn't trying to kill you, was he? It was a warning shot.'

Leeming was rueful. 'I suppose so.'

'And did he actually resist arrest or simply fight back when you tried to take the shotgun from him? Don't answer,' he went on quickly, raising his palm to cut off his companion's response. 'Just take time to mull it over. Manders is a surly fellow with less respect for the police than he ought to have. But does he deserve to have criminal charges brought against him and thereby lose his job? That's the decision you have to make.'

'He fought like the devil.'

'So did you, Victor. You overpowered him. That wounded his pride.'

'Manders deserves some kind of punishment.'

'Wait until you've had a shave,' advised Colbeck. 'You may feel a little more benevolent after that.'

Lydia Quayle arrived early at the house and was shown straight upstairs to the bedroom. To her delight, she saw that Madeleine was seated in a chair with her head in the book. Her gift had had the desired effect.

'How far have you got?'

'I'm about halfway through.'

'Shall I tell you what happens?' teased Lydia.

'No, no,' cried Madeleine, 'don't you dare!'

'You're enjoying it, that's the main thing.'

'It's a miracle. I finally found a book that could hold me for more than a couple of minutes. Thank you so much, Lydia. I've never read any of Trollope's books before.'

'*Barchester Towers* is my favourite. I suppose that you should have read *The Warden* first but I couldn't wait to introduce you to the sequel. It kept me laughing for hours. The characters are so wonderful.'

'I didn't realise what I was missing,' said Madeleine, putting the book beside her. 'Since I started painting, I've more or less stopped reading novels. When Robert and I first met, he used to lend me books from his library – most of them by Charles Dickens. Now that I've discovered Trollope, I've got back my enthusiasm for reading.'

'That's a relief. I was afraid you'd throw the book at me as soon as I walked in through the door.'

They laughed. Lydia greeted her properly and gave her a kiss. Madeleine talked excitedly about the novel. She seemed to have forgotten that she was in the later stages of pregnancy and that her visitor really wanted to know how she felt. They chatted amiably for a long time. The doorbell then clanged below.

'That will be the doctor,' said Madeleine, adjusting her dressing gown. 'Please don't go, Lydia. Wait outside for a while. We've so much to talk about and, when the doctor has gone, I'll be able to tell you what he said about me.'

Lydia moved to the door. 'I'll leave you alone, then.'

'Oh, there was one thing . . .'

'Yes?'

'Immediately after you left, someone called here.'

'Who was it?'

'It was a gentleman, apparently. I didn't see him myself.'

'What did he want?'

'He wanted to know who lived here.'

Lydia was shaken. 'And this happened yesterday?'

'It was less than a minute after you'd gone,' said Madeleine. 'It was almost as if he'd been waiting outside for you to leave.'

When they finally got within sight of the station, Colbeck saw something that warmed his heart. Held in place by a man, a small child was perched on a horse as it was being led along. A woman trotted beside them. It was an image of family life that spoke to Colbeck. The adults, he assumed, were the parents of the little girl and her giggles of delight showed how much she was enjoying the ride. The father then lifted her off and handed her to his wife. After kissing both of them fondly, he led the horse on its way.

It was only when they got closer that Colbeck realised he'd been looking at Harry Wills and his family. He hailed the railwayman and the latter stopped. The detectives caught up with him.

'Was that your daughter, Mr Wills?' asked Colbeck.

'Yes, Inspector, that was Helen with my wife, Letty. We'd love to buy Helen a pony but, since we can't afford one, I gave her a ride on Samson instead.' He patted the horse. 'You're much too big for her, aren't you?'

Colbeck recalled the money he'd found hidden away at Bedloe's home. If it eventually found its way to him, Wills would be able to buy a pony, after all.

'What are you doing in Dorchester?' asked Wills.

'We were tracking down a suspect.'

'Did you make an arrest?'

'No,' said Leeming, sourly, 'we had bread and cheese instead.'

'Don't listen to the sergeant,' said Colbeck. 'He's just joking.' Wills was peering at his face. 'And I apologise for not having shaved this morning,' he went on, running a hand over his bristles. 'Are you going to do some more shunting?'

'Yes,' replied Wills. 'Samson is slowly getting better.'

'I thought that trains were supposed to replace horses,' said Leeming.

'For the most part, they have, Sergeant. But there's still work for the horse and I'm glad.' He stroked Samson's neck. 'They're a joy to work with. Talking of which, you'll have to excuse me. There are wagons waiting to be shifted.'

Wills went off in the direction of the marshalling yard, leaving the detectives to go on to the station. They bought their tickets and, since there was a wait, settled down on a bench on the platform.

'At least, *this* one wasn't presented by Mr Feltham,' said Leeming.

'You should never mock philanthropy, Victor.'

'Is that what it is, sir?'

'On reflection,' said Colbeck, 'it's probably not. It's one of the many gifts that Feltham has bestowed upon the town to buy popularity. He may be acting from impure motives but the people of Wimborne nevertheless get the benefit.'

'I'd loved to have been there when the superintendent roasted him.'

'Yes, it would have been an interesting spectacle.'

It was Leeming who stroked his bristles now. Before he'd married, he'd been the proud owner of a bushy beard and regretted the fact that his future wife had disliked it intensely. Estelle had forced him to shave it off. One day's growth of beard made him nostalgic. Reality then intruded. He remembered why they were there.

'We're running out of suspects, sir,' he said. 'I was convinced that Manders was the killer, then we both came round to the view that Jack Elwell was our man.'

'The superintendent picked him out as well.'

'Who does that leave?'

'Oh, we're not short of contenders, Victor. There's that crossing-keeper in West Moors and I daresay that you've still got vestigial doubts about Satchwell.'

'Something about the man worries me, sir.'

'And we haven't eliminated Copsey, that old shepherd. Did he really find the corpse by accident or did he help to put it there?'

'I'd forget Copsey, sir.'

'Why?'

'Because Manders and Elwell both had good reasons to kill Bedloe. The shepherd didn't. What did he stand to gain?'

'That's a good question.'

'I think we should look closer at Tullidge and Satchwell.'

'Then let me add two more names.'

'Who are they, sir?'

'Alice and Betsy,' said Colbeck. 'One of *them* could have murdered Bedloe.'

Rebecca Tullidge always enjoyed a visit to Wimborne on a market day. It got her away from the isolation of her home and allowed her to join the crowds that thronged the square. The noise and bustle brought her fully alive and she didn't mind having to carry a large basket that got heavier and heavier as she bought more groceries. It was her first taste of freedom for a week and she savoured it. Her pleasure was tinged with regret, however. The market had offered much more than the pleasure of haggling and buying. In the past, it had given her the chance to see John Bedloe. Though they never actually met, he'd always be at a particular spot so that they could exchange a glance and a secret smile. Such moments had been treasured by her. It was thrilling to have such an important private moment in a public place and it atoned for his absences.

It was all over now. She would never again see him, resplendent in his uniform, standing on his usual corner and waiting for her to pass. There would be no secret smile to share. Whenever she came to the market from now on, she would miss him. Yet there was still much to cheer her in the experience. Simply being part of a mass of people was exciting. Starved of company at the lodge, she drew comfort from the constant jostling and the babble of many voices.

After buying some potatoes, she decided reluctantly that it was time to go home to face complaints that she'd been away too long. The prospect was daunting. Her brief escape was over for a week and there was no smile from John Bedloe to sustain her until she next went to market. Rebecca began to push her way through the hordes. Then, when she least expected it, something remarkable happened. He was there, after all. She saw his uniform first, then his broad shoulders as he elbowed his way towards her. Impossibly, Bedloe had come back to her.

The cry of joy died in her throat. When he got close, she saw that it was not her lover, after all. It was another railway policeman, the one Bedloe disliked. She'd met him once or twice but didn't really know him. Rebecca tried to turn away but he'd already caught sight of her.

'Good morning, Mrs Tullidge,' he said.

'Oh, hello,' she replied.

'This must be a change for you.'

'It is, Mr Satchwell.'

'You must have a lonely life out there at the lodge.'

'It suits us.'

'It wouldn't suit me or my wife,' he said. 'We like to see people all round us. Most of the time, the only people you see are the ones who shoot past you in trains.'

'Someone has to mind the crossings.'

'Oh, I agree. You provide a vital service. I know how easily deaths can occur at unmanned crossings. We should be grateful to you and Mr Tullidge.'

Wanting to get away, Rebecca lacked the skill to detach herself from the conversation. She was, in any case, mesmerised by his uniform. Staring at that, she could almost believe that she was talking to Bedloe.

'How long have you been there?' he asked.

'Michael has lived there much longer than me,' she replied. 'He and his first wife moved in years ago. It was only when she died that . . .'

'I understand. Did he always want to be a crossing-keeper?'

'No, but he liked the house that came with the job.'

'Yes, that would be a temptation,' said Satchwell. 'What did he do before he got the job?'

'He did all kinds of things before he got work on the railway. Michael grew up on a farm so he started off as a labourer. That meant he was out in all weathers. He didn't like that so he looked for something else.'

'I don't blame him. Born on a farm, was he? Where was that?'

'God's Blessing Green.'

Though it was always a pleasure to visit Madeleine Colbeck, she didn't leave the house with her usual sense of contentment. Lydia Quayle was pulsing with suppressed anger. It was not directed at her friend and had not been on display when she was seated at the bedside. All the time she was talking to Madeleine, however, she was thinking about the man who'd called at the house on the previous evening. The fact that he rang the bell almost immediately after she'd left the house was significant. It confirmed something that had been at the back of her mind for some time. Lydia was primed for action. It was time for a confrontation.

The maidservant opened the door to her and smiled in recognition.

'Oh, good morning, Miss Quayle,' she said.

'Good morning, Dora.'

'It's very nice to see you again.'

'Thank you. Is Miss Myler in?'

'No, I'm afraid she isn't. She went off to the library but won't be long.'

'In that case,' said Lydia, determinedly, 'I'll wait.'

And she stepped into the house.

After a proper shave and a late breakfast, the detectives felt much better. Colbeck was able to look in a mirror without flinching and Leeming's demeanour brightened after the meal. He decided that he would mix tolerance with leniency. When the two of them went to the police station, they had William Manders unlocked from his cell and taken to the room where he'd been interviewed earlier. He regarded the detectives with a compound of resentment, curiosity and a grudging respect.

'Did you have a good night, Mr Manders?' asked Colbeck.

'No,' grunted the other.

'Why was that?'

'I'm being locked up for something I didn't do and the bed in that cell is so hard that I preferred to sleep on the floor.'

'That can't have been any worse than the church pews in which *we* slept,' said Leeming, soulfully. 'I don't want another night like that again.'

'There's no need to bother Mr Manders with *our* problems, Sergeant,' said Colbeck. 'They shrink into invisibility beside his.'

'When do I get out of here?' grumbled Manders.

'We're coming to that.'

'Mr Findlay said that he'd speak to you.'

'And so he did. Like a good employer, he supported his staff.'

'What did he say?'

'He spoke well of you.'

'But he only sees what you show him,' said Leeming. 'If you'd fired a shotgun at *him* and started a fight, he might take a different view.'

'*You* started the fight,' argued Manders.

'No, I didn't.'

'Yes, you did.'

'You punched me in the stomach.'

'That's enough,' said Colbeck, intervening with a decisive gesture. 'Bickering will get us nowhere. Mr Findlay told us that you'd have something to say.'

Manders was about to unleash a stream of expletives but managed to hold them back. A night in custody had effected a slight improvement in his manners.

'I'm sorry,' he said to Colbeck.

'The apology should be directed to the sergeant.'

Manders looked at Leeming. 'I'm sorry for what happened.'

'Do you always shoot at trespassers?' asked Leeming.

'No, I don't.'

'Then why pick on me?'

'I knew why you'd come and, since I didn't want to be bothered with questions about John Bedloe again, I thought I'd have some fun. It was a mistake,' he added, 'and it could have led to an injury. I apologise for shooting, Sergeant. It was stupid of me. I deserved a night on the floor of the cell.'

It was not just a form of words. Manders held his gaze as he spoke and they could both hear the sincerity in his voice. Leeming was still not appeased.

'Why did you resist arrest?'

'I didn't want to be charged with something I didn't do.'

'You should have come quietly.'

'If you hadn't punched me, I might have done.'

Manders was ready to apologise but he was not going to grovel in order to secure his freedom. He felt that he had some right on his side. Colbeck agreed with him to some extent but he left the decision entirely to Leeming. The sergeant kept the prisoner waiting for a long time.

'What you did,' he said, eventually, 'was not only stupid, it was illegal. The police force is not there to provide amusement. We're not targets in a booth at the annual fair. Our job is to protect people – and that includes you – from physical attack or some other unlawful act. As a gamekeeper, you're in a position of authority and are called on to enforce rules of trespass. A person like you, Mr Manders, should be the first to acknowledge the need for a police force and to respect it—'

Leeming broke off because he felt as if he were impersonating Edward Tallis and that shocked him. His admonishment nevertheless had its intended effect. It caused Manders to nod in agreement and look almost sheepish. He was at last viewing the incident from the sergeant's point of view.

'I made a terrible mistake,' he admitted.

Leeming glared at him. 'Then you must expect punishment.'

After leaving the market, Rebecca had managed to get a lift from a farmer who had to drive past West Moors on his way home. Dropped off at the crossing, she went into the lodge to face a stern interrogation. There was no word of thanks for making the effort to do the shopping. All that Tullidge could do was to fire questions at her.

'You're late,' he said, clicking his tongue in disapproval.

'I was as quick as I could be, Michael.'

'I expected you back half an hour ago.'

'There was a lot to buy,' she said, heaving the basket onto the table.

'I think you wasted too much time gossiping.'

'No, I didn't. There was nobody I knew. I only spoke to one person.'

'Who was that?'

'Mr Satchwell, the railway policeman.'

He tensed. 'What did you talk to him for?'

'I couldn't help it. He came up to me.'

'Did he ask you about . . . what happened here on Saturday?'

'No, he didn't.'

'So what did he say?'

'I only spoke to him for a couple of minutes.'

'He must have asked *something*,' pressed Tullidge. 'What was it?'

'It doesn't matter.'

'Come on,' he said, banging the table. 'What did he ask you?'

'He asked me what it was like to live here.'

'Why did he do that?'

'He said it must be lonely. I told him that it suited us.'

'Go on.'

'That was all, really.'

'There must have been more. Policemen are all the same. They're always poking their noses into other people's business. Satchwell is like the rest of them. He can't stop snooping.'

'He was very polite, Michael.'

'You should have walked away from him.'

'I couldn't do that. It would have been rude.'

'We keep ourselves to ourselves, Becky.'

'I know,' she sighed.

'Remember that next time.'

'He was just showing some interest, that's all. He asked me what you did before you got this job and I told him you'd been a farm labourer.'

'That was years ago,' he said, angrily. 'I'm a railwayman now. I've come up in the world. Don't tell anyone what I did in the past, especially not someone like Satchwell. I'm a crossing-keeper. That's all he needs to know.'

'Yes, Michael.'

'Hold your tongue, woman.'

'I'm sorry,' she said. 'I didn't mean to upset you.'

But she'd unwittingly done just that. Rebecca had been unfairly castigated by her husband and – to add to her distress – she had no idea why.

It had been a new departure for Victor Leeming. He'd appeared in court to give evidence on many occasions but he'd never before been asked to act as judge and jury. Colbeck was always ready to give him responsibility and he'd let the sergeant take the lead in the meeting with Manders at the police station. It had given Leeming a feeling of power that was tempered by fears of emulating the superintendent. The last thing he wanted to do was to act and think like Edward Tallis. When he gave his judgement, therefore, he didn't impose a maximum penalty on Manders. Displaying mercy, he gave the man a dressing-down before deciding to dismiss all charges. When they were alone, Colbeck congratulated him.

'Well done, Victor,' he said. 'Manders can run all the way back to the estate now and tell Mr Findlay that he simply owes you the cost of a new top hat.'

'I'll choose the most expensive one in Dorset.'

'I hope that it eludes the same fate as its predecessor.'

Leeming chuckled. 'I'll duck faster next time.'

'The superintendent would have wanted his pound of flesh from Manders.'

'I know, sir. He'd have wanted him dragged through the streets on a hurdle and whipped every inch of the way – and all because of a hole in a top hat.'

'He'd see it as tantamount to a heinous crime,' said Colbeck. 'It's one of the reasons I won't be telling him very much about what happened here this morning. My view is that you were a veritable Solomon.'

'Thank you, sir.'

They'd just left the police station and were trying to pick their way through the crush in the square. The only way to be heard above the hubbub was to raise their voices. Wimborne on market day was pleasantly chaotic. It was Leeming who noticed someone fighting to get to them.

'Here comes the chief spy,' he warned.

'What does Satchwell want, I wonder?'

'He's after some crumbs of information to carry back to Mr Feltham.'

'Oh, I think the superintendent put a stop to all that.'

They stepped into an alleyway so that they had a minimal degree of privacy. Satchwell eventually reached them and said that he'd been looking for them for some time. The railway policeman was not for once in search of news. He'd come to impart it and did so with eagerness.

'I went to that shed close to where Bedloe was found,' he said. 'You'll never guess what I found inside. It was a mattress cut into tiny pieces.'

'Thank you for telling us,' said Colbeck. 'We might well take a look at that. Was there a knife left behind?'

'No, Inspector.'

'That's interesting.'

'I spoke to Mrs Tullidge earlier on,' said Satchwell. 'She'd come to do her shopping.'

'Yes,' said Leeming, 'there'd be far less choice in West Moors. It could never offer anything on the scale of Wimborne.'

'I learnt something you ought to know.'

'And what was that?'

'Her husband grew up on a farm.'

'That doesn't surprise me,' said Colbeck. 'He has the build of a labourer and a weather-beaten face. Working where he does must be a much less hardy existence.'

'I'm not sure why you're telling us about him,' Leeming interjected.

Satchwell smirked. 'Tullidge was born in God's Blessing Green.'

'Don't mention that accursed place to me!'

'And I remembered something that Bert Maycock told me.'

'What was that?'

'Sim Copsey lives in the village,' said Satchwell, as if expecting a round of applause. 'It's a tiny place. He'd have known Tullidge from the time he was born. In other words, they must be friends. Could that be the reason Copsey came to West Moors on Saturday night?'

The lengthy wait had sapped much of Lydia's ire. Back again in a house where she'd known such contentment, she was invaded by pleasant memories. All around her were the packed shelves of her friend's library, the various authors arranged neatly and alphabetically. On the wall above the little fireplace was the painting they'd brought back from a holiday in Florence. That, too, prompted soothing reminiscences. When she'd left Madeleine Colbeck, Lydia had been powered by an unladylike rage. It had slowly been reduced to a sense of mild irritation.

When she finally arrived with a bag of books, Beatrice Myler was delighted to see her friend there. After a warm embrace, she kissed Lydia on both cheeks then ordered a pot of tea. When Lydia said that she might not be staying long, her protests were waved away. They sat down opposite each other.

'Well,' said Beatrice, 'this is a lovely surprise.'

'I came for a reason.'

'Of course, you did. You came to see me and I couldn't be happier. They asked after you at the library, by the way. They know your taste in reading as well as they know mine.' She squeezed Lydia's hand. 'Oh, you're so welcome!'

'I need to ask you a question, Beatrice.'

'Ask anything you like.'

'Please be honest with me.'

'What a dreadful thing to say!' cried the other. 'I'm always honest with you. It's been the basis of our friendship. I confide things in you that I wouldn't divulge to anyone else in the world. You know that.'

'Yes, I do.'

'Then what's all this nonsense about honesty?'

Lydia needed a moment to compose herself. She was already starting to lose her confidence and somehow had to stop it ebbing away. She recalled the moment when Madeleine had told her about the stranger who'd called at her house. It had been like a slap on the face to Lydia. She felt the sharp pain yet again. It emboldened her.

'Did you have me followed?' she asked.

'What an absurd question!'

'Did you, Beatrice? It means a lot to me.'

'I can't think what's got into you.'

'It's the fear of betrayal,' said Lydia, her anger now rising. 'I thought that somebody was following me a couple of days ago but, when I turned round, nobody was there. I had the same feeling yesterday. It was . . . very uncomfortable. Yet when I suddenly looked behind me, once again there was nobody there.'

'Then it was only a figment of your imagination, dear.'

'Oh, no, it wasn't.'

'I should forget the whole thing.'

'You'd like me to do that, wouldn't you?'

'What do you mean?' said Beatrice, defensively. 'I like nothing more than to make you happy, Lydia. Frankly, I can't understand why we're having this unseemly conversation. Let's end it this second.'

'I can't do that, I'm afraid.'

'Why not?'

'You know very well. The person who followed me went too far yesterday. He called at the house I'd visited to find out who lived there. Then he came back here, no doubt to report to you. Don't deny it,' she went on as Beatrice began to twitch and flutter. 'You paid someone to spy on me.'

'It wasn't like that at all, Lydia.'

'Oh, yes, it was.'

'Let me explain.'

'I just couldn't believe that you'd sink so low.'

'I was curious,' said Beatrice, abandoning all attempts at evasion. 'That's all. When you love someone, you want to know everything about them. There's nothing untoward in it, Lydia. It was simple curiosity.'

'All that you had to do was to ask me.'

'All that *you* had to do was to tell me.'

There was anger in Beatrice's voice as well now. She'd shaken off her usual sweetness and was looking at her friend as if about to accuse her of a terrible crime. Lydia responded by raising her voice.

'I didn't dare tell you,' she said, 'because you wouldn't understand.'

'Oh, I understand it perfectly. You've been sneaking off to see that "friend" of yours who's married to Inspector Colbeck. It all started when you got dragged into the murder investigation. *That's* when Mrs Colbeck got to work on you.'

'Madeleine did nothing of the kind!'

'She's obviously a conniving little madam.'

'Beatrice!'

'The moment I set eyes on her, I knew that she'd cause trouble.'

'She stood by me at a time when *you* didn't.'

'It was only because she wanted to lure you away from me.'

'You *drove* me away, Beatrice.'

'I didn't want you involved in all that mess. It was disgusting.'

'It was my family,' yelled Lydia. 'I couldn't just walk away.'

'Why not?' demanded the other. 'You did it once before – you came to me.'

Lydia took a deep breath. 'That's true.'

'And I hoped you'd do so again.'

'So did I for a time,' confessed the other.

'But there was a gap between us that just wouldn't close. It was there every time we met. I knew there was somebody else, Lydia, some manipulative woman trying to win you over and I just had to find out who it was. It was my right. I was entitled to know who was holding you back from me.'

'Nobody has been holding me.'

'I could almost see her grasping hands around you.'

'That's a ludicrous idea.'

'It's that Mrs Colbeck, isn't it? She wants your friendship.'

'Beatrice—'

'She wants to have all the things that we shared when we lived here in the same house. Can't you see how cruel it is to me?' wailed Beatrice. 'I gave you everything. What can a woman like that possibly offer you?'

'Madeleine is having a baby,' said Lydia, calmly.

Beatrice was stunned. 'A baby?'

'It's something your private detective didn't find out, isn't it?'

'She's having a baby?'

'Yes, and Madeleine needs friends at a time like this, especially since her husband is away from London. We enjoy each other's company. It's as simple as that. I've grown very fond of her.'

'You used to be fond of *me* once!'

It was the howl of a dispossessed woman. Beatrice had lost and she knew it. She'd been forced to see the friendship between the two young women in a very different light. Madeleine Colbeck had not enticed her friend away at all. Lydia had gone of her own volition and there was nothing that Beatrice could do to stop her. She could – and had in the past – offer her all kinds of blandishments. They no longer had the same appeal. Having lost her own family, Lydia yearned to belong to another one and she'd found it. The prospect of a child changed everything.

They sat there in silence until the maid brought in a tea tray and set it down. Knowing their respective tastes, she poured two cups of tea and added the requisite amount of milk and sugar to each one. After a little bob, she left the room. Lydia looked around the shelves once more, keenly aware that she'd never set foot in the house again. She was no longer welcome. Pleasant memories that had washed over her earlier were now replaced by thoughts of Beatrice's tantrums and jealousy and capacity for disapproving so strongly of something that Lydia wanted that the latter had invariably bowed to her wishes. They'd lived together on the older woman's terms. It was an unspoken agreement. Had it not been for the murder of her father, Lydia would have stayed there without even imagining that there could be an alternative life for her.

As a result of her friendship with Madeleine, she'd now done so. She'd seen the bloom of motherhood and the glow of fulfilment that it brought. In spite of the dangers and fears that came in its wake, she was given a new vision of her future. Madeleine had reminded Lydia that she was still a young woman, still capable of bringing her own children into the world, still able to create a family of her own. Beatrice was too shrewd and watchful to miss the signs. Sensing the threat, she'd sought to identify it in order to get rid of it. But she was far too late. It was over.

She reached for her cup and stirred in the sugar. Lydia followed suit.

'I'm sorry that it has to end this way, Beatrice,' she said, softly.

'So am I,' whispered the other, 'so am I.'

'Do you wish me to keep in touch?'

'What's the point?'

The gap between them suddenly stretched to an unbridgeable width. Each drank her tea in isolation as if she were the only person in the room. When she'd finished, Lydia rose to her feet and moved to the door.

'Wait,' said Beatrice. 'When is the baby due?'

* * *

Madeleine was caught completely off guard. Having been dozing contentedly in her bed, she was awakened by painful movements she'd never felt before. One hand on her stomach, she used the other to grab the bell beside her and ring it frantically.

CHAPTER SIXTEEN

Having hired a trap in the town, Colbeck elected to take charge of the driving. Victor Leeming had the freedom to look around and see bits of the surrounding countryside that he'd not been able to enjoy before.

'Dorset is starting to grow on me,' he said, admiringly.

'I thought you were missing home.'

'I'm missing Estelle and the children, sir, but that always happens. I'm not missing the filth and fog and villains who lurk in dark corners. No matter where you are in London, you're never far away from criminals of one kind or another.'

'Dorset has its supply of those, Victor.'

'Yes,' said the other, 'but they're small in number and largely confined to petty offences. Constable Maycock showed me his beat book. The only arrests he's made in the last month are for drunkenness, breach of the peace, assault, stealing fowl and urinating over a statue.' He laughed. 'If it was a statue of Mr

Feltham, I'd have let him off. It'd still be a petty offence. We have to deal with serious crime every day.'

'John Bedloe's murder was a serious crime.'

'It's the exception to the rule.'

'Would you rather be working here in rural tranquillity?'

'No, sir, I'd fall asleep within days.'

Colbeck smiled. 'So much for the beauty of the open countryside!'

'It's lovely to look at, sir, but nothing ever *happens*.'

They drove on until the West Moors lodge finally came into sight. Leeming had doubts about the value of their trip and felt they should be looking elsewhere.

'We ought to put Satchwell himself under the microscope, sir.'

'But he's actually trying to help us.'

'That could be a means of throwing suspicion on to someone else.'

'He stumbled on a coincidence that deserves examination,' said Colbeck. 'Two men were in the vicinity of the murder scene on Saturday night. One of them was Copsey, who has never adequately accounted for his presence there, and the other is Michael Tullidge, who lives nearby. If there's a connection between them, we need to find out what it is.'

'I can tell you the connection, sir.'

'Can you?'

'Yes – neither of them had a motive to kill Bedloe. We should be looking for someone who was obsessed with the idea of revenge.'

'We found two of those – Manders and Elwell.'

Colbeck pulled on the reins and brought the horse to a halt beside the shed.

Leeming sized it up. 'Is this the place Satchwell told us about, sir?'

'Yes, Victor. He's been doing our job for us.'

'I still don't trust him.'

When they'd got out of the trap, Colbeck put the sergeant to the test, asking him to find a way to unlock the shed. It took Leeming less than twenty seconds to discover where the key had been hidden. Slipping it into the lock, he twisted it until the door swung open. They looked in at the tattered remains of the mattress.

'It's exactly as Satchwell described,' said Colbeck.

'I think I'd prefer the church pew to a night on that. Somebody must have attacked it in a real frenzy.'

'But why do it *after* the event, as it were? Having disposed of Bedloe, why didn't the killer simply stroll across here and use his knife on the mattress there and then?'

'Maybe he was eager to get away as fast as possible.'

'That's one explanation, Victor.'

'Can you think of another?'

'Yes,' said Colbeck, 'this is not the work of the killer but of someone else.'

'I know who you're talking about, sir – one of those women.'

'Which one was it – Alice or Betsy?'

'Suppose that one of them *was* the killer. You thought that was possible.'

'I did and it would certainly simplify matters.'

'It would mean that our journey here was in vain,' said Leeming. 'Tullidge and Copsey would be off the hook.'

Estelle Leeming had left her mother to pick up the two boys from school. After making her way across London, she got to the house and was looking forward to the prospect of seeing Madeleine and having a long rest. In the event, she got no further than the front door. The servant who answered the bell was white with anxiety.

'Hello, Mrs Leeming,' she said. 'I'm afraid that you can't come in today.'

'Why not?'

'The doctor is here.'

Estelle was alarmed. 'Is Mrs Colbeck all right?'

'She's gone into labour.'

'Already?'

'There are complications. Mrs Colbeck is being moved to hospital.'

'Oh dear – that's terrible!'

Estelle was in a dilemma, desperate to know what was going on yet feeling she'd only be in the way if she insisted on entering the house to await news. She thanked the servant and turned away. Her immediate thought was that Colbeck should be told. He'd never forgive himself for being away at such a critical moment. Estelle had no means of contacting him but she knew someone who might be able to get in touch. Under the pressure of circumstance, she did something she couldn't normally afford and waved down a cab.

It was some time since Colbeck had spoken to the crossing-keeper and Tullidge's manners had not improved in the interim. He was as rude and unhelpful as ever. Leeming was impressed by the way that the inspector questioned him without once raising his voice or losing his temper.

'Let's go over it once more,' said Colbeck.

Tullidge scowled. 'Why waste my time?'

'Don't you want this murder to be solved, sir?'

'Makes no difference to me.'

'Oh, I think it does. I'll wager that you've had dozens of people coming here to see exactly where it happened. Do you want that to go on? The sooner we catch the killer, the sooner the children will stop re-enacting the murder in fun down there on the line. It's unhealthy to let them do that kind of thing, Mr Tullidge. It puts gruesome ideas into their heads. It also makes them trespass. Is that what you want?'

'No, it isn't.'

'Then it's high time you started to help,' said Leeming.

'I'm on duty.'

'So are we.'

Tullidge looked from one to the other. Both were clearly intent on questioning him. They couldn't be ignored. He decided that it was better to listen to them and make their visit as short as possible.

'Ask me what you want to know, Inspector,' he said.

'What did you do after you left the pub on Saturday night?' said Colbeck.

'I told the superintendent that.'

'Tell us.'

'I left there after several pints of beer and got back around ten-thirty.'

'Your wife said it was eleven.'

'Becky now says it was ten-thirty. Ask the superintendent.'

'That's rather difficult. He's in London at the moment.'

'Why did you leave the pub earlier than usual?' asked Leeming.

'I felt like it,' replied Tullidge.

'Do you often do things on impulse?'

'What d'you mean?'

'Well, I don't know exactly what you do out here, Mr Tullidge, but it's obviously governed by a strict timetable. Every day must

315

go like clockwork. It must be the same when you're off duty. You keep to regular times.'

'Saturday was different.'

'Really?'

'I wasn't feeling well.'

'That's the first time you've mentioned that,' said Colbeck. 'If you'd felt sick, you'd surely have mentioned it to the friends you spent the evening with at the Waggon and Horses. I spoke to them. Neither Mr Rawles nor Mr Delafield recalls your saying anything about feeling unwell. Why is that?'

'Look,' said Tullidge in exasperation, 'all I did was to have a drink with two friends. What am I supposed to have done wrong?'

'You lied about why you left and where you went.'

'I'd been drinking. I was confused.'

'Is that why it took you an hour to get back home?'

'It was only half an hour. Becky will tell you.'

'We'll talk to her in due course. Right now, we have another question for you. Do you know a man named Simon Copsey?'

'No, I don't.'

'Yet he was brought up in the same village as you.'

'I left there years ago.'

'You must have known him. He's a shepherd.'

'I'd had enough of farming, Inspector,' said Tullidge. 'It was hard, grinding work for low pay and little time off. Working on the railway is a lot better.'

'The reason we ask about Copsey,' explained Leeming, 'is that he was right here on Saturday night. He and his dog found the dead body.'

'So I heard.'

'What was he doing in this neck of the woods?'

'Ask him.'

'And why deny knowing him when he lived in God's Blessing Green at the same time as you? I've met Copsey. He's not a man you'd easily forget. And I've been to the village,' he went on. 'It's one of those places where everybody knows everybody else. You see, it occurs to us that the only reason Copsey would come here is that he wanted to see a friend, and the only friend he's likely to have in West Moors is someone from God's Blessing Green.'

'I may have known him years ago,' said the other, vaguely. 'I forget names.'

'Is the railway company aware of that?' said Colbeck. 'You're uncertain about times and unreliable when it comes to names. Those are two very poor qualifications for the job that you do.'

Tullidge became truculent. 'I get no complaints.'

'You'd get plenty from me, if I employed you.'

'And from me,' added Leeming.

'The LSWR is very particular when it comes to appointing crossing-keepers. They expect such people to have clear heads and good memories.'

'Why don't you just leave me alone?' shouted Tullidge.

'We're hunting a killer. When we do that, we don't leave *anyone* alone.' Colbeck consulted his watch. 'According to the timetable, there's a train due in five minutes. If you can remember how to do it, I suggest you close the gates.'

Caleb Andrews was sitting in his living room with a newspaper when he heard the clatter of hooves. Through the window, he saw a hansom cab pulling up outside. The sight put unexpected energy in his old legs. Casting the newspaper aside, he was out of the chair instantly. He opened the front door in time to see Estelle Leeming paying the driver. Andrews rushed over to her.

'Has the baby come yet?' he asked. 'Has my grandson been born?'

'No, Mr Andrews – there's been a problem.'

'What sort of problem?'

'Give me a moment,' she said.

She handed over the last of the money and the cab drew away from the kerb.

'What's going on, Estelle?'

'Can we go inside the house?'

'Yes, yes, follow me.'

When they got inside, she explained what had happened when she'd called at the Colbeck house earlier. As far as she knew, the baby had not been lost but a crisis had occurred and the doctor had to be sent for.

'Complications?' he asked. 'What sort of complications?'

'I don't know.'

'Poor Madeleine!'

'I think that her husband should be told,' said Estelle. 'He wouldn't forgive us for keeping anything as important as this from him.'

'I agree. Robert should be here.'

'The quickest way would be to send a telegraph to Wimborne. I thought of going to Scotland Yard and speaking to the superintendent but Victor says he's an ogre. I'm too frightened to go. I'd be afraid that he'd refuse.'

'We can forget him,' said Andrews, reaching for his coat. 'There's another way to get the message through and that's to deliver it in person. I'll do that.'

She was amazed. 'You'll go all the way to Dorset?'

'I'd go all the way to the North Pole for my grandson. First of all, I'll get over to the hospital to see what's wrong with

Madeleine. There's no point in charging off unless I have some details to pass on.'

'You're right.'

'Thank you for coming here, Estelle.'

'You were my only hope.'

'I'll be on a train to Wimborne very soon.'

'Be sure to give Victor my love, won't you?'

'He's going to need it,' said Andrews. 'If Robert is hauled off the case – and I'll insist that he is – Victor will be in charge of a murder investigation on his own. That will be a real test for him.'

Leeming felt sorry for her. He pitied any woman married to Michael Tullidge and forced to share a narrow, dull, repetitive life. Having suggested that the sergeant spoke to her, Colbeck stayed outside to watch the trains go by and to keep the crossing-keeper occupied. In her husband's presence, Rebecca would be constrained. Even without him there, she was parsimonious with words.

'You told the inspector that your husband got back here on Saturday night around eleven o'clock. Is that right, Mrs Tullidge?'

'Yes, it is,' she replied.

'Yet you claimed it was ten-thirty when you spoke to Superintendent Tallis.'

'That's right.'

'Why did you change your mind?'

'I got the time wrong.'

'I can't believe that you did, somehow,' said Leeming. 'When the inspector went to the Waggon and Horses, he met a Mrs Vout.'

'Yes, her husband is the landlord.'

'She's very fond of you.'

'We're good friends.'

'Would you say that she knows you well?'

'Yes, Sergeant.'

'According to her, you're a rock for your husband. Without you to help him, he'd never be able to do his job properly.'

'That's not true at all. Michael is very good at his job.'

'I'm only reporting what Mrs Vout told the inspector.'

'Well, Maggie was wrong.'

It was evident to Leeming that he'd get no criticism of Tullidge out of his wife. She was too afraid to tell the truth. Rebecca had a look in her eyes and a defensive posture that he'd seen before when he'd called at houses where wives had been battered by their husbands. Even with broken limbs and smashed faces, the women had been reluctant to make complaints. They endured suffering in order to keep another assault at bay. Leeming didn't think that Tullidge actually beat his wife but he could see that the man had a strong hold over her.

'Do you know a man named Simon Copsey?' he asked.

'No, I don't.'

'He's better known as Sim Copsey. He's a shepherd.'

'I've never heard of him.'

'He's lived in God's Blessing Green all his life. Your husband was born there, I gather.'

'Yes, he was.'

'So he must obviously have met Copsey at some time.'

'I expect so.'

'He denies it.'

'Then he *didn't* meet this man.'

'You accept your husband's word without question, do you?'

'Yes, I do.'

'Then I wish my wife did the same,' he said with a grin. 'It would save a lot of arguments. You're a rare woman, Mrs Tullidge. You think your husband is a saint.' He saw her mouth twitch involuntarily. 'That kind of devotion is inspiring.'

Rebecca was getting increasingly restive under his questioning.

'I don't see why you have to ask me these things.'

'It's a matter of routine, Mrs Tullidge.'

'I can't help you.'

'As a matter of fact, you already have.' She was startled. 'I asked about Copsey because he was the person who stumbled on Mr Bedloe's dead body.' There was a second twitch around her lips. 'What was a man who lives in God's Blessing Green doing down here on Saturday night?'

'I don't know.'

'We think that we do, Mrs Tullidge. We have one answer.'

'What is it?'

'He came to see someone from the same village – in short, your husband.'

'No,' she said, 'that can't be right.'

'Why not?'

'Michael would have told me about it.'

'Does your husband confide *everything* in you?'

'Yes, he does,' she said, unconvincingly.

'I could never do that with my wife,' he confessed, 'because it would upset her to hear about some of the things I've seen and done. I protect her from knowing any sordid details. It's what she prefers.' He studied her face and she was palpably ill at ease under his scrutiny. 'Mrs Vout told the inspector that you were a brave woman.'

'I wouldn't say that.'

'Your friend said you're never afraid to go out in the dark.'

'I . . . do have to go out in the evenings.'

'Doesn't the murder make any difference?' he asked. 'A man had his life snatched away from him only a few hundred yards from here. That would scare most people, Mrs Tullidge. They wouldn't dare to go out in the dark on their own.'

'No, they probably wouldn't.'

'The killer might come back. Have you ever thought about that?'

'Yes, I have,' she admitted.

'Then you were right to do so because he did just that.'

She gasped. 'How do you know?'

'The inspector and I looked into that shed further down the track. There's a mattress in there. We believe that it was used by Mr Bedloe and a woman friend of his. Well, it's no use to anyone now,' he explained. 'The killer returned and slashed it to bits.'

Rebecca's worst fear had been realised. The killer had come back, after all. What if she'd been near the shed when he was there? Would she have suffered the same fate as Bedloe? Rebecca was in his power. Supposing he came back to make demands on her? How could she possibly cope? Panic seized her and she began to tremble violently all over. Before Leeming could move, she suddenly went weak at the knees and collapsed in a heap on the floor.

Lydia Quayle was in a state of confusion. Simultaneously, she felt a sense of loss and a sense of gain. The loss arose from the severing of her friendship with Beatrice Myler. Only now that she'd finally broken away could she appreciate how much the older woman had done for her. When Lydia had been driven away from her family, Beatrice had been there to help, soothe and offer an alternative life for her. The two of them had been supremely satisfied with that life. It was only when the murder of Lydia's father had allowed the real world to intrude that she saw what she was missing and, through Madeleine Colbeck, had learnt to enlarge her vision. When she lived with Beatrice, she looked, dressed and behaved older than she really was. Madeleine had reminded Lydia of her true age.

Although she was dogged by regret, therefore, she felt liberated. In escaping from Beatrice's shadow, she could do what she wanted at last. And she now could do so without having to conceal anything. The idea that she'd been tailed by a private detective had wounded her deeply and the pain had increased when Beatrice had tried to justify it. There was no need for subterfuge with Madeleine. Their friendship was open and unenforced. They simply loved each other's company. With that thought in mind, and secure in the knowledge that nobody was following her this time, she made her way to the house to call on Madeleine. A shock awaited her.

Caleb Andrews was highly critical. Having devoted most of his working life to the London and Birmingham Railway and, after its amalgamation, to the London and North Western Railway, he always looked down on other railway companies. His greatest scorn was reserved for the Great Western Railway but he found plenty to sneer at among its rivals. The journey to Wimborne gave him the opportunity to deride the LSWR. To begin with, the train was late and, when it did leave the station, it did so with the kind of sudden jerk that he would never have subjected his passengers to when he was on the footplate. The compartment was no more than adequate and the seating less than comfortable for a four-hour journey. Had he not been on an errand of mercy, he could have grumbled happily all the way to his destination.

As it was, his mind was focused on his daughter. He'd arrived at the General Lying-In Hospital in a state of alarm. Though a doctor had kindly given him a brief description of his daughter's problem, Andrews had not been able fully to understand it. He chided himself for his woeful ignorance of the details of childbirth. His wife's pregnancy had been entirely without mishap and he'd hoped that Madeleine would enjoy a similar experience. Clearly, that was not going to happen. One thing that would give her some peace of mind was the presence of her husband and that was the mission that Andrews set himself. He didn't care at what stage the investigation was. Colbeck had to abandon it. Because he was still somewhat in awe of him, Andrews had never really quarrelled with his son-in-law or tried to interfere in his domestic life. This time it was different. If the inspector hesitated for a second, Andrews was going to issue a demand. Whatever happened, he was not going to return to London without Colbeck.

'Are you sure that you're all right, Mrs Tullidge?'

'Yes, yes,' she whispered.

'The sergeant told me what happened.'

'I'm fine now.'

'I don't think that you are.'

'Going to market today tired me out.'

'There's more to it than that,' said Colbeck, gently. 'Isn't there?'

Victor Leeming knew his limitations. He was able to lift Rebecca onto the sofa and to revive her with a glass of water but he suddenly felt out of his depth. Something had upset the woman at a deep level and he lacked the skill to draw the truth out of her. When he heard a train coming, he knew that Tullidge would be occupied so he slipped out of the lodge, told Colbeck what had happened and changed places with him. Leeming would now distract the crossing-keeper while the inspector took on a more delicate assignment.

'Anything you tell me will be in strict confidence,' he promised her. 'Your husband will not hear a word of it.'

'I've nothing to say, Inspector,' she murmured.

'Oh, I believe that you do and, until I hear what it is, I'm going to keep coming back here time and time again. I admire your loyalty to your husband but we are dealing with a case of murder, Mrs Tullidge. That takes precedence over anything else. Don't you agree?' She gave a reluctant nod. 'We both know that your husband took the best part of an hour to get home from the Waggon and Horses on Saturday night. Even if it had been only half an hour, I'd still want to know how he spent it. Wouldn't you?'

'Michael explained that.'

'He came up with a paltry excuse, Mrs Tullidge.'

'I accept his word.'

'With respect,' he said, softly, 'that's what you've been trained to do because you're too afraid to question it. But you gave yourself away when the sergeant was in here with you. When he mentioned that the killer had been back, it was too much for you and you fainted.'

'I didn't feel well.'

'Let me suggest *why* you didn't feel well, Mrs Tullidge.' She looked anxiously towards the door. 'It's all right. Your husband won't come in. The sergeant will see to that. You have to make an important decision. Are you going to keep the truth hidden for the rest of your life and let it gnaw away inside you? Or are you going to put the murder victim first, as you should do?' She let out a yelp. 'Yes, I know it's difficult. It must be agonising for you and

I do sympathise. But I'm convinced that you can help us to solve this case, Mrs Tullidge.'

'No, no, I can't.'

'Think about that missing hour on Saturday night,' he suggested. 'It must surely have crossed your mind that there's one reason why your husband took so long to come back here. He was committing a murder.'

He could see the tears welling up in her eyes and thought for a moment that she was about to agree with what he'd said. Instead, she lost all control. Weeping piteously, she flung herself into his arms and clung on with desperation. Colbeck had provoked a response but it was not the one he'd expected. What he'd just learnt was that Rebecca Tullidge had been the woman Bedloe had expected to see on Saturday. The discovery shone a whole new light on the investigation.

Though he was supposed to be on duty, Satchwell couldn't resist taking time off to report to Feltham. The future mayor deserved to hear the good news. Unfortunately, he was nowhere to be found at first. Satchwell eventually ran him to earth near the minster.

'I found you at last,' he said, gratefully.

'And you don't find me in a good mood,' warned Feltham. 'I've just wasted over an hour trying to persuade Councillor Naismith to vote for me. He refused point-blank to commit himself.'

'I thought that he'd already done so, sir.'

'So did I.'

'What changed his mind?'

'Godfrey Preece must have got at him.'

'Then I can tell you something that might coax him back.'

'Really?' said Feltham. 'Then I want to hear it.'

'Arrests are in the offing.'

'How do you know?'

'I did something you thought impossible,' said Satchwell, swelling with pride. 'I solved the murder.'

He went on to explain how he'd linked together the two people who'd been at or near the murder scene on Saturday night. As he told his story, Satchwell convinced himself that Tullidge and Copsey had acted together to commit the crime, even though he could advance no credible motive for their doing so. For his part, Feltham was too delighted with the revelation to look too closely into it. The murder had been solved and the town had been cleansed. It was the fresh impetus he needed for his campaign. All he needed to do was to make sure that he reaped the full benefit of good publicity.

'Well done!' he said, shaking Satchwell's hand. 'Have the two arrests actually been made yet?'

'One of them certainly has, sir. They'll have gone for Tullidge first. I daresay that Inspector Colbeck and the sergeant are on their way to arrest Sim Copsey now.'

'Are you *certain* about that, sir?'

'Yes, I am.'

'Did she confess?'

'Mrs Tullidge didn't need to put it into words.'

'No wonder her husband wanted to kill Bedloe.'

'But he didn't, Victor.'

'He had the strongest motive possible if his wife was—'

'Her husband was unaware of what had been going on,' said Colbeck.

'What makes you think that, sir?'

'If he *had* known, Mrs Tullidge would have been murdered

327

as well. You've met him. Can you see a man like that letting her stay alive?'

'No, I couldn't,' said Leeming. 'He'd kill her *and* Bedloe.'

'Mrs Tullidge is nursing a terrible secret. It's no wonder she's in such a state. She's terrified that her husband will find out.'

'I can't say that I'm sympathetic, sir.'

'Why not?'

'She committed adultery.'

'I think she was driven to do it, Victor. She was deeply unhappy.'

'That's no excuse, sir.'

'I'm not trying to excuse it, simply to understand it. When I met them for the first time,' admitted Colbeck, 'it never crossed my mind that Mrs Tullidge could have been involved with John Bedloe. She seemed so completely under the thumb of her husband. She hardly moves without his permission.'

'She was taking a terrible risk.'

'I think she realises that now. The fact that she was prepared to take that risk proves just how much she must have loved Bedloe. Well,' he continued, 'we have at last identified one of his conquests.'

'Yes,' said Leeming. 'We know who Alice is now.'

They were in the trap as it headed towards God's Blessing Green and the sergeant was marvelling at the way that Colbeck controlled the horse with such ease. It was something he'd signally failed to do when he was holding the reins.

'What did you notice about him?' asked Colbeck.

'Tullidge?'

'Yes. While I was trying to calm his wife down, you spent a fair amount of time in his company.'

'It was not by choice, sir. He's a miserable devil.'

'What else?'

'He's as dull as dishwater,' said Leeming. 'I'd hate to live in a small house with someone like that. He's oppressive.'

'I think you missed something.'

'Did I?'

'Tullidge had been drinking.'

'You'd never have guessed it.'

'He's learnt to disguise it, Victor. In his job, he has to. If he was caught touching alcohol on duty, it would be the end of his life as a crossing-keeper.'

Michael Tullidge could hardly contain his fury. Conscious that he was being detained on purpose by Leeming, he wanted to go into the lodge to hear exactly what Colbeck was saying to his wife. Whenever he tried to do so, another train would be due and he'd have to attend to his duties. When the detectives finally departed, he rushed into the building only to find that Rebecca was no longer there. She appeared to have slipped out of the building altogether. It was some time before she turned up again. Tullidge looked as if he wanted to strike her.

'Where've you been?' he demanded, waving a fist.

'I went for a walk.'

'Why?'

'I had a headache.'

'You didn't tell me.'

'You'd have stopped me going.'

'And so I would have. You were away most of the morning.'

'We needed things from the market.'

He peered closely at her. 'You've been crying.'

'I told you. I had a headache. I was in pain.'

'You never cry.'

'Well, I did this time.'

She tried to move away but he grabbed her by her shoulders.

'What did you tell that inspector?'

'He was kind to me.'

'I'm asking you what you told him.'

'It was what you made me say, Michael,' she replied. 'I told him that you got back here at half past ten on Saturday and that it might even have been earlier than that. You'd had a lot to drink so I put you straight to bed.'

'What did he say to that?'

'He said nothing at all.'

'You were in there a long time with him.'

'It didn't seem like it. He's a real gentleman. He was very considerate.'

Tullidge sneered. 'That's just a trick to get you to talk,' he said. 'I didn't take to him at all – or to that pig-faced sergeant of his. What did *he* ask you?'

'He wanted to know about a man named Copsey.'

'And what did you tell him?'

'I'd never heard of him. That's the truth.'

'He's a shepherd,' said Tullidge. 'He lives in God's Blessing Green. I must have met him when I was there but I don't remember him. Those days are long gone. I never want to work on a farm again.'

'What *do* you want, Michael?'

It was as if he'd never heard the question. He went off into a kind of trance and his eyelids flickered. All that she could do was to wait until he suddenly became aware of her presence again. His anger surged again.

'Where've you been, woman?'

Rebecca was worried. 'I've already told you that once.'

* * *

They got to Manor Farm without incident. Having arrived there thoroughly jangled the last time, Leeming was gratified to have more composure now. They found the old shepherd sitting on an upturned bucket as he munched his way through some bread and cheese. As his head nodded vigorously, the remains of his hat came perilously close to disintegrating altogether. Copsey stared at the inspector.

'I've seen ye somewhere afore.'

'Yes,' replied Colbeck. 'I bought you some beer at the Jolly Shepherd.'

'I niver forgets a gintl'mun.'

'Then you'll remember me as well,' said Leeming.

'Niver seen ye afore in my life,' claimed Copsey before emitting a loud cackle. 'I remembers ye now, Sergeant. Ye wanted to know what I was a-doing in West Moors last Saturday.'

'We've come to ask the same question.'

'Then ye'll get the same answer.'

'We don't want any more lies.'

'I went to see my sweet'eart.'

'If you're going to stick to that story,' said Colbeck, brusquely, 'you'll have to come with us to the police station in Wimborne. You're well known there, I gather. We were warned that you had a habit of telling outrageous lies.'

'It's no lie,' insisted Copsey.

'Then give us her name at once and we'll go and speak to her.'

The shepherd spat out some cheese. 'No, no, you can't do that!'

'Does she reside in West Moors?'

'Yes, she does.'

'Then we'll take you with us and knock on every door until we find this poor woman who's fallen under your spell.'

'She doesn't exist, Inspector,' said Leeming.

'I know that, you know that and Mr Copsey also knows that. To expose his lie, I suggest that we drag him off there right now.'

He and the sergeant grabbed an arm apiece and lifted Copsey bodily from the bucket. As they carried him across the farmyard, his legs were flailing around.

'Put me down,' he demanded.

'Your sweetheart is waiting for you,' taunted Leeming.

'She 'as an 'usband.'

'Then he'll be most interested to meet you.'

'Wait!'

Copsey's yell brought Sam to his aid, yapping at the detectives but unable to stop them carrying his master towards the trap. Copsey came up with a whole battery of alternative explanations for his visit to West Moors and they rejected each one. It was only when they threatened to refresh his memory by dipping him in the water trough that he gave in. They lowered him to the ground. Sam nestled against him.

'Bert Maycock niver man'andled me like that,' he complained.

'You've never been a suspect in a murder enquiry before,' said Leeming.

'I killed nobody.'

'So what were you doing in West Moors that night?'

'No more evasion,' cautioned Colbeck, 'or we'll be very angry. We've already spoken to Michael Tullidge and we know that you and he grew up in the same village. *He* was the reason you went there on Saturday night, wasn't he?'

'Is that what 'e told ye?' asked Copsey, slyly.

'He gave us his story. We'd like to hear yours now.'

'Otherwise,' said Leeming, 'we'll drown you in that trough.'

Sim Copsey turned to his dog for advice but all that the animal could do was to crouch down on the ground in submission. The shepherd decided to cooperate. Beckoning them to follow, he led them through a cluster of farm buildings and outhouses until they came to a large hut. Though he had a cottage in the village, he also had the use of the hut at the farm if he needed to stay over at night. It was a ramshackle place with gaps in the roof and a door that was almost falling off but it was clearly prized by Copsey. He took them inside and they recoiled from the almost overpowering reek. At the far end of the hut was an area concealed behind a curtain made of old sacking. The shepherd pulled it back like a conjurer revealing the assistant whose disappearance he'd apparently contrived minutes earlier.

A large pot stood on a table. Beside it were a number of Kilner jars. Under the table was a sack of potatoes. Other sacks stood beside it. Copsey tapped the largest of them with his finger.

'Malted barley is the main thing,' he said, smirking, 'then there's all kinds of secret bits and bobs I puts in it.'

'What are they for?' asked Leeming.

'Can't ye guess?'

'He's making poteen,' said Colbeck, 'or something like it, anyway.'

Copsey picked up a Kilner jar. 'Would ye like to taste it?'

'No, thank you.'

'What about ye, Sergeant?'

'I value my life too much,' replied Leeming. 'Is that what took you to West Moors on Saturday?' Copsey nodded. 'Were you selling some of your foul potion to Michael Tullidge?'

'I was. 'E's got a taste for it,' said Copsey. 'I took some more last night.'

'You were right, Inspector. Tullidge had been drinking.'

'It doesn't leave such a smell in the mouth as beer.'

Leeming turned to Copsey. 'Is this what you do when you're not looking after sheep?'

The shepherd grinned. 'It's my 'obby and it brings in a few pennies.'

'How long have you been supplying Tullidge?'

'It must be a month or two.'

'Then he may have been drinking on duty for some time,' said Colbeck. 'That's serious. We'd better get back there, Sergeant. A man like that is a menace if he's left in charge of people's safety.'

Leeming was downcast. 'I thought we came here to arrest a killer.'

Colbeck walked across to the table, opened a jar and sniffed it.

'We may have found a killer, after all,' he said. 'It's this.'

It had started with an occasional nip when he was off duty but it gave him too much pleasure to be rationed. Michael Tullidge, hitherto addicted to beer, had slowly fallen into the habit of staving off the boredom of his daily round by drinking a small amount of gin. While his wife was in the kitchen, he sneaked off into the garden and unlocked the little shed at the bottom of it. Hidden behind some implements was the little stone bottle that Copsey had sold him the night before because Saturday's supply had already run out. Tullidge had a long gulp of the gin and felt it course through his body. Revived by the taste and fortified by its effect, he hid the bottle, left the shed and locked it up. As if in a daze, he wandered across to one of the crossing gates and closed it. After doing the same on the other side of the track, he leant against the gate and went off into a reverie.

Minutes later, a train approached from Poole Junction, puffing furiously away and expecting to tear past the crossing without impediment. But, all of a sudden, there was an obstruction on the line. At the last moment, a man seemed to wander into the path of the locomotive and was hit with irresistible force. Michael Tullidge was killed instantly and it would never be known if he died completely by accident or by design.

The detectives returned to West Moors and saw a hideous scene. Though it stayed on the rails, the train had come to a halt further up the track and many of the passengers were leaning out to see what had happened. The crossing gates were closed but a small audience had gathered outside each one to stare in horror. Someone had covered the mangled remains of Tullidge with a tarpaulin and railway policemen – including Satchwell – were trying to drive people away. Jumping out of the trap, Colbeck ran across to Satchwell and asked for details. When he'd heard them, he rushed into the lodge to see how Rebecca Tullidge was coping. Sitting bolt upright on the sofa, she was being comforted by Margaret Vout. There were no tears in Rebecca's eyes just a look of glassy disbelief. Her days at the crossing were over.

Colbeck quickly rejoined the sergeant and told him what he'd learnt.

Leeming was astonished. 'Tullidge committed suicide?'

'That's not at all clear. Witnesses say that he just wandered in front of the train as if he'd forgotten it was coming.'

'Copsey's gin may have had something to do with that.'

'There's nothing we can do here, Victor,' he said. 'We need to get back.'

'But where are we going, sir? We set out with two suspects in mind and we don't have a single one left.'

'Yes, we do.'

'Well, I don't see one,' said Leeming.

'Look at that tarpaulin and think what's underneath.'

'It's what's left of Tullidge, sir.'

'Copsey saved John Bedloe from being sliced apart like that,' recalled Colbeck, 'and he showed me the exact position in which the body had been laid across the lines. I should have remembered that.'

'You said it was as if someone wanted to crucify him.'

'It meant the killer had a Christian upbringing.'

'Jack Elwell had that.'

'So did someone else.'

'Who are you talking about?'

'The person who *did* kill Bedloe,' said Colbeck, working it out in his mind. 'When I took him to Dr Keddle's house, he went down on his knees beside the corpse. I thought he was offering up a prayer for the soul of his cousin. In fact, he was probably asking God for forgiveness.'

'Harry Wills?'

'Yes – it has to be him.'

'But he had no motive, sir.'

'Oh, I think he did, Victor, and it's time we found out what it was.'

Caleb Andrews sat impatiently on the bench donated by Ambrose Feltham and cursed the London and South Western Railway. It had given him a bumpy ride to Wimborne and, he'd just been told, there'd been a fatality on the line at West Moors. Finding his son-in-law had not been as easy as he'd hoped. When he'd first reached the town, he'd discovered where Colbeck was staying but there was no sign of him at the King's Head. He therefore left a message there to the effect that he would wait at the railway station until the inspector finally appeared. Having resigned himself to the possibility that he might be there for a long time, he had the pleasant surprise of seeing a trap heading at speed towards the station. Someone who looked remarkably like his son-in-law was holding the reins. Andrews dashed out of the station to greet him.

Astounded to see who was there, Colbeck brought the trap to a skidding halt.

'What's happened?' he asked, jumping from the vehicle.

'I've come to fetch you, Robert.'

'Has the baby been born yet?'

'No,' said Andrews. 'Maddy's gone into labour but there's a problem.'

'What's wrong with her?'

'The doctor said that the baby had turned round and it might be a case of – what did he call it? – a breech delivery. That's more difficult so they've taken her to hospital. She needs you.'

Colbeck was consumed with guilt. While he'd been charging around the Dorset countryside, his wife was undergoing all manner of pain and danger. When she'd been moved to hospital as a precaution, it must have caused her great alarm. What she'd hoped would be a relatively straightforward birth in her own home had now become something more complex. Colbeck could only guess at her distress.

'I'll have to go, Victor,' he said. 'You must take over now.'

'Don't worry about me, sir. I'll make the arrest.'

'Take the train to Dorchester and confront him. If he's not at work, he may be at home. I have his address here.' Pulling out his notebook, he opened it to the relevant page. Leeming hastily copied the information into his own notebook. 'If you feel you need help, call at the police station beforehand.'

'Forget about me, sir. You go back home as soon as you can.'

'Thank you.'

'Mr Andrews is the one to thank,' said Leeming, turning to the old man. 'But for you, the inspector wouldn't have known that there was a problem.'

'He's lucky that he knows it now,' said Andrews, waspishly. 'It took the LSWR ages to get me here. Why couldn't you solve a murder near the London and North Western Railway? Their trains always run on time and nobody ever steps in front of them.'

When it had been opened almost a century earlier, it was known as the Westminster New Lying-In Hospital. Just over fifty years later, it was rebuilt on the east side of York Road in Lambeth. Constructed of white brick and ornamented with stone pillars, it was a neat, square building that rose to four storeys. As she gazed up at it, Lydia Quayle found it elegant and reassuring. The first person she met as she went through the door was Estelle Leeming.

'What's happened?' she asked.

'Mrs Colbeck is comfortable. That's all they'd tell me.'

'Weren't you allowed to see her?'

'Only close family members can do that, Miss Quayle.'

'Do you know exactly what's wrong with her?'

'I don't, I'm afraid, but they wouldn't have moved her here unless they were concerned. I've been hanging on in case of any news.'

'What about Inspector Colbeck? He should be here.'

'He will be,' said Estelle. 'I'm certain of that.'

Both the driver and the fireman of the locomotive that had hit Michael Tullidge had been shocked by the incident. It took them some time to recover. When they felt well enough, they drove away but at a much slower speed, leaving the victim behind but carrying the memory of his death with them for ever. Colbeck and his father-in-law meanwhile, had caught a train at Wimborne Station and set off for London. When they got to West Moors, the inspector noticed that Satchwell had taken over the duties of the crossing-keeper. Andrews averted his gaze from the tarpaulin that covered the remains of the deceased.

'Every driver has nightmares that one day he'll kill someone,' he said.

'The circumstances here are particularly tragic.'

'At least they've opened the line for use again.'

'As you know,' said Colbeck, 'there'll be a full enquiry into the accident but the priority is to get the trains running again. That's what they've done.'

He'd pressed his father-in-law for details of Madeleine's condition but could only get very limited information out of him. What he did realise was that a breech delivery, where the baby emerged backwards from the womb, presented difficulties and that major surgery might be involved. He scolded himself for not being there during the crisis and for letting his wife down. Andrews didn't need to add his own criticism. Colbeck was patently suffering.

'Thank you for coming,' he said, touching his father-in-law's arm.

'Somebody had to do it.'

'I can't tell you how grateful I am. As soon as I saw you there, I knew that there was an emergency of some sort.'

'It *was* an emergency,' agreed Andrews. 'Nothing else would have made me spend eight hours travelling on this railway. It's an ordeal.'

* * *

Though he was pleased with the confidence shown in him, Victor Leeming was not entirely persuaded by Colbeck's claim that Harry Wills must have been the killer. The only time that the sergeant had seen the man was when he was giving his daughter a ride on a horse. Jack Elwell and William Manders had both looked as if they were capable of a murder and Michael Tullidge had been in the same category. Wills, however, was a quiet, inoffensive family man. Could he really be the person who'd murdered John Bedloe then hacked a bed and mattress to pieces as a symbolic gesture?

When he got to Dorchester, Leeming found that the railwayman had left work because his shift had ended. He therefore went on to the address that Colbeck had given him. Letty Wills was not at all surprised that a detective should come in search of her husband. She knew that the investigation was in progress and that Wills had asked to be kept abreast of it.

'Harry is not here at the moment,' she said.

'Do you know where he is, Mrs Wills?'

'I expect that he's gone to the grave. He often does that when he leaves work.'

'Which churchyard is it in?' asked Leeming. 'I really do need to speak to your husband as a matter of urgency.'

'Oh, it's not in any churchyard, Sergeant. It's in a field.'

Harry Wills stood in silence for a long time. Nobody ever came there. The field was railway property and he'd sought permission to use part of it. He'd selected a quiet corner for the burial. The wildflowers he'd placed there earlier still topped the little mound. Beside the grave was the fresh earth that he'd tamped down with his spade. In doing that, he'd felt that his work was complete. Wills eventually decided to go home but, when he turned round, he discovered that he was not alone. Victor Leeming was standing directly behind him.

'Inspector Colbeck introduced us,' said the sergeant. 'I've been sent here to arrest you for the murder of your cousin.'

'Nobody should be arrested for killing that monster,' said Wills.

'The law is the law, sir.'

'Do you know what he did – what he *tried* to do with my wife?'

'I hope that you're going to come quietly.'

Wills pointed at the grave. 'He was responsible for this.'

'Your wife told me that you'd buried a horse here.'

'It was not just any horse,' said Wills, passion igniting his eyes. 'It was the dearest and most lovable old animal you could ever wish to meet. Trojan was my best friend and he really was a Trojan. When I took him shunting, it was a joy to work beside him. He knew exactly what to do. Yes, he only had a couple of years left in him, I know that. After a lifetime of toil, he deserved his retirement.' His voice became steely. 'Then my cousin, John Bedloe, got up to his tricks. He tried to lead my wife, Letty, astray and she was frightened. I went to see him and we had a fierce row. Do you know what he did to spite me?'

'I think I do, Mr Wills. He killed your horse.'

'He did more than that. He made Trojan suffer. Instead of shooting him in the head, he maimed him badly and let him bleed to death. This is where I found him,' said Wills, pointing at the grave, 'so this is where he was buried.'

'Did you report Bedloe to the police?'

'Yes, but I had no evidence. John denied it and that was that.'

'So you took the law into your own hands.'

'That's exactly what I did,' said Wills with a laugh. 'I followed him. I knew he'd do to other women what he tried to do to Letty so I watched him for months. When he went to West Moors on

Saturday night, I took my chance and I got my revenge. It was very sweet, I can tell you.'

'Why did you go to his cottage and hack his bed to pieces?'

'That's where he gave vent to his lechery.'

'He did the same in that shed. We saw what you did there.'

'John Bedloe was a liar and a threat to any pretty woman. He even dared to molest his cousin's wife. But it was what he did to Trojan that made my blood boil, Sergeant. He swore that it was somebody else but I knew better. That's why I put a corkscrew through his tongue. He won't tell any more lies.'

Leeming took out the handcuffs. 'It's time to go, sir.'

'Let me show you something first,' said Wills, kneeling down and shovelling earth away with his hands. 'I stole the murder weapon from John's cottage.' He pulled out the shotgun and shook off the dirt. 'This is what killed Trojan.'

'I'll take that, if you don't mind.'

'But I do mind,' said Wills, aiming it at him. 'What's to stop me from shooting you? I'm sure that Trojan won't mind sharing his grave with you.'

'Now, don't do anything stupid, sir.'

Wills was beyond reason. Leeming could see that. He could also see the wisdom in Colbeck's suggestion that he might want to get support from the police station. Leeming now felt horribly alone. A gentle, law-abiding Christian had somehow been turned into a vengeful killer. Roused to a fury, he really looked as if he was ready to fire the shotgun. Leeming acted swiftly, hurling the handcuffs into his face then diving at his waist to knock him to the ground. The shotgun went off, discharging its pellets harmlessly into the air. Wills fought back but Leeming was stronger and far more determined. It was only a matter of time before he subdued him. He eventually had the man lying face down on the ground with his wrists held firmly together behind his back by handcuffs.

Leeming hauled him to his feet and held him right next to the grave.

'Say goodbye to Trojan, sir.'

At Colbeck's insistence, the driver took the cab at a gallop through the darkened streets of London. When they reached the hospital, Colbeck leapt out and thrust money at the driver before running towards the building. Grumbling at being left behind, Andrews followed at a more sedate pace. Colbeck, meanwhile, was pushing open the front door and running into the building. Lydia jumped up from her chair.

'Good evening!' she said.

'What's happened?' he asked, breathlessly. 'Is Madeleine well?'

'She's still in labour, apparently.'

'Have you spoken to her?'

'They wouldn't let me see her, Inspector.'

'Where is she?'

'It's somewhere on the first floor.'

Given directions, Colbeck went haring down the corridor then started to take the steps in batches of two. Andrews came in and saw what his son-in-law was doing. He turned to Lydia.

'I'm not going to race him,' he said.

'You're entitled to visit her as well, Mr Andrews. You're her father.'

He sat down. 'I think I know who Maddy would most like to see now.'

The journey there had been the worst part. Madeleine felt very uncomfortable in the cab, especially when it hit a pothole or turned a corner sharply and threw her against her companion. She'd become even more aware that she was carrying a baby. The strangeness of the hospital had disturbed her at first because it was so unlike the bedroom in which she'd spent most of her time. The sudden loss of privacy was worrying. Even more upsetting, however, was the fact that something was wrong. Though she'd had it explained to her, she felt that they were holding something back. There were dangers about which they were not telling her.

She'd gone into labour hours ago but nothing seemed to be happening. The nurses seemed content to leave her alone for short periods before coming back to check on her. Then there was a long gap when nobody came and she wondered if they'd forgotten her. She felt lonely, uncomfortable and disregarded. Then someone did come in. It was a nurse and she brought an unexpected visitor. She left Colbeck alone with his wife.

'Hello, Madeleine,' he said, coming to her.

'Robert!'

'How are you?'

'I'm all the better for seeing you.'

'I'm so sorry that I wasn't here when it happened.'

'Don't say another word,' she said, indicating the chair beside the bed. 'Just sit there and hold my hand.'

He did as she asked and the anxiety slowly oozed away out of both of them. They were together again. Madeleine could face anything now.

Edward Tallis was so used to upbraiding him that he began to yell at Leeming as soon as he came into the room. It was moments before he realised that he should instead be congratulating the sergeant. It was the day after the arrest. The murder had at last been solved, Harry Wills was in custody and Leeming was in the unprecedented position of deserving unqualified praise. Tallis waved a sheaf of papers.

'Your report makes excellent reading,' he said.

'Thank you, Superintendent.'

'There are too many spelling mistakes and you lack Colbeck's command of grammar but I'm prepared to overlook those solecisms. The fact is that you made the arrest all on your own. The commissioner will be passing on his congratulations but I wanted to be the first to do so.' Leeming shook the proffered hand. 'Tell me honestly,' Tallis went on, 'would you have been able to solve the crime if Inspector Vallence had led the investigation?'

'No, sir.'

'Why not?'

'He'd never have picked the killer out as Inspector Colbeck did.'

'Perhaps not, but at least he'd have stayed for the duration of the enquiry.'

'It would still be going on.'

Tallis stroked his moustache. 'Is there . . . any news?'

'They're still waiting, sir.'

'Where is Colbeck?'

'He's at the hospital. By rights, he should be here but he insisted that I came on my own to . . . see what your reaction would be.'

'I think he knew only too well. This deserves a celebration,' said Tallis, opening the cigar box on his desk and taking out a large cigar. 'Will you join me?'

'Yes, please,' said Leeming, eagerly.

Tallis kept him waiting. After cutting the end of his cigar, he lit it, took a series of puffs and was soon sending clouds into the air. He then set the cigar down in an ashtray and took out a second box from the desk. Flicking it open, he revealed a row of substantially smaller cigars.

'Since you're not used to smoking,' he said, condescendingly, 'it would be cruel to offer you a larger one. It would be too much of a challenge for you.' He thrust the box at Leeming and smiled. 'One must accept one's limitations.'

'Yes, Superintendent,' said the other, wistfully.

Neither of them had realised how long Madeleine could be in labour. Both she and her husband began to grow impatient and it was well over a day and a half before there were clear signs that delivery might at last take place. Colbeck and Andrews had been in the waiting room for what seemed like an eternity. When Lydia Quayle came back to the hospital again, she brought good news. Lucas, her younger brother, had written to her. He had somehow persuaded his siblings that it was wrong to contest their mother's last will and testament. Lydia was still telling them what it meant to her when the doctor came into the room.

'It's all over,' he said. 'We managed to turn the baby so there was no need for a breech delivery. Mother and daughter are well.'

'Daughter!' said Andrews. 'I was certain that it would be a boy.'

'She's a beautiful girl, sir.' He beckoned Colbeck. 'You can see your wife now, Inspector.'

Colbeck was on his feet at once, following him along a corridor and into a room. Madeleine was lying in bed with the baby in her arms. She looked pale and exhausted but was clearly overjoyed.

'Come and meet your daughter, Robert,' she said.

He knelt beside the bed and kissed each of them gently in turn.

'I'm so proud of you, Madeleine.'

'Father is going to be disappointed.'

'I'm not,' he told her. 'I always hoped for a girl and now I have one. I just couldn't be happier, Madeleine. We're a family now.'

THE CIRCUS TRAIN CONSPIRACY

1860. Following a string of successful performances, the Moscardi Circus is travelling by train to Newcastle for their next show. Amongst the usual railway hubbub the animals have been loaded, the clowns, now incognito, are aboard and Mauro Moscardi himself is comfortable in a first-class compartment with a cigar. Yet a collision on the track with a couple of sleepers causes pandemonium: passengers are thrown about, animals escape into the night and the future of the circus looks uncertain.

When the body of a woman is discovered in woodland next to the derailment, Inspector Colbeck is desperate to lend assistance, believing the two incidents might be connected. It is up to Colbeck to put the pieces together to discover the identity of the nameless woman and unmask who is targeting Moscardi's Magnificent Circus.

To discover more great books and to
place an order visit our website at
allisonandbusby.com

Don't forget to sign up to our free newsletter at
allisonandbusby.com/newsletter
for latest releases, events and exclusive offers

[f] **Allison & Busby Books**
[t] **@AllisonandBusby**

You can also call us on
020 7580 1080
for orders, queries
and reading recommendations